MW01389090

CHILDREN OF THE SCROLL

RICK TABOR

To Colleen and Darren,
Thanks for being
awesome friends &
Neighbors!
Love -
Rick Tabor

LONG OVERDUE

This book is a work of fiction. Names, characters, places, and incidents are the product of the authors' imagination or are used fictitiously. Any resemblance to actual events, locales, or persons, living or dead, is coincidental.

Cover design by Heather Nelson

First Edition: December 2024

Title: Children of the Scroll

By: Rick Tabor

Description: First edition.

ISBN 979-8-9913593-2-0

Printed in the United States of America.

CHILDREN OF THE SCROLL

RICK TABOR

Ancient magic is found in the modern world –
no one is ready for it.

For Angela, whose sacrifices for us
and our family has taught me much about love.

Genesis 1:26-27

Then God said, "Let us make mankind in our image, in our likeness, so that they may rule over the fish in the sea and the birds in the sky, over the livestock and all the wild animals, and over all the creatures that move along the ground."

So God created mankind in his own image, in the image of God he created them; male and female he created them.

Genesis 2:20-23

The man gave names to all livestock and to the birds of the heavens and to every beast of the field. But for Adam there was not found a helper fit for him. So, the Lord God caused a deep sleep to fall upon the man, and while he slept took one of his ribs and closed up its place with flesh. And the rib that the Lord God had taken from the man he made into a woman and brought her to the man.

Then the man said, "This at last is bone of my bones and flesh of my flesh; she shall be called Woman, because she was taken out of Man."

1

ALLIANCE

7:55 AM
June 3, 1988
Tel Aviv, Israel

Ivan Sokov sipped his espresso across from his lovely wife. The couple sat at a small table in the cafeteria of the R&D facility of Israeli Defense Systems outside of Tel Aviv. He gazed through a floor-to-ceiling window in the small cafeteria and onto the hot, grassy landscape outside the building. Orina was reading the latest issue of *The Journal of Applied Material Science* while drinking a bottle of sparkling water. Ivan was a tall, handsome man with a perpetual tan, thick dark hair, and a boxer's physique. Orina was of medium height with hazel eyes, brown hair pulled back into a ponytail, and a slim runner's build. The two of them had just finished their 5-mile run 30 minutes earlier on the hiking trails that led through the arid countryside on the large property owned by the company. They were both stained with sweat.

A pair of determined steps clicked and thumped across the tiled cafeteria floor. Ivan and Orina looked up to see a young lady with short brown hair and glasses approaching them. She was wearing black pants, a long-sleeve white blouse, and medium heels. Accompanying her was an olive-skin security guard carrying a Desert Eagle handgun in a holster on his hip.

"Good morning, Ms. Fischer," Ivan said cheerfully. He stood from his seat and motioned for her to sit with them at the table. "I've always said that the definition of 'on time' is 5 minutes early, and that 'on time' is actually late. So, thank you for arriving on time."

The security guard gave a slight nod to Ivan and returned to his post at the front desk.

"Good morning, Ms. Fischer," Orina said. "It's so nice to meet you in person. Was your flight from New York eventful?"

"Very nice to meet both of you in person as well, Mr. and Mrs. Sokov," Eva said, "and yes, it was a bit eventful. We landed at 3 a.m., more than 6 hours late."

"I'm so sorry to hear that! You must be absolutely exhausted," Ivan said.

"Nothing that a double espresso won't cure," Eva said. "Besides, in my line of work, I generate a ridiculous number of international airline miles, and delays are unavoidable when dealing with airlines."

"Petra, please get our guest a double espresso," Ivan asked the cafeteria worker.

"Right away, Mr. Sokov," responded the waitress.

"Thank you, Mr. Sokov," Eva said.

"Please, let's continue on a first-name basis," Orina said. "We hope you will eventually think of us as good friends."

"I'd like that very much, Mrs. Sokov – I mean, Orina," Eva said.

"Eva, we've done our homework on your background and reputation as an ancient antiquity dealer," Ivan said. "I would be surprised if you haven't done the same on us and our little company. Please, tell us what you know about our growing enterprise. We'll fill in the gaps."

Eva felt like she was under a very bright spotlight on a very small stage. "Well, I know you're the founders of a growing company that supplies military products to the Israeli Defense Force. Your financial records are confidential since you aren't publicly traded. I would definitely *not* call your company 'little' since, according to my sources, you broke the billion dollar mark in sales last year, up over 20 percent from the previous year."

Eva continued as the corners of Ivan's mouth curved into a slight smile. "Orina, you're the Chief Technology Officer, and Ivan, you're the CEO. Israeli Defense Systems. I'm surprised the name wasn't already taken. I bet it's pretty memorable to the Israeli Defense Force procurement agents."

Ivan chuckled, and Eva smiled politely. Eva continued, looking directly at Ivan.

"My sources also tell me that you met at Tel Aviv University, where you obtained a BS and an MBA in International Business."

She turned her attention over to Orina.

"And you obtained two PhDs - one in material science and another in computer science, in the emerging area of artificial intelligence. Am I boring you yet?"

Ivan and Orina looked at each other, smiled, and gently applauded approvingly. "Nicely done, Eva," Ivan replied. "So, to get down to brass tacks, as the Americans say, we are obviously interested in your very special skills as a dealer in valuable antiquities."

"But why would a military products company be interested in an antiquities dealer?" Eva asked.

"You are undoubtedly familiar with the various examples of powerful ancient mythical and/or legendary items that were reported to exist throughout the history of man," Ivan said. "Mjölnir, Thor's Hammer. King Arthur's sword, Excalibur. Archimedes' death ray, and so on. It is almost certain that most of these mythical items are purely fictional nonsense. But we are looking for items that are not fictional, not just a myth. We're looking for items that possess powers beyond our understanding."

The waitress delivered the double espresso to the table. Eva blew on the beverage to cool it before taking a long slow sip.

"You're correct," Eva said. "Those are fairy tales that have been told by different cultures and religions to entertain their children at night, or worse, propaganda fantasies to bolster the stature of their culture or beliefs. Nobody's wielding Excalibur or Thor's Hammer any time soon."

"And that brings us to our demonstration for the morning!" Ivan said, clapping his hands together loudly with a smile. He pulled a pale brown ram's horn – a shofar – from his briefcase and pushed it across the table to Eva. "This is one of the seven shofars that Joshua's army used, along with the Ark of the Covenant, to destroy the walls of Jericho after a weeklong siege. As you probably already know, a shofar is a musical horn used in Jewish rituals."

Eva first looked at the shofar on the table without touching it, then pulled a lighted magnifying glass from her purse and examined it. "The Walls of Jericho event was discredited almost unanimously by archeologists as never having taken place," Eva said.

"As the English would say – 'The proof is in the pudding.' You may handle it, but I wouldn't blow into it or try to play it indoors if I were you," Ivan said.

After a few minutes of examining, Eva said, "Thank you, though it appears to be just a simple, albeit very old, polished ram's horn."

"Then let us taste the pudding!" Ivan said, grinning widely.

Orina picked up a VHS video camera and walked to the door leading to an outdoor patio. Ivan walked next to Eva and opened the door for the two ladies, allowing the warm summer air to flow into the cafeteria as they exited. As the door swung closed, he reached quickly back into the cafeteria to a small table and grabbed three sound-dampening earmuffs. A short walk around a large berm of rocks led them to a flat, open savannah. A small cinderblock shed interrupted the view of the dried grassland. Ivan gave a flamboyant gesture and a bow toward the structure as Orina began videotaping the two from a distance. He then stepped closer to Eva.

"Eva, this is your objective. Examine it, then attempt to push it down," Ivan said.

Puzzled, Eva walked around the small structure, no bigger than a walk-in closet, and moved her hand across the cinderblocks.

"Appears to have been recently constructed," Eva said in a quiet voice. She put both hands against the structure and pushed as hard as she could, but with no effect. "It appears to be quite sturdy."

"Now, hold onto your earmuffs until we all get into position," Ivan said as he handed both Eva and Orina a pair of earmuffs.

Ivan handed Eva the shofar. He gently took her arm and guided her to a spot about 25 feet away from the structure.

"I will get into position away from you and the structure and raise my hand," Ivan said, pointing back to the structure. "When I lower my hand, I will point the shofar at the structure and blow. Now this next part is very important. Do NOT point it anywhere aside from the structure. Understand? This would be a good time for us to put on our earmuffs."

After they fitted their earmuffs, Ivan stood next to Orina, raised his hand, and brought it down quickly. Eva blew into the horn, aiming towards the wall. The sound waves projecting from the horn became visible as pressure waves distorted and compressed the air hitting the wall. The force caused Eva to stumble backwards, her shoes slipping on the gravelly surface, but she continued to stand and blow. Cracks formed in the mortar and the cinderblock structure cracked and crumbled before her, leaving a cloud of dust rising from the rubble. She stopped blowing, her lung capacity expended.

"Are you kidding me?!" Eva exclaimed with a child-like joy, attempting to catch her breath. She turned the shofar over in her hands and examined it again. "Definitely not a simple polished ram's horn."

Eva removed her earmuffs, allowing them to hang over her wrist as she stared at the shofar.

"Unfortunately, we've been unable to find the other six shofars, nor, of course, the Ark of the Covenant," Ivan said, removing his earmuffs, "but according to the famous Steven Spielberg movie, that one is locked away in a government warehouse somewhere in the United States." Ivan smiled. "We don't understand exactly how this shofar works but, naturally, you can easily envision the military applications if we were able to reproduce this effect. And that is exactly what my lovely wife is currently attempting to do. Worst case scenario, we may sell it as a stand-alone one-of-a-kind weapon."

"Incredible," Eva said, expecting to feel power pulsing through the item as she held it. She was disappointed that it felt cold and hard, just like a simple, polished ram's horn.

"Naturally, all of what I have told and shown you fall under the confidentiality agreement you have already signed," Ivan said. "And now we come to the real reason we have asked you to meet with us here, Eva."

Ivan gestured politely towards Orina.

"We acquired this shofar completely by chance. A tour guide found this in the desert while giving a tour to a group of American tourists, one of which was a friend of Orina's aunt. Fortunately for the tourists, the guide blew the horn for the first time at a boulder, and no one was hurt."

"Had my Aunt Aila not contacted me, we would never have known about the horn's existence," Orina explained. "I decided we should become more intentional in acquiring such items as a small part of our weapons development program."

"After seeing the evidence for such artifacts, you can understand why a woman of science such as my lovely and brilliant wife, and a man of enterprise, such as myself, would be interested in finding more of these items. We would like to offer you a yearly retainer of one million US dollars per year for the next two years. During the next two years, we want you to work for us full-time, identifying items like this and searching for more. If you can acquire one and Orina agrees based on her test results that it has military value, we will pay you a bonus of 5 million US dollars per item. If Orina does not believe it has value to our company, then you are welcome to sell the item elsewhere and keep the profits for yourself. If the arrangement proves fruitful, you can count on us to continue the relationship past the two-year term. Does this sound reasonable to you?"

Eva paused for a second, then smiled.

"You had me at sonic shofar and a million dollars a year. When shall I start?"

"How does today sound?" Orina asked. "We'll have our research team send you the list of potential artifacts we've identified as distinct possibilities and what notes we have. Unless you already have a few that come to mind?"

"As a matter of fact, I've been researching a Buddhist scepter that, according to legend, renders the bearer invulnerable," Eva replied. "Oh, and then there is this Scroll that I've been daydreaming about."

2

FRAGMENT

Five Years Later
May 11, 1993
Prague, Czech Republic

Eva Fischer sat across the table from Rabbi Kohn in a tiny restaurant – *Table Poutine* - while her two hired bodyguards stood nearby. The restaurant was dimly lit with modern eclectic décor. A bust of Bedřich Smetana stared out from an alcove built into the wall, while recessed purple lighting shone gently from under shelves and tables. A colorful cubist mural in the style of Josef Čapek embellished the wall to the left of the circular booth, while historical pictures of the Czech Republic covered a wall to the right, including an autographed color photo from Martina Navratilova, a photo of Soviet tanks rumbling down a Prague street in 1968 while buildings burned in the background and a painting of the sun setting behind the Baroque church of St. Nicholas.

A violinist sat in a chair near a window overlooking the street and played a Czech folk song. Eva sipped a Cabernet Sauvignon from the

Hustopeče region of the recently formed Czech Republic, savoring the tones of black currant with hints of dark chocolate and tobacco. She had paid the owner a handsome fee to rent the entire restaurant for the evening. An attractive blonde waitress wearing a tight-fitting red-striped shirt and a short black skirt delivered plates for both the rabbi and Eva.

"Thank you, Aneta," Eva said. "Bon appetit, Rabbi Kohn."

Eva took a bite.

"Yum! Bramboračka s bramboráky," Eva exclaimed. "I just love the mushroom and meat gravy that comes with these!"

The rabbi was a short, rotund man with white hair and a neatly trimmed white beard, wearing a black suit and a hoiche – a black, high-crowned hat with a brim. He smiled pleasantly at Eva as she enjoyed her potato pancakes.

"Though I've never eaten here before, I appreciate your willingness to take my recommendation on the entrée and, more importantly, for inviting me to dinner this evening," Rabbi Kohn said. "This dish is one of my personal favorites. By the way, aren't your bodyguards going to eat?"

"They don't eat while they're on duty," Eva said. "Now, Rabbi Kohn, I bet you're wondering why I would fly you out here, rent a restaurant, and pay you $500/hour to watch me devour a plate of potato pancakes."

"I must admit, I'm quite curious."

Eva took another bite of pancake drenched in gravy. "Incredible! So delicious." She continued, "Alright, now for the grand reveal – what can you tell me about the original copy of the Sefer Yetzirah?"

The rabbi looked down at his meal and then squirmed in his seat, apparently uncomfortable with the question and the blunt delivery.

"Don't be shy," Eva said. "I just want to compare notes."

"Well, although this tome has a great deal of history and tradition surrounding it, the short story is that according to historical documents and Jewish tradition[1], the original Sefer Yetzirah originated

---

1. Sepher Yetzirah Paperback – March 29, 2018 by Abraham (Author), One-Eye Publishing (Editor), Isidor Kalisch (Translator)

directly from the Jewish patriarch Abraham himself, although modern scholars are not in complete agreement on this. If it existed, the original copy would likely be in the form of a scroll made out of parchment – a type of paper made by scraping the skin of an animal such as a sheep. According to Rabbi Saadia Gaon, the purpose of the scroll's author was to convey how everything in our universe was created. Unfortunately, the original copy is believed to no longer exist. Our oldest copies are from about the second century AD."

"Ah, but don't forget about Judah Loew ben Bezalel, the Maharal of Prague[2] who lived in the 1600s," Eva chimed in. "This was a very special rabbi indeed! In addition to being a Talmudic scholar, a Jewish mystic, a mathematician, an astronomer, and a philosopher, he was also a rabbi here in Prague, just like you. He led his congregation during a dark time for the Jews – a time of blood libels, where Christians falsely accused Jews of using the blood of their children for dark rituals. It was also a time of pogroms – organized massacres of Jews in the Prague ghettos[3]. But Rabbi Loew had a very interesting defense for these attacks, didn't he? He created a golem – a creature made from clay on the banks of the Vltava River[4] – a creature that would protect the Jewish people from the blood libels and the pogroms."

Eva continued, "The legend goes on to describe how the golem had superhuman strength, how he could become invisible and summon spirits of the dead. But how, exactly, did he create this golem?" When the rabbi didn't answer, she said, "Well, it is speculated, or perhaps a more accurate description would be, rumored, that Rabbi Loew enchanted the original Sefer Yetzirah written by Abraham to make it even more powerful."

Eva took another bite of her potato pancakes and again gave a

---

2. https://www.newworldencyclopedia.org/entry/Judah_Loew_ben_Beza
lel#google_vignette
3. https://en.wikipedia.org/wiki/History_of_the_Jew
s_in_Prague#:~:text=At%20East-
er%20in%201389%2C%20which,fled%20to%20Poland%20and%20Hungary.
4. https://theculturetrip.com/europe/czech-republic/prague/articles/the-legend-of-the-golem-of-prague

slight moan to the heavens. Swallowing, wiping her mouth on her napkin, and then looking into Rabbi Kohn's eyes with a serious gaze.

"Rabbi Kohn, I didn't invite you here to teach me about the scroll. I want the scroll in my possession."

Without breaking her gaze, Eva asked, "You said that the original copy is believed to no longer exist, correct?"

"Yes, that's correct, Ms. Fischer," the rabbi said.

"Oh, please, Rabbi Kohn! Call me Eva. I hope that you consider me a friend at this point," she said, and then she took another sip of Czech wine from her glass.

"Of course, thank you, Eva," Rabbi Kohn said. As he spoke, a drop of sweat flowed down his forehead into his right eyebrow and then fell onto his cheek. He wiped it away nervously with his napkin.

A Louis Vuitton satchel rested on the bench seat next to Eva, and she casually reached over and flipped open the flap, pulling out a large photograph. Eva looked at the photograph and then purposefully placed it face up on the table between the two of them, sliding it towards Rabbi Kohn.

"Rabbi, this photo indicates that the original Sefer Yetzirah exists and that you are, in fact, its proud owner," Eva said. The photo showed Rabbi Kohn standing at a podium with a small scroll rolled open, reading the text using a Torah pointer. The Hebrew text was clear enough to be read in the photo if one used a magnifying glass.

"Where did you get this photo?" Rabbi Kohn asked.

Eva finished chewing another bite of potato pancake and swallowed, washing it down with another sip of wine. "That is not important, Rabbi. The important part is that two of my other bodyguards - who you have not met - are, as we speak, searching your synagogue for this important and valuable artifact."

Rabbi Kohn quietly gasped.

"Eva, believe me when I say that you must get your men out of there immediately!"

At that moment, the walkie-talkie of one of Eva's bodyguards in the restaurant beeped. The guard clicked a button on the device, and gunfire could be heard, followed by a man screaming. A second man spoke quickly, "I have the artifact and am on my way to you. Some kind of creature was protecting the scroll. Able is presumed dead. Smith out." The sound of a motorcycle engine cranking and then revving came from the speaker, and then the device became silent.

Eva wiped her mouth with her napkin, looked into Rabbi Kohn's eyes intently, and quietly said, "How exciting! You've created a golem using the Sefer Yetzirah, haven't you?"

Rabbi Kohn replied, "You must return the scroll to the synagogue. You don't understand what you're up against. This creature will not rest until you are all dead and the scroll is returned." The two bodyguards looked at each other with raised eyebrows and then back at the rabbi.

Eva calmly looked at the two bodyguards and said, "Jones, dismiss the restaurant staff and join me at the van. Cain, you are with the rabbi and me. Oh, and give me your knife." As one of the bodyguards stepped towards the kitchen, the other pulled a black tactical knife from a sheath strapped to his thigh and handed it to Eva.

"Rabbi Kohn, we're leaving, and you're coming with us as insurance. Come along now. Don't dally." Eva motioned for him to walk in front of her using the black, razor-sharp tactical knife as her pointer. "Step lively, now."

The rabbi extracted himself from the booth and walked to the door. The sound of a motorcycle approaching could be heard in the distance as Cain opened the rear door of the black Mercedes Benz S class to allow the rabbi to enter. Eva went to the other rear door and entered the vehicle from the dark street, save for a few street lamps and orange barricades equipped with flashing yellow lights around a gapping manhole undergoing construction.

The sound of the R100 BMW motorcycle grew louder as Smith rounded the corner of a nearby street. He parked the bike behind the Mercedes and walked to Eva's window. Eva rolled down the window with a quiet whirring sound and Smith handed her a scroll rolled onto two ornately decorated wooden rollers.

"Get in the front. Quickly!" she hissed as she accepted the scrolls and rolled up the window.

As Smith jogged around the rear of the Mercedes to comply, a dark, amorphous figure dropped from the four-story roof of the restaurant, landing on the trunk of the vehicle. After recovering from the impact, Eva turned in her seat to look out the rear window. A 6-foot-tall gray figure resembling a statue created by a 12-year-old out of clay reached down from atop the trunk, grabbed Smith's skull, and crushed it with a horrifying crunch. Blood and gray matter oozed from between the creature's fingers as it flung the dead bodyguard to the sidewalk.

"Get us the hell out of here!" Eva yelled to Cain, who needed no further encouragement and was already gunning the engine.

The rear tires smoked and chirped wildly as they revved against the cobblestones, but no forward motion resulted. The creature had grabbed the rear bumper with one hand and was simply holding the car in place. Eva started yelling. "Get out of the car and shoot that fucking monstrosity!"

Hesitantly, Cain took his foot off the accelerator, drew his Glock from its holster, and stepped outside the car. As he was firing, Jones walked out of the restaurant and began firing. The crossfire would have shredded a normal human being, but while the bullets left small holes in the skin of the creature, they seemed to have little effect on its well-being. Cain emptied his Glock and searched for another clip. As he removed the clip from the holster, the creature leaped over the car, landed next to him, lifted him by the neck, and tossed him through the restaurant window.

The creature then ripped the rear door off of the vehicle to find Eva with the tactical knife on the jugular of Rabbi Kohn.

"Get away from me, or I'll cut his throat!" she exclaimed.

But instead of walking away, the creature bent downwards, grabbed the bottom of the Mercedes, and flipped it over onto its back, crushing Jones, who had reloaded and was now firing his weapon into the creature again. Eva and the rabbi were tossed about in the rear of the vehicle like a pair of marionette dolls. When the car stopped rocking back and forth, the creature reached through the rear door and grabbed Eva by her wrist, causing her to drop the knife in pain. In her other hand, Eva still held the scroll. Pulling Eva out of the vehicle, the creature held her up over his head and snatched the Sefer Yetzirah from her hand, but in the one-sided tug-of-war, a small fragment of parchment tore away from the artifact, remaining in Eva's grasp. Stepping quickly to the open manhole next to the flashing yellow pylons, the creature dropped her down into the darkness and sludge. The creature lifted the heavy manhole cover with one hand, and dropped it snugly into place over the opening.

3

FACTORY OF DEATH

July 7, 2019
Wuhan, China

The humid jungle night was peppered with hungry horseshoe bats chasing moths and flying beetles through the tree canopy. The sounds of fluttering thin leather wings filled the air. This gentle cacophony was joined by the guā guā of frogs partially submerged in scattered pools of murky brown water.

A young horseshoe bat peers through the darkness with eyes well adapted to the darkness but unable to see well because they are partially obscured behind her nose leaves. Instead of using her eyes, she projects ultra-high frequency squeaks from her throat and focuses these sounds with her nose-leafs, allowing her to precisely map her surroundings using echolocation with her large ears[1]. Movement in the air detected by the Doppler-shifted echoes returning from a flying

1. Surlykke, A., Boel Pedersen, S. & Jakobsen, L. Echolocating bats emit a highly directional sonar sound beam in the field. Proceedings. Biological sciences/The Royal

beetle draws her to her prey, which she pulls into her mouth mid-air using the fingers at the tip of her wing. She munches on the beetle hungrily and swallows.

The act of eating stimulates her bowels, and soon, she defecates again in mid-air. Unbeknownst to the young horseshoe bat, she is a natural reservoir for numerous viruses[2]; many evolved for easy transmission directly to other mammals, like human beings. On this day, one of those viruses - a deadly virus - is a passenger in the falling scat. The fecal matter falls between the leaves of a fig tree and onto a ripened fig that has fallen from the tree above to the ground. A young, masked palm civet chews on a leaf nearby in the darkness of the forest undergrowth. With a very long tail, the body of a cat, a long snout, and a face resembling that of a raccoon, the civet is attracted by the sound of falling feces. Thinking it might be a beetle, he trots to the freshly seasoned fig, breathes in the tasty aroma of the fruit of the forest, and devours it greedily.

Over the next few days, the civet develops a fever and runny nose and takes a night off from hunting. During this time, the virus hijacks his cells, converting them into miniature facilities for replicating RNA virus soldiers, thereby guaranteeing the virus's survival. For the human race, however, he has become a biological factory of death.

* * *

December 6, 2019 | Wuhan, China

The smell of out-of-season mango was irresistible to the young male civet. Mango trees normally yielded their delicious fruit between April and September in China, yet surprisingly, he smelled his favorite fruit here in December. As he bit into the fruit, the live-capture trap snapped shut behind him like a guillotine. Instead of separating its head from its body, this guillotine separated the civet from its jungle

---

Society 276, 853–860, doi: 10.1098/rspb.2008.1505 (2009). See also: Qiao Zhuang and Rolf Müller, Phys. Rev. Lett. 97, 218701 (2006), Published November 22, 2006

2. https://www.cdc.gov/coronavirus/2019-ncov/daily-life-coping/animals.html

home and soon would separate life from more than 7 million human beings[3].

The next morning, a bushmeat dealer arrived and transported the masked palm civet along with his other captures of the night to the Huanan Seafood Wholesale Market, where he sold them to Zhang Wei, one of the more than one thousand tenants in the 12-acre market filled wall to wall with small open-front shops.

In 2019, the Huanan Seafood Wholesale Market was a wet market, selling fish, meat, produce, and a variety of other foods. The freshest meat, of course, came from live animals which were slaughtered and butchered in the shop right in front of the customer, hence the descriptive word "wet" in the name "wet market". In addition to the benefit of the freshness of the resulting meat, the viewing of the slaughter of a living animal contained a certain element of entertainment to some customers. And if you were interested in bushmeat from wild animals, then one of the freshest shops to visit was owned by Zhang Wei, who wielded his cleaver and skinning knives with artful and entertaining precision. As careful as Zhang was, he occasionally cut himself or received a bite from one of the live wild animals that he handled every day.

Today, the young male masked palm civet that he was about to sell slipped briefly from his grasp and gave him a nasty bite on the wrist, injecting virus-saturated saliva into his bloodstream. His customer bent over with laughter as Zang Wei fired off a string of curse words. Angry at having been embarrassed in front of a customer, he also cut his index finger while butchering the civet, allowing even more of the deadly civet blood to mingle with his bloodstream.

* * *

December 10, 2019 | Wuhan, China

Zhang Wei awoke in the middle of the night feeling like he had been run over by a truck. His joints and muscles ached, and he had a

3. https://www.worldometers.info/coronavirus/

headache. He wrapped a blanket around him and went to the kitchen, where he brewed a pot of yanhusuo. He poured the steaming brown liquid into a cup and sipped it as he walked back to bed, noticing that strangely, he was unable to taste the pungent bitter brew.

The next day, Zhang Wei awoke, coughing violently. His throat was sore, and the ache in his muscles and joints was worse. He was having difficulty breathing and became concerned. After getting dressed, he pulled on his jacket and drove to the local hospital. After registering, he found a spot in the waiting room and continued coughing. He noticed that two others were coughing in the waiting room, including the customer who had laughed at him when the masked palm civet had bit him. Several hours later, a doctor examined him and told him that he would be staying in the hospital for a night or two because he had contracted pneumonia.

Unfortunately, Zhang Wei did not respond well to the treatments that the doctors provided, and two days later, at the age of 54, he suffocated to death within days of the other two patients who were also coughing in the waiting room.

4

TO BE SAFE

April 14, 2020
Skokie, Illinois

Ross Newman rolled onto his side, propped his surgically masked head on his hand, and looked at his surgically masked wife, Lilith, lying on her back, reading a book on her iPad.

She looked back at him and asked, "Whatcha thinkin'. . . ?"

Ross replied, "I'm worried. I've been reading the news, seeing how unprepared we are as a nation – not enough masks, not enough ventilators, not enough beds in the hospitals, the dead laying on floors of ER hallways like we've just been bombed – and then watching Tyvek-suited orderlies piling the bodies of the aged, coronary patients, and asthmatics who caught COVID into refrigerated semi-trucks parked in the backs of hospitals. This is a real pandemic. And with your asthma, I'm beyond terrified. People with lung problems like yours are dying left and right when they catch COVID. It's incredibly contagious – even when those around you don't have symptoms – so we have to assume we will all contract this virus at one point or another."

Ross took a deep breath.

"As much as neither of us likes the thought of being apart, I think the smart thing for you to do is temporarily isolate yourself in the basement. It's got a TV, a fridge, treadmill, bathroom with a shower, and a comfy bed. Of course, we'll have to move your files, desk, and chair down there, but there's space. I'll buy a hot plate and a small microwave, and you'll be set. We'll even cook for *you* for a change and provide kitchen-to-basement grocery delivery," Ross said through his light blue surgical mask.

"It almost sounds like you're looking forward to a vacation away from me," Lilith said with a mock pout.

"Well, I do have reservations booked for Tahiti with two Swedish volleyball players, but that's only in the interest of improved international relations," Ross said with a glint in his eye.

Lilith playfully punched him hard in the arm.

"Ow, that actually hurt!

"Maybe you can have your Swedish volleyball players massage it down for you," she said and pretended to be engrossed with the screen of her iPad.

"You know that I never, ever want to be without my girl, don't you? I literally would not be able to go on living if you caught this virus and left me. My life would be over. I love you too much."

"I feel the same, Ross," she said quietly through her surgical mask.

"This will not be easy. I don't like the thought of being apart from you at all. They are working on a vaccine, but who knows when they'll have one. In the meantime, we have to do everything we can to protect you."

"It stinks, but I suppose it is the right thing to do," Lilith sighed. She continued, "Perhaps as a way of saying goodbye, and since it might be a while until we – you know – do the wild thing again, what would you say to a roll in the hay – masks on, of course, before you put me in my quarantine prison? After all, COVID is not a sexually transmitted disease, right?"

"Well, this is a little awkward, but the Swedish volleyball players are waiting in the next room," Ross joked.

Lilith's hand moved under his shirt and down the front of his pants.

"Careful, you'll be called for penetration under the net..." Ross whispered.

"If you want to play volleyball, we have to put the pole up. Oh look, it's already up!" Lilith whispered with a smile, sliding her head beneath the sheets.

"Uh, Lilith, you don't seem to have your mask on anymore," Ross said quietly as he threw his own mask onto the floor.

After several minutes under the sheets, Lilith mounted Ross, teasing him with exaggerated slowness, thrusting ever-so-luxuriously and lustily, using him like a living toy. Soon, Ross could take no more of the teasing, and he abruptly rolled her over onto her back, pounding into her with an animal urgency. She came before he did, forcing him to slow his thrusting to allow her to pace herself for maximum climax as she bit the pillow and then moaned into it. Once she had completed her orgasm, he became even more urgent, slamming his hips into her until he also released, jerking and lurching above her before she felt his full weight relax onto her.

Ross whispered into her ear, "I love you, darling."

And Lilith whispered back, "I love you, too."

5

AN INVOLUNTARY SNEEZE

April 15, 2020
Skokie, Illinois

"Is there anything else I can get you, Mom?" Brian called through the basement door after delivering her office chair while wearing a surgical mask.

"A vaccine? A cure for asthma? A deserted island where we can all go to escape this madness?" Lilith replied. "No, I'm fine. I'm very lonely, but aside from that, I'm fine, thank you, Bri-Bear."

"I'm in charge of dinner tonight, so do you have any special requests for a favorite meal?" Brian asked.

"How do you feel about a frozen lasagna, burned parmesan broccoli, and garlic bread?" she replied through the door.

"Your wish is my command, Queen Mother," Brian replied, using his best British butler accent.

Lilith replied from the top of the basement stairs in a high-pitched, whiny British accent, "Oh, and *do* bring me a glass of my favorite zinfandel and have the new wine taster taste it for me. Such an unfortunate incident with the last wine taster – all of that foam shooting out of his nostrils and such. Strychnine should be completely against the rules in treacherous court poisonings. I was absolutely mortified – and all in front of Napoleon Bonaparte!"

Brian continued with his fake butler accent and a smile, "Of course, Your Majesty. I agree, strychnine is almost as bad as strangling – the blood, the kicking, the flailing and such, and almost always during the main course, which simply makes an enormous mess with the plates and drinks being kicked about."

"I love you, Bri-Bear, and thank you for putting up with all of this," Lilith said in her normal voice.

"I love you, too, Mom. I miss you already."

"I miss you more, Bri-Bear."

About an hour later, Brian's 13-year-old sister, Emily, carried a tray with a plate of lasagna, garlic bread, and "burned" broccoli to the basement door. As she approached, a sneeze burst from her unexpectedly. Although she was wearing her surgical mask, and although her father had taught her how to properly wear a mask, the nose piece was pulled down from her nose, leaving the mask covering only her mouth. As she sneezed, aerosolized microscopic droplets of saliva and mucous from her nose floated in the air, several of them settling on her mom's plate of food. Without realizing what she had done, she knocked on the basement door and called out, "Dinner's ready, Mom!" and then placed the tray on a small table in front of the door. Moments later, Lilith climbed the stairs and brought down the tray of warm food, looking forward to watching the Season 3 premiere of *Westworld* on HBO.

* * *

April 18, 2020 | Skokie, Illinois

Lilith's alarm began buzzing loudly at 7:00 a.m. She reluctantly reached over and turned it off, noticing that her shoulders were sore. A wicked headache throbbed to the beat of her heart.

She pulled back the covers, sat up on the side of the bed, and pulled on her pajamas. Walking to the bathroom, she looked at herself in the medicine cabinet mirror.

"Wow, Lilith, you look like something that a drunk, three-legged cat dragged in. For the love of God, you're living by yourself in a basement. How the hell have you managed to catch anything? This is not fair, God, definitely not fair."

She opened the medicine cabinet, grabbed a bottle of ibuprofen, and took two of the little blue gel capsules with a handful of water from the faucet. She texted Ross that she wasn't feeling well and went back to bed. As an accountant working out of her basement, the Petersons' taxes would just have to wait.

Lilith awoke again at about 3 p.m. that afternoon. This time she was shivering under the two blankets and the bedspread and sheet – shivering so hard that her teeth were chattering. She rolled out of bed and stumbled to the medicine cabinet, taking three ibuprofen instead of just two. She texted Ross upstairs to ask him what the thermostat was set to. He replied that it was set to 72 and asked how she was doing. "Not good" was her short reply.

Seeking relief, she turned on the shower, waited for it to warm up, and stepped into the warm water, full body shivering. At last, some relief, she thought. After about 10 minutes of partial relief in the shower, she took her temperature. 103.2 F.

There was a knock on the basement door followed by a loud voice from Ross.

"Honey, what's going on with you? Are you okay?"

"I'm not feeling good. My temperature is 103.2, and I've just taken some ibuprofen. Going back to bed," Lilith said.

"Do you want me to take you to the ER or urgent care?" replied Ross through the door.

"Let me ride this ibuprofen until tomorrow morning and see if I don't start feeling better," she said. "Is anyone else sick upstairs?"

"Emily seems to have a mild cold but nothing major," Ross said. "Call me immediately if you get worse, baby, no matter what time it is. Okay?"

"Okay. Going back to bed now. Love you," Lilith said.

"Love you, too. Feel better," Ross said.

Hoping the ibuprofen would take effect soon, she went back to bed and eventually fell asleep. She awoke a little after seven in the evening, shivering again, but not quite as bad, still aching all over. She was also hungry and texted Ross for some chicken soup. Three more ibuprofen later, Brian brought her a bowl of chicken soup, steamy hot. After he departed with a "Get well, Mom. We love you," far from the playful British accent interaction a day ago, Lilith opened the door and gingerly carried the soup down to her easy chair. She took a big spoonful, blew on it to cool it off and delivered it to her mouth. There was no taste whatsoever. She couldn't taste it at all! When she tried to swallow the soup, it was as if her throat was swollen. She began to choke on the soup and cough, though it sounded more like a bark than a cough.

Terrified, she texted Ross.

"I can't taste the soup. I think I have COVID. Please take me to the ER."

6

HOSPITAL, OVERWHELMED

April 18, 2020
Skokie, Illinois

Ross and Lilith arrived at Health Harbor Hospital within 15 minutes of her text. The ER waiting room was filled with patients, many of them coughing underneath their masks. Hand sanitizer stations were set up every 25 feet around the waiting room and near the entrance. A nurse was stationed just inside the door. She asked each patient entering the ER waiting room to answer 11 questions about whether or not they had experienced specific symptoms of COVID within the past few days. After seeing the mass of people in the waiting room area, Lilith and Ross began to worry even more.

As their three hours in the ER waiting room continued, Lilith began to cough blood from her throat. Thankfully, they heard "Lilith Newman" called out by one of the nurses holding a chart. Ross put his arm around her and escorted her through the motorized doors of the ER entrance and into a triage room. The nurse, however, told Ross that he would have to wait in the ER, as even family members were not allowed into the treatment areas. Ross kissed her forehead through his surgical mask. Lilith went on without him.

The nurse took her vitals, reviewed the file that one of the administrative assistants had prepared with Lilith's medical history and personal information, and escorted Lilith back to a curtained ER room. A cacophony of medical conversations filled the air as masked and often face-shielded health workers strove to treat the overwhelming influx of the first wave of pandemic patients.

After another hour of waiting, Lilith began to struggle for breath. She searched for her albuterol inhaler in her purse, which she had already used several times during their stay in the waiting room. She again took the salmon-colored dispenser and breathed out, then pushed the dispenser and pulled air mixed with albuterol through the inhaler through her inflamed throat and into her lungs.

At that moment, a young man in green scrubs pulled aside the curtain and entered the treatment area with a young woman wearing light blue scrubs. Both were wearing green surgical masks, a face shield, and blue nitrile gloves. The doctor didn't waste any time. He didn't have time to spare. People were dying all around him.

"I'm Dr. Linkletter, and this is Margi, who will be assisting me today. Are you Lilith Newman?" Dr. Linkletter asked.

"Yes, doctor," she replied

Dr. Linkletter continued, "Lilith, you have COVID. Because of your history with asthma, you are considered to be an 'at risk' patient. Your oxygen level is at 85 percent, your heart rate is at 120 bpm, and your temperature is at 102.7. None of these are where we want them to be. Now, as we are sailing in uncharted medical waters with this new virus, we'll be treating you with dexamethasone – a steroid - via IV drip. Margi, please get that started for Lilith immediately and set her up with a low-flow oxygen mask. Dexamethasone is an anti-inflammatory that we hope will reduce the inflammation in your throat and lungs and get this disease under control. It's the best treatment that we've seen at this early stage of the virus."

"If we don't see a reduction in the swelling in your throat soon, which I am quite concerned about at this point," Dr. Linkletter continued as he shined a flashlight down her throat, "then there is the very real possibility that you may need a ventilator. I'll be back in a few hours to check on you, Lilith, after the dexamethasone has a little time to work its magic. Dr. Linkletter left while Margi inserted the IV drip needle into Lilith's left arm and provided her with an oxygen mask. Lilith was grateful for the cool, pure oxygen breeze around her mouth and nose.

Lilith shared the news by cell phone with Ross. After she hung up, Ross bowed his head in the ER waiting room and prayed silently for the love of his life.

During the first hour, Lilith's temperature dropped to 101.5, her oxygen level increased to 87 percent, and her heart rate dropped to 108 bpm.

Unfortunately, none of these numbers improved during the following hour.

Two and a half hours later, Dr. Linkletter returned, looked at Lilith's vitals, and informed her that they were going to put her on a ventilator. Lilith pushed the speed dial for Ross' number.

"They are putting me on a ventilator," Lilith said, "I'm scared."

"I love you, Lilith," Ross said.

"I love you, too, Ross," Lilith said. "Oh God, they're going to put me under now."

After being isolated from her family and on a ventilator for five days, Lilith took her last breath in the intensive care unit of Health Harbor Hospital.

7

ESCAPE AND HIDE

May 11, 1993
Prague, Czech Republic

After dropping Eva into the open manhole, the golem quickly carried Rabbi Kohn and the Scroll through the darkness of Prague's narrow streets and back alleys to the Formace Synagogue, where the rabbi led a small congregation in what is known as the Josefov.

The Josefov, or Jewish Quarter, is located between the Vltava River, which, according to legend, is where Rabbi Loew, the Maharal of Prague created a golem out of clay during the 1600s to protect the Jews. The unsavory history of the Josefov area of Prague began in the 13th century when Jewish people were ordered to leave their scattered homes in and around Prague to concentrate them into the quarter of the city. The Prague Jews were, over the centuries, banned from living anywhere else in Prague, and as the Jews were exiled from Germany, Spain, Moravia, and Austria, they migrated to this section of Prague, creating evermore crowded conditions. As if this segregation wasn't enough, the ghetto inhabitants were forced to submit to changes to buildings and streets depending upon the mood of whichever ruler governed them. The latest of these reconstruction events occurred between 1893-1913, when a number of buildings were leveled, and streets were re-routed regardless of the desires of the inhabitants.

The golem entered the synagogue through a back entrance and placed Rabbi Kohn on his feet just inside the entrance, and the Scroll onto a small table near the rear of the synagogue. Rabbi Kohn began pacing through the synagogue, pacing in an agitated state and talking to himself. As he walked in the darkness, he nearly tripped and fell over the body of 'Able', one of the mercenaries whose screaming he heard over the walkie-talkie, as this nightmare began. He reached over to the wall and turned on an overhead light, illuminating the body lying in a pool of blood on the floor. It looked as though the man had received a point-blank hit from an 8 lb cannonball, but Rabbi Kohn knew the source of the impact – his golem's fist. He looked at the golem standing silently near the doorway.

"Golem, close and lock the back door to the synagogue," Rabbi Kohn said.

The golem obediently closed and locked the door.

"There is no choice in the matter," Rabbi Kohn said, still in distress, "I have to leave with the Scroll and my wife at once. If I stay here, the people that Eva is associated with will come after the Scroll again and again until they have it. At any and all costs, the Sefer Yetzirah must be kept out of the hands of those who don't understand its purpose."

The rabbi stopped pacing and prayed.

"Adonai, help me protect the holy words of our Father Abraham as they are written upon this blessed Scroll. Please give me wisdom to protect it from those who wish to steal it from your people."

A sense of calm washed over the rabbi, and a plan came to him like a gentle ocean wave. He said to the golem, "Follow me," and he walked out the rear door of the synagogue into an alleyway. He stopped once the golem was outside on the cobblestones, and the golem stopped, as well. Rabbi Kohn then turned to the golem and pulled a small pocketknife from his pants pocket. Examining the creature's chest, he searched for and found the letters that he had written there when he created it several years ago on the banks of the Vltava River under the light of a full moon – אֱמֶת.[1]

"Golem, you have faithfully worked for me here at the synagogue for several years and protected both me and the Scroll, and I am grateful for your service," the rabbi said.

The golem looked down at Rabbi Kohn without a trace of emotion.

Working quickly, he used the pocketknife blade to scrape away the aleph (אֱ) converting the meaning of the word from "truth" to "dead" in Hebrew[2]. When the last traces of the letter were removed from the golem's chest, the golem shivered, moaned quietly, and then crumbled into a pile of dried clay. Rabbi Kohn then spread the clay particles around into the cobblestones, recovered the Scroll, and walked quickly to his home.

He entered his bedroom to find his wife sleeping peacefully in their bed. He sat on her side of the bed and turned on the lamp on his wife's nightstand.

"Vera," he said, gently shaking her shoulder. "Vera, we have to leave."

Her eyelids opened, then closed again.

"Albert. What time is it, Albert?" she mumbled.

"It's 11:30, darling. You must get up, pack a few days-worth of clothing and then we have to leave – tonight. There are people searching for us who want to hurt us," he replied.

Vera sat up suddenly, startled awake at his words. "What are you talking about, Albert? What people want to hurt us?" she said.

"The golem defended me from people who took the Scroll from the synagogue tonight. They are all dead, but there are more people who will be coming soon. You have to trust me, and you must do what I say quickly. And don't forget to pack your passport. I had to send the golem back to the dust of the earth tonight. There may have been witnesses to their deaths at the hands of the golem, and we

1. The Hebrew word אֱמֶת translates to "truth" in English.
2. The Hebrew word מֶת translates into death in English.

simply can't take the chance that we'd be connected to their deaths in some way," Albert said.

"I knew that monstrosity would come to no good!" she exclaimed, leaping out of the bed to begin packing. "Sure, he was good at cleaning the synagogue at night and cooking meals – and all without leaving the synagogue, but he has almost been discovered on several occasions and now here we are leaving our home to escape thieves?"

"These were no ordinary thieves, Vera. Tonight, the golem protected the Scroll from being stolen by a very wealthy and powerful woman with armed mercenaries. Now they are all dead in the street in front of the *Table Poutine*, and it won't be long until the police will be knocking at our door to ask a variety of awkward questions, the least of which will be, 'Why is there a dead mercenary in your synagogue?' Worse yet, I'm almost certain that this woman will be followed by others, if they aren't already here. And if the Scroll ends up in the wrong hands, there is no telling what kind of destruction might be unleashed upon the world," replied Albert.

Vera and Albert packed their bags and drove quickly through the night from Prague to Munich, where they purchased tickets to Chicago. Rabbi Kohn and Vera stayed with relatives in Skokie, Illinois (about 15 miles north of Chicago), and quietly donated the Scroll to the Bara Synagogue under the leadership of Rabbi Aaron Meltzer, who took an oath to protect the Scroll with his very life.

Rabbi Meltzer kept the Scroll in a safety deposit box in the Northshore Bank and Trust for several years. Concerned that the Scroll was too far away from his immediate purview at the bank, and in a believable ruse to replace his aging and decrepit podium, the rabbi paid a carpenter to build a podium with a secret compartment in the base, large enough to contain something of the dimensions of the Scroll. Given the amount of money the carpenter was going to be paid for the work, he gladly signed an NDA to never reveal the nature of the work that had been done, under penalty of $100,000 for breaking his silence. All diagrams of the carpenter's project were given to Rabbi Meltzer upon completion of the work. The rabbi burned the documents in his fire pit and relocated the Scroll to its new home in the base of his podium.

Albert and Vera Kohn moved to Jackson Hole, Wyoming, later that year and opened Grand Teton Coffee and Bagels, a coffee and bagel shop in the downtown area. The venture was profitable and delicious, and it gave them the privacy they sought as they lived out the rest of their lives.

The snowstorm on January 3rd, 2000, was one hell of a way to start the new new century, dumping 13 inches of snow on the city of Skokie, Illinois. Unbeknownst to Rabbi Meltzer, his cholesterol had been above 240 for the last seven years, and this, combined with his relatively sedentary lifestyle, had created a 95 percent blockage of the left anterior descending artery in his heart. This artery is often referred to as the widowmaker for its propensity to deliver death quickly and unexpectedly to men, thereby turning their beloved spouses into widows. Had Rabbi Meltzer conducted a yearly check-up with his physician, his condition would have been detected and corrected with medication, but Aaron didn't like going to the doctor unless something was causing him a serious problem.

Thus, on the morning of January 4, 2000, merely four days into the brand-new millennium and six hours after the end of the snowstorm, Rabbi Meltzer put on his snow boots, snow pants, warmest coat, and battery heated gloves and grabbed his snow shovel. He began shoveling the heavy, though beautiful, 13-inches of snow from the sidewalk in front of his synagogue along with several of the synagogue's neighbors.

As he shoveled, he began to feel indigestion from his breakfast of eggs, bacon, and toast. A few minutes later, dizziness set in, and he collapsed, face down in the deep snow. None of his shoveling neighbors saw him collapse, as they were too busy shoveling their own sidewalks. The wind that day blew just enough fresh snow over the rabbi to hide him from view, and the owner of the Scroll died in the snow in front of the Bara[3] Synagogue, taking the location of the Scroll to his grave.

3. This word, transcribed from the Hebrew word בָּרָא, means "created".

8

THOSE WHO WERE LOST

April 25, 2020
Skokie, Illinois

Barry Spearman, Funeral Director at the Lakewood Funeral Home in Skokie, and Dante Moretti, Mortuary Technician at the same establishment were dressed for the grim times. It was Dante's sixth day on the job, and Barry was teaching him the ropes. Each man wore a disposable white, Tyvek body suit covering themselves from head to toe, with a perimeter around the face lined with an elastic cord. Their hands were covered by blue nitrile gloves and a blue surgical mask covered their mouths and noses. Six face shields hung from hooks in the back of the windowless, white panel van emblazoned with a large professional sign painted on each side. The sign read "Lakewood Funeral Home – Dedicated to the Ones You Love" posted under a large photo of a granddaughter hugging her grandpa.

Barry was driving the van to the former Moskowitz Meats refrigerated meat storage facility that had been converted by the city into a temporary morgue due to the number of deaths created by the COVID outbreak.

Barry, a tall gentleman with a thick white mustache and carefully coiffed, white hair combed back into a look suitable for Wall Street, was usually impeccably dressed in a business suit and tie. Today, Barry was wearing only a button-up white dress shirt due to the additional warmth of the Tyvek suit. Dante, meanwhile, was a medium-height young man with jet-black hair woven into dreadlocks. Dante was a bodybuilder whose biceps were larger than many folks' thighs. Underneath his Tyvek suit, he wore Under Armour track pants and a shirt with a picture of Arnold Schwarzenegger urging people to hit the gym.

"Now, when we get there, we'll need to wear the transparent face shields and bring the frosted face shield in with us on the gurney, just in case," Barry explained. "For times when the morgue doesn't have the body in a body bag, we made a face shield for the deceased that we sanded with 120 grit sandpaper. After all, we don't want to get our face shields mixed up with someone who has just died from COVID, do we?"

"Makes sense to me, Boss," Dante said.

"You probably don't know this, but the simple act of transporting a body – loading it on the gurney, bouncing it around a bit in the back of the van, and so forth – is enough to expel droplets of moisture remaining in the lungs out into the air. And since I'm 72-years-old, and, by the way, planning to retire at the end of the year, the last thing I need is to breathe in a droplet of COVID-infected corpse spray."

"Woah, boss, you're retiring this year? Well, congrats, man. I don't blame you for being careful. Hell, I'm young, but I'd like to get older, so I'll also take a pass on the COVID-infected corpse spray too."

"This is the place," Barry said, as he drove into the loading area of the former meat storage facility and backed up to a point near a ramp leading to a rear door. On the door face was a duct-taped piece of cardboard with a large magic marker print that displayed: "Cook County Temporary Morgue. ID Required for Access."[1]

---

1. https://www.cdc.gov/mmwr/volumes/70/wr/mm7046a5.htm

The two men got out of the van and walked to the back. They opened the rear doors. Fitting their face shields on their heads and over their surgical masks, they pulled the gurney out of the van and rolled it up to the back door, where they pressed a white button, activating a loud buzzer inside the building. Soon, a worker opened the back door and asked for ID. Both men offered their driver's licenses and their funeral director and embalmer ID cards, and the worker escorted the men inside, where the cold soon caused their face shields to fog, creating some difficulty in seeing where they were going. They passed through row after row of hastily constructed but sturdy industrial shelves, with about 30 percent of the shelf space holding COVID pandemic casualties.

Barry looked around in grim amazement and said, "Lord God in Heaven! In my 45 years as a funeral director, I've never seen so many body bags before – so many dead."

Dante said, "Looks like we're about to become very busy."

"Take a few deep breaths and focus on the one person that we're here for," Barry said, holding up a lone finger. "Look at my finger. Keep saying to yourself, we're here for Lilith Newman."

"Yeah. Sure. Got it," Dante said as his eyes scanned the racks of body bags.

Finally, the temporary morgue worker stopped at a low shelf where a body bag containing a small person was being stored. The edge of the shelf underneath the body bag was labeled QC-27. The worker looked at the paperwork provided by Barry, then he unzipped the body bag to examine the toe tag. Finding that the information on the toe tag matched the paperwork that Barry had provided, the worker gave them a thumbs up, allowing them to move Lilith's body to the gurney. The worker and Barry both signed the paperwork, leaving two copies in possession of the morgue. The frosted face mask wasn't needed, as Lilith's body was being transported in a body bag.

Respectfully, the two men gripped the gray polyethylene bag on each end and moved her to the gurney, strapping her in gently. They then rolled her to the van and began the journey back to Lakewood Funeral Home.

9

ASHES TO ASHES

April 26, 2020
Skokie, illinois

THIS REFRIGERATED STORAGE IS FOR
HUMAN REMAINS ONLY. STORAGE OF
FOOD AND DRINK IS PROHIBITED

Dante Moretti opened the door to the refrigerated storage area used for human remains about to be cremated. Dante stepped into the cold storage area and walked to the sturdy wooden shelves containing cardboard coffins, wooden coffins and, these days, plastic body bags. Finding Lilith's body bag, he looked to make sure that the paperwork matched the papers contained in a transparent folder heat-sealed to the body bag, as well as to the toe tag present on Lilith's right toe.

He then raised the hydraulically actuated gurney surface to the level of the shelf upon which she had been placed and slid the body bag over onto the gurney, securing the strap that prevented her from accidentally falling off. Dante lowered the gurney and pushed it out of the refrigerated room down a short hall to a door. He knocked on the door, and heard someone say quietly, “Come in.”

Dante’s Tyvek attire combined with surgical mask and nitrile gloves presented no comfort to Ross, who sat in the small waiting room, waiting to identify Lilith’s body prior to cremation. He walked over to the open door, accompanied by Barry Spearman, now in suit, tie and a black surgical mask covering his thick white mustache.

“Ross, could you please stand on the blue X to maintain a safe distance from her?” Barry asked, a request he provided to far too many grieving family members recently.

Ross stepped back a few feet. “Sorry about that. It’s just that I didn’t have a chance to say goodbye to her while she was in the ICU.”

Barry nodded at Dante, who remained silent behind his surgical mask. Dante stepped toward Lilith’s body bag and unzipped the upper portion of the bag, revealing her face for Ross.

“That’s my wife, my lover, my best friend, the love of my life, and the mother of my children. That’s Lilith Newman,” Ross said, choking as he spoke, with tears streaming from his eyes down onto his surgical mask.

Barry nodded again at Dante, who zipped the body bag back up.

Barry asked quietly in his baritone voice, “Ross, this is hard to ask at this moment, but just to confirm, you’d still like for Lilith to be cremated, correct?”

“Cremation is what Lilith wanted, so I will respect her wishes, yes. If it were up to me, I would put her in the most beautiful and expensive casket that you have and bury her in a mausoleum fit for the Queen of England,” Ross said.

“Ross, I have one more verification step that we need to take,” Barry said as Dante handed him a numbered, stainless steel ID tag. “Could you please verify that the number on that ID tag matches the number on Lilith’s cremation paperwork? If it matches, could you please sign at the bottom of that paperwork?” Barry asked.

Ross nodded, signed, and returned the ID tag to Dante.

“Dante, please take Mrs. Newman back, now,” Barry said, referring to the cremation unit. Barry stepped forward and gently closed the door to the hallway, allowing Dante to return to the task at hand. He then handed Ross a box of tissues.

Dante pushed the gurney down the hall through a set of swinging doors to the cremation unit, where a conveyor table inlaid with stainless-steel rollers awaited. He hummed an odd, almost musical tone as he pushed the gurney into the room. He placed a foldable sheet of cardboard onto the steel rollers and raised the hydraulic lift to match the gurney height with the conveyor leading into the door of the cremation unit, also known as a retort. Dante then positioned himself on the same side as the foldable cardboard and grabbed two of the built-in handles on the body bag, pulling Lilith and the bag over onto the foldable cardboard box.

He then folded the box sides upward and interlocked them to create a temporary cardboard coffin. Taking one of the pre-folded cardboard lids, Dante placed it over the opening of the cardboard coffin. Finally, he placed the numbered ID tag on top of the coffin lid, directly over where Lilith's head was positioned. Dante then opened the door to the retort and pushed Lilith, her body bag, and the cardboard coffin into the unheated furnace. He lowered the firebrick insulated door to the furnace until it was about three-quarters of the way down and pressed a button labeled "Ignite."

The button actuated a ventilation fan above and to one side of the furnace, followed by six natural gas-fired burners – three on each side of Lilith's body. Dante watched as the cardboard surrounding Lilith's head burned away, followed by the plastic of the body bag. Finally, the hair, scalp, and skin of her head became visible and began to burn away on the firebrick surface where she lay. As soon as he saw this, he was confident that the furnace was operating properly, and he closed the door of the retort to let it run through its programmed fire and cool down sequence.[1]

* * *

1. Source: Barie Fritz, funeral director consultant.

April 27, 2020 | Skokie, Illinois

The next morning, Dante entered the retort room humming his tuneless song. He checked the internal temperature of the retort and then pressed the button to open the door to the retort. A wave of warmth entered the room from the interior of the retort chamber. Dante grabbed his heat-resistant wire brush push broom and pulled the ashes mixed with fragments of Lilith's bones into a stainless-steel cool-down tray. After the mixture cooled for a few minutes on a table, he put on a pair of nitrile gloves and searched the mixture for the identification tag, metallic surgical implants, screws, jewelry that might have been forgotten and the like.

Finding nothing of significance other than the identification tag, he carefully shoveled the ashes and fragments into a stainless-steel blender, locked the lid in place and flipped the switch[2]. Dante began humming his musical tone again, and the source of the tune became apparent. His humming was a perfect match for the frequency of the blender.

Flipping the blender switch to the off position, Dante continued his humming, unlocked the lid and poured the pulverized contents into a plastic bag. He taped the stainless-steel identification tag to the top of the bag and carefully slid the bag into a purple urn that the family had picked out for her remains. He also placed a small beige envelope with Lilith's wedding ring into the urn atop the bag of ashes.

* * *

April 28, 2020 | Skokie, Illinois

The purple urn containing Lilith's ashes rested on the altar of the small chapel of Lakewood Funeral Home. Ross had chosen to schedule a memorial service for Lilith soon after her cremation, due to the many on-going restrictions, social distancing and recommended limitations on public gatherings. The funeral home was even reluctant

---

2. Source: Barie Fritz, funeral director consultant.

to publish an obituary for Lilith, because social gatherings – even at funerals – were discouraged under the guidelines of the Center for Disease Control, and an obituary in the newspaper simply represented an open invitation to gather. Because of this, Ross had only invited about 15 of Lilith's friends and family, and no obituary was published.

All but two of these guests were present as he, his two children and Carly, his sister, sat in one of the two pews at the front of the chapel. Because of the fact that she had flown on a plane to attend, Carly sat the recommended six feet away from Ross and the children. The two who were not present had contracted COVID and had called to excuse themselves. Of the chapel's 14 pews, all but six of the pews had been roped off with blue velvet rope. Attached to the middle of each rope was a sign that read:

PLEASE RESPECT SOCIAL DISTANCING GUIDELINES.
THIS PEW IS CURRENTLY CLOSED.

At the front of the chapel, on a 50-inch television screen, a variety of photographs of Lilith with her family were being played, about one every 10 seconds – Lilith in the hospital holding Brian right after he was born, letting a giggling young Brian squish his birthday cake frosting in her face, holding Emily as a baby with her bottle in her mouth, swinging Emily in a toddler seat on the swing set in the back yard, driving a motor boat with the wind whipping her hair, graduating from college with her accounting degree, in her wedding dress having rice thrown at her with Ross running down a sidewalk, on their honeymoon on a beach in Hawaii. A Pandora playlist of Lilith's favorite musical groups was being played – Gwen Stefani, Newsboys, U2, MercyMe, Taylor Swift, and others – at a respectful background volume for those in attendance.

At 7:05 pm, the music stopped, and Barry Spearman stepped up to the podium.

"We welcome everyone in our chapel today, as well as to those viewing online via our chapel webcam. We are here today to pay our respects and celebrate the life of Lilith Grace Newman. Lilith leaves behind her beloved husband, Ross, and her beloved children, Brian and Emily, whom we know are experiencing the most difficult day of their life," Barry said. "I would like to ask anyone who might wish to celebrate Lilith or express their love and appreciation for her to please do so from the podium at this time."

Ross stood and walked somewhat shakily to the podium, carrying a box of tissues. "I met Lilith when I was in college, delivering bread part-time for Grandpa's Oven Fresh Bread Company. Lilith managed a small grocery store in Champaign, Illinois, and the first time I saw her open the garage door for my truck, it was like the clouds parted to reveal a glowing beautiful angel. I stood in the back of my truck with my mouth wide open until, with a smile on her face, she said to me, 'Are you here to deliver bread, or are you going to stare at me with your mouth open for the rest of the day?' I somehow managed to snap out of my stupor and delivered the bread, and I couldn't wait to make that delivery every week for the next six weeks. At week six, like Jacob working for the hand of Rachel, I finally worked up the courage to ask her out, and she said, 'Well, it certainly took you long enough!' which caused me to drop the entire pallet of honey buns."

After those in attendance stopped laughing, Ross continued.

"I always tell people that from the very first time she saw me, she was mainly interested in my buns - but that's just a silly joke - with a grain of truth. I married way up when I married Lilith – sort of like a monkey marrying a princess. She will always be my best friend, the mother of our children, and my dream girl."

Ross wiped his eyes with a tissue and said, "I think I have to sit down, now, before I become a blubbering idiot."

Several others came up and shared funny stories and stories of Lilith's generosity and time volunteering at church in Sunday School for Ross and Emily's classes. The stories and visiting at a socially acceptable distance wrapped up at about 8:30 that evening. After the last guest left, Barry presented Ross with Lilith's ashes in a beautiful purple urn inlaid with flowers and a cross in gold leaf.

Ross carefully set the urn in the exact center of a mission-style cherrywood coffee table, then sat in the middle of the adjacent couch, and looked at the urn with tears in his eyes. Emily sat down next to her dad and put her arm around him, laying her head on his left shoulder, tears clouding her view of the urn. Ross' sister, Carly did the same on Ross' right shoulder. Brian sat down in a gray and teal wing-back chair and pulled tissue after tissue out its green cardboard dispenser, wiping his eyes and nose. Ross waited until his family, now reduced in number by a very important one, regained some degree of control, then he picked up the urn containing the remains of his beloved with both hands, stood up and led his family through the glass front doors of the funeral home into the night.

The stars twinkled overhead with the unspeakable beauty of God's creation, but tonight the Newmans' hearts were filled with unspeakable grief. Aunt Carly drove them back to a home that would never be the same again.

10

ANATOLY AND ALEXEY

8:05 PM
April 5, 2001
Moscow, Russian Federation

Anatoly Dezhnyov sat on the brown brick steps of his townhouse and peered down Nagatinskaya Street, waiting for his next "customer." The street was deserted, and the dusk was gaining momentum towards night as a black rat scampered across the sidewalk from somewhere underneath his stairs into the gutter. He watched with mild amusement the sight of its hips and shoulders furiously wiggling above the curb in the darkness as it made progress to the storm drain, where it disappeared.

"Run little krysa, run!" he chuckled in mock excitement.

Looking across Nagatinskaya Street, across a field covered in litter, used tires, plastic vodka bottles, used condoms and illegally dumped concrete rubble, he could glimpse the Moscow River, a rank flow of gray ooze, today adorned with oil slicks and reeking of dead fish and the occasional dead pigeon. He reached into his jacket pocket and pulled out a pack of Belomorkanal cigarettes and his Zippo lighter, which he had proudly purchased at a flea market earlier this year. It was just like the one his dad used. He removed a cigarette from the packet, put it between his lips and lit the cigarette with the Zippo, closing the stainless-steel lid with an almost elegant flip of his wrist, thereby extinguishing the flame. He placed the package of cigarettes and the lighter back into his jacket pocket as he inhaled the pungent smoke from the cigarette, squinting his eyes as he did so.

The hissed words, "Are you Shorty?" caused Anatoly to jump and he dropped his cigarette from between his gray-tinged lips onto the steps, releasing sparks of ash. He looked up and saw a young man grown old with addiction and vodka, with torn, dirty clothing looking expectantly at him in the growing darkness.

Anatoly whispered angrily, "Yes, you idiot! Never call me by that name again or it will be the last time you buy a rock from me, you filthy junkie. Now shut up and show me the money."

The junkie reached into the pocket of his trousers, looked around and said, "Here you go, Shorty." Anatoly stood up to punch the man, but a Makarov pistol appeared from his trouser pocket, pointed at Anatoly's face.

"Sit down, *Shorty*." The junkie dragged the pronunciation of the last word out sarcastically. Anatoly sat back down onto the steps, his anger boiling.

A pair of yellow and blue police cars pulled around the corner of the street and parked diagonally in front of the steps. Two police officers stepped out of the vehicles and walked quickly up the stairs to Anatoly. They both drew telescoping batons, briskly extended them and began to beat him. He raised his arms to protect his head, so they beat him on the chest and belly. He lowered his arms to protect his abdomen, and they switched to his head. The last thing that he remembered before the welcome darkness of unconsciousness was the police informant junkie saying, "Good night, *Shorty*."

* * *

7:14 AM | April 7, 2001 | Matrosskaya Tishina, Moscow, Russian Federation

Anatoly slowly opened his swollen eyelids and found that he was naked, lying on a fold-down plate made of iron in a narrow cinder block cell. He wondered, "Is this iron plate going to be my bed?" An iron door painted dark green appeared to be the only egress or entrance. A rat crawled from a hole in the floor at the back of the cell. He realized that this must be the toilet. Pain buzzed through his head, face, arms, shoulders and abdomen. He looked down and saw that his abdomen was covered in dark black and purple bruises, of which there was blacker and more purple than his original flesh tone. He wondered how long he had been unconscious – one day? Two days?

After he managed to sit up, with great difficulty, he managed to swing his legs over the side of the fold-down iron table. Squeezing himself between the edge of the bed and the cinder block wall, he felt something furry brush against his foot and then a sharp bite on his ankle. Adrenaline shot into his bloodstream, and he furiously lifted the iron table up onto the wall. Holding the plate there with pain burning through his arm, he saw five rats scampering about his cell. He latched the plate to the wall and examined his ankle, which was bleeding. The sound of a squeaky-wheeled cart grew louder and then stopped outside in the hallway. About belly-high, a small door opened in the sickly green door and a bowl slid in on top of the door.

"Here is your breakfast, dog!" a voice said, and then began counting down. "Five... Four.. Three... Two..."

Anatoly painfully leapt to the door and grabbed the bowl with both hands as the jailer spoke the word "One. " At that point, the small door slammed shut.

"Why am I here?!" yelled Anatoly.

From the other side of the sickly green door came, "Really? You don't have a clue about why you are here? How about this, then? In addition to the fact that you are a drug dealer, your moron brother illegally tried to escape from Mother Russia across the border into Finland a month ago, and the Fins returned him back into Russian custody, just like the Finish cowards always do. So now you and your entire family are considered to be traitorous scum. Please allow me to welcome you to the Hotel Matrosskaya Tishina[1] conveniently located near the center of the friendly and welcoming city of Moscow. We absolutely guarantee that you will give us a five-star rating at the end of your stay, or I will personally make your stay right with vigorous beatings from our hospitality team."

The voice on the other side of the sickly green door then began to laugh deliriously, as though this was the funniest thing he had ever said in his life. Soon, the laughter devolved into a fit of phlegm-laden coughing, which slowly moved away from Anatoly's cell along with the squeaky-wheeled cart.

* * *

1:13 PM | April 10, 2001 | Matrosskaya Tishina, Moscow, Russian Federation

For the first time, after lunch, Anatoly was herded into the yard of the prison and allowed to walk among the other prisoners. Unsure of himself and still in pain from his police beating, he walked as far away from the other inmates as possible to a shadowy corner of the prison yard. There, he sat down on a small patch of crab grass and hung his head almost between his knees. Voices from several other inmates grew louder as they approached, accompanied by three jailers, who were silent. Anatoly raised his head and watched them as they walked towards him.

"Hey! New guy, we have a present for you!" yelled the largest of the group of five. "Some of Russia's finest vodka, just for you!"

This gained the full attention of the other inmates, many of whom began to walk towards Anatoly's corner to watch. One of the jailers handed the large prisoner a plastic flask of Stoli vodka along with something else, something that gave off a brief silver flash of reflected sunlight as it passed between the jailer's hand and the prisoner's hand.

1. https://en.wikipedia.org/wiki/Matrosskaya_Tishina

A large crowd of prisoners had now congregated around Anatoly, as though they knew what was about to happen. They began to chant "Vasily! Vasily! Vasily!" beginning quietly at first, then growing in volume as Vasily, the large muscular prisoner, held the bottle of vodka high in the air and strutted back and forth for the growing crowd, whipping up their enthusiasm with his showmanship.

"Boys, hold the new guy down so we can warm him up with a little Stoli vodka," the large prisoner said. Vasily's four assistants stepped over to Anatoly, who tried to rise to his feet. He immediately received a punch to his already broken nose, putting him down forcefully on his back. The four men each took hold of a limb and held him down on the ground.

"Here you go, Traitor. Stoli vodka!" the large man said, pouring the clear liquid onto Anatoly's face and head. But Anatoly quickly realized that instead of vodka, it was charcoal lighter fluid.

"No! Don't do this to me! I'm not a traitor to my country!" Anatoly yelled as the liquid wet his face and then he sputtered and choked as the fluid got into his mouth and spilled down his throat. He could barely see because the liquid was stinging his eyes, but he managed to glimpse Vasily, pulling out Anatoly's Zippo lighter, then thumbing the metal gear to spark the wick. Vasily kissed the side of the shiny stainless-steel Zippo and tossed it onto Anatoly's chest, whereupon his captors released him, hooting and laughing as they jumped away from the combustion.

The flames made a whump sound as they spread to his face, hair, mouth, throat, and neck - and then the screaming and flailing began.

* * *

12:45 PM | Five Years Later | Moscow, Russian Federation

The sickly green door to his cell opened and Anatoly was greeted by coughing, followed by the jailer standing before him hocking a pale-yellow chunk of phlegm onto the floor. He said, "Congratulations! Today you rejoin our growing and vibrant Russian society again, though you are always welcome to visit our beautiful Hotel Matrosskaya Tishina at any time again in the future. If you haven't already done so, please be sure to sign up for our frequent stayer's program, where you can enjoy special offers such as avocado-lighter fluid fire facials to make your hideously disfigured face look even more swollen and hideous."

Anatoly responded, "I hope that, as the main proprietor of this shithole, you are able to take full advantage of *that* facial, as well as the prison-jizz-diahrrea-body-soak. If either of us needs their face fixed, it's you, you lung-loogie-chunking son of a bat-faced-whore. As for my frequent-stayer points, please feel free to shove them up your wrinkled old ass with that rat-shit-coated mop of yours – mop-end first, of course, Alexey."

"I wouldn't have it any other way, my friend. My, you are full of piss and vinegar today, Anatoly! I must admit, I will miss that flame-broiled, earless, hairless cauliflower face of yours," Alexey said.

"And I will miss your hacking, hocking, that damned squeaky wheel that you have never oiled in the five years I've been here, and of course, your maggot-infested oatmeal every morning," Anatoly said.

"The secret is to scoop them straight out of the bottom of the garbage can so that they are as fresh and juicy as the day they were hatched," Alexey said. "Goodbye, old friend."

"Goodbye, old friend," Anatoly said. "See you again in a year."

* * *

12:45 AM | One Year Later | 20 Kilometers East of the Finland / Russian Federation Border

The night was near freezing as the aurora borealis danced in the night sky above in brilliant, flaming, green curtains of light. Anatoly and Alexey watched as their Finnish contact, Tuullikki, pulled aside the camouflaged netting and opened the hatch to the tunnel leading beneath the Finland/Russia frozen border to freedom.

"Get in! I will follow," Tuullikki whispered.

Anatoly and Alexey followed her instructions and climbed down the ladder below the surface of the earth and into the narrow tunnel leading to their freedom. Anatoly stepped down off of the wooden ladder onto the solid, but damp, floor of the tunnel, bending down to begin the long crawl to freedom. The tunnel was only about three feet tall by three feet wide with two miniature rail tracks that could be ridden on small, hand-powered flatbed carts for the entire distance to freedom. Anatoly heard the hatch close above him and then heard the circular dog wheel spin and the pins sliding into place followed by Tuullikki's climb down the ladder into the enlarged chamber with Alexey and Anatoly.

She sat down on the damp tunnel floor preparing for the long journey ahead and asked in Russian, "So, let's address the elephant in the tunnel first thing, shall we? Anatoly, what the hell happened to your face?"

Anatoly was used to this question by now, and replied, "The jailers in the Matrosskaya Tishina commissioned some of their pet prisoners to hold me down, douse my face with charcoal lighter fluid and light it on fire with my own Zippo lighter. It took me about five minutes to put the fire out before I collapsed into unconsciousness. Two years later, I managed to kill each and every one of the bastards that did this to me. The first was by poisoned oatmeal. The second was electrocuted naked in the shower. The third was by rabies – honestly, that was the most difficult one to achieve, using blood from a rabid bat that I captured – the fourth one I simply hired three prisoners to stab him to death. These first four men were *only* the men that held me down for the act of immolation. The masterpiece of my quintet of prison murders was saved for Vasily, the man who actually did the deed. I simply bribed one of the guards to allow me to have access to his cell for an hour. Access to the man who poured charcoal lighter fluid on my face, in my mouth and on my head and then used my own Zippo lighter to set me on fire. For Vasily, I returned the *warm* love that he gave to me, but I used *much* more lighter fluid. *Much* more. Of course, I used my Zippo lighter. The rats enjoyed a tasty barbeque that night," Anatoly said.

Tuullikki sighed from deep within her lungs and said, "You Russians are all a bunch of sick bastards. I don't know why we continue to help you escape. But I suppose the money makes it all worth it in the end." Then, she pointed to the three carts resting on the floor of the chamber and said, "Let's go."

* * *

Alexey and Anatoly both eventually made their way to the United States. Anatoly settled in Chicago, where he became a very successful, albeit illegal, drug distributor. He also conducted private investigation work for dubious clients who paid top dollar for his investigative talents. Alexey settled in Skokie, Illinois, where he worked as a butcher, mostly as a legitimate businessman handling pork, beef, and chicken.

But every now and then, and not often enough to satisfy his personal greed, he delved into the highly profitable processing of *human* meat, mostly for the purpose of making people disappear.

11

STAINED GLASS AND GRAFFITI

June 1, 2020
Skokie, Illinois

Brian Newman added two cans of peas to the basket from Aisle 5 and began his masked trip to the next items—four zucchinis and a white onion—from produce. He took the job as a shopper in April at Mitchell's Pantry just as people were beginning to have their groceries delivered to the trunks of their cars in special parking spots just outside the store during the COVID pandemic.

Since the beginning of the pandemic just a few months earlier, Brian's life had been turned upside down in ways that he never would have imagined a year earlier. Most of all, Brian missed his mom. Everyone in his family caught COVID in March, beginning with Emily, then mom, then dad, then Brian. But now mom was gone, leaving a gaping black hole in the middle of their family. Brian recalled how his mom loved the color purple and how there were still snuggly purple blankets, purple sweaters, and purple socks and slippers scattered around their home.

Brian's thoughts were interrupted as he completed his customer's shopping cart with the addition of a box of frozen hamburger patties. His phone had been dinging for the past few minutes, and it indicated that his previous customer was waiting for him in spot number five. He pushed that customer's shopping cart towards the front of the store and into the parking lot. A Land Rover awaited him in spot five with the back hatch open. Like all but a few in these pandemic days, the driver was wearing a mask. This one was emblazoned with the Chicago Blackhawks logo.

"I have an order for Mr. Atchison." Brian called out.

"That's me!" the driver nodded.

Since there were three bottles of wine in the cart, Brian added "Can I please see your ID, sir?" The driver pulled off his baseball cap to reveal a shock of thinning platinum white hair and responded, "Does this count as a valid form of ID?"

If only he had a dollar for every time he'd heard that joke, he could retire.

"Sorry, sir. I have to obey the law. If you hold your ID up to the window, I'll take a photo of it," Brian replied.

The good-natured baby boomer held up his ID as requested for the photo and then poked a five-dollar bill through the crack in the window. "Thank you, sir," responded Brian, accepting the tip. Brian pulled the cart back into the store and lodged it snugly into the other carts. He walked over to the employee entrance, clocked out, and began his walk home.

Brian's dad, Ross, worked as an IT support manager at a medium-sized chemical company just off of I-94. Lilith's death was not only emotionally devastating for the Newman family, it also impacted them financially, and it was decided that Brian would get a job at Mitchell's Pantry to help out the family, and that dad would begin working a second job - installing security cameras and Plexiglas shields between cubicles for essential workers. Essential workers were people who were essential for maintaining the function of the country's infrastructure such as doctors, nurses, defense contractors, farmers, grocers, and even people who installed cough shields to prevent the spread of the virus.

Brian's walk home from Mitchell's Pantry brought him past several mostly shut down strip malls, the recently closed Lou's CrossFit Gym, the now-empty Peking Duck restaurant, and the abandoned Bara Synagogue. Brian had always admired how beautiful the synagogue building was on the outside, in spite of being abandoned. Rumor had it the last rabbi stole more than $70,000 from congregational donations but that he was never convicted because of lack of evidence in the congregation's sloppy bookkeeping practices. Due to ongoing lawsuits, the building continued to languish in a legal no-man's land – not able to be bought or sold or even used or rented by a new congregation. In the light of the beautiful day combined with the fact that he had no homework, Brian decided to walk around the synagogue and admire the ornate stained-glass windows.

"¡Buenos dias, Brian!" Mr. Fuentes, the property keeper, called out.

"¡Buenos dias, Señor Fuentes! ¿Como estas, hoy?" replied Brian, who enjoyed practicing his Spanish with the elderly gentleman. Brian pulled his mask up so as not to inadvertently expose Mr. Fuentes to any virus that he might have picked up at the market. Gabriel Fuentes did the same, but out of concern for his vulnerable age.

Gabriel was using a solvent, a scrub brush, and a pair of rubber gloves to scrub off the last few nights of graffiti from the stonework on the exterior of the building. In addition to mowing the yard, fixing leaks, and trimming the hedges, removing graffiti seemed like a job that never ended for Mr. Fuentes, and to Brian, it seemed incomprehensible that someone would deface such a sacred and beautiful structure as this one.

"I was on my way home from my job, the sun was shining, the skies were blue, and I thought I'd walk around the building to look at the stained glass. I guess I needed a little cheering up today," Brian related. "I hope you don't mind."

Mr. Fuentes replied with a laugh.

"Of course not, amigo! ¡Mi casa es tu casa!"

The two began to walk around the synagogue together. In addition to a bright yellow Star of David, there were other panes depicting horns being blown, a menorah, a partially unrolled Torah, a dove in flight, a burning bush, two stone tablets containing the ten commandments, a scene of the Red Sea being parted, and a series of windows depicting the creation of the world. In a pane in the highest place on a western wall of the synagogue, presumably above the podium within, was a rendering of the creation of man by God.

"Would you like to see the windows from the *inside* of the synagogue, Brian?" Mr. Fuentes asked.

"Wow! That'd be amazing! Am I allowed to go in?" Brian asked.

"Si, Señor! But only if *I* let you in," responded Mr. Fuentes, wagging his finger back and forth, as he walked with Brian to the entrance of the synagogue.

On arriving at the front door, he began fumbling through a large ring of keys. Finding the one he was looking for – a bright brass key with the Star of David molded into the bow of the key – he placed it into the lock and twisted it. The door opened with a creak, and stale air pushed past Brian's face.

The two entered the tall, wide, metal doorway and inside was a visual contradiction – the holiness of brilliant, beautiful beams of multi-colored light coming from the stained-glass windows and shining onto wooden pews and the main platform contrasted with the graffiti on the walls and the broken furniture on the floors.

"Mr. Fuentes, you ever work inside the synagogue?" Brian asked.

"You mean, why is there graffiti everywhere and broken furniture, if you are the caretaker?" responded Mr. Fuentes.

"They must not let you work your magic indoors," Brian said.

"Yes, they only let me work inside when there is a roof leak, a plumbing problem or something else similar occurs. No indoor cleaning allowed, no indoor painting, no removal of indoor graffiti allowed, because they want to keep my time to no more than two days a week, and to do the absolute minimum to avoid complaints from a neighborhood that can only see the outside of the building," Mr. Fuentes said.

"That's a real shame, this place is quite beautiful inside."

"Feel free to look around, Brian. Just try not to break anything and don't go into the basement. I need to finish removing the graffiti from the outside of the building," Gabriel said, and then he headed towards the front door calling out, "Be sure you finish looking around by 5:30 – that's when I have to lock up."

"Will do, Mr. Fuentes. Gracias," replied Brian.

Brian watched Mr. Fuentes exit the massive front door and then turned to the incredible scene before him. He wondered how vagrants were breaking into the synagogue to desecrate the sanctuary like this.

Above the platform at the rear of the sanctuary was the stained-glass rendering of the creation of man, with Adam rising from the bank of a river, shins covered in earth, pale blue light with twinkling stars flowing into Adam's mouth, giving him life. It was truly impressive and unquestionably the best window in the entire building.

Brian walked towards the platform and up to the podium. He walked around behind the podium to face the pews and just take in the enormity of the room. In this lighting, even the graffiti had a certain measure of beauty. He looked out onto an imaginary congregation and in his best rabbi imitation proclaimed "Shalom, my friends! May God bless you all!" As he emphasized the last word of his very short sermon, his knee bumped into an ornamental veneered Star of David under the podium and a small cabinet door opened. He kneeled down to look inside the cabinet, and at the back of the podium was a small, leather scroll with the following symbols inlaid in gold leaf on the outer cover of the scroll[1]:

ספר יצירה

Brian was startled by footsteps behind him, and he quickly hid the small scroll in the front of his pants underneath his sweatshirt. When Brian turned, the footsteps seemed to be coming not just from behind him, but also from underneath him, as though there was a basement below the platform. Quickly and quietly, he walked away from the podium and out of the synagogue. He sought out Mr. Fuentes on the grounds and told him that he needed to head home, and then showed him the scroll.

---

1. ספר יצירה transliterates from Hebrew into English as Sefer Yetzirah and means "book of formation".

"Looks like you found yourself a souvenir, amigo! I don't see any harm in keeping it since all of the important scrolls and sacred items were moved to another temple several years ago. Also, the grafiteros and banditos have long taken everything else of value, except for the stained-glass windows," Mr. Fuentes said.

"Gracias, Señor Fuentes. I suppose I will have to learn Hebrew in addition to Spanish so that I can read this scroll," Brian joked.

12

A REVELATION AND A WARNING

June 2, 2020
Skokie, Illinois

Brian waited until the following morning to really examine the old leather scroll. The entire scroll was written in Hebrew and, therefore, indecipherable to Brian. Along nearly every margin in the scroll were blocks of carefully hand-printed letters in what also appeared to be Hebrew. The scroll was rolled onto two dark wooden rollers. The short handles were ornately carved to depict puffs of wind blown from the circular wooden plates. The wooden plates were engraved with stars, birds, fish, cattle, and a kneeling man. When fully unfurled, the 4-inch-wide scroll stretched about 10 feet across most of the length of his room on the carpet. The "parchment" of the scroll whispered as it was unrolled and rubbed against the carpet. A texture was present on the scroll, making it look like thin leather.

Brian used his phone to search for "ancient paper" and found that animal skin was used long ago as a type of parchment, leaving exactly the defects he witnessed. There were four sections of parchment sewn together using some sort of thread, as though the maker of the scroll couldn't find enough parchment of good quality and needed to add lengths from other skins. A piece was missing near the beginning of the scroll, with a tear evident in the parchment across a block of Hebrew writing. When held up to the light, the skin was translucent in some sections, opaque and white in other sections, and pale yellow in others. When sunlight from the window struck the marginalia at the right angle, pale red flecks sparkled in the dried ink.

Brian carefully re-rolled the scroll. He Googled "Jewish bookstores in Skokie, IL." Several websites listed books and scrolls written in Hebrew. Brian figured if the store sold Hebrew language books, then the proprietors ought to be able to read Hebrew. Although Brian could drive, his family didn't have a car to spare, and his dad was at work, so he chose the closest bookstore on the list – three miles away. He put the scroll into a gallon Ziploc freezer bag, then put the bag into his backpack and hopped on his bike for a ride through a chilly but gentle mist that had formed since the previous day.

Unsure if he'd be able to trust the bookstore's owner, Brian's first stop was a nearby Kinko's, where he made a copy of the scroll's first ten 'pages'. He folded these copies in half and slid them into his backpack.

Feldman's World of Judaica was part of a strip mall that also contained an H&R Block tax service, Goldblum's Jewelry, a New Balance shoe store, and Marcy's Cold Slab Ice Cream Parlor. Brian parked his bike in a nearby rack, pulled up his surgical mask and walked through the glass doors. An old-fashioned bell dinged above Brian's head as the door opened. To his right was a small bay of prayer shawls. He observed an area of similar size displaying silver candlestick holders, plates, cups, wall hangings, and blue glass and ceramic items. Immediately in front of him was a glass display case containing jewelry. A sign on the display case proudly boasted, "More than 10,000 Judaica Books in Our Collection." Judging from the numerous tall shelves behind the display case, Brian might have offered a higher estimate. A few of the shelves bowed precariously downward with the weight of dusty tomes.

On top of the display case was a cash register straight from the previous century's Great Depression. Behind the cash register stood a short, white haired gentleman wearing gold-rim glasses and a surgical mask, palms resting on the display case, evaluating Brian with an amused gaze.

"Shalom, my young friend. How may I assist you today?" greeted Mr. Feldman in a quiet but friendly voice.

"Are you the owner of the store?" Brian said.

"Yes, my name is David Feldman. And to which famous scholar do I have the honor of speaking?"

"My name is Brian," he replied, intentionally omitting his surname. "I've found an old scroll, and I think it's written in Hebrew. I was wondering if you might be willing to look at it and give me some idea of what I've found?"

"Where did you find the scroll?" Mr. Feldman asked.

"In an abandoned building," Brian replied, avoiding the fact that he had found it in an abandoned synagogue in which he was technically trespassing.

"Can I see the scroll? I'll be glad to help you if I can," indicated Mr. Feldman.

"I've brought a copy of the first few sections of the scroll," Brian said, pulling the copies from his backpack and handing them to Mr. Feldman.

Mr. Feldman glanced at the copies and his eyebrows immediately rose with a look of alarm.

"Well, to start with, you are correct that this scroll is written in Hebrew," he said.

He turned to the next page and mumbled something in Hebrew and reviewed the other copied pages, continuing to mumble under his breath in Hebrew as he did so. Every now and then, David's generous white eyebrows rose with interest as his brass Torah pointer, shaped in the form of a pointing finger, scanned the copied pages in sync with his intelligent brown eyes moving behind the gold-rim glasses. After several minutes of studying the copies, Mr. Feldman spoke again.

"What you seem to have here, my young friend, is a heavily annotated copy of the Sefer Yetzirah, which, in English, means 'the Book of Formation.' Without seeing the actual scroll itself and based upon the style of the Hebrew alphabet used, this scroll appears to be ancient. The very interesting part of this scroll is that it has hand-written instructions in the margins that look like the beginning of a very dangerous ritual – a ritual used for creating life or bringing the dead back to life. This scroll belongs in a synagogue under the watchful eyes of a rabbi, not in the hands of a Gentile. A young Gentile at that."

"If it can bring the dead back to life, why would that be dangerous?" Brian asked.

"Young man, I have a very simple answer for you: have you ever seen a movie where someone brought back to life is *not* dangerous? Let me think – *The Mummy*, *World War Z*, *Dracula*, *Dawn of the Dead*, *Zombieland*, *28 Days Later*, *Frankenstein*, *Pet Sematary*, and *Salem's Lot*. Shall I continue? Now I realize these movies are fiction, but even fiction is based upon a kernel of truth, at some level."

"Hmmm. Perhaps you have a point," Brian said.

"I would happily pay you $2,500 for the scroll just to ensure it's returned to its rightful home in a synagogue," he said. "I'm almost certain that the right congregation, or perhaps even the Chicago Jewish Historical Society, would be willing to pay you much more, but the most important thing for you to do with this scroll is to get it back into the hands of the Jewish people."

Then Mr. Feldman looked intently into Brian's eyes and admonished in a hushed tone, "I can't stress enough how dangerous this scroll might be to someone who is untrained or, worse, to someone with malicious intent."

Brian considered the implications of Mr. Feldman's words.

"Uh . . . Thank you for your help, Mr. Feldman. I'll think about your offer and let you know." Brian mumbled as he clumsily pulled the copies of the scroll back together, re-folded them and slid them back into his backpack, stumbling out the door. As he exited, instead of chiming, the old-fashioned doorbell simply clanked once, like a pair of manacles.

13

SOIL WITH NOTES OF MUSHROOM

June 2, 2020
Skokie, Illinois

Anna Weisel played contentedly in her sunny backyard under the less-than-watchful eye of her nanny, Amanda. Amanda was sitting at the patio table making big plans for her wedding day on her employer's laptop. At the age of three, Anna was a precocious, blonde-haired, blue-eyed adventurer, with a backyard that was beginning to lose its novelty. She chased a monarch butterfly to the short hurricane fence on the property line between her house and the abandoned Bara Synagogue.

The butterfly hovered back and forth at the edge of the fence line and then bounced through the air over the fence to a patch of flowers growing in the middle of a fairy ring of white mushrooms. The fairy ring formed a perfect circle in the lawn almost directly below the stained-glass window depicting the creation of Adam. The gate to the chain link fence perched open just a few inches, left open by Amanda after their stroll around the neighborhood. Anna pushed the gate open just a bit further and toddled through towards the butterfly.

She carefully stepped over the ring of mushrooms and the monarch flew away from his perch on a patch of dandelions in the middle of the ring. Anna plopped down just inside the ring and picked a few dandelions for her mother and held them in her left hand. Examining the large, pretty mushrooms, Anna pulled one from the ground and bit off the cap, chewing and swallowing. It was savory and nutty, and she decided to have another. Anna then carried her bouquet of dandelions back to her yard, where Amanda was looking at floral arrangements for her wedding on her employer's laptop.

Mr. Fuentes pushed his wheelbarrow to the back of the synagogue and parked it near the fairy ring. The Weisels had left their gate open again, and having met them and their beautiful daughter Anna, he walked over and closed and latched the gate to help keep her from wandering. He'd noticed the fairy ring yesterday and put it on his mental list of things to do for today. Although the fairy ring was beautiful, the mushrooms were larger today, and even the lawn out of sight at the rear of the synagogue deserved to be fungus-free. He put his leather gloves on, grabbed his hoe and uprooted the fungi, raking up the mushroom remnants and mixing them into a pile of moist soil near the maintenance shed to compost.

That evening, Anna complained of a stomach ache. She vomited and then had explosive diarrhea. Her parents drove her to the Skokie Hospital Emergency Room, where they promptly administered IV fluids and rushed her to the pediatric intensive care unit. On the way to the ER, Anna's mother had called Amanda to ask if Anna had eaten something unusual that day. Oblivious, Amanda responded that she had not. Anna's mother spent the night in a chair by her ICU bed. Legend has it that if you step into a fairy ring, you can disappear. As little Anna slipped into sleep for the last time in her very short life, she dreamed of chasing a playful butterfly, picking dandelions, and eating delicious amanita phalloides - Death Cap mushrooms[1].

1. https://en.wikipedia.org/wiki/Amanita_phalloides

14

A VIOLENT DEATH

11:14 PM
JUNE 2, 2020
SKOKIE, ILLINOIS

Brass chugged the remainder of his fifth beer of the evening. He set the mug back down with an exaggerated, slow, gentle controlled motion on the coin-inlaid, epoxy-coated bar of The Barbeque Pig Lounge.

"Brass" was Peter Schiller's Northside Skulls nickname, given to him for the set of brass knuckles that he kept at the ready in his pocket. He had used them on numerous occasions and tonight he slid them out of his pocket, pulled them over his fingers, and examined them in the glow of the dim lights of the dive bar. Four Nazi swastikas regaled the brass knuckles – one for each knuckle.

An electrical buzzing filled his head – a buzzing that was not the result of alcohol. He thought to himself that this was the perfect night for a beat-down.

"Hey Brass," Snake whispered, "you wanna get arrested again? Put those away before someone calls the cops.[1]"

Snake sat on the next stool over, watching a countdown of *The Best Football Plays in History* on one of the screens above the bar. "Snake" was also ironically known as Joseph Schweinekopf, which in German translates to "pig head," but no one in their right mind called Snake "Pig Head" or Schweinekopf. Instead, Joseph's nickname arose from a rattlesnake tattoo that began with its tail tipped with five human skulls as rattles on Joseph's lower back, slithered up his spine, wrapped itself around his neck, and finally bared its fangs on his chest.

"I'll put them away, but they wanna come out and play later," Brass said.

"Why don't we just call it good for the night? I've got to get up at 5 am tomorrow," replied Snake.

"Alright, you fucking pussy, let's get you home to your mommy," snarled Brass, who pulled out a $20 bill and slapped it on the bar. The two walked out a side door into an alley, lit up smokes and began walking to their motorcycles parked at the back of The Barbeque Pig Lounge.

A door opened about 25 feet in front of them, pouring light into the dark alleyway. David Feldman stepped down the steps carrying a garbage bag tied at the top. He cracked open the top of a dumpster with some difficulty using one hand and tossed the full bag of garbage in with the other, letting the green plastic lid slam shut.

"Hey, Grandpa Jewstein! Give us your fucking money and maybe we'll let you live!" Brass threatened.

"I'm sorry, I don't have any money. I-I-I just came outside to take out the garbage," Mr. Feldman stammered.

Brass reached into his front pocket, pulled out his brass knuckles and slid them onto his hand.

"Come on, Brass, I've got a really bad feeling about this. Let's leave this guy alone," Snake hissed.

---

1. https://www.hankenlaw.com/blog/2024/07/carrying-brass-knuckles-is-illegal-in-illinois/#:~:text=Carrying%20a%20concealed%20weapon%20without,%2C%20or%20-sawed%2Doff%20shotguns.

"Open that door, take us inside and give us all the fucking money you've got, and we'll let you go back to taking out the fucking trash," Brass said.

"But I, I only have perhaps 40 dollars inside," stammered Mr. Feldman.

"Show me!" hissed Brass, as he grabbed David by the collar and pulled him up the stairs to the door. Mr. Feldman shakily typed in the keypad code and opened the door. Brass shoved him through the door into a small kitchen. A table with two chairs was arranged to one side, and several books written in Hebrew lay open on the table. Mr. Feldman walked unsteadily over to the counter, opened a cabinet, pulled down a coffee mug with the Hebrew alphabet on one side, and pulled out two 20 dollar bills. Brass yanked them out of his hand and stuffed them into his pants pocket, tossing the coffee mug on the floor, where it instantly shattered.

"Show me the rest of the place," growled Brass.

Mr. Feldman walked Brass through the small apartment, where he opened a china cabinet, pulled out a silver menorah and used it to break several of the glass panes in the cabinet, then threw it to Snake. In the lone bedroom, Brass pulled open the nightstand drawers, scattering pharmacy bottles, books and reading glasses across the floor. Then he walked over to a small chest of drawers and began pulling the drawers out and dumping them on the floor.

"Where is the rest of the cash, asshole?!" yelled Brass.

"I have given you everything I have!" pleaded Mr. Feldman.

"Oh, wait! There is one more thing of value. Open the thin drawer at the top of the chest there in the middle. There is a small plastic bag with old coins in it. They are valuable and you could sell them!" Mr. Feldman said.

Something inside Brass snapped, and an unrelenting rage exploded, channeling itself through his brass knuckles. He began pummeling David Feldman's head and face with his brass-accessorized fist. The last image that registered from Mr. Feldman's right eye was that of a muscular arm covered in tattoos of demons and swastikas, punching him again and again. The demons were laughing as he lost consciousness. At some point, Snake joined in using the menorah for several blows, but the bloody, grapefruit-sized impact crater pounded into the left side of Mr. Feldman's face and skull was violently crafted by Mr. Peter Schiller and his brass knuckles.

15

A VISION AND FOOTSTEPS EXPLAINED

11:27 PM
June 2, 2020
Skokie, Illinois

Brian was laying on his back on his bed, looking at the ceiling fan and planning how best to enter the synagogue without a key. How had all of the graffiti artists gained entry? Suddenly his vision blurred, and then refocused. When he could see again, it felt as though he were floating above three men, one man punching another man on the floor while another man watched. The victim of the assault was the bookstore owner.

"Mr. Feldman!" he tried to yell. "Stop!"

But nothing came from his lips. Blood sprayed into the air with each punch, drifting downward through the air and onto the floor, Mr. Feldman, and the assailant. The man watching hit Mr. Feldman with a silver candlestick holder once or twice. Brian had the passing thought that the holder was called a menorah. The names "Brass" and

"Snake" entered his mind unbidden, and as Mr. Feldman died, his view returned to his room's ceiling fan.

He felt an urgent *calling* from the Scroll (with a capital "S", as he now thought of it), which he pulled from his backpack. It was warm to the touch, which surprised him, and this caused him to drop it on the carpet. The Scroll rolled open on the floor, revealing the copious hand-written marginalia that were now glowing in pale red.

Brian needed answers now more than ever, and the vision and the behavior of the Scroll made his plan to find the source of the footsteps he had heard in the synagogue even more urgent. He had a hunch about the owner of the footsteps but didn't want to curse it by saying it out loud, even to himself.

The nearly full moon hung in the sky shining through his bedroom window, forming an elongated trapezoid of light on his floor. He quietly opened his bedroom window fully and slid over the windowsill onto the grass in his Converse sneakers and black hoodie, then closed it again. He put the Scroll into the Ziploc bag again and then into his backpack along with a small but powerful flashlight. The handles of a pair of bolt cutters protruded from the top of the backpack.

He walked quietly down the street until he reached the abandoned synagogue. There, he slowed, looked around carefully to make sure that no one was watching, and then quietly walked into the shadows of the abandoned Bara Synagogue. As he walked down the side of the building, he came to a set of concrete stairs that led downward. He silently followed these down into the darkness to the basement door at the bottom of the cracked concrete stairs. A dim light shone from a small, frosted, wire-reinforced window in the door. He carefully tried to turn the door handle, but it was locked. Brian opened a zippered pouch on his backpack and pulled out a hooked, flat paint scraper. He put his shoulder against the door and slid the flat section into the gap between the door and the door jamb, wiggling the hook of the scraper downwards and pushing the latch out of the hole in the strike plate. Holding the scraper in position, he relaxed his pressure on the door, allowing it to swing open. Someone was waiting for him in the hallway.

"By all means, come in," a man said, wearing a green plaid robe, pajama pants and slippers leaning against the hallway wall with a Glock in his right hand and a glass of red wine in his other. He was about 45 years old, of medium build, 5'10", with jet black hair peppered with gray, and dark brown eyes.

"Come in and close the door behind you," he said, gesturing with the gun. "Let's get to know each other a little better before I call the police."

Brian closed the door behind him and held his hands up, palms facing the man. The man again gestured with the gun, this time for Brian to walk past him through a doorway in the hall. The hallway floors were smudged with shoe and dolly wheel marks, perhaps left by careless movers. Most of the fluorescent light tubes in the ceiling were either flickering or dead – only a few remained to light the hallway. The room appeared to be what was formerly a conference room but had none of the furniture you'd expect, save for a projector attached to the ceiling. Instead, the room was furnished with three comfortable chairs, an end table for each, and an ottoman for the chair facing the whiteboard/screen area. A refrigerator stood in one corner of the room, and a hot plate and microwave were located on a long table to one side of the room.

"Please sit down," the man intoned. Brian took off his backpack and set it on the floor next to the chair. The man sat down in a chair across the room and rested his wine glass on a small table next to the chair. He continued to point the Glock at Brian. Resting on the long table was an open laptop with live video images from around the synagogue.

"Why don't you begin by telling me who you are and why you're breaking into my 'home,'" he said, adding air quotes with his left hand.

"My name is Brian Newman, and I'm here to learn more about a Scroll that I found in the synagogue on Monday," Brian replied.

"Exactly what *kind* of scroll did you find in my synagogue, Brian Newman?" the man in the plaid pajamas said.

"The kind of Scroll that brings people back to life," replied Brian.

"Interesting," the man said.

"Well, this is according to David Feldman who was a Judaica bookstore owner. You were the rabbi of this synagogue, weren't you?" replied Brian.

"Guilty as charged. Rabbi Wendell Rosenburg, at your service. But why are you referring to David Feldman in the past tense?"

"The Scroll gave me a vision of Mr. Feldman being beaten to death a few hours ago. It was the worst thing I've ever seen."

"Perhaps it was just a nightmare?" Rabbi Rosenburg asked.

"No, it was too real to be a nightmare, it was as though I was projected out of my body to the exact location where the beating was happening. I couldn't say anything or touch anything, but I *saw* everything. And when I was returned to my room, the Scroll was very warm to the touch, and the marginalia were glowing red."

"That . . sounds . . terrible," the rabbi said slowly and quietly.

After a moment of reflection, Wendell continued "Would you mind if I looked at the Scroll?"

This time, Brian paused, studying the rabbi's face, then he came to a decision. "I would feel better if you put the gun away," Brian said.

"Yes, of course," Wendell said, and he slid the gun into a pocket on the right side of his chair.

Instead of pulling out the copies of the Scroll, Brian pulled out the Scroll itself, packaged in the gallon Ziploc freezer bag and handed it to the rabbi. Wendell placed the freezer bag onto the conference room table and carefully opened it.

"Brian, this is very old!" he exclaimed while gently unfurling the small scroll. As he opened it further, he commented, "A piece is missing here at the beginning. Do you have it somewhere?"

"I noticed that, too," Brian agreed. "Sadly, I do not."

"Where exactly did you find the scroll in the synagogue?" the rabbi asked.

"This is a little embarrassing, but I, um, I was pretending to give a sermon from the podium. I bumped my knee against it and a hidden panel opened underneath. The scroll was inside the hidden panel."

Wendell continued examining the Scroll, reading to himself during the next hour or so, then finally said, "This appears to be a very old version of the Sefer Yetzirah but with detailed instructions in the form of marginalia on how to create a human being from clay and earth or perhaps even how to bring someone who is dead back to life. It also appears that a ritual was performed to give the Scroll itself a lifeforce of its own, though I'm not sure exactly how that was done, because it is not described in the Scroll or even in the marginalia, which seems to be in a different handwriting and ink from the original, older main text. This lifeforce attribute, combined with its mission to protect the Jews, could explain why the Scroll chose *you* as its owner – so that you would create a golem to defend someone in need of protection or perhaps even vengeance. Whatever the reason, I believe that this Scroll can only be owned, and therefore used, by someone with righteous intent."

"I don't care about vengeance or defending other people, I just need you to help me bring my mom back to life – back to her family," Brian said.

"You should care, Brian. You should care very much. This Scroll might have plans for your mother that you simply don't understand yet," Rabbi Wendell Rosenburg said.

16

INGREDIENTS AND DEALS

1:02 AM
June 3, 2020
Skokie, Illinois

Rabbi Wendell Rosenburg watched as Brian wiped his eyes with the back of his sleeve and sighed.

"Brian, you must understand something about the Book of Formation," Rabbi Rosenburg explained, "legend has it that mystic rabbis have used the principles in it combined with a lot of mysterious hand waving to bring people back to life. But those same legends also indicate that the result is mostly only a shadow of what that person was when they were alive – usually no more than what is known as a golem, capable of following simple instructions or protecting the Jewish people from enemies. You would need a very special set of 'ingredients' to bring life to a being that was even somewhat recognizable as your mother."

Wendell used air quotes to accentuate the word "ingredients."

"What sort of 'ingredients' would you need?" Brian asked.

"If you simply want to create a mindless golem, for example, something to act as a protector or laborer, then all you need is clay, and water, combined with a very complex ritual involving incantations and the letters of the Hebrew language," replied Wendell.

"Okay, but what about my mom?" Brian asked, bluntly. Before Wendell could respond, Brian further clarified. "So that she comes back exactly the way that she was?"

"In that case, you would ideally need her body or at least portions of the body such as the heart or head or such," Wendell said.

Brian responded with sadness in his voice "Mom was cremated."

"I think that a person's ashes might actually work," Wendell said. "But the even bigger problem is that because you are attempting to create or form a woman, you will need a rib from a man. Remember that God created woman from the man's rib.[1]"

"Could I give her one of my ribs?" Brian asked.

"That is quite touching, Brian. Unfortunately, the removal of a rib from a person would require a surgeon and an operating room with nurses and an anesthesiologist, a recovery room and the Almighty knows what else," Wendell said.

"Um, what about a rib from a man who is dead?" Brian asked, more to himself than to the rabbi.

"I suppose, in theory, that could work, but this discussion is pointless, since we aren't going to conduct a formation ritual," Wendell said.

"How would you feel about making a deal with me?" Brian asked. "If you conduct a formation ritual for my mother, I will give you the Scroll. If not, I will find someone else who will perform the ritual."

Rabbi Rosenburg locked eyes with Brian and asked, "You're dead serious here, aren't you? And I admire it. I really do. But just to be clear – if I perform the ritual of formation to bring your mother back, you will give me the Scroll?"

Brian replied, "Yes."

"Even if the result is not what or who you were expecting? Even if it doesn't work at all?" Wendell asked.

1. Genesis 2:20-23

Brian replied again, "Yes."

Rabbi Rosenburg held out his hand to shake Brian's.

"Then you have a deal. I'll begin making preparations."

"What about the missing piece of the scroll?" Brian asked.

Wendell responded, "It shouldn't matter, the first page simply repeats a variety of well-known Jewish praises to God – almost like a preamble. I should be able to fill in those blanks."

"Rabbi Rosenburg, I think I know where we can find a rib. What if we took it from David Feldman? He must still be in his apartment. But, I guess it's kind of pointless."

"Why's that?"

"What are we gonna do, cut into him?"

Brian looked at Wendell expectantly.

"Don't look at me! I'm not leaving my fingerprints on a crime scene. Besides, I think I'm gonna throw up just thinking about it."

"We need a surgeon, or a dentist, or a—" Brian's voice was becoming increasingly desperate. Rabbi Rosenburg cut him off.

"Ever hear that joke, a rabbi, a surgeon, and a high school kid walk into a crime scene?" Wendell said with a big laugh. "We don't need a surgeon, Brian. We need a *butcher*."

"Yes!" Brian agreed. "But who'd be willing to do an assignment like this?"

"Let's just say... I know a guy," Wendell said, a smirk rising on his face. "And his marinated ribeye steaks are the best I've ever grilled."

* * *

1:33 AM | JUNE 3, 2020 | SKOKIE, ILLINOIS

"Privyet, uh, hello? Who call and wake me up so early?" mumbled a man with a heavy Russian accent over the cell phone's speaker. Rabbi Rosenburg heard the man begin coughing hoarsely and then the sound of him spitting.

"Privyet, Alexey. I'm so sorry to wake you this early in the morning. You may not remember me, but I am Rabbi Rosenburg, and I wouldn't call you this early, but I have an emergency," Wendell said.

"Rabbi Ribeye! Of course, I remember! What kind butcher emergency does rabbi have this time in morning, especially thief rabbi?" Alexey said.

"It's the kind of emergency that only a well-paid butcher can address," the rabbi said.

"Well-paid? How can Alexey help, my Jewish friend?" Alexey said, his tone suddenly now friendly.

"We need someone who can keep their mouth shut forever and someone who can cut a rib out of a dead man, with no questions asked," Wendell said.

"Sounds like - how you say in America? – just another Tuesday - for Alexey," Alexey said. "What payment you offer Alexey for rib?"

"I can give you $3,000," the rabbi said.

"Alexey need $10,000 for this type job," Alexey said.

"Alexey, I can't spare that kind of money!" Wendell exclaimed.

"Alexey not Jewish charity. Alexey taking big risk. Alexey like America. I do what I want here. No police, no KGB looking over shoulder. This is $10,000 worth of risk," Alexey said.

"Fine! We have a deal. You get me the rib. I pay you $10,000. Cash. But you have to do it tonight."

"Tell me where and I go now," Alexey said.

17

A BONE TO PICK

2:22 AM
June 3, 2020
Skokie, Illinois

Brian left the synagogue wondering how an unemployed rabbi could have $10,000 in cash just lying around. He quietly picked up his bike and rode it for nearly three and a half miles in the moonlit streets to David Feldman's address. The address given to Brian by Rabbi Rosenburg was a brownstone that had been converted into two apartments, each with its own entry door in the front and one near the back. The brownstone was next door to The Barbeque Pig Lounge, but between the two was a long dark alley.

In an attempt to be as quiet as possible, Brian walked his bike down the dark alley, hoping to find a back door to Mr. Feldman's apartment. He was still unsure as to whether the "vision" that he had seen was real or just the result of having fallen asleep and into a nightmare. In any case, getting caught would be a very good thing to avoid.

Alexey was leaning against the stairs next to Mr. Feldman's apartment, smoking a cigarette. Brian leaned his bike against the wall of the apartment and quietly walked over to the butcher.

"You have money for Alexey?" Alexey asked.

"Here is a $2,000 down payment," Brian said. "You get the rest once the job is done."

"As agreed," Alexey said.

Brian walked up the steps and found a keypad lock on the door, but the door was open with the latch resting against the striker plate. Brian listened for any sounds from the inside but could hear nothing. As quietly as he was able, he pulled the door open and stepped into the apartment. He searched for a light switch and pulled it up, illuminating a kitchen/breakfast room. Alexey followed him into the apartment. Fragments of a blue coffee mug were scattered around the floor. They both walked silently into the next room and turned on the overhead light. It was in complete disarray, especially the small china cabinet, where several of the glass doors were broken and crystal glassware lay scattered on the floor. Realizing now that his vision was not simply the result of a sleeping nightmare, Brian gritted his teeth at what he would find next.

They walked to the entrance of the bedroom door, which was open, and Brian quietly called into the dark room, "Mr. Feldman? Are you OK?"

He felt along the wall and found a switch, hesitating at what he might find. Turning it on, he found what was left of Mr. David Feldman, laying on his right side, his head and face caved in on the left side, and a pool of blood absorbed into the beige carpet, staining it nearly black. The light in his right eye was gone, but it stared lifelessly up at Brian, nonetheless.

Brian and Alexey looked around the room. The carpet was covered in bloody footprints from, presumably, pairs of boots. Brian shuddered, dropped to his knees in the doorway and gagged but managed to keep his mostly digested dinner down.

"Oh, dear God! What kind of monster would do such a thing to such a nice old man?" Brian whispered to himself.

Alexey whispered, "Worst kind of monster – human monster."

But the question now closer to home for Brian was what kind of monster would further desecrate Mr. Feldman's body as they were about to do?

"A son who loves his mother, that's who," Brian whispered to himself.

"What you say?" Alexey asked.

"Never mind, just get the rib and let's get out of here," Brian said.

Alexey carefully tip-toed near the wall, avoiding as much of the blood spatter as he could to arrive behind Mr. Feldman, carrying the tools of his trade in a small leather bag. Thankfully, the vast majority of the blood and spatter had flowed forward toward the front of his body. Alexey knelt on a relatively clean spot on the carpet behind Mr. Feldman and used scissors to cut through his shirt and undershirt. Then he used his fingertips to find the bottom of his rib cage and the lowest rib.

Alexey selected a very sharp, 6-inch curved boning knife from his leather bag and inserted it just above the lowest rib, slicing through skin, muscle, and fat along the top of the rib from the front of the lower chest to the middle spine. He repeated the process with a cut below the same rib. Blood followed gravity towards the floor along his back.

He then laid the knife on Mr. Feldman's hip and reached into his leather bag, removing what appeared to be branch-cutting shears. He opened the shearing blades as wide as they would go and inserted them, one on top and one on bottom of the rib that he had made incisions around, and as close to the spine as possible, and he forced the blades closed, creating a stomach-turning crunching sound. A few minutes more with the boning knife, and the rib released with a squelch from Mr. Feldman's chest cavity. He cut most of the flesh away from the bone, and then laid the rib on top of Mr. Feldman and pulled out two of the kitchen garbage bags, placing one inside the other, followed by insertion of the rib and knotting the two sacks to avoid dripping blood. He then handed the packaged rib to Brian, who placed the packaged rib in his backpack, looking away almost the entire time.

Finding the sink in the adjoining bathroom, Alexey washed the head of the shears, the 6-inch boning knife, the scissors, the branch cutting shears and his hands and put the items back into his leather bag. He then found a bottle of rubbing alcohol and a rag, soaking the rag with rubbing alcohol and then wiping every surface that he could remember that they might have touched with the rag – door and drawer handles, the light switch, the bathroom sink handles, the soap dispenser, the knife sharpener, and even the sink, saving the incision area for last.

Alexey and Brian then snuck quietly out of Mr. Feldman's front door, shutting it and ensuring it was locked behind them. Brian pulled the remaining $8,000 from his backpack, passed it silently to Alexey, quietly mounted his bicycle, and rode home.

As Alexey walked to his gray 2012 Honda CRV, he pulled out a flip phone and made a phone call to an old friend.

Speaking in Russian, Alexay said, "Wake up, Anatoly, you mutant-cauliflower-faced, son of an octopus and a skunk."

"Well, privyet to you, you lung-loogie-hocking anus of a flea-infested camel!" Anatoly said. "Thank you for waking me at three in the morning."

"I have some information that might be useful to you. I have just done a very special job for a very special rabbi. What will you pay me for this information?" Alexey asked.

18

LOOSE ENDS

4:27 AM
June 3, 2020
Skokie, Illinois

Brian again quietly slid the window to his bedroom open and climbed inside. He put his backpack under his bed, stripped down to his underwear, tossed his clothes and shoes under his bed, and slept for a few hours, exhausted, until his alarm sounded at 6:30 a.m. the next morning.

"Brian? I've fixed scrambled eggs, hashbrowns, and toast this morning," called Brian's dad through the door.

Brian pulled on his Chicago Bears pajama bottoms and a black, short-sleeve shirt, washed his hands and face in the hallway bathroom, and joined his dad and Emily at the breakfast table. The eggs were still steaming on his plate. His dad was sipping a cup of coffee and reading the news on his iPad, while his sister texted friends on her phone. Brian sat down and began to eat, although after last night, he wasn't very hungry.

"Hey, bud, are you okay this morning? You look a little pale," Brian's dad asked.

"Honestly, not feeling too hot. I think I'm gonna go back to bed."

Brian's dad got up, walked over to Brian, and put his cheek against Brian's forehead. He was not a big believer in thermometers, saying that he had one built right into his cheek.

"You don't seem to have a fever," Ross said.

Emily slapped the back of the freshly opened ketchup bottle to accent her hash browns and was rewarded with an unexpectedly large red glob of ketchup on her plate. Brian looked at the oozing red glob and began to gag, rushing to the bathroom and just barely making it to the toilet to vomit up half a pitcher of yellow bile.

Brian heard from behind him, "You are definitely *not* okay, buddy. Stay in bed and try to feel better. Don't push it. I've got to go to work or I'll be late. Call me if you need me, okay? Okay? I hope you feel better today, Brian. And tell your sister to focus on her remote classes. Have a good day. I love you guys,"

Ross grabbed his sack lunch, phone, wallet, and keys and walked out the door to the garage.

"I hate these online classes," Emily said. "I hate having to wear this stupid mask outside of the house. I hate COVID. And I miss Mom."

"I really miss Mom, too," Brian said.

Brian wiped his face on a cold, wet washcloth, went to the kitchen, and scraped his eggs and toast into the garbage.

"Well, at least turn on your laptop," Brian said. "Make it look like you're paying attention. I'm going back to bed."

"Feel better, Brian."

"Thanks, sis. Goodnight."

Brian returned to his bedroom, locked his door, and changed into new clothes. He pulled his clothes from last night and his backpack out from under his bed. Again, he opened his bedroom window and stepped outside, walking over to the fire pit. Fortunately, the fire pit was on the opposite side of the house from where his sister was attending her virtual class, so she couldn't see him place his clothes into the fire pit, douse them with Matchlight Firestarter, and set them ablaze with a long neck lighter.

The last thing remaining was his backpack, which he reluctantly put into the fire pit, adding a squirt of Matchlight for good measure on any pieces that had survived the first round.

Hopping on his bike, he rode down to the abandoned Bara Synagogue and parked his bike near the basement entrance. Brian knocked on the basement door and waited. Rabbi Rosenburg cracked open the door, looking around to ensure that no one else was with Brian. Brian walked in and Wendell closed and locked the door behind him.

"How did it go last night?" Wendell asked.

"Well, while you were sleeping, Alexey and I collected the rib from David Feldman," Brian said in a matter of fact tone. "I almost lost my cookies. Well, I finally did this morning, but Alexey performed the job perfectly, gave me the rib, cleaned up after himself, took the money and then we both left."

Brian handed the rib wrapped in kitchen garbage bags, but Wendell was reluctant to take it.

"Thank you for the $10,000, Rabbi. I don't know how I will ever repay you. I suggest we put this in your freezer or your refrigerator until you need it."

Wendell took the packaged rib and grimaced as he walked into his living room, putting it into an empty vegetable drawer in the bottom of his fridge.

"Dearest Almighty, I pray that this brings Brian's mom back. I am beginning to feel like a grave robber!" Wendell said to himself.

Wendell walked back and sat next to Brian.

"There will be a full moon this coming Saturday night," Wendell said. "That will be the best time for me to conduct the ritual of formation. Bring me the ashes of your mother between now and then so we will be ready. In the meantime, I will prepare the platform and conduct the appropriate purification rituals so that I will be able to conduct the ceremony."

Wendell quickly lifted his index finger.

"Oh, I almost forgot," Wendell said. "I'm going to need a pint of your blood. It's for a part of the ritual where I have to apply certain letters of the Hebrew alphabet to the forming body of your mother. These letters will be embedded into her skin, sort of like tattoos."

"Tattoos! My mom didn't have tattoos?"

"Sadly, there is no way to avoid them, Brian," the rabbi said.

Brian sat down in one of the chairs and felt all of his energy pour out of him onto the floor. He was completely exhausted.

"Is there anything else that I need to do?" Brian asked. "Besides, you know, the whole pint of blood thing."

"You can pray, Brian," responded the rabbi. "Pray a lot. Now go get some sleep. Tomorrow you can come back here, and I will draw the blood that I need."

Brian peeled himself out of the comfortable chair, walked out of the basement door and rode his bike home. Sleep came to him the instant his head hit the pillow.

19

BLOOD

4:45 PM
JUNE 4, 2020
SKOKIE, ILLINOIS

Brian sat down in the chair in Rabbi Rosenburg's "living room" in the basement. The chair was covered with several bath towels.

"Not to insult you or anything, but do you know what you're doing?" Brian asked.

"Absolutely!" Wendell replied. "Before I became a rabbi, I majored in biology at Northwestern and had a part time job with an animal study developing anti-cancer drugs using rats. I took blood from the rats once a week."

"So, what made you decide to become a rabbi?" Brian asked.

"I couldn't get a job that I enjoyed as a biology major. Unless you spent another five years to get your PhD, you had to either become a lab technician or a teacher. There's nothing wrong with these jobs, but neither are my cup of tea, unfortunately. I suppose I blame my original poor career choice on being young and naive. When I heard that there was money to be made as a rabbi, and since I've always been good with people, I was ordained and went to rabbinical school and began working with the congregation here."

"Money in being a – at the risk of receiving a more painful blood draw, can I ask a more sensitive question?" Brian said.

"Such as - you'd like to know if I stole money from my congregation?" replied Wendell.

"I heard Alexey last night . . ." Brian said.

"And he was correct. Yes, I stole money from my congregation. The love of my life, my best friend, my lover, my wife – Isabella – contracted a rare blood cancer, and the treatments were very expensive. The bills were far beyond what I could ever pay on my salary as a rabbi, but I had to do whatever was necessary to keep her alive. In spite of my best efforts, however, she died. After she died, my home was foreclosed upon, my crime of theft was discovered, and I became a pariah to my congregation and friends. So, now you know why I'm living illegally in the basement of an abandoned synagogue."

"Is she the reason you want the Scroll?" Brian asked.

Rabbi Rosenburg looked down at the ground before he answered. "Yes. At this point, you of all people should understand the meaning of 'whatever is necessary.'" He continued, "If the Sefer Yetzirah is successful at bringing back your mother, perhaps you'd consider helping me bring back the love of my life?"

"If this works, yes. Unless you intend to make this phlebotomy extra painful as payment for me being nosy. Let's draw some blood."

Wendell pulled a stool close to Brian's left arm and put on a pair of nitrile gloves. He opened a package of cotton makeup circles and poured rubbing alcohol onto one of the circles. He used the dripping makeup circle to swab the inside of Brian's left elbow. Next, he pulled an oversized rubber band out of a package labeled 'SUPERSIZE BANDS' in big red letters and tied it around Brian's left bicep.

"I use these to keep my garbage bags from slipping off of the garbage can. Drives me nuts when that happens. But don't worry, these haven't been around a garbage bag, at least not yet," Wendell said.

"Whatever is necessary," Brian replied.

Wendell grabbed a piece of tubing resting on a paper towel on the end table next to the chair. Connected to one end of the short piece of tubing was a small needle.

"Fish tank tubing?" asked Brian.

"Good guess. Yes, but sterilized with rubbing alcohol," Wendell said. "And now you will feel a small stick."

"Yowser!" Brian exclaimed, as the needle entered his vein.

"Hold still! Sorry about that. The rats never complained, at least not in English, but they were restrained so they wouldn't bite me," Wendell said, who was holding the short tubing in a crimped fashion. He reached over and grabbed an 8-ounce bottle and deftly inserted the open end of the tubing into the bottle. Brian watched as the bottle steadily filled with his blood. The flow slowed and the rabbi removed the rubber band tourniquet from Brian's arm, restoring the flow again. Wendell then crimped the tubing to prevent the bottle from overfilling and set the blood-filled bottle back on the end table.

He grabbed a paper towel and placed it under the tubing as he pulled the needle from Brian's arm. A few drops of blood drained from the needle onto the paper towel. Wendell gathered the towel, tubing, and needle carefully and put them into the trash. He put a cap onto the bottle of Brian's blood.

"Success!" Wendell said, as he put a Band-Aid on the puncture site. "Well, that went much better than I thought it would. Unfortunately, that's not the last 'ingredient' that we need for the ritual."

"What do you mean, 'that's not the last ingredient'? Brian asked.

"I was reading the ritual this morning, and you're not going to like this," Wendell said.

"What?"

"During the ritual, we will need a full-length photo of your mom, and you're not going to like this either, but . . . an index finger, freshly cut from a living person."

"You've got to be kidding me?! Are you serious?"

"Yes, I'm absolutely serious. The sacrifices that must be made for this complicated ritual are critical to whether your mom ends up as a robot or very close to a human being. Each and every ingredient is very important, Brian. To quote you - 'Whatever it takes.'"

Brian looked into Wendell's eyes, which were completely serious. Then Wendell burst into laughter. "No, I'm completely messing with you. But you should have seen the look on your face! Priceless," laughed Wendell.

"You are a complete and utter asshole," deadpanned Brian.

"Yeah, that's what my wife, Isabella, used to say on a daily basis. But in all seriousness, don't forget the photo of your mom. I really do need that so I can give it my best effort at sculpting."

20

FORMATION MOON

3:14 PM
JUNE 6, 2020
SKOKIE, ILLINOIS

Rabbi Rosenburg opened the maintenance shed used by Mr. Fuentes, the property keeper, and located a spade and a five-gallon bucket. He handed both to Brian, who took them to the pile of vermilion soil next to the shed and filled the bucket using the spade. The soil was rich, loose, and networked with small white tendrils or roots. Brian didn't give much thought to this, and as he encountered a worm or two, he removed these by hand and tossed them to the side.

He carried the full bucket into the basement and then back up a set of interior stairs into the main sanctuary and up onto the main platform near the podium. The two had chosen this route as being the least likely to attract attention from people on the street and sidewalk near the front entrance. A plastic tarp was spread over the surface of the platform, and Brian poured the soil into a pile onto the surface of the tarp next to a number of packages of pale grey, natural clay purchased from Amazon by the rabbi. Brian repeated this several times until the rabbi indicated that they had enough soil for the ritual.

Rabbi Rosenburg examined the full-length photo of Brian's mom, Lilith, that Brian had provided for the ritual. Brian's dad (Ross), Brian, and his sister Emily were all in the photo with her. Lilith looked young for someone who had a 16-year-old son and a 12-year-old daughter. She was a beautiful woman – slim of build, brown hair that cascaded over her shoulders, petite in height, and looking at the photographer with hazel eyes that twinkled with life. The backdrop for the photo was the zoo on a sunny fall day, filled with the bright reds, oranges, and yellows of maple leaves. Wendell took a pair of scissors and carefully cut the figure of Lilith away from the rest of her family and away from the maple leaves that formed the backdrop of a happier day for Brian's family.

As Brian watched, Wendell wiped his balding head with his hand, surprised at the amount of nervous moisture present, then dried his hand and head with a white dish towel. He opened a drawer in a cabinet in the main sanctuary and brought out a white silk yarmulka rimmed with gold embroidery – a Jewish skullcap – and placed it upon his head. From the same drawer, he pulled out a white shawl with blue lines and wrapped this around his shoulders. Next, he removed two tefillins – small cube-shaped black boxes made of leather attached to leather bands and containing four hand-written texts from the Torah.

Wendell then recited a blessing in Hebrew. He placed the arm tefillin around the bicep of his left arm – wrapping the leather strap holding the box around his arm seven times and then six times in a specific pattern around his fingers. He then recited another blessing in Hebrew as he placed the head tefillin on his head around the kippah with the fabric box positioned on his forehead. Upon completion of this, two leather bands of the head tefillin hung down from the knot at the back of his head and over his shoulders. Wendell then reached into the drawer again and removed a pen made from a reed, a bottle of ground gallnuts, and the bottle of Brian's blood, placing all of these on the pedestal.

The rabbi picked up a pitcher of water and carried it, along with the edited photo of Brian's mom, to the pile of soil and natural clay. There he placed the photo within sight on one of several small stools that surrounded the ingredients. Next, he retrieved the heavily annotated Sefer Yetzirah from his vest pocket and began singing methodically in Hebrew as he walked around the ingredients, making small bowing motions as he walked. After several minutes of reading aloud, Wendell placed the open Scroll on a small folding table that they had brought in for this purpose. Brian had been assigned the task of unfurling the Scroll but was admonished by the rabbi to do absolutely nothing else during the ceremony with the exception of retrieving Mr. Feldman's rib from the fridge at the right moment during the ritual.

Rabbi Rosenburg took the purple urn containing Lilith's ashes from the pedestal and carried them to the clay and soil. Removing the lid, he carefully poured the ashes onto the pile of other ingredients, chanting in Hebrew as he poured. He then began the laborious process of kneading the natural clay, the soil, and Lilith's ashes together, slowly forming the material to be used for Lilith. Several readings in Hebrew and nearly two hours later, the creation material appeared as a reddish mound in the center of the tarp on the platform. Wendell then used his hands to begin forming a detailed effigy of Lilith from the red clay there on the blue tarp, with beams of light from the waning sun pouring through the stained-glass windows onto the grim work.

At some point, the rabbi produced a set of sculpting tools and used these to produce details that his hands and fingers alone were simply incapable of achieving. After several more hours, the clay sculpture was complete. Brian thought the likeness of his mom did not present itself as Michelangelo's marble David – so realistic that if it stepped off its dais, no one would be surprised – however, the details of the rabbi's work were quite impressive, given the brief time he had spent. Her fingers and toes had nails and spaces between the digits, her hair contained the sort of detail that a second-year art student might have included, her nose had nostrils, and her mouth had lips. A strange channel was carved into the side of the statue's chest, and Brian instantly knew its purpose. But it was her eyes that were the true works of art. Wendell had spent nearly 45 minutes on the eyes alone, and although they were staring up from her prone position on the floor towards the ceiling, it was as if they were seeing into heaven.

After Wendell completed the effigy, Brian ached to say something to the rabbi – "Thank you," "She looks amazing!", or "Do you think this will work?" - but he continued onward as a silent assistant, as instructed. Wendell again picked up the annotated Sefer Yetzirah and began reading in Hebrew, walking around the prone clay figure, and gently bowing as he spoke. It was impossible not to notice that the annotations around the margins of the pages were again glowing red.

The rabbi suddenly stopped chanting and turned to Brian, silently pointing to the side of his chest, and then waving him away. Brian knew it was time for Mr. Feldman's contribution, and he walked quickly to the basement refrigerator, found the "package" and returned, unwrapping the rib for the rabbi to use. After further chanting, Wendell took the rib from Brian and placed it into the channel carved into the side of her chest, sealing the rib into place with the surrounding clay.

At this point, the rabbi ceremoniously washed his hands in a blue and white bowl of water resting on one of the stools surrounding the effigy and dried them with a white towel. He reached into his pocket and pulled out a necklace forged from silver with the Hebrew letters:

אמת.

The word transliterates to "emmet," meaning "truth." Wendell took the stylus made out of a reed and gently fitted the necklace under the back of her neck in a tunnel that he had shaped for this purpose. He fastened the clasp, centered it upon her chest and read the word in Hebrew, breathing the word onto the effigy's face. After a moment where it seemed that he was meditating, the rabbi gathered together the bottle of Brian's blood, the ground gallnuts, and an agate mortar and pestle. He poured some of the ground gallnuts into the mortar, then some of Brian's blood. He then used the pestle to mix and further grind the gallnut powder even finer for several minutes in the blood, and then dipped the reed stylus into the resulting mixture, leaving the stylus in the mixture while he repositioned the Scroll for further chanting.

Once the Scroll was in position (marginalia still glowing red) and using the reed stylus wet with Brian's blood mixed with gallnut powder, Wendell began to painstakingly "write" Hebrew letters onto Lilith's effigy while chanting from the glowing marginalia of the Scroll. This portion of the ritual required another two hours, and when the rabbi had finished, Lilith's natural clay and soil effigy looked as though a calligraphy artist had spent weeks applying large Hebrew letters onto its "skin." He gently pulled the photo of Brian's mom from his jacket and placed it atop the silver necklace around her neck.

Rabbi Rosenburg raised himself painfully to his feet, picked up the Scroll and read the glowing red marginalia in Hebrew again, walking around in a circle around the clay sculpture lying before them both, chanting and repeatedly bowing as he walked. Then he knelt and read from the Scroll for the last time, in the end saying something that sounded like "Amen." He gently rolled up the Scroll and placed it on a stool near the effigy, then rose, patted Brian on the back and silently gestured that they should leave the sanctuary.

The hour was late, and the full moon was shining through the stained-glass window onto the platform. The image formed was of Adam rising from the muddy bank of a river, his shins covered in earth, and a pale blue light with twinkling stars flowing into Adam's mouth. Slowly, the moonlight through the stained glass inched towards the sculpture of Lilith.

21

MOM?

6:00 AM
June 7, 2020
Skokie, Illinois

The alarm on Brian's nightstand buzzed twice before Brian quickly pressed the "off" button. He'd been awake for the past two hours, staring at the ceiling, trying to go back to sleep. Did it work? Would she even remember him? What if she were nothing more than a golem, as Rabbi Rosenburg had warned she might be? What would he do then? How could he end her life again if she were simply a vegetable? Perhaps even worse – if she were truly his mom back from the dead with all of her memories, how would he tell Dad – "Hey, Dad, a rabbi and I brought Mom back to life. Isn't that great? She's got Hebrew alphabet tattoos all over her and I had to steal a dead man's rib to make it happen, but hey, let's order some pizza. The family's back together!"

It was time to find out.

Brian rolled out of bed, quickly dressed in fresh clothes, threw on his COVID mask, and snuck out of the window. He could still see the full orange moon as it sank slowly towards the horizon. He rolled his bike down the sidewalk for a few steps, mounting it in front of the neighbor's house. Across the street, a dog began barking at him from the backyard, letting all who would listen know that Brian was there. He grimaced but rode to the synagogue and parked his bike near the basement entrance. The door was unlocked. He quietly entered, hoping to avoid waking Wendell. He crept down the hallway back up the stairs to the first floor. Silently, he approached the platform. A slender woman sat with her knees pulled against her chest and her arms wrapped around them, looking down at the ground in front of her, completely naked. Hebrew alphabet tattoos and mud covered her body and a small silver necklace glinted in the emerging morning light through the stained-glass windows.

After what seemed like an hour, Brian quietly spoke. "Mom?"

The woman shifted her eyes slowly to Brian's face, and a small smile arose at the corners of her mouth.

"See if she will put on this robe," Rabbi Rosenburg said as he pushed the robe into Brian's back.

"Ahh!" Brian exclaimed, jumping, turning and holding up his hands in a defensive posture. A pair of startled doves fluttered from the rafters, flew across the ceiling, circled several times, and then came back to rest on a rafter where they had spent the night.

"I didn't mean to startle you – sorry about that," the rabbi whispered. Wendell held a steaming mug of coffee in his right hand and with the other, he handed Brian a thick black robe.

Brian walked hesitantly and fearfully across the platform toward Lilith and placed the black robe around her. Then he offered his hand to help her stand up. She looked at his hand like it was the first hand she'd ever seen, then examined her own. She stared at her hand for quite some time, as though it were a gate to infinity, and then reached out to grab Brian's hand. Hebrew letters adorned her hand, arms, torso, and legs as mahogany-colored tattoos, written in Brian's own blood. As he helped her rise, he thought that her grip was strong, warm, and wet, as though she had just been delivered from an enormous womb.

After she stood up, Brian gently wrapped his arms around his mom in a gentle embrace and began to sob. He couldn't help it – he had lost her forever, and now here she was – back with him again. After a moment of this, Lilith returned the hug, with her eyes closed and an expression that was difficult to interpret.

When Brian regained control, he stepped back and looked down at the place on the tarp where she had been formed. The spot from which she rose displayed a perfect outline of her back, not just in the now dried mud used to fashion her, but as though an intense, source of energy had emanated from her – gently toasting the underlying carpet to leave a negative image of her hair, shoulders, spine, buttocks, legs, and heels printed on the carpet. Brian tied the front of the robe closed and led her towards Wendell, who was still cupping his mug of steaming coffee. He continued to look at Lilith with awed amazement, mouth slightly open.

Lilith stopped in front of Wendell and examined him.

"Mom, this is Rabbi Wendell Rosenburg. He used a special scroll that I found called the Book of Formation to bring you back to life. You died a few months ago from COVID."

Brian stopped talking. He was about to cry again, and didn't want to complicate her reentry into the world any more than he had to. Lilith remained silent but placed her tattooed hand gently against Wendell's face, as though to say thank you.

Brian continued to hold her hand and led her downstairs to the conference room-turned living room. Letting go of her hand, he poured her a glass of water. She drank until the glass was empty. Wendell led her to a shower in the women's bathroom in the basement, adjusted the water temperature, and then went to cook them all some breakfast.

Lilith silently took a shower and washed her hair. As she bathed herself, soil and mud streamed down her body and down the drain. In spite of her silence, she seemed to be returning to normal.

22

PATIENCE REWARDED

Evening of June 6, 2020
Queens, New York

Eva Fischer held the glowing cigarette to her mouth with the three remaining fingers of her right hand and pulled nicotine-laden smoke through the glowing tobacco and into her lungs. A half-empty glass of Cabernet Sauvignon awaited her next sip on a small glass-topped table next to her chair. This was her last cigarette of her second pack of the day. She sat on the second-story deck of her townhome watching the passenger jets pass overhead, like clockwork, every 30 seconds preparing to land at LaGuardia airport in Queens, New York. She had lived in her townhome for the past 16 years and although loud, the rumble of the jets had become soothing and predictable.

As the next jet came within earshot, she took a sip of wine and listened carefully. "Tail-mounted engines," she said. She had turned the constant passage of jets overhead into something of a game – using only the sound of the jet, she guessed whether the plane had tail-mounted engines or wing-mounted engines. This particular rumble contains fluctuations and is slightly lower in volume than the previous jet, which had wing-mounted engines. The fluctuations are caused by turbulence occurring near the tail of the jet. She casually looked up to confirm this was the case. She was correct. A wing-mounted jet has louder engines and almost no fluctuations in the sound of the thrust. She'd become quite good at this silly little game.

Eva had two missing fingers on her right hand. The incident happened when she was reaching into a narrow space of a Buddhist temple in Thailand, searching for a Buddhist dorje[1]. This particular dorje was a ceremonial wand created by Buddha himself. Ancient writings indicated that the wand would allow the owner to become indestructible. If only she had found the wand *before* her hand had met the young cobra. Fortunately, the cobra had only bitten her pinky and ring fingers of her right hand. Since she was so far away from anything resembling a medical facility, she immediately took her machete and chopped these two fingers off, wrapping the wounded digits tightly with a cloth. She then waited until the cobra exited the cubby hole and chopped its head off in retaliation. She never suffered a single symptom from the snake bite venom, and although she did not find the dorje, she mounted the cobra in striking position, and it now sits in her parlor as a conversation piece. The taxidermist had done wonders restoring the snake's head to its body after its death.

Eva took another sip of wine, finished her cigarette, squishing the butt under her fur-lined moccasin and kicking it down into her very tiny backyard. She continued reading the latest issue of *Archeology Magazine*, finished the last of her wine, and stepped through the sliding glass door into the dining room of her townhome. She poured another glass of cabernet and walked up the stairs to her bedroom. Her bedroom was equipped with curtains designed to admit no light and reduce sound from the outside into the room, thus helping her with annoying and frequent bouts of insomnia. As she opened the door, however, a red glow faintly permeated the room.

1. https://projecthimalayanart.rubinmuseum.org/essays/dorje-discovered-by-dorje-lingpa/#:~:text=The%20dorje%20(vajra%20in%20Sanskrit,object%20and%20aid%20-for%20meditation%20.

There upon the wall, framed and mounted under glass, was the missing piece of the Sefer Yetzirah scroll, with glowing red marginalia.

"The Sefer Yetzirah is busy tonight," Eva whispered to herself. Eva pulled her phone from her back pocket and pressed the phone number for Anatoly Dezhnyov.

23

LILITH 2.0

8:14 AM
June 7, 2020

Lilith stepped out of the shower onto the fuzzy shower mat. Brian averted his eyes and handed her a towel. Wendell knocked on the bathroom door, carrying clothes and a cup of coffee. Brian opened the door, took the clothing and coffee, and thanked the rabbi.

"Breakfast's ready if you and your mom are hungry," Wendell said.

"I don't know about Mom, but I'm starving. We'll be there as soon as she is dressed," replied Brian.

Brian brought the clothing into the small changing room/bathroom used by the synagogue's former clergy. He laid them on the bench near the shower and turned his back to allow her to dress in private. Lilith tried to speak, then coughed. Her coughing grew worse until it appeared that she was gagging.

"Mom, are you okay?" Brian asked. Although she was naked, Brian continued to watch as she coughed up a white mass. Tendrils parted her lips, and she opened her mouth. This initiated a coughing sequence which ended with Lilith vomiting a white mass onto the floor. The tendrils writhed and began to find purchase on the bathroom tile floor, moving the white form along towards a grilled drain in the floor. Brian kicked the creature onto the drain and watched as it broke apart and slithered down the slots in the drain like tiny snakes. He looked back at his mom, asking again, "Are you OK?".

Lilith coughed several more times, then cleared her throat and said "I'm okay. Thank you. And thank you for my second chance, Bri-Bear."

"You DO remember me!" Brian said with tears streaming down his face at being called the nickname that his mother had used for him since he was three years old. Had she not been naked, Brian would have given her another hug. Instead, he simply looked into her eyes and saw that she was crying also.

Brian had previously brought several changes of clothing and some toiletries from his mom's closet and bathroom to the synagogue in preparation for this possibility. Brian stepped out of the room as Lilith selected a bra, panties, and a long-sleeved violet dress. She put them all on, then slipped on a pair of brown sandals. Lilith looked at herself in the mirror and brushed her hair. As she brushed, strands of hair began to move on their own in almost imperceptible, gentle waves.

The smell of potato latkes filled the synagogue basement as Lilith and Brian joined Rabbi Rosenburg in the conference room. Wendell placed scrambled eggs, lemon muffins, and toast on the table for his guests alongside the potato latkes.

"I hope that you are both hungry," he said as he placed plates on the table. "Coffee, anyone?" he offered.

Brian held out his cup, and Wendell poured. Lilith picked up her cup and examined it. It was emblazoned with Van Gogh's *The Starry Night* painting in blue, yellow, and white swirls. Eventually, she, too, offered her cup to Wendell to fill with steaming coffee, blew on the surface, and took a sip.

"I'd like to know exactly how I am alive again," Lilith asked.

"It's a long story, Mom," Brian answered. Then he launched into how he found the Sefer Yetzirah, Mr. Feldman at Feldman's World of Judaica, the glowing marginalia, giving his own blood, and then the very elaborate ritual that Rabbi Rosenburg carried out using the ashes from her cremation. He left out any mention of Mr. Feldman's rib, as he was more than a little squeamish about mentioning that part of the story or the fact that she was carrying around a dead man's rib in her body.

"Thank you, Bri-Bear. I suppose that explains the strange tattoos and the silver necklace. By the way, I have tried to take the necklace off, but as much as I want my hands to do so, they simply won't cooperate."

"Yes, both the tattoos and the necklace are part of what is keeping you alive," Wendell said. "If you or someone else removes or breaks the 'shem' – the necklace that you are wearing – you will die. It is probably for the best that you do not share that last piece information with anyone else. Honestly, I am completely astounded that the Scroll and the ritual worked at all."

"So, Wendell, my mom coughed up what appeared to be some sort of white, writhing, fibrous thing earlier. I kicked it down the drain. Any thoughts on what that might have been?" Brian asked.

Wendell thought about it for a moment and then replied: "Sorry, I can't think of any reason for that to have occurred, but then this is my first attempt at bringing someone back from the dead using the Sefer Yetzirah, or for that matter, any other means, so I wouldn't exactly consider myself an expert."

"Well, I hope you both enjoyed the breakfast," Wendell said, gathering plates. "I think it's time to let the two of you do a little catching up."

"Before you go, would you mind if Mom spends the night here with you?" Brian asked. "I need to prepare Dad and Emily for their reintroduction to Mom."

"That shouldn't be a problem at all, Brian," Wendell said.

The next few hours of being together felt as though Brian's mom had never died. It was hard to do, but Brian said goodnight and assured her he'd be back tomorrow, this time with the whole family.

On his way out of the synagogue, Brian encountered Rabbi

Rosenburg in the hallway. Brian grasped Wendell's shoulders, looked him in the eyes, and said, "Thank you, Rabbi. Thank you! Beyond any words, thank you. This is the best day of my life - having my mom back. We had a deal. The Scroll is yours."

24

LILITH'S DREAM

12:33 PM
JUNE 7, 2020
SKOKIE, ILLINOIS

In her dream, Lilith entered the dimly lit bar and sat down next to an overweight man with a tattoo of a snake with bared fangs on his chest framed by the "V" formed by the unzipped top of his leather jacket. She ordered a beer and began watching reruns of motocross racing on the TV above the bar. As she dreamed, she knew that the overweight man preferred to be called "Snake." She also, somehow, instinctively knew that this man had helped to brutally kill David Feldman for the simple reason that he was a Jew. She also knew David was a kind old gentleman who had helped her son better understand the ancient Scroll. A Scroll that no longer belonged to Brian but to Rabbi Rosenburg. She didn't know *how* she knew these things – but she did, and she moved about the dream with a type of sixth sense of every detail around her.

Snake eventually stopped watching the motocross rerun and

turned to Lilith, looking her up and down hungrily. He placed his hand on the fabric of her purple dress covering her thigh and asked, "How would you like to come home with me so we can get to know each other a little better?"

In her dream, Lilith responded in a way that she never would have responded in real life, "I thought you'd never ask, big boy."

His hand tightened on her thigh, and moved under her dress, but she pushed it away with surprising strength.

"Not here," she whispered. "Take me to your place and this little girl will give you more than you can handle."

In her dream, Snake pulled a $10 bill out of his jacket, laid it on the bar in front of Lilith - never taking his eyes off of her - then took her hand and walked her out of the bar, and down the alley. As they passed Mr. Feldman's brownstone, Snake glanced at the door but said nothing. They finally arrived at his 2003 Harley Davidson Road King in the back parking lot. He picked Lilith up and placed her on the pillion. He mounted the front seat of the big bike, started it up, and they roared away, the big bike's engine blatting loudly in the otherwise silent night.

In her dream, the night air was warm, and Lilith wrapped her arms around the large man as they rode. The wind lashed her hair wildly, like a maniacal cat-of-nine-tails. Soon, Snake pulled the bike down a narrow alley past a two-story garage and parked the bike. Lilith dismounted first, then Snake. He gestured for her to climb the narrow stairs outside the small garage, and she obeyed. In her dream, she glanced back to see Snake following her, his sick grin leering in the dim light. She looked back and licked her lips.

At the top of the stairs, he pulled a key from a retractable keychain and opened the door to an upstairs apartment over the garage. The garage/apartment combo was situated separate from the small cracker box-style home commonly built in the late 1950s in the city of Skokie. In her dream, Snake flipped on a light switch and pulled her inside the apartment, shut the door, and pushed her hard up against the door, putting his mouth over hers and inserting his tongue into her mouth. In her dream, she wrapped her arms around his neck as fibrils extended from her forearms and grew into his neck and skull.

In her dream, Snake had finally begun to realize that Lilith was not the girl she seemed to be, and he tried to pull away, but the mycelium fibrils wrapped around Snake's neck and punctured his skin with hundreds of tiny stingers. In her dream, Lilith bit Snake's tongue off and spit it out onto the floor. Mycelium fibrils grew from her nostrils and mouth and flowed into his mouth, stinging as they grew. The death cap venom injected into Snake was too much for him to overcome, and Snake began to convulse and moan unintelligibly as blood flowed from his mouth in a crimson waterfall onto the tattoo of the rattlesnake on his chest. Lilith released the mycelium, allowing them to occupy their new residence in Snake, as she watched him fall to the floor of his dingy garage apartment. Lilith squatted on the floor next to Snake, looked into his eyes, and said, "This is for David Feldman." He continued to seize, jerking about as though a thousand volts of electricity were coursing through his body. The convulsions eventually ceased and Lilith continued to watch as the life drained out of Snake's eyes.

The dream continued, and Lilith searched Snake to find a lighter, which she used to light his furniture, clothing, and drapes. She then tossed the lighter onto Snake's burning figure and stepped out of the door from which she entered and out into the night.

25

ROAD KING

2:36 AM
June 8, 2020
Skokie, Illinois

Wendell awoke abruptly, realizing he'd just experienced a vision from the Sefer Yetzirah—much like the ones Brian had described. Based on his limited readings in the area, it occurred to him that he might have been astrally projected to Lilith's location by the Scroll.

He pulled back the bedding, swung over the side of the bed, and threw on his pajamas and robe. Opening his nightstand drawer, he brought out the Scroll and unrolled it. The marginalia were glowing red. Wendell returned the Scroll to the nightstand. He grabbed a flashlight and walked down the hall to Lilith's room. He opened the door quietly, shading the beam of the flashlight to allow only a pencil-sized beam of light to pass through his fist. Scanning the room with the reduced beam, it eventually illuminated the bed. The blankets were pulled to one side, and the bed was unoccupied.

"Looking for me?" Lilith said from behind the rabbi.

Wendell jumped suddenly and dropped the flashlight.

"Uh-um, yes. I was just checking to see if you were okay. You have had a very unusual 'experience,' after all," he replied, using air quotes for the word "experience."

Wendell picked up the flashlight and turned on the hallway light. Lilith stood before him dressed in her purple dress and sandals, her hair mussed.

"Are you going somewhere?" he asked.

"No, I think I've been sleepwalking. I had a horrible nightmare and then woke up in the conference room, no longer in my pajamas, but instead wearing this dress and my sandals. I don't remember having changed clothes," she replied.

"What kind of nightmare was it?" Wendell asked, suspiciously.

"I only remember that it was very disturbing – something about a stranger in a bar, a motorcycle, and a fire," she replied as she yawned. "I think I'll go back to bed, if that's okay with you, Rabbi Rosenburg?"

"Of course, Mrs. Newman," replied the rabbi.

"Oh, please call me Lilith, Rabbi," Lilith said, waving her hand towards Wendell as if they had known each other for years.

"Thank you, Lilith, and please call me Wendell."

"Thank you, Wendell. I will."

Lilith stepped lithely past Wendell into her bedroom, emitting the unmistakable aroma of smoke as she walked by.

Wendell walked down the hall to the basement door leading out to the stairs. He opened the door, noting that although he had locked it prior to retiring for bed, it was unlocked now. Walking up the stairs to the side of the building, he found a 2003 Road King — engine still hot — leaning against the side of the synagogue.

26

HISTORY LESSON

8:47 AM
JUNE 8, 2020
SKOKIE, ILLINOIS

Wendell looked at Brian and Lilith and said, "It is my belief that although we were successful at bringing your mom back to life, she now serves the Scroll in the manner of what is known as a golem. According to legend, the purpose of a golem created by a mystic rabbi has been to defend and avenge its people – the Jews. For thousands of years, this has been part of the purpose of Sefer Yetzirah, to bring life from inanimate matter such as mud or clay, but more than this, to create a servant or a defender when the Jews needed protection from those who persecuted them. That being said, the Sefer Yetzirah is not in and of itself an instruction manual for the creation of life, but only contains some of the principles needed for the creation of life."

"In one example of these legends, it is said that the late 16th-century rabbi of Prague known as the Maharal of Prague, created a golem out of river mud and that this golem defended the Prague

Jewish ghettos from antisemitic attacks and pogroms. The Scroll is now controlling Lilith to avenge the very brutal death of David Feldman. I would imagine that the need for vengeance is especially intense since one of David's own ribs was used to create her."

"What the hell did you do!" Lilith exclaimed. "How did you two obtain a rib bone from David Feldman?!"

"Mom, please try to understand my desperation. Your family desperately loves and needs you. *I* love you and *I* need you, and we did what was necessary to bring you back. Besides, it's not like he needed it anymore."

"Dear God, I AM a monster!" Lilith exclaimed.

"Both of you, please calm down," Wendell said. "Think of the time you both spent together yesterday. Brian, you said that it was the best day of your life. There is no reason that you can't at the very least have more of that sort of time with your mother."

"I suppose that's true, but Wendell, the vision that you just shared with us ended with only one of Mr. Feldman's murderers being avenged. There were two murderers in the vision or – what did you call it? – oh, yeah, astral projection that the Scroll gave to me. This means that mom isn't done yet."

"I agree. I think that your mom may have another busy evening ahead of her," Wendell said.

"What about the fibrils that came out of her?" Brian asked. "What you described from the vision sounds like what she coughed up yesterday just before she began talking. What the heck are they?"

"I have a theory," Rabbi Rosenburg said. "Follow me." Wendell rose from his chair, followed by Lilith and Brian. He walked out of the synagogue basement door out to the gardener's shed. Next to the shed was the soil that they had used as part of Lilith's creation. Rising from the soil were six white mushrooms.

"Hola, Brian! Hola, Rabbi!" Mr. Fuentes exclaimed.

"Hola, Mr. Fuentes," Brian and Wendell replied, nearly at the same time.

"So, Mr, Fuentes, you knew that Rabbi Rosenburg was living in the basement of the synagogue?" Brian asked.

"He needed a place to stay, and since no one else was using it –

look, I've needed a place to stay before. I know that feeling. So I help the Rabbi a little," Mr. Fuentes replied, holding a finger to his lips.

"Tell me, Gabriel, do you know anything about these mushrooms?" Wendell asked.

"Si, they are very poisonous - el sombrero de la muerte. They have been growing in the lawn. I hoe them, and put them here to compost," Gabriel said.

"The hat of death – death cap mushrooms?" Brian asked.

"Well, I just become more of a monster every minute," Lilith said.

"Perdoname, señorita, but we have not met," Gabriel said.

"Oh, hello, I'm Brian's m-. . . math teacher, Lilith."

"El gusto es mio, Lilith, I am Gabriel Fuentes."

"So nice to meet you, Gabriel, and thank you for this wonderful soil."

"De nada," Gabriel said with a puzzled look on his face.

27

BRASS

12:23 AM
June 9, 2020
Skokie, Illinois

Brass popped the cap off his seventh Heineken dark lager for the evening, took careful aim, and flipped the cap with a snap of his thumb into a grey metal pail decorated with skull and crossbone stickers. The cap rattled against a few hundred other caps half filling the pail. He turned his attention back to changing the brake pads on his jet-black 2019 Harley. The bike rested atop a lift table in his one-car red brick garage adjacent to the alley behind his cracker box rental house. Next to the front tire of the Harley lay his swastika brass knuckles. Posters of Burzum, Mayhem, and Absurd were taped or thumbtacked to the walls, and Metallica's *Master of Puppets* surged from a set of speakers mounted in the rafters. A large red Nazi Swastika flag hung over a window inside the small building. A 2016 Indian Chief Dark Horse was parked next to his Slaver poster. Almost more valuable to him than his motorcycles, however, was a gold-colored cloth Star of David with the word "Jude" printed in the middle. This was mounted in a frame and hung next to his Nazi flag.

The news of Snake's death in the fire was not surprising to Brass. He was always smoking and falling asleep drunk in whatever position he happened to be sitting or lying. The surprising thing was that someone had bitten his tongue off before the fire was set. Sure, there were a lot of people who hated Snake. Someone had surprised Snake, and that someone was likely a woman that he was kissing right before the bitch bit his tongue off. So, the god-damned question was, how could a woman, even a big woman, have overpowered a big man like Snake? Brass heard the sound of a Harley off in the distance and wondered if he was about to find out. He slid the swastika knuckles onto his right hand and listened.

This time, Lilith realized that she was not dreaming, but under the control of a vengeful, supernatural Scroll. She dreaded what was about to happen but was helpless to do anything that might prevent it. It was as though she was simply along for the ride inside of another person's body as the Road King blatted noisily down the quiet street. She turned the bike down an alleyway and pulled it into the backyard, aiming the bike at the entry door of the garage building. Light shone through dusty plaid curtains covering the small window in the door. She revved the engine hard, raced the bike towards the door, and jumped off the bike at the last second onto the grass, rolling to cushion her momentum. The bike smashed through the door and the handlebars crashed through the aging frame of the doorway, continuing through the door and into the small garage building. An angry curse burst from inside the building, followed by the sound of the engine sputtering to a stop.

Lilith rose from the lawn and walked towards the jagged hole where a door once stood. She stepped into the small garage and stopped. The 2003 Harley Road King stood with its front tire crumpled against a lift table, and entangled with a second black motorcycle, which had fallen off the table during the impact. She quickly looked around, but Brass was not present anywhere in the shop.

A creaking sound from above was her only warning as Brass dropped from the rafters, his brass-knuckled fist smashing into the side of her neck as he landed behind her. Lilith hit the clay floor hard, landing on her back, head ringing. She felt a heavy knee plow into her chest and then saw the tattooed arm raise up to throw the first punch. Her new body, however, had other plans. Mycelium snaked from her left hand to wrap around his arm as it came down. She felt the mycelium injecting venom into him. She saw the brass knuckles on his hand and, with her right hand, began snapping his fingers one by one, his screams echoing with each sickening snap.

After they were broken, she pushed him off of her with a strength that she had never known in her previous life, and pulled the brass knuckles off of his mangled hand as he continued to scream. She released the mycelium to their new host, placed the brass knuckles on her own right hand, looked him in the eyes and said, "This is for David Feldman." Then she caved in the left side of Brass' head. As Brass was losing consciousness, the last image to light his retina was his own swastika brass knuckles, used against him. Tattoos of the Hebrew letters Ayen, Samech, and Nun were spaced evenly upon her arm as it eked out its revenge.

Lilith removed the brass knuckles, opened Brass' dead mouth, and shoved the foul weapon into the back of his throat. She searched Brass' pockets and retrieved a set of keys and a Zippo lighter. She then opened the gas tank of the tilted and mangled Harley, allowing it to drain on the floor. Her fingers touched the garage opener button as she started the engine. Then she lit the Nazi flag on fire and rode her new bike back to the synagogue.

28

DECISION

8:30 AM
June 12, 2020
Skokie, Illinois

"Mom, it's time for Dad to meet you," Brian said.

"Don't you think he might object that I am now technically, though most certainly unwillingly, a murderer? That I'm controlled by the magic Scroll to do its whim on a regular basis, and I can apparently extrude poisonous tendrils when threatened? For all I know, I could be cooking dinner one night, taste the food with my finger and accidentally poison my entire family!"

"Look at the bright side – you don't seem to have asthma anymore," Brian said with a smile. "And you have a motorcycle."

Wendell put his hand up to cover his smile.

"Don't you even *think* about laughing at this situation, Rabbi Rosenburg! Not even a smile!" Lilith said, and Wendell slipped out of the room muffling his laughter with fake coughing.

"I don't think you're a murderer," Brian assured. "I think you're a holy protector. Those jerks deserved to die after what they did to Mr. Feldman. Without the Scroll, they probably would never have spent a day in prison. I'm *proud* of who you are."

"And based on how you handled those two thugs, I personally think you're a real badass," Wendell said, slipping quietly back into the room.

"Those are very nice things to say, guys, but I'm not proud of being a killer, even if I'm a righteous vigilante killer," Lilith said. "I mean, what if the Scroll decides it wants to send me to Israel to hunt down antisemite terrorists or to Germany to kill the last living Nazi guards from Auschwitz?"

"I don't think the Scroll will do that, Lilith," Wendell said. "You are connected to the Scroll, but I'm the owner now. I think it will only protect Jews that I'm connected to. I mean think about it, when Brian owned the Scroll, he connected the Scroll to David Feldman after he met him. The Scroll, in turn, provided an astral projection to David's crime scene so that we could use David's rib to bring you back to life, and then bring justice to Brass and Snake. Bottom line: I think the Scroll does righteous justice, through Lilith, but ultimately serves the owner of the Scroll and always protects the Jewish people."

"So, you're saying that since you aren't connected to any Jews who were murdered in Auschwitz, or because those responsible are already almost all dead, it won't have me hunting down geriatric Nazis?" Lilith asked.

"Right."

"And probably won't send her to the Middle East either?" Brian asked.

"Well, as it turns out, I do have an aunt living in Tel Aviv," Wendell said, "but she's quite old, a genius at bridge, makes Italian cream cake to die for, but not likely of much value to possible enemies of the nation of Israel."

"What if we gave the scroll to Dad?" Brian asked. "Then Mom would only be serving justice, if any, to those who threatened Jews who we're connected to. By the way, we don't know very many Jewish people."

"I hear ya but don't forget, I have someone I'd like to bring back, too," Wendell said. "Though I'm still on the fence about it. Forgive me if I selfishly maintain ownership of the Scroll for now. But let's get back to the original question – should your dad be introduced to Lilith 2.0?"

"I vote yes," Brian said.

"I vote yes, too," Wendell said.

"Well, I would really like to have more time with the love of my life, and my family, but I don't want to bring the dangerous baggage that comes with me," Lilith said.

"I think you need your family to make that decision with you," Brian said. "I'll make the arrangements to have 'two special guests' over for dinner."

29

FAMILY AGAIN

8:30 PM
June 12, 2020
Skokie, Illinois

". . . and now you've heard the entire story," Brian said to his dad and Emily, after more than two hours of relating the events surrounding his mom and answering their many, many questions.

"As you requested at the beginning, I've listened to your story without too many interruptions or objections. Is it my turn to speak?" Ross asked.

"Yes," Brian said.

"You have probably ruined your life forever," Ross said, rather bluntly. "The police may be on the way to arrest you this very moment. What were you thinking, son? Breaking into a murder scene. Hiring a butcher to cut out a rib? Stealing an ancient scroll? You know this was all very reckless, don't you?!"

Ross's face was bright red. It seemed like he stopped just to catch a breath of air.

"This could mean years in prison for you," Ross continued, "and if they do arrest you, now it's not just Lilith, the love of my life, but my only son! Brian, I simply can't take any more loss. It's literally all I can do to hold myself together after your mom died, and the *only* reason I'm holding it all together is because I can't let the two of you down."

"Dad, my actions haven't really hurt anyone, and because of those actions Mom is back! Think about it - she's with us again! We're a family again. I don't regret any of those questionable steps, and I'd do them all over again to bring her back. Besides, what I've done can't be undone. Dad, you've got nothing to lose. Everything you've lost is back. Waiting for you. Just give her a chance. I know it's hard to believe, but she's really alive again. She's here."

"It's just so unbelievable," Ross said to his son, tears welling up in his eyes.

"She's really alive again, Dad," Brian said.

"When can we see her?" Emily finally chimed in. She looked far more excited, more convinced, and more hopeful than her father.

"I was hoping we could all meet her and Rabbi Rosenburg over dinner tomorrow night here at the house," Brian said. "We'll just meet them and talk to them. Dad. Please?"

"Well, I know that I, for one, after everything we've been through, could certainly use a miracle," Ross said. "I just hope and pray that we have a miracle on our hands, not a curse. I'm taking a leap of faith here, Brian. Ask them to come for dinner. And I'd like to see this Scroll."

Emily squealed and began jumping up and down, hugging her dad.

Neither Ross nor Emily got much sleep that night.

* * *

6:00 PM | JUNE 13, 2020 | SKOKIE, ILLINOIS

Brian opened the front door of their home and ushered Rabbi Rosenburg in.

"Dad, Emily, this is Rabbi Wendell Rosenburg. Rabbi Rosenburg, this is my sister, Emily, and my dad, Ross Newman."

"Very nice to meet you, rabbi," Ross said, as he shook Wendell's hand.

"Nice to meet you, Rabbi Rosenburg," Emily said as she gave him a polite hug.

"But where is the miracle lady?" Ross asked.

"She is very nervous about this and wanted to wait outside until Brian was done introducing me," Wendell said.

Wendell opened the door again and waved for Lilith. She stepped through the door, wearing a hood so as not to draw attention to herself during their walk from the synagogue. Brian shut the door behind her, and Lilith tentatively pulled back the hood with both hands, allowing Ross and Emily their first view of her face. There, for all to see, were the Hebrew letters Aleph and Tav, one on her right cheek and the other on the left side of her neck. Hanging below her chin was the silver necklace spelling out the Hebrew word for "truth" - אמת. Her hazel eyes looked at each of them nervously.

"Lilith?" Ross asked, his voice trembling.

"Mom?" Emily asked.

Lilith nodded and looked down at the floor as if she were about to be scolded or, worse, rejected.

Ross stepped slowly towards Lilith and held out his arms. Lilith began to sob, stepping into his arms. Ross matched her tears, and so did Emily who now joined their hug.

After a long embrace, Ross held Lilith by the shoulders and looked into her eyes.

"I have been dead without you, darling," Ross said. He looked at Rabbi Rosenburg. "Thank you, from the bottom of my heart. I don't know how any of this is possible, but thank you."

Wiping his eyes on his sleeve, Ross smiled and said, "Well, is anyone else here hungry besides me?"

There was an enthusiastic round of agreement as he led them into the dining room and then held Lilith's chair for her to sit. Ross brought Lilith and Wendell each a glass of wine while Emily and Brian brought in steaming bowls of shrimp scampi, buttered sweet potatoes with pecans, gumbo, and sauteed Brussel sprouts with bacon. The appetizing and comforting smells of delicious home cooking filled the kitchen and the dining room along with the sounds of animated voices and laughter. Lilith offered to help, but Ross insisted. *No. You're the guest of honor.*

Ross led the family in grace before digging in.

"Dear Lord, bless this food to the nourishment of our bodies, and help us to serve you through its nourishment. Thank you for our guest and our family gathered around this table, and we give you thanks for the miracle that you have provided us in bringing Lilith back to our family. In Jesus' name, we pray, amen," Ross again teared up and his voice cracked as he said the last few phrases of the blessing.

After everyone had started eating, Ross looked over at his wife.

"Lilith, do you remember everything about your life up to the point of your death?"

"Well, based upon my conversations with Brian so far, everything seems to be in order in the memories department, so – nice work, Rabbi Rosenburg," she replied.

"Thank you, Lilith," mumbled Wendell through a mouthful of Brussel sprouts.

"How about while you were, well, you know – dead?" Emily asked. "Do you remember where you went? Did you meet Grannie and Pawpaw in Heaven?"

"Sorry sweetie, I don't remember anything from while I was dead at all," Lilith said. "Perhaps that's for the best."

"What about these fibrils you produced when you were under the Scroll's control?" Ross asked. "Can you make them anytime you want? Is this like a Spiderman thing?"

"I've tried to produce them on my own, but nothing happens," Lilith replied.

"Does anyone have any thoughts on how we will re-introduce her back into society?" Ross asked. "I mean, we can't just say – hey, remember when Lilith died? Good news - she got better! Or, 'surprise! I met a new lady on eHarmony who happens to look and act exactly like my dead wife, except maybe a little over-the-top with the Hebrew face tattoos.'"

"You could say I'm your Swedish volleyball player," Lilith said with a smile.

"Wow!" Ross exclaimed. "He really did keep your memory intact!"

"But you're right, we'll have to put some serious thought into how I'm reintroduced. My big comeback tour," Lilith said. "But that assumes you're all gonna let me live with you again. That basement still available?"

"Well, the last tenant was a real 'dead' beat if you know what I mean," Ross said. Wendell choked on a bite of sweet potato as Brian groaned in feigned agony.

Lilith began to stand up.

"Wendell, it seems that Ross here didn't miss me that much, after all," Lilith deadpanned. "I think we'll be leaving now."

Ross laughed and quickly motioned for her to sit down. "No, no, no, I'm just kidding darling. Please don't go."

"That's more like it," Lilith said. "Please pass the shrimp scampi, if Brian hasn't already wolfed it all down. Oh, and do I really have to spend the night in the basement tonight, darling?"

Lilith put her hand on Ross's thigh.

"I may have seen a mouse down there yesterday," Ross said. "I can't allow *anyone* to sleep down there until that problem has been fully resolved. The Skokie Health Department could give us a citation. I think it's probably best, and this is strictly from a safety perspective, for Lilith to sleep in our bed."

Emily and Brian looked at each other and rolled their eyes at the same time as the rabbi smiled.

Once everyone had eaten their fill, Wendell politely excused himself and walked back to the synagogue. As he walked, he felt truly happy that he was able to be a part of bringing Lilith back to her family. And new comforting, reassuring thoughts filled his mind about bringing his beloved and beautiful Isabella back into his arms again.

Meanwhile, Ross led Lilith upstairs to their bedroom. There were rose petals scattered around the room and several candles lit.

"I guess you did miss me after all," Lilith said, holding his hand. "When did you do all of this?"

"Earlier today, darling," Ross said.

"But what if I didn't pass the Lilith test?"

"Then you wouldn't be in our bedroom right now," replied Ross.

"Of course. I suppose I better do something to make up for lost time, then," Lilith said, unbuttoning Ross' shirt.

"Wait. One more thing," Ross said as he knelt to one knee and opened a box with Lilith's wedding ring. "Will you marry me, again?"

"Sure you don't want to see if all my systems work, first?" Lilith teased.

"You are still you, my love," Ross said. "That's what matters."

"Then my answer is still yes," Lilith said as she slipped her ring back on and admired it. "How about now? Can we make up for lost time now? Please, please, please?"

"Definitely the same girl I married the first time," Ross said, smiling as Lilith unbuttoned his shirt, kissing his neck and chest as she went.

30

ON THE RADAR

10:06 PM
JUNE 13, 2020
QUEENS, NEW YORK

Eva Fisher's cell phone rang with the sound of an old-school telephone jangle. "Anatoly, give me some good news," she said.

Anatoly responded with his heavy Russian accent.

"Well, assuming we have an actual golem, the Sefer Yetzirah golem seems to be in Skokie, Illinois. There have been three deaths reported in past few weeks. The first was Jewish man by name of David Feldman – skull was crushed with swastika brass knuckles during what police describe as home robbery. That's where it gets interesting. Very dear friend removed a rib from the dead man. My friend was hired by rabbi, not the killer."

"Because the rabbi is trying to make a *female* Sefer Yetzirah golum..."

"Well, Mr. Feldman's death was followed by death of motorcycle gangster by name of Joseph Schweinekopf, AKA 'Snake.' Joseph's tongue was bitten off, he was poisoned with massive quantities of Death Cap mushroom, and then his garage apartment set on fire and burned to ground before fire department could control it. Next murder victim was guy by name of Peter Schiller, AKA 'Brass'. Mr. Schiller was also motorcycle gangster and member of Northside Skulls, a neo-Nazi group in Skokie. Would you like to know motorcycle gang Mr. Schweinekopf rode with?" Anatoly asked.

"Let me guess – the Northside Skulls?" Eva said.

"Give lady a Cuban cigar!" Anatoly said. "And guess what else? Mr. Schiller died because skull was crushed with some sort of swastika brass knuckles. Oh, and I'm sure that this is also just coincidence, but Mr. Schiller also poisoned by massive quantity of Death Cap mushroom poison."

"Definitely not a coincidence," Eva replied.

"Definitely not," echoed Anatoly. "Oh, I almost forgot to tell you about one more dead person. A 3-year-old girl - Anna Weisel – also died, but she died before the three men. You want to guess how she died?"

"Death Cap poisoning?"

"Da. And do you want to know where Anna lived?"

"Let me guess - next to a synagogue?"

"You are genius, Boss."

31

BUYERS

6:15 PM
June 14, 2020
Tel Aviv, Israel

Ivan Sokov stood before the full-length windows of his office on the 41st floor of the Azrieli Center Triangular Tower in downtown Tel Aviv, a snifter of Louis XIII cognac in hand. His wife, Orina, wore a formal Valentino Garavani evening dress paired with black Louboutin stilettos. Both were elegantly attired for a very important dinner that evening.

The view of the city below gave Ivan a visceral tingling sensation in his testicles – he felt like a bird of prey, hunting with unmatched vision for his next money-bloated rabbit in the pulsing heart of the vibrant and growing city. For decades, Ivan's biggest "rabbit" had been the Israeli Defense Force, to which they sold war-hardened communications, computers, laptops, and explosive drones and fighter aircraft upgrades. The decades had turned Ivan and Orina into billionaires, with Ivan still in charge of the business side of the company and Orina still in charge of research and development.

Israeli Defense Systems, also known as IDS, was the couple's company, and it was an instrumental part of making Israel one of the most powerful nations on Earth. But his most profitable venture to date, so he believed, would finally launch in the next few months – artificially intelligent, autonomous explosive drones, weapons that even China or the United States had not perfected yet. The product line, codenamed "Devastator," would be offered in three sizes:

- A small drone designed to deliver a grenade-sized fragmentation explosive,
- A medium sized drone designed to deliver an armor-piercing explosive for use against tanks and troop carriers, and
- A large drone designed to deliver a punch similar to a Hellfire missile.

A version even exists that allows for the drones to be launched from tanks. All of the delivery systems used artificial intelligence developed by IDS. The AI was designed to identify targets based upon facial recognition, uniform or clothing type, military aircraft, tank or vehicle type, possible hiding places for vehicles, and weak points in infrastructure such as bridges, railroads, power stations, fuel storage depots and the like. No radio link to an operator is required, and the drones had been, so far, impossible to jam electronically because they relied on terrain recognition rather than GPS - simply fire and forget.

"The South Korean contingency from Hyundai Rotem has arrived in the lobby," Orina said.

"Good, and so begins the start of a beautiful relationship," Ivan said.

"I just read that Kim Jong Un launched their second brand new nuclear attack submarine yesterday," Orina said. "That's two in less than a year."

"Excellent. That should grease the skids for upgrading their K2

Black Panther tanks with our tank-launched Devastators," Ivan said. "Is everything ready for tomorrow's proving ground demonstration?"

"Of course, darling. Has my incredible attention to detail ever let you down?"

"No, and may I also say that you are the most beautiful woman that I have ever laid eyes upon, especially in that dress."

Ivan's hand traveled down her bare back, over the silk fabric, resting on the cleft of her ass.

Orina gently pulled his hand away from her backside, put it to her lips and kissed it, then admonished him.

"Ivan, not now. Do you know how much trouble I went through pouring myself into this dress? Let's save that kind of fun for *after* our dinner tonight."

Their flirtatious conversation was interrupted by a phone call to Ivan's private cell phone. He picked up the phone from his desk, looked at the caller ID, and answered without hesitation.

"Good morning, Eva. How is my favorite antiquities and artifacts dealer today?"

"Good evening, Ivan. I have some news that I think you will find very, very interesting," Eva said.

"Eva, I have to let you know that I'm about to go to dinner with a very important customer, so my time is literally a great deal of money at the moment."

"I've found the Sefer Yetzirah scroll."

Ivan pushed a button on his cell phone to bring Orina into the conversation on speaker.

"That's fantastic! I just put you on speaker. Orina, Eva said she found the Sefer Yetzirah scroll – the original one. You have it in your possession?"

"Good evening, Orina. I don't have the scroll in my possession, and that's why I'm calling you. I need two of your corporate operatives to come to the United States to assist in extracting the Scroll," replied Eva.

"Now wait a second, why would you need my corporate operatives to come illegally into the United States to conduct an illegal military exercise on US soil to acquire a defenseless little scroll?" Ivan asked.

"Because the Scroll is under the protection of a golem – a female golem," Eva said.

"Reeeally?" Orina said.

"We agreed that if I were to provide you with the original Sefer Yetzirah Scroll handwritten by Abraham and annotated by the Maharal of Prague, you would pay me five million US dollars. However, now, not only do I know *where* the Scroll is, I also have *proof* that the Scroll works, *and* I can lead you to a female golem created by the Scroll – essentially, a super soldier created to protect the Jewish nation of Israel if placed in the right hands. I'm going to need more money for what I'm bringing you – a lot more money. By the way, did I mention that she has special *powers*?"

Her last statement was followed by the audible hiss of smoke being pulled through her Virginia Slims cigarette into her lungs.

"Special powers?" Orina asked. "What kind of special powers?"

"She has the ability to kill her enemies using Death Cap mushroom poison, and my guess is that she does this by extruding fibrils from her body in some fashion that I don't yet understand. I haven't personally seen her in action, yet, but one of her victims had mycelium wrapped around his neck and another victim was found with his hand trapped in the stuff and all of his fingers broken."

"Mycelium? You mean fungus fibrils?" Orina asked.

"Well done! I see that you paid attention in Biology 101, Orina. Exactly," answered Eva. "And it looks as though the special powers were introduced entirely by a fortuitous accident. We have evidence that points to Death Cap mushrooms being present in the soil or clay used for the creation ritual. And do you know what that means for your super soldier dream, Mr. and Mrs. Sokov?"

The phone became silent for a moment.

"Ivan? Orina? Are you still there?" Eva asked.

"Yes. Yes, We're still here." Orina paused and then said, "It means that we could create an army of super soldiers with a variety of special powers by including small amounts of different biological materials. If a fungus yields the ability to create mycelium that can be deployed rapidly during a battle, along with the ability to poison an enemy, then perhaps a piece of a crab shell could provide the soldier with a built-in personal armor, or perhaps a the gills of a fish might enable the soldier to swim underwater, or the feathers of a bird might allow the soldier to fly, and so on. The possibilities are quite interesting to think about."

"Quite interesting indeed," Eva said. "But speaking of interesting, about that payment. I'm thinking north of one hundred million US dollars, at least," Eva said.

"Give us a minute, Eva," Ivan said. "I'm putting us on mute for a moment."

"There's no need to negotiate, just give her what she's asking," Orina said. "This could be worth billions if what she says is true. Naturally, we will want proof that it works before we pay her. We'll get that all written up. There will be essentially no downside for us."

"Who cares about the Devastator anymore," Ivan said. "THIS could make us the most valuable company on the planet."

Ivan who pushed the speaker button again.

"Will $125 million work for you, Ms. Fischer?" Ivan said.

"That is," Orina quickly chimed in, "assuming we can *prove* that the golem has the special powers you claim she does in the tactical arena, *and* that we can demonstrate that the Scroll can create another golem."

"I'm not sure I'll be able to buy that small island off of Fiji, yet, but I think that will work," Eva replied. "You have a deal, my friends."

32

2005 AND THE CIRCLE OF LIFE

4:11 AM
May 2, 2005
12 miles east of Camp Eggers, Afghanistan

A mist of cold rain gently settled on the five U.S. soldiers as they hiked in the dark toward their mission objective, roughly 7,000 feet above sea level in the mountainous terrain east of Kabul. Earlier, a UH-60 Blackhawk helicopter had encountered small arms fire from what appeared to be a camp of about five Taliban fighters. Responsibility for locating and neutralizing these fighters now rested squarely on Naval Special Warfare Officer Ross Newman, positioned at the center of the patrol.

Ace — a towering black man with giant muscles honed by thousands of hours in the gym — whispered in a voice just loud enough to carry, "Say, Crosshair, when's that sweet lady of yours gonna pop out that baby boy?"

Ross had acquired the nickname 'Crosshair' when he put a 5.56 mm round through a mounted 50-cent piece at 100 yards, winning a

$100 bet with a fellow Marine sniper as well as the admiration of most of the troops stationed at Camp Eggers who quickly heard the story. Bored troops, it seems, come up with the best entertainment.

Ross replied, "Thanks for asking, Ace. I know that you are asking simply out of heartfelt compassion for me being so far away from my wife who is about to give birth to my first-born child, and *not* because you think my wife is hot and that you are basically a giant, muscle-bound, testosterone-engorged penis, right?"

Ace replied, "Oh, yes sir. Absolutely, sir. My compassion for your unfortunate and very sad family situation brings water to my eyes nearly every night, sir. And for the record, if you ever have trouble in the sack with that fine lily white woman of yours, I could have compassion for that situation, as well, if you know what I mean."

The other three men in the line began laughing.

"Well, the fact is, she is due any day now," Ross said.

"What y'all plan on naming him, sir?"

"I want to name him David, as in David and Goliath, but Lilith wants to name him Brian," replied Ross.

Ace chuckled, "Well, it looks like you've got yo'self a Brian, then."

After the laughter died down, Ross activated his Precision Lightweight GPS Receiver to assess their progress toward the objective.

"Looks like we're 'bout a mile away from the reported campsite," Ross said quietly. "Let's go quiet from here on in. Hand signals only."

* * *

The misty rain stopped falling about halfway to the objective, but the cloud cover remained, leaving the soldiers in the gray gloom of dawn as they marched forward. The dusty, dead grass path came to a ravine, which divided two sections of the mountain by a distance of about 30 feet.

Ross motioned for Ace and Peach (named for his thick Georgia accent) to examine the bridge. He motioned for the other two men to get down on one knee so as to reduce their profile to a possible enemy sniper. The three men then scanned the mountainside, seeking any indication that this might be an ambush. Ace removed a mirror with a small light on a telescoping handle from his jacket as the pair squatted down, looking for trip wires between the rails and IEDs underneath the wooden bridge. After a quick search, Ace gave the all-clear sign.

Peach rose to a standing position and stepped onto the wooden bridge. As his boot landed, a sniper's bullet impacted his chin, traveled through the back of his throat, severed his spine, and killed him instantly. Droplets of blood flew through the air as the sound of the sniper rifle report finally arrived at the teams' eardrums. As Peach fell backwards onto his back, Ross shouted, "Take cover!" and grabbed Peach's jacket by the shoulder, dragging him behind a low rock.

The other men quickly found cover behind low lying rocks. The sound of AK-47 gunfire and bullets impacting against stone, the wooden bridge and the arid, crusted earth filled the air around them. Ross pressed his fingers to Peach's carotid artery, confirming he was dead, then rolled his body onto the low stone where he had taken cover.

"I need you to keep fighting with us even after you have died, dear friend," Ross whispered. Then to the rest of his team he shouted, "Draw their fire, but stay under cover! I'll take them out one-by-one!"

The slope of the mountain made it possible for Ross to stretch out behind the added cover provided by Peach's body. He did so and placed his sniper rifle at the bottom of Peach's body armor, searching for flashes from the AK-47s in the dawn's early light.

Soon he saw what he was looking for, flashes, and behind those irregularly shaped flashes, he was just able to make out a charcoal turban against the shadowed arid mountain rock. He put his sights on the turban and pulled the trigger. The fighter's head flopped backward, and he went down. Ross repeated this procedure three more times. Each time, the sound of AK-47 gunfire died down and then eventually resumed. After the death of the fourth fighter, the AK-47 fire ceased. Ross knew that the sniper was waiting for them to relax, to believe that the danger was over, perhaps even to continue their journey across the bridge, but he signaled his men to remain silent and remain down, behind cover. He knew that the sniper was simply biding his time.

The sun slowly rose from behind the mountain located to their six. As it did, the mountain's shadow behind them crept steadily down the slope ahead, inching closer to the sniper's hiding place. Ross waited patiently, scanning the moving curtain of light against the slopes ahead. A twinkle of reflected light at about 15 degrees to his right revealed the position of the sniper's scope. Ross placed his crosshairs on the now visible turban of the Taliban sniper, adjusted for the updraft that unfailingly came with the sunrise against the mountainside and pulled the trigger. Through his scope, he saw a patch of blood splatter against the rocks behind the turban. He watched as the sniper rifle slid down the side of the mountain.

* * *

The campsite of the five fighters was simply that – a small campfire with the usual chainak, or Afghan teapot, some provisions and a rocket propelled grenade launcher with four rounds. That evening, Ross spoke with Lilith via satellite phone and learned that their son, Brian David Newman, had been born the night before at 8:30 p.m. in Skokie, Illinois. He weighed 7 pounds, 5 ounces, and had hazel eyes just like his mom. The time of Brian's birth matched, to the minute, the time of Peach's death, though Ross would never reveal this to either his wife or his son.

33

BAIT

2:16 AM
June 20, 2020
Skokie, Illinois

Eva drove the black panel van containing the equipment needed to the Bara Synagogue and parked it on the street. Included in the needed equipment were Mauricio and Alex, two of Israeli Defense Systems' "corporate operatives." Mauricio and Alex, of course, were not their real names. Their US passports were government-grade forgeries, virtually indistinguishable from a real US passport. The two men had flown in from Israel four days ago and had been preparing ever since. They cased the abandoned synagogue, acquired blueprints of the interior layout, and learned everything relevant about Rabbi Wendell Rosenburg, who they discovered was living illegally in the basement of the synagogue. Some of the other equipment was shipped via private jet from Israel and now resided in the back of the black van. The black van, bought with cash, now bore two large magnetic signs reading: **"Creative Plumbing – Call 847-555-9633 for Emergency Service."** The signs were affixed neatly to each side of the sleek 2022 Mercedes-Benz Sprinter. Inside, all three occupants were dressed in black, their outfits completed by black armored military vests.

In the back seat, Mauricio opened a small plastic case and retrieved a hand-sized drone, which he handed to Alex. He opened a laptop, clicked a few icons, and the small drone began to whir in Alex's hand. Alex opened his window, letting the drone glide out into the night toward the synagogue. Watching his screen, Mauricio guided the drone as it approached the synagogue wall and maneuvered toward a security camera from the side. A small arm extended from beneath the drone, spraying black paint over the lens. Mauricio repeated the process five more times, using the drone to neutralize all of the Rabbi's exterior electronic eyes.

Eva then quietly backed the van over the curb, across the lawn to the stairs leading to the basement. The three then quietly exited the van and strode quickly to the basement stairs. At this point, all three pulled on spandex balaclavas. Alex knelt at the door, pulled a ring of master keys from his backpack, examined the lock, and searched for a Trudoor skeleton key on the ring. Quietly, he inserted the key in the lock and opened the door.

Wendell stood in the middle of the hallway wearing blue plaid pajama bottoms and a Chicago Cubs pullover shirt, pointing his Glock at Alex.

"You should probably tell me who you are and why you're breaking into—" Wendell started, but two small flashbang grenades rolled between Alex's legs. He turned his back on them and covered his ears.

As the grenades burst into a flash of light, smoke, and a deafening noise, Alex pounced like a cougar onto the disoriented rabbi, grabbing the gun hand and twisting it to point back at his chest, causing him to release the gun. Mauricio and Alex then pulled the rabbi off of the floor and walked him quickly into the conference-room-turned-living-room and sat him down in one of the chairs. Eva pulled zip ties from her backpack and secured Wendell's hands and then his ankles together.

"Wendell, did you know that it only requires eight pounds of force to tear a person's ear off?" Eva asked. "Strangely, that's about the same amount of force that's required to open a bag of potato chips. Although I'm not particularly squeamish, the lack of two of my fingers on my right hand makes the task a bit more complicated for me. To ensure that it is done correctly, my friend Mauricio here will demonstrate."

As Eva stepped aside, Mauricio stepped forward, reached out his right hand, firmly gripped Wendell's left ear, and ripped it off, tossing it onto the conference room table. Wendell screamed in agony. Blood poured from the wound and onto his Cubs jersey. He began to moan.

"Why are you doing this to me?" Wendell screamed between moans.

"Oh, darling, please," Eva cooed with false sympathy. "We don't care about *you*. We want to see your friend. You're just the bait for our little golem trap."

Eva pulled a strip of tape from a roll of duct tape and placed it firmly over the rabbi's mouth.

Mauricio and Alex threw their backpacks onto the table and began unloading parts that looked like some sort of strange weapon.

34

A TRAP SPRUNG

2:39 AM
June 20, 2020
Skokie, Illinois

Lilith woke quickly, pulling on jeans, a long-sleeve shirt, and sneakers. It was more accurate to say that the Scroll had taken control of her, with Lilith—the passenger—merely along for the ride. She couldn't speak and had no control over her body.

"Lilith, are you okay?" Ross asked. She didn't respond. He walked over to her and tried shaking her, but she looked into his eyes dispassionately, pulled his hands off of her shoulders, and firmly pushed him aside with a strength far beyond Ross's own.

Ross yelled loudly, "Brian! I need a little help here! Wake up, throw on some clothes, let's go!"

Lilith leaped down the stairs and ran out the front door with Ross still pulling on his shoes. He ran after her in his pajamas and shoes, but she was too fast. She continued sprinting down the sidewalk towards the synagogue. Ross went back to the house and changed into his jeans and opened the gun safe, retrieving his Sig Sauer P365 and its holster. He pulled on a light jacket.

"Where did she go, Dad?" Brian asked.

"Follow me," Ross responded.

They both set off sprinting down the sidewalk towards the synagogue.

* * *

Lilith arrived at the synagogue and without hesitation, ran around the black van and down the outdoor basement stairs. She opened the unlocked door to the basement hallway and walked quickly down the hall. Lilith noted that the furniture from the conference room littered the hallway as she stepped up to the conference room door and opened it.

Eva had positioned herself behind Wendell in his chair, furthest from the door, with his own Glock pressed against his temple. Lilith was shocked and horrified to see all the blood on the side of the rabbi's face and to see his ear right there on the floor in the middle of the room. A large, dark blood stain covered the left side of Wendell's shirt. The conference room was devoid of any furniture save the chair in which the rabbi sat or, better put, strapped against his well. Mauricio and Alex stood on either side of Eva, each holding a strange 4-cylindered gun of some sort.

"One more step and I'll blow Wendell's brains across the room," Eva said.

Lilith couldn't believe it, but against her will, her body stepped forward. *What am I doing? What are WE doing?* As she entered the room, first Mauricio, then Alex fired their net guns at her. Lilith's hands strained at tearing the webbing but only a few broke under her efforts. Instead, she straightened her fingers out of the net and shot a wad of fibrils across the room, hitting Alex square in the chest. The fibrils injected a deadly dose of Death Cap poison. Alex, initially ignoring the pain, fired his tactical dart gun, followed by Mauricio hitting her in the legs and abdomen with two darts apiece. These darts, however, contained not only a tranquilizer, but a powerful fungicide. Mauricio pushed a button on a small plastic remote-control box and the nets contracted, restricting her ability to move, and then consciousness slipped from her grasp. Lilith collapsed on the floor, wrapped in military-grade, contractible spider silk netting. Alex also dropped to the floor, convulsing, overwhelmed by the poison. Within seconds, he was no longer breathing.

* * *

Ross and Brian finally arrived at the basement door to the synagogue. They heard a voice down the hallway and Ross pulled his Sig Sauer out of its holster. The two moved down the hallway, approaching the voice.

"I can't believe she killed Alex from across the room," a man's voice mumbled quietly.

"And, on top of it all, she broke at least three strands of military-grade spider silk in this net. Those things are five times stronger than steel," Mauricio mumbled to himself.

Ross entered the conference room, Sig Sauer at the ready. Mauricio was adjusting the netting around Lilith even tighter.

"Lay down on the floor!" Ross commanded. "Now!"

Mauricio looked at Ross and slowly complied. Ross handed Brian a large pocket knife.

"Brian, start cutting the netting away from your mom," Ross said.

As Brian unfolded the knife, a loud puffing sound came from behind Ross, followed by a second. Sharp pain shot through Ross's butt and upper thigh, while Brian felt a similar sting in his shoulder. Moments later, a heavy wave of drowsiness swept over them both, pulling them into unconsciousness like dark waves crashing on a black sand beach.

"Really, your mom?" Eva said. "Oh, I'm so sorry to have interrupted such a touching family gathering. Load her into the van and be careful not to touch any of the mycelium fibrils – they are lethal, as Alex can attest to. I'll see if I can loosen Rab."

"On it, Boss," Mauricio said.

Eva walked over to Wendell.

"Now, would you like for Mauricio to rip off your other ear, or would you like to tell me where the Sefer Yetzirah Scroll is?" Eva asked.

She tore the duct tape from his mouth with the three fingers of her right hand, peeling away dried blood from his left cheek. He moaned softly as she searched under the cabinets, found a bottle of cabernet sauvignon, uncorked it, and poured herself a glass. Turning away, she pulled down her balaclava to take a generous sip.

"Let me state this as simply as I can," Eva continued, "when Mauricio returns, you will lose the other ear if you haven't given me the location of the Scroll."

The blood from Wendell's wound had begun to flow again in earnest when the tape was ripped painfully from his cheek and mouth.

In spite of this, the rabbi asked quietly, "If I tell you where the Scroll is, will you allow the three of us to live?"

"Yes, I will, and you can prance off to the police and tell them that someone took your golem and your magic scroll that brings people back to life."

Eva began to laugh as though she had said something incredibly funny. At that moment, Mauricio walked into the room, threw Alex's body over his shoulder, and walked it down the hall.

"Be careful not to touch the mycelium on his chest, you Neanderthal!" Eva yelled.

Eva continued, "Now, as I was saying, Rabbi – I agree to let you and her family live, IF you tell me where the Sefer Yetzirah Scroll is."

"Before I tell you, what do you intend to do with the scroll?" Wendell asked.

"Let's just say that I always have interested buyers for valuable antiquities such as these," Eva said.

"I would humbly beg that you do not take Lilith from her family," Wendell pled for mercy. "She died several months ago, leaving the family heartbroken and lost. There is no question in my mind that the Almighty put the Scroll into our hands to allow me to bring her back to them. Please, just take the Scroll and leave Lilith here."

"And have a supernatural being trying to kill me for the rest of my life? Yeah, no, I'll pass. Besides, the buyer is expecting both the Scroll and the golem."

"Then at the very least, please don't harm her family."

"If you tell me where the Scroll is, then I won't harm you – any further – or her family," Eva said.

"I suppose that I have little choice," the rabbi said. "The Scroll is in the podium upstairs, in a secret compartment underneath. You open the compartment by pressing the Star of David on the left side at the bottom of the rear leg. Press it hard, or it won't open."

Carrying the glass of wine with her, Eva walked to the door. "Now, don't you go anywhere, Rabbi Rosenburg. I'll be right back." She smiled icily as she walked out of the room to retrieve the Scroll.

She entered the stairwell to the sanctuary and turned the light on. Continuing up the stairs, the fluorescent bulb in the overhead light buzzed and shattered, raining fragments of glass around her. Eva paused to regain her bearings and allow the surge of adrenaline to dissipate there in the darkness. Determined, she resumed her climb up the stairs and was overcome with a sudden sense of dizziness, that the stairs and in fact, the space around her was somehow stretching and twisting.

She instinctively grabbed the handrail with both hands to keep from falling down the stairs. Her wine glass fell and shattered on the concrete and metal steps. It felt as if someone had shot *her* with a tranquilizer dart, perhaps even one laced with LSD.

"Stop it, you contemptuous roll of sheepskin! You will *not* escape me this time!"

Gradually, the dizziness passed, and she continued cautiously up the stairs to the almost imperceptible line of light shining under the door at the top, then she opened the door to the main sanctuary.

Pale light from the waning crescent moon shone through the stained-glass windows, and the sanctuary was unnaturally dark. She felt the wall next to the doorway and found a switch, pulling it up with no effect. Cautiously, she crept towards the podium. The moonlight faintly projected on the tarp a scene from the stained-glass window - Adam rising from the muddy bank of a river, his shins covered in earth, with blue light twinkling with stars flowing into

Adam's mouth. The image overlapped remnants of soil, clay, and other ingredients used during the ritual to create Lilith. Eva knelt down and examined the remains of the ritual, yet to be disposed of.

A small movement of something pale and hairy covering the pile of soil, like white grass caught her attention. She bent towards the soil and saw tiny white fibrils thrusting their way out of the soil and joining together. The fibrils wormed their way towards one another to form something that looked like an insect, perhaps a large ant. She realized with panic that the Scroll was trying to form something to protect itself.

Fear gripped her instantly as she thought of Alex, now in the back of their black van, dead. She leapt to her feet and stepped over to the podium, seeking the Star of David at the bottom. She found it and pressed it - hard - but nothing happened. She pressed it again and again, this time reaching up into the podium in search of the secret compartment. She pressed it again and rather than hearing it, she felt a slight click in the wood. Looking fearfully at the soil, numerous white ant-like creatures were making their way to her – some on six legs, some on five, legs, some on three. Some with large mandibles, others with triple needle-like stingers protruding from their tails – a macabre platoon of venomous animatrons. She pushed the star again and desperately pulled on where she believed the compartment in the podium was. She felt the click again and pulled hard, finally releasing the door to the compartment.

There was the Scroll.

One of the mycelium ants had reached her shoe. She cried out in fear and kicked it away, then pulled the Scroll from its hiding place, but it was hot and burned her hand as she removed it. She dropped it as more of the ghastly pallid ants drew near. The Scroll rolled off the podium, inexplicably moving toward the ants instead of away as if it were alive—seeking refuge among its ghostly protectors. Her eyes darted to the hourglass: only a few grains of sand remained, signaling the impending end—whether it meant her death or the success of her mission.

The ants surged like an undead tide, scrambling to grip her shoes. She kicked the podium over onto the tarp, ripping her shirt off in one swift motion. With a gymnast's precision, she stepped onto the overturned podium, balancing on its edge like a beam. Wrapping the shirt tightly around her hand like an oven mitt, she reached down, snatched up the Scroll, and leaped off the tarp onto the platform, her heart pounding as she outpaced the advancing swarm.

She looked back at the tarp and saw that one of the mycelium ants had now grown wings and was flying towards her erratically, as though the wings hadn't fully formed yet. Terrified, she ran, jumping off the platform, to the door of the basement stairs, forcing herself through it, slamming the door shut behind her.

The heat from the Scroll was beginning to work its way through the layers of her shirt, but she cradled it and hurried down the stairs, carefully closing the door at the bottom after her.

When she got back to the conference room, Mauricio was wheeling in an expensive-looking Plexiglas box on a gurney. The 1.5-inch-thick box had been designed with silicone seals infused with hexaconazole, a fungicide, and an air handling system with one-way valves and 25-micron filters to prevent escape of mycelium from the box.

"I hope that this box can hold her," Mauricio said. Then he looked over at Eva, leered, and exclaimed, "Looking good, Boss!"

In her panicked flurry of actions, Eva had forgotten she was now wearing nothing but her bra—her jersey having been sacrificed to insulate the Scroll.

"Stop gawking at me and get the golem into the box," Eva said. "We have deadly mycelium ants coming our way."

"Mycelium ants?" Mauricio asked.

"Yes, ants made from Death Cap fungus and created by the Scroll for protection," Eva replied. "Now, work faster!"

Eva picked up one of the tactical tranquilizer guns, looked at Wendell, and said, "Sorry about the ear, darling. I noticed on the back of your ear in very small print it said, 'Refrigerate after Removing' and I just really wouldn't want it to go past its expiration date. No hard feelings, it was the only way to bring the golem to me."

With that, she shot him in the arm with the tranquilizer gun.

Wendell tried to fight the drugs, but blackness covered his consciousness like a thick curtain. Eva watched as Wendell fell asleep.

"I'm definitely going to ask Orina for one of these IDS tranquilizer guns," Eva said. "They are so much better than the ones I used to use. With those, it was shoot a man and 15 minutes later, the guy finally starts to yawn. But these IDS darts work in seconds!"

"I heard they use a tranquilizer drug cocktail developed in Russia," Mauricio replied. "Oh, just so you know – not everyone wakes up after these darts. Sometimes the person dies from an overdose."

"I see. A little like 'Russian roulette,' then," Eva said with a smile. "Oh dear, I hope we didn't overdo the darts with the golem."

"We'll find out in about two to six hours or so," Mauricio said.

Eva and Mauricio, both wearing leather gloves, carefully avoided the extruded fibrils on Lilith's hands as they loaded her and the Scroll into the Plexiglas box. Securing the lid, they activated the attached air cylinder and double-checked the airflow. Hurriedly, they rolled the box into the hallway and toward the van. As they pushed and pulled together, Eva's eyes caught a pale white ant crawling up Mauricio's shoulder.

"Mauricio – on your shoulder!" Eva said, pointing at the ant.

Mauricio saw the ant in his peripheral vision and quickly brushed it off with his gloved hand, then stomped on the two-inch-long abomination.

"Die, you filthy piece of shit!" Mauricio exclaimed.

They continued to scan for the deadly ants that Eva had experienced until they reached the bottom of the exterior basement stairs. The gurney was electric, and originally designed for heavy coffins with built-in electric treads used for climbing stairs. At the top, the gurney matched up to the back of the van and another set of electric treads loaded Lilith into the back of the van. They both got into the van, and quietly drove away.

35

TIME RUNNING OUT

7:27 AM
June 20, 2020
Skokie, Illinois

Brian awoke with his cheek planted against the cold tile floor; nose bent to one side. He blinked several times in an attempt to clear his vision and shake off the effects of the tranquilizer dart. A dull pain in the back of his shoulder reminded him that a dart needed to be removed. He reached back, found the offending cylinder, and pulled it from his shoulder. Hunching up from the floor on his elbows, he examined the dart with blurred vision and then tossed it across the floor.

Brian began to stand and got as far as his knees. A dizzying wave of vertigo caused him to sit back down. Ross lay to one side of where Brian was sitting, and the darts were both still embedded in him. He pulled them both out and threw them aside. He shook his dad several times with no result. The vertigo had subsided, so he made another attempt at standing, this time successfully, though he steadied himself against the nearest wall. Seeing Rabbi Rosenburg still zip tied, he found a knife in the kitchen and cut his bonds. This did not awaken Wendell. Brian gently shook his shoulder. Moaning, the rabbi slowly returned to the world of consciousness. Brian looked at the wound created by the commando knowing it would require medical attention soon. He only hoped it wasn't too late to be reattached.

"Dad! Wake up, Dad! We've got to get Rabbi Rosenburg to the emergency room!" Brian shouted. Thankfully, Ross Newman was still breathing but wouldn't open his eyes.

"Do you have any triple antibiotic, gauzes, medical tape, bandages, or rubbing alcohol?" Brian asked.

"Yes, in the locker nearest the sink in the bathroom," Wendell said, "but I will take care of it. Just help me stand and make sure I don't fall down."

Brian helped steady Wendell as he carefully got to his feet. The rabbi looked over at Ross, again checking that he was breathing properly. He began second-guessing himself, wondering if his breathing was slower than the last time he checked.

"Thank you, Brian," Wendell said. "I'll be fine and I'll work on my head in the bathroom. Right now, I'm worried about your father. You should continue to try to wake him. Try making a hard fist, then rub your knuckles into his sternum. Rub it hard so as to cause pain. The sternum is the bone that runs down the middle of his rib cage."

"Are you sure you are able to stand?" Brian asked. "Can you make it to the bathroom sink?"

"I'll manage. Wake your father up, or I'll have to call an ambulance."

Brian followed the instructions from the rabbi. Ross moaned slightly. Brian repeated the process with the same result. Brian grabbed a hand towel and drenched it in cold water, then wiped his dad's face. Ross breathed in deeply and coughed several times, finally opening his eyes.

"Thank God!" Brian said. "We were about to call 911."

While Ross slowly regained consciousness, Brian made coffee, knowing that they would need it for what was about to come. Ross slowly stood up and then promptly leaned onto a garbage can and vomited. Brian offered his dad the wet towel.

"Take it slow, Dad. Based on how one dart affected me, I'm amazed you're even able to stand up, after two of those things."

Ross sat in the chair for a few minutes. Before the coffee had finished brewing, Ross mumbled his first sentence.

"Pass me a cup of that coffee. It smells like – consciousness."

Rabbi Rosenburg entered with his wound now bandaged with gauze and tape.

"I'll take a cup of consciousness as well," Wendell said.

"Consciousness delivered," Brian said as he handed each man a cup of steaming coffee.

"Should you be walking around, Wendell?" Ross asked.

"My ear hurts like hell, but I took some ibuprofen before I disinfected it with rubbing alcohol, and it's beginning to kick in."

"Well, we need to get you to the emergency room and have that ear sewn back on ASAP," Ross said.

"Finish your coffee first," Wendell replied. "I have some information that I learned while the two of you were taking involuntary naps. First, the name of the woman is Eva. I don't know her surname. Eva only has three fingers on her right hand. Next, the name of the man who shot Lilith with some sort of net gun and then with tranquilizer darts is Mauricio. Another man named Alex also shot her with a net gun and tranquilizer darts, but Lilith shot a glob of fibrils at him, and he did not survive. Finally, Eva seems to be some sort of antiquities expert who earns money by delivering valuable artifacts such as the Scroll to buyers. She said she had a buyer arranged for both the Scroll *and* Lilith."

With increased urgency, Ross and Brian jogged unsteadily back home to retrieve the car, Emily, and the supplies Ross had instructed Brian to gather. Once ready, Ross drove them all—including Wendell's severed ear, carefully packed on ice—to the Skokie Hospital emergency room. There, they left Emily to assist Wendell in getting the medical attention needed.

When they got back in the car in the parking lot of the emergency room, Ross opened up his laptop and clicked on an application called

C-Track. A map appeared on Ross's screen of a location on the south-side of Chicago. Two dots blinked in the middle of the map - a red dot and a blue dot.

"Dad, is one of those what I think it is – Mom's location?" Brian asked.

"Yes, the red dot is your mom's location, and the blue dot is the van's location. I had your mom's wedding ring modified slightly in case she was required to conduct any midnight special operations for the Scroll, and less than a week later, I'm very glad I did. It looks like she is no longer in the van," Ross said.

"It looks like they've stopped in Wisconsin," Brian said. "What are they doing there?"

"No idea," Ross said.

"Does she know about the tracker in her ring?[1]" Brian asked.

"No. The battery needs to be recharged about once a month and I was planning to talk to her about the tracker when the battery got low," Ross said.

"But how are you tracking the van?" Brian asked.

"I attached a magnetic tracker under the front bumper as we passed the van going down the basement stairs. There are certain advantages to having an IT guy on the team," Ross said with a grim smile. "Everything we talked about earlier is in the back of the car, right, Bri?"

"Yes, sir."

"Then let's go get Mom back," Ross said.

Ross furrowed his brow, worried that they would transport Lilith somewhere else by plane or discover the tracker before they could rescue her – IF they could rescue her.

---

1. Tracking devices small enough to be placed in a wedding ring are possible, though they require recharging, according to Darrin Pryke, information technology expert.

36

TRAPPED

11:17 AM
June 20, 2020
Milwaukee, Wisconsin

Lilith—the passenger—became aware of her eyes opening inside the transparent container. She pressed both hands against the lid and pushed, but it wouldn't budge. Panic surged through her. If she could scream, cry, or beat the walls of her coffin in terror, she would have. Instead, the crushing fear of her confinement overtook her, making it hard to breathe. Her mind went into a trance, replaying that dreaded day that was the very source of her claustrophobia.

* * *

6:07 AM | August 14, 1985 | Carpentersville, Illinois

Hank Wright stood at the controls of the asphalt milling machine, grinding away the surface of 4.5 miles of the gently curving Millsworth Road. The resurfacing project was already six weeks behind schedule due to uncooperative weather conditions during the summer. A large dump truck rolled slowly forward, matching his speed, and allowing asphalt grindings from the long conveyor arm of the milling machine to fall into the back of the dump truck. Behind him, a bulldozer followed, scooping up the loose asphalt the milling machine had missed. Sixteen hours later, Hank checked the clamps on the milling machine and gave a thumbs up to the oversized flatbed truck driver, sending it to the equipment yard. This was the third day in a row that he'd worked double shifts.

Running late, and covered in asphalt dust, Hank wearily crawled into his Ford F150 pickup truck and began driving to pick up his daughter, Lilith, from church movie night. At the tender, but often emotional age of 11, he needed to get her home so she could be rested for school the next day. Her mother, April, was out of town teaching dentists how to use the new Accubond 2300 UV-cure apparatus and resin for filling cavities. After a 20-minute drive, he pulled into the church parking lot and walked into the gymnasium. Lilith was the last one there and came running to give him a big hug. Hank loved the fact that no matter how strongly he smelled like asphalt after a long day, she would always give him hugs. They climbed into the driver's side of the pickup truck and began the drive home.

"How was your day in school, Baby-Bear?" Hank asked.

"Fine," Lilith said.

"You look a little sad. Are you okay?" Hank asked, yawning.

"Well, I was walking down the hall with Kelly and Heather, arm-in-arm, and Emery came along and wanted to cut in to hold my arm. We told her to go away, and then later she was talking to her friends, and they were looking at me during lunch and giving me the stink-eye. They did that all – Dad! Look out!" Lilith exclaimed as the truck began to weave.

She looked over at him and his eyes were closed and his head leaning on the steering wheel as the F150 left the road and began to roll, the sounds of bushes being crushed, and metal crunching overlaid onto the sounds of Lilith screaming. Lilith lost count of the number of times the truck rolled over and over. Finally, the truck's roll began to slow, and at last came to a stop with the roof settling onto a boulder, denting it into the cabin space and folding the metal into the side of her dad's skull and pressing it against the steering wheel.

She spent the next two days unable to open the doors or windows buried in the bushes down in a ditch, trapped with her dead father. As an adult, she still had nightmares about being trapped in the truck cabin, crying, with her father's right eye bulging from its socket, staring at her in unceasing wakefulness as penance for falling asleep at the wheel.

* * *

11:19 AM | JUNE 20, 2020 | MILWAUKEE, WISCONSIN

In the first instant of realization that she was trapped in what was effectively a transparent coffin, Lilith-the-passenger was terrified. Slowly but surely, she was reassured and calmed by a presence that she didn't understand, but somehow instinctively knew emanated from the Scroll.

Lilith pushed upward again in an attempt to break open the lid with no success. Lilith continued observing and found herself examining the thin silicone seam of the lid. She then focused her gaze through the Plexiglas and made out the warped image of the recently deceased Alex lying next to her box, eyes open, looking back at her, froth drooling from his mouth onto the grey carpeted floor. For an instant, the view of Alex's face brought back the view of her father's face in the truck. Again, the Scroll calmed her and helped her to not be afraid.

Other equipment, including the four-barreled net guns rattled audibly next to her. She saw a blue blanket wrapped around a cylindrical object and immediately knew this was the Scroll. She stilled her movements and listened, hearing fresh air being pumped into the container. She felt hair-thin mycelium fibrils stranding from her fingers and into the coffin. She knew that they were snaking their way toward the outlet of the air flow. She sensed them entering the small hole, and then sensed that they couldn't fit past the 25-micron fritted stainless steel filters. The fibrils retreated from the air outlet and reabsorbed themselves back into Lilith's leg.

Lilith-the-passenger thought there was nothing else that could be done, but Lilith raised her hand close to her face, making her palm visible. Thin gill-like structures slowly grew from her palm. Lilith slowly and carefully placed her hand back down to her side, palm up, where she sensed millions of spores being released. The 10-micron spores wafted into the air and followed its flow upward into the small outlet, then through the 25-micron filters and out into the cargo area of the 2022 Mercedes-Benz Sprinter van. As the van moved at 75 miles per hour up I-94 towards Milwaukee, Mauricio unknowingly breathed in several hundred of the spores, where they lodged themselves into his warm, wet, waiting lungs. The Scroll wrapped in the blue blanket lit up brightly, shining through the blanket and gently illuminating the back of the van.

* * *

The Israeli Defense Systems building in Milwaukee was a glass, 15-story cube surrounded by an eight-foot tall, hurricane fence with three strands of barbed wire strung along the top. The windows of the building were programmed to become opaque or transparent depending upon the interior temperature of the room behind any given window. This provided a constantly changing exterior appearance depending upon the position of the sun and the weather. The programming changed depending upon the season, special holidays and the like.

The black Mercedes van pulled up to the guard house in front of the building. Eva rolled down the driver's side window and provided her driver's license and Mauricio's IDS employee badge. The guard asked to view the contents of the van, waited for Eva to step out of the van and then walked around to the rear. Eva opened the rear doors, providing a view of Lilith in her transparent transport container, the Scroll wrapped in Eva's jersey, the dead body of Alex, the net weapons, tranquilizer guns, M16 rifles, air cylinders, a gurney, and various other pieces of equipment that they had brought with them. Lilith banged repeatedly on the interior of her coffin, but the guard ignored her.

"You lost Alex?" the guard asked.

"Unfortunately, the subject in the transport container proved more capable than we expected," Eva replied.

"Sorry to hear that, Ma'am," the guard replied. "Please proceed to the unloading dock and have a nice day."

Eva climbed back into the van and drove down the entrance ramp to the underground shipping and receiving dock where she positioned the van for unloading. Workers dressed in dark gray coveralls unloaded the van and carted Lilith's container to a laboratory, where her air supply was replaced by a technician.

The Scroll was placed in a plain metal toolbox and carried to a laboratory adjacent to the laboratory in which Lilith was being stored.

Mauricio removed the magnetic signs from the van and sent them with Alex to the building's incinerator. He then drove the van to a car-crushing facility. As he passed through Milwaukee, his breathing grew more labored, and he started to cough. He attributed it to the high pollen count, which had worsened after completing his delivery. He waited until the van was completely crushed and loaded onto a flatbed truck for shipment to a steel refinery. Once complete, he paid the owner of the facility with $6,000 in cash, after which he was given a ride back to the Milwaukee IDS building, his coughing growing worse.

* * *

"The van drove away from where Mom is to an auto scrap yard, and then the van dot stopped registering," Brian said. "Mom's dot is stationary in a building called Israeli Defense Systems."

"Let's keep heading toward Mom," Ross said. "We're only about 30 minutes away now."

"Do you think this Israeli Defense Systems is the buyer that Wendell mentioned?" Brian asked. "Why would they want mom?"

"Think about it, if you were the Israeli military, why *wouldn't* you want Mom?" Ross rebutted. "A badass soldier wholly determined to protect the Jewish people. She's the ultimate weapon."

"That's a good point," Brian agreed.

"And what if you could use the Scroll to make more badass soldiers?" Ross continued. "Build an entire army."

"But wait," Brian said, scratching the back of his head. "They don't own the Scroll – Rabbi Rosenburg does."

"True. But they literally have the Scroll in their possession. What makes you think that they don't own it already or can't make that switch?"

"Rabbi Rosenburg told me that the Scroll can only be used by someone with righteous intent. I can't imagine that anyone who breaks into someone's house and steals the Scroll by force would have righteous intent. And since the Scroll fought back by calling Mom to defend Rabbi Rosenburg, I don't know. I feel like it's gonna stay on our side."

"Let's hope so, son. Let's hope so," Ross said.

* * *

"Mauricio, are you okay?" Eva asked.

Mauricio didn't answer. Just continued coughing. Finally, he stopped coughing long enough to reply in a hoarse voice, "It's either allergies or I've managed to catch COVID."

"You better not have," Eva said, lacking any empathy. "Get yourself to the infirmary and get tested for COVID right now. And put your mask up over your nose."

"Probably a good idea," Mauricio replied. "I'll head there now."

Eva checked the transparent box again for signs of tampering or cracking, but all appeared to be in order. She went into the adjacent laboratory and brought back the metal toolbox containing the Scroll.

She looked through the box, right into Lilith's eyes, and said, "Who would have thought, after all these years, it would be so easy to capture both you and the Scroll? Do you know how long I've been patiently waiting and searching for this? Thirty-seven long years. I had it in my grasp thirty-two years ago, but a different golem - a crude golem made only from clay - ripped it from my hands and threw me down an open manhole in Prague, leaving me for dead in the sewer. A piece of the Scroll tore away in my hand when he snatched it from me. It took hours for me to find my way to another open manhole, limping along through the disgusting sludge in the dark with a broken ankle. By the time I managed to return to the synagogue, the rabbi, the Scroll, and the golem were gone."

Eva continued, "I've acquired many artifacts and antiquities in my life – a few of them with powers or enchantments - most of them simply valuable or beautiful or both. And all of them available to the highest bidder. But the Scroll – yes, this deceptively humble roll of sheepskin - brings the power to create life from something as common as mud, and not only life but super soldiers. In my employers' hands, Israel might even subjugate the entire Middle East with an *army* of golems like you. No more war – something nations have been negotiating, battling, and conquering each other for since the dawn of the Jewish people thousands of years ago. I like to imagine that that peace will be largely because of me. I'll have to invite you to my Nobel Peace Prize ceremony."

Lilith-the-passenger listened in horror, not wanting to be any part of any war, or any killing mission, or any super-soldier army. She wished she could simply be back home with her family. In this moment, she didn't feel like a super soldier. She felt like that scared high school girl, trapped and helpless in the F-150, praying for escape.

37

OUT OF THE BOX

12:28 PM
June 20, 2020
Milwaukee, Wisconsin

Mauricio knelt over the toilet in the men's room and vomited. His vomit consisted of yellow liquid and white fibrils that looked like very fine spaghetti. He thought to himself: definitely COVID. Vomiting was one of the symptoms, right? But he didn't have anything for breakfast that even remotely looked like spaghetti.

He felt a little bit better after vomiting. Mauricio rose, flushed the toilet, unlocked the bathroom stall, and walked over to the sink to wash his face. Turning on the faucet, he splashed his face with water and then dried himself with paper towels. He stared at his reflection in the mirror, running his fingers through his hair. Though there was no breeze in the bathroom, his hair seemed to shift ever so slightly. Was it his imagination? He blinked hard, then looked again. That's when he became a passenger in his own body. He tried to say, "What the hell?" but no words escaped. All he could do was watch as his body turned, opened the bathroom door, and walked down the hall toward the elevator.

* * *

2:24 PM | JUNE 20, 2020 | MILWAUKEE, WISCONSIN

Ross parked the SUV on the side of a dirt road leading to a fenced-in electrical transformer station and hiked through a wooded area to a position where they could see the Israeli Defense Systems cube building. Peering through binoculars, they watched as a car approached, stopping at the security guard gate. The occupant of the car provided a photo ID which the guard scanned. Soon the aluminum arm swung open, and the car passed through and then down a ramp out of sight.

"There must be parking in the basement levels," Ross said.

"That guy at the gate is not the only security guard," Brian said. "Look just to the left of the building, near the fence."

"Well, look what we have here – an autonomous security robot," Ross said.

At the spot where Brian had indicated stood what appeared to be a grey 4-wheel all-terrain vehicle suitable for use in riding along trails, however, there was no seat for a person, only a three-foot pole containing built-in cameras, a remote-controlled light, and presumably other sensing devices. A flashing blue light was affixed to the top of the pole.

"How do you know it's autonomous?" Brian asked.

"There are robocop products like this that have been introduced in parking garages and shopping malls," Ross said. "I don't know about this one in particular, but they usually are limited to cameras and speakers. I think that we should assume that this one is armed in some way, perhaps even with a taser."

"There are also cameras about two stories up on the sides of the building," Brian said. "What are we going to do about those?"

"I have a plan," Ross said, with confidence. "It's not a perfect plan, but I can't think of a better way in. Here's what I'm thinking."

* * *

8:33 PM | JUNE 20, 2020 | MILWAUKEE, WISCONSIN

A black Mercedes S class followed by a black Lincoln Navigator, both with heavily tinted windows, pulled up to the security gate and the driver of the Mercedes lowered his window.

"Here is my ID card and Mrs. Sakov's ID card," the driver said.

"Could you please roll down the rear window so I can have a look?" the guard at the gate asked.

"Of course," responded the driver.

The guard stepped to the rear of the vehicle and looked inside. He looked into the intelligent green eyes of Orina Sokov.

"Good evening, Mrs. Sokov."

"Good evening, Mitch," Orina said. "How's the IDS-26 security bot working out for you? Any suggestions for improvement?"

"Pretty good, so far, but to be honest, the refresh rate is a little slow on the infrared camera. The optical cameras are just fine. It's more annoying than anything else."

"I'll send your suggestion to the IDS-bot team tomorrow. Thank you for testing it out for us," Orina said.

"Happy to help, Boss," Mitch said.

The guard gave Orina's ID badge back to her and stepped back to the driver's window. "Could you kindly open the trunk, sir?" he asked the driver.

"Of course," the driver said, taking his badge back from the guard and placing it back in his jacket pocket.

The trunk opened with a gentle thunk and the guard looked at the luggage but did not open any of the bags. Closing the trunk, Mitch opened the gate and waved them into the compound.

The procedure was repeated for the Lincoln Navigator, which contained three IDS corporate operators and their associated support equipment.

* * *

9:03 PM | JUNE 20, 2020 | MILWAUKEE, WISCONSIN

Orina folded her hands behind her back and surveyed the IDS tactical arena from the skybox. The arena spread across two acres, and at five stories high it functioned as a secret and secure test lab and training facility for new weapons, small explosives, drones, and equipment and tactics for soldiers. The view of the IDS building from the outside was somewhat misleading, appearing as a cube from ground level or above. In actuality, in addition to the 15 stories above ground level, the facility extended another 10 stories below ground. Five of these stories were dedicated to the tactical arena.

The tactical arena contained small brick structures, berms, pools of water, trees, bushes, and several raised platforms. The walls of the arena were lined with quarter inch steel, and painted beige along the bottom 10 feet of the wall. Above that point, the walls were painted pale blue, including the ceiling. The skybox extended from the ceiling on the west side of the building. A large flat screen mounted to one side of the room was divided into four quadrants with an overhead view of the entire arena.

"I see that my three corporate operations men are ready at the south end of the arena," Orina observed. "When will the golem be released?"

"They are bringing her in now," replied Eva.

Orina opened the metal toolbox in which the Scroll was being stored. She put on a pair of oven mitts and pulled the Scroll out of the box, placing it on a benchtop on the south side of the large room. She then rolled open the Scroll and an uncharacteristic look of amazement shone on her face as she saw the glowing red Hebrew writing all along the margins of the parchment.

"I've never seen anything like this," she said.

On the north end of the arena, a door slid open, and three men wheeled in the transparent coffin containing Lilith. The men left the coffin and stepped back out of the door, which slid shut again. An audible beep began counting down, and after four beeps, the final sound was that of a buzzer. The buzzer was accompanied by the activation of eight small thermite devices attached to each of the latches holding the coffin closed. The thick Plexiglas top of the coffin flew up and clam-shelled open violently as Lilith pushed it off of her, her claustrophobia fueling her anger. Unaware of its influence in the moment, the Scroll was strengthening her resolve. She sat up and then leaped over the side of the box.

"Impressive, that lid alone weighs over a hundred pounds," Eva said. "Especially impressive for someone who only weighs about 120 pounds."

The three corporate operations soldiers had begun moving from the south end of the arena to the north end in a V-formation, assault rifles at the ready.

"We don't know if she will hold up against bullets, Orina," Eva said.

"You sound concerned, perhaps even worried about her," Orina said. "I need to understand what my new toy can handle – *before* she is sent into battle. We know she can be tranquilized, given a high enough dosage. We know that her strength is not unlimited since she couldn't escape the Plexiglass box and she couldn't break free of military-grade, contractible spider silk netting."

One of the soldiers had climbed to the top of a two-story platform. He knelt down, rested the rifle barrel on a section of railing and aimed at Lilith from his sniper vantage point. A brief burst of fire from the barrel accompanied by the unmistakable sound of gunfire indicated that he had taken the shot. Lilith fell backward as the bullet impacted her shoulder. She rolled out of the line of fire next to a short wall. Her motion was being tracked by several cameras. Orina and Eva watched as one of the cameras focused on her sitting with her back against the wall. Fibrils extruded from her left shoulder, pushing the now mushroomed bullet out of her body. The fibrils fell away from her shoulder along with the slug. Lilith's face grew grim.

Lilith raced from cover to cover, advancing on the soldiers as they fired at her, none of the shots finding their target. As the soldier in the lead position changed his ammunition clip, Lilith raced up to him and punched him hard in the throat, causing something to snap in his neck. He dropped his weapon and dropped to his knees, trying to restore air to his lungs. Lilith shot him in the face with a wad of fibrils and leapt to acquire better cover from the bullets being fired at her.

* * *

Brian cut the last wire in the section of hurricane fence and put the bolt cutters on the ground beside him. Reaching in his backpack, Brian pulled out a small, remote-controlled, four-wheeled camera-bot and placed it on the ground. He activated the remote-control box, and a small screen came to life, showing a live view of himself kneeling on the ground in front of the camera-bot. He pulled the fence open and pushed the camera-bot through the opening, looking over at his dad laying on a grassy berm with his thirty-aught-six that was a gift from his father resting on a log. Ross nodded to Brian, who launched the camera-bot with a quiet, high-pitched whine. He drove the bot around the building and across the path of the IDS-26 security bot, which began to follow the camera-bot to the opposite side of the building.

The bot began to repeat the message, "STOP. YOU ARE TRESPASSING. I AM AUTHORIZED TO USE DEADLY FORCE."

Ross waited until the IDS-26 security bot was on the opposite side of the building, then fired three carefully aimed hollow-point rounds into the transformer powering the Israeli Defense Systems cube. The bullets mushroomed as they passed through, exiting the opposite side and leaving a hole about two inches in diameter. Fluid drained rapidly from the container, causing it to overheat and short-circuit in a violent explosion of sparks. The cube compound was instantly plunged into darkness.

Ross sprinted to the cut section of fence being held open by Brian. They both raced in the dark to the vehicle entry point leading to the underground parking garage.

38

FULL COURT PRESS

9:21 PM
June 20, 2020
Milwaukee, Wisconsin

Mauricio descended the stairs, passing the door marked "L2 Parking," then "L3 Drone Technology," until he reached "L4 Tactical Arena Roof, Skybox, and IT Servers." With a quick swipe of his badge, he unlocked the door and stepped into an air-conditioned hallway. The corridor was lined with doors labeled for computer servers, audio/visual equipment, and offices. At the end of the hall, he arrived at a door marked "Skybox." He pressed his badge against the black pad, watched the light shift from red to green, and opened the door.

As he entered, Orina said, "Mauricio, this is a private meeting, please leave at once."

Mauricio continued forward towards Orina, who opened her satchel and retrieved her Jericho 941F handgun.

"Leave now, Mauricio, you are interrupting an important meeting," Orina said, pointing the weapon at him.

Mauricio continued towards her, and Orina fired her weapon. Mauricio stumbled backwards and looked down at his chest. The hole in Mauricio's chest extruded fibrils and a 9 mm bullet shaped like a mushroom. The fibrils and bullet fell to the floor. At that moment, the lights went out, leaving only a dim red glow from the marginalia of the open Scroll faintly illuminating the area near the table.

* * *

In the initial darkness, Lilith thought that all was lost. But slowly her eyes revealed everything faintly in shades of green. The soldiers, glowing in green hues, appeared disoriented in the dark. It became clear that darkness wasn't part of the exercise, as her enemies lacked infrared goggles.

She stepped out from behind the wall where she was taking cover and silently approached the soldier she had killed, picking up his assault rifle. Quietly she aimed the rifle at the soldier on the raised sniper platform and fired into his left eye. His body fell from the platform and landed at the feet of the last living corporate operative, who jumped back in a panic and fired in Lilith's general direction before diving for cover. Lilith-the-passenger felt burning pain in her back as two of the bullets from the operative's last volley hit their target. Her fingers found one of the bullet-holes but couldn't reach the second. Quickly, the pain subsided, and she felt fibrils pushing the mushroomed bullets out of their original entry points.

Meanwhile, the last remaining operative, had unzipped his pack and recovered a flare. He pulled the cap from the top, exposing a sandpaper-like surface, and then rubbed the lighter button of the flare stick against this surface, creating a blinding, spark emitting pink light. Briefly stepping out from behind the artificial concrete rock where he had taken cover, he hurled a brilliant, smoking flare onto the steel grating of the elevated platform's floor. A moment later, he repeated the action with a second flare, casting dim pink light into a cone-shaped area beneath the platform and illuminating the lifeless body of his fallen comrade. Crawling under a section of waist-high plastic ferns, he lay motionless, his rifle trained on the lighted area, waiting in ambush.

* * *

Ross and Brian raced down the ramp to the underground parking in the basement of the building. A woman in high heels and a green dress was walking to her car, her badge swinging back and forth across the side of her purse.

Ross pointed the rifle at her.

"As much as I hate to do this, you need to give us your badge right now," Ross ordered, keeping her at gunpoint.

"Ye-yes, of course," the woman stuttered. "Here it is. I don't have much money, but you are welcome to whatever I have. How'd you get in here?"

Brian took the badge.

"I need the keys to your car," Ross said, ignoring her question. "Brian, get me the packing tape."

The lady obediently handed Ross her key fob.

"Now come with us," Ross said.

Her high heels clicked as she walked, and Ross grabbed her by the elbow, directing her towards a shadowy area in the stairwell. Brian and Ross taped over her mouth, and then taped her hands and feet together.

"Ma'am, I'm really sorry about having to do this, but your company has kidnapped my wife, and we really need her back," Ross said.

The two took her phone, key fob, and badge and proceeded down the stairs.

* * *

In the near-total darkness, Orina fired another shot in Mauricio's general direction, each explosion momentarily illuminating the room with the fiery flash of the muzzle. Using these fleeting bursts of light to adjust her aim, she landed at least three rounds squarely into Mauricio's chest.

As Orina fired, Eva dropped to the ground, crawling behind her to a set of drawers beneath a window overlooking the tactical arena. Blind in the darkness, she felt for the second drawer from the top, yanked it open, and found the device she had once seen demonstrated with devastating effect. Pulling it free, Eva rose to her feet, aimed to her right—away from Mauricio and Orina—and briefly squeezed the trigger. The Israeli Defense Systems Dragonfire flamethrower prototype roared to life, shooting a stream of ignited fuel toward the window and setting the carpet ablaze.

As the fire lit the room, Eva shouted, "Orina, get behind me!"

She didn't need to be told twice, but as she was moving behind Eva, she yelled, "Whatever you do, don't damage the Scroll!"

"Follow my lead and stay behind me!" Eva shouted as she moved towards the north side of the room, keeping the conference room table between Mauricio and leaving the Scroll resting on the benchtop on the south side of the room.

Mauricio moved to the north side of the room, but on the opposite side of the table. Once Eva had lured him far enough away from the Scroll, she pulled the trigger on the Dragonfire and sprayed the burning liquid onto Mauricio. Surprisingly, he didn't scream in agony, but as the flames immolated him, his steps towards Eva and Orina became a stumble. Suddenly Mauricio began to emit long howls of inhuman anguish, something like a cross between a scream and the moans made by someone whose tongue had just been cut from their mouth. He stumbled forward towards Eva, but she and Orina backtracked, moving away from him. Finally, he fell face down onto the carpet, the skin melting off of his head and hands, small holes emitting flame from within him as though he were stuffed full of mycelium and now it was burning inside of him.

At that moment, a shot rang out from the opposite side of the room. Eva looked over at the door and saw Ross looking through the scope of his 30-ought-6 directly at her, Brian standing behind him. She stepped backwards and almost tripped over the dead body of Orina, blood still pulsing out of a crater in the right side of her head, chunks of her brain and skull sliding down the now shattered window on the east side of the sky box.

"Put the flame thrower down," Ross commanded. "Now!"

Eva slowly put the Dragonfire down on the floor and raised her hands. The room was now dimly lit by firelight.

"There is no need for further violence," Eva said. "I surrender."

* * *

Lilith peeked around the edge of the short wall where she had taken cover to see the brilliant pink light emanating from the steel grill of the platform. Stealthily, she moved away from the platform, moving from cover to cover, and then she began to walk the edge of darkness surrounding the platform.

Reaching the spot where she had last seen the soldier, Lilith picked up a rock and hurled it into the darkness behind his position. She watched as his head and assault rifle rose cautiously above the plastic ferns, the weapon aimed toward the sound of the impact. Lilith-the-passenger was puzzled when her body quietly leaned the assault weapon against a tree, then knelt and began moving toward the soldier unarmed. It was as if her body had turned this into some sort of game, deliberately evening the odds by setting the rifle aside.

When she came within about 25 feet of the soldier, she entered the ferns. The rustling of the ferns was unavoidable. The soldier turned, saw her, and began firing. At least four bullets strafed her abdomen as she ran and leapt onto him, grabbing the rifle and tossing it aside, dragging a severed trigger finger with it. She grabbed him by the throat and felt her fibrils flowing around his neck from her hand, releasing their poison into him. Before he lost consciousness, his hand came up from his leg sheath with a tactical knife, stabbing it into her chest. Lilith-the-passenger felt the awful pain. If she could have, she would have screamed, but Lilith's body simply waited a few seconds for the soldier to succumb from the poison and then allowed him to drop dead to the ground. She gripped the tactical knife with her right hand and pulled it out of her chest. Again, the pain was excruciating for Lilith-the-passenger. She then sat down amongst the ferns while her body healed itself.

After several minutes, her recovery complete, she stood in the dim, pulsing pink light of the flare. Stepping over to the soldier, she searched him for anything that might open the arena exit. Her efforts yielded an ID card and a small plastic box with two buttons. Pressing one, she heard a door slide open about 40 yards away. Retrieving the assault rifle taken from the corporate operative, along with a tactical knife and its sheath, she strapped the sheath to her thigh, slid the knife into place, and jogged toward the exit.

After leaving the arena, she quickly found the stairs leading upward and followed them to a door marked 'Skybox.' Swiping the ID badge, she entered the hallway and made her way to the door with the same label. Another swipe let her into the room, where Ross, Brian, and Eva stood near the conference table. From across the table, the thirty-aught-six remained trained on Eva.

"Mom!" Brian exclaimed, but Lilith did not respond. Instead, she strode purposefully around the table to Eva. She pulled out the tactical knife, raised it above her head and slammed it deeply into the top of the conference room table. Then she walked to the side bar where the Scroll rested, set the assault rifle against the side bar, and gently rolled the Scroll back onto its ornate wooden rollers. When this was complete, she laid the Scroll in front of Ross and fainted on the carpet.

"Brian, check to make sure she's still breathing," Ross said.

Brian bent down and carefully rolled her onto her back, noting the bullet holes in her shirt and the healed skin beneath. Then he put his cheek near her nose and mouth.

"She's still breathing, Dad."

"Here, keep it pointed at this bitch," Ross instructed his son, handing him the rifle. "Bring the Scroll and the flashlight that we found in the drawer. If she so much as looks at you funny or yells for help, shoot her in the back. Eva, you'll be taking point. Brian, you follow her close behind with that rifle pointed at her spine with your finger on the trigger. Got it?"

With that, Ross picked up Lilith and carried her over his shoulder. Eva did exactly as she was told.

Battery-powered emergency lights illuminated the stairwell and hallways, making their way to the parking garage easier. As they passed the duct-taped, green dress woman in the stairwell, she let out several muffled *mmmffs* through her nose—until her eyes caught the rifle aimed at Eva's back. Then she fell immediately silent. Stepping into the garage, they noticed many of the cars that had been parked there were now gone. A blue light pulsed somewhere among the painted steel support pillars, cutting through the dimness.

"Security robot," Ross whispered, as he pulled Eva back into the stairwell, with Brian following. "Let me have your backpack, Brian."

Brian held the gun on Eva with one hand and slipped his backpack off with the other. Ross gently leaned Lilith against a wall and then took the pack, unzipped it, and pulled out the duct tape, peeling off a generous amount.

"Hands behind your back."

Eva complied with Ross's request. He was not gentle as he wrapped the tape around her wrists, ankles, and mouth. He carried Eva down to the next landing below the garage entrance and lay her down, not so gently, on her side in a puddle.

"This puddle is the least of what I'd like to do to you for kidnapping the love of my life," Ross said. "Stay away from my family. If I ever see your face again, you won't live to see another day, Eva Fisher."

Ross made his way back up the flight of stairs and pulled the key fob out of his pocket to examine it.

"A Range Rover - I've never driven a Range Rover before. Perfect car for the job at hand," he said quietly to Brian.

Taking the key fob, he then opened the door to the stairs. The flashing blue light was still on patrol off in the distance, still obscured by pillars.

"There's the car," Ross said pointing to a Range Rover about 50 yards away. "Grab your backpack and the gun, son."

Ross again lifted Lilith and put her over his shoulder. He took another look for the security robot, and seeing that it was still out of sight, he began a quick, silent walk towards the vehicle, Brian right behind him. When he was close to the Range Rover, he attempted to push the unlock button, but with Lilith over his shoulder, he accidentally pushed the lock button. The SUV beeped twice.

"Damn it," Ross whispered.

Looking more carefully at the fob, he pushed the unlock button and heard the locks gently click open. He opened the rear door and loaded Lilith into the back seat, closing the door as quietly as he could. The flashing blue lights were closer now and headed in their direction. Ross and Brian opened the front doors and got in, again closing them as quietly as possible. They scrunched down in the seats in an attempt to avoid alerting more security, in the form of humans - with guns.

The security robot passed their vehicle and rolled onward towards the stairwell door, which had not closed properly behind them.

"Dad, I think that bot is about to find the lady with the high heels," Brian whispered.

"I think you might be right," Ross replied in a whisper. "Let's see if it opens or closes the door."

The robot approached the stairwell door, extended an arm to grip the handle, and pulled.

"Welp, that's our cue," Ross said. "Put your seat belt on."

Ross buckled his seat belt and pressed the Range Rover's start button. The security robot swiveled its optical stalk, searching for the source of the noise, but Ross was already flooring the accelerator. Tires squealed as the SUV shot forward, barreling toward the ramp. Without slowing, he smashed through the security arm beside the guardhouse and sped down the road toward where they'd left their own vehicle.

They switched to their SUV and sped away from the still-darkened Israeli Defense Systems cube building, heading home.

39

OFF THE GRID

9:14 AM
June 21, 2020
Skokie, Illinois

Wendell was finishing his toast with blackberry jam when he heard a knock on his hospital room door. This knock, however, was not the usual double tap followed immediately by a nurse pushing open the door. It was four knocks followed by a polite pause for a response.

"Come in, Ross!" the rabbi said.

The door opened and Lilith strolled in with a big smile on her face behind her mask, followed by the rest of her family, also all wearing surgical masks. Then came the barrage of questions.

"How are you feeling?" Lilith asked.

"Were they able to reattach your ear?" Brian asked.

"Before they started the surgery, did you ask for a Vulcan ear with WiFi?" Ross asked.

"DAAad!" Emily said, rolling her eyes.

"Sorry, that's neither *ear* nor there," Ross said.

Emily nudged her dad in the ribs, smiling under her mask.

Lilith approached Wendell's bedside and leaned in to give him a gentle hug, her mask pressing softly against the side of his face that hadn't undergone surgery.

"Thank you, Lilith," Wendell said. "It is so good to see all of you. I'll attempt to answer in the order the questions were asked. First, I'm feeling pretty good, largely because of the excellent pain medications that modern science has been so kind to provide. Second, they are quite optimistic that the ear will be fine, although there was a great deal of discussion about making sure that some of the very tiny veins were reattached properly in order to prevent the ear from filling with blood. As for question number three: They don't offer the Vulcan ear with WiFi, at least not in this hospital. But given a choice between the elephant ear with Dumbo flight capability, the cat ear with 180-degree rotation, and my own boring but thoroughly abused human ear, I stupidly chose the last one. Nostalgia I guess. Now, I suspect that your recent events have been much more interesting than mine, so please tell me all the juicy details that I missed."

"Rabbi Rosenburg," Ross started, "it's a very long story, and there will be plenty of time to tell you all about it when we get on the road."

"On the road?" Wendell asked.

"Yes, the people who assisted Eva worked for Israeli Defense Systems, a multi-billion-dollar company headquartered in Israel and, oddly enough, a facility in Milwaukee, too," Ross explained. "Can you guess why they might be interested in the Scroll and Lilith?"

"Oh, dear God, no," Wendell said. "Military applications?"

"Yes, and that means that we all have to get the hell out of Dodge ASAP. When can you travel?" Ross asked.

"Assuming the surgeon gives me his seal of approval, I can leave sometime soon after lunch," the rabbi said.

"And if he doesn't?" Ross asked.

"I can leave sometime soon after lunch," Wendell said with a grin.

"Alright, that gives us a little time to get back to the house, pack up the SUV with essential items," Ross said. "Please text Brian with a list of essentials that you will need for a few months of 'vacation time.'"

"Sounds great," Wendell said, pausing for a second. "Wait, where are we going?"

Ross bent down next to his good ear and whispered, "For tonight, we are going to stay at a local motel that takes cash. Then, when the banks open tomorrow morning, we'll withdraw as much as we can without generating a report to the US Treasury Department – about $9,500. Then we'll drive to my sister's house in the hill country of Texas. She lives in a large house out in the middle of nowhere with cottages that she rents out to newlyweds for their honeymoons. It's a little bit like a romantic dude ranch, with horse riding, fishing, swimming, and such, and even though this is normally the peak of wedding season, COVID has pretty well shut down her business. Okay. We're heading back now. See you in a couple of hours."

* * *

"Well, that was an interesting night at 'The Comfy Coachman Inn,'" Brian said, as the entire family and Rabbi Rosenburg drove out of the city limits of Skokie, Illinois on their way to Greyhill, Texas.

Their departure from the hospital was uneventful. Wendell's surgeon cleared him, the nurses completed some paperwork, and nobody seemed to notice anything odd about Lilith, not even the tattoos on her face.

"I think they need to rename it 'The Lumpy Roachman Din' to provide a more accurate description of the lumpy mattresses, lack of clean sheets – or perhaps anything at all, for that matter - and paper-thin walls," Lilith said.

"Oh, come on, it wasn't that bad," Ross said. "Don't forget the complimentary chair in the room that you could brace under the doorknob as a makeshift deadbolt. That was almost as nice as staying at the Ritz, if you ask me."

"If by Ritz you mean sleeping in an empty box of Ritz crackers, I fully agree," Lilith said.

"Exactly," Ross said with a big smile, enjoying the familiar comfort of these playful back and forths with the love of his life.

The conversation then turned to the events that Wendell and

Emily had missed during his stay in the hospital. Ross and Brian related their 'Mission Impossible' rescue of Lilith and the Scroll, while Lilith filled in the blanks for her time in the Plexiglas box and the arena.

"But why didn't the Scroll kill Eva at the end?" Brian asked.

"It seemed almost like the Scroll felt that it was safe, at that point, and that there had been enough killing," Lilith said. "But I also think stabbing the knife into the table in front of Eva was a clear warning for her to leave us all the hell alone."

"Yeah, that was pretty impressive how deep you buried that knife," Brian said.

"So why do you think you fainted right after that?" Ross asked.

"The best I can come up with is that the Scroll sensed that the battle was over," Lilith said. "I'm not sure I have a better answer than that."

"Maybe next time you could ask the Scroll to wait until we get you into the car, so I don't have to carry you up three flights of stairs and across a parking garage before it turns you into 120 pounds of dead weight?" Ross joked.

"Are you saying I'm overweight?" Lilith asked in mock shock.

"No, no, just that I'm desperately out of shape, dear," Ross recovered.

"Nice save, honey, nice save," Lilith said.

"How are you doing back there in the back of the bus, Wendell?" Ross asked.

"Oh, I'm fine," Wendell said. "Just thinking."

"What are you thinking about?" Brian asked.

"How Israeli Defense Systems is not gonna give up. They're gonna keep coming after Lilith and that Scroll.

"Well, that's why we're driving 20 hours to Greyhill, Texas," Ross reminded him. "We need to put some distance between us and the bad guys. And we'll keep using cash to stay off the grid."

"But that won't be enough," Wendell said. "They will eventually find us again, and we will need to be ready. Ready to fight. I'm thinking that if those assholes want a war – sorry, excuse my language, Emily."

"A swearing rabbi?" Emily said, waving him off. "Oh, I'm totally on board with that."

"We're gonna need help," Wendell concluded.

"What did you have in mind, Wendell?" Ross asked.

"I think we might need to *make* some soldiers," Wendell said.

"Like, clone Mom or something?" Brian asked.

"Not exactly. To bring Lilith back to life, we needed a set of very special ingredients – her ashes, the rib from a man, Brian's blood, clay, soil, water, a very special synagogue, a full moon, the Scroll, and an elaborate ritual," Wendell explained. "But to make a simple golem – basically a robot soldier with super strength – I think all we would need is clay, water, the Scroll, and the ritual. I suppose what I'm suggesting is that we make a golem for extra protection. When he isn't being used, he could simply stand in a closet. Ultimately, he would be completely expendable, unlike Lilith."

"Thank you, Rabbi," Lilith said.

"Now that's a very interesting thought, Wendell," Ross said. "Very interesting indeed."

40

HAVEN

7:22 AM
June 24, 2020
White Dress Ranch, Greyhill, Texas

Ross awoke from the first truly restful night's sleep he'd experienced in several weeks. The road trip had resulted in two nights in dumpy little motels with uncomfortable beds and pillows, but his sister had apparently spared no expense to provide the most comfortable beds and pillows for her honeymooning guests.

Ross raised himself up on one elbow to gaze at Lilith, lying beside him, still sleeping. He had always thought that she looked like a Greek goddess, with every feature of her face perfect and perfectly beautiful. One of the prices paid for her reanimation was the large Hebrew letters tattooed across her body and her face. The tattoos looked as though a professional tattoo artist had created them rather than a rabbi, so Ross couldn't complain about the quality, especially since they had been part of the process that had brought his beautiful wife and best friend back to him. He was getting used to the tattoos. She was peacefully sleeping while he watched her breathing slowly in and out, ever so gently moving the sheets.

Lilith drew a slow, long breath and then released it, then her eyes fluttered open in the gentle sunlight that was filtering through the lace curtains in the room. She saw that Ross had been watching her sleep.

She yawned, smiled, and said, "Good morning, handsome. Have you been awake for long?"

"Only a few minutes, gorgeous. Just long enough to fall a little more in love with you, but not long enough to bring you coffee, if that's what you're wondering."

"No, but now that you mention it, coffee sounds good."

"Let's go down and get some breakfast, then," Ross said.

Ross made coffee in the room while Lilith showered. They both got dressed, had two small cups of joe, put on their surgical masks, and went downstairs to the restaurant for breakfast.

They were staying in a sprawling, white plantation-style mansion that Carly and her husband, Dennis Smythe, had built as a 40-room hotel after purchasing the ranch in the heart of Texas Hill Country. The property also featured five honeymoon cottages, a non-denominational chapel adorned with stunning stained-glass windows and seating for about 200, as well as horseback riding, fishing on the Blanco River, and hiking trails

Unfortunately, Dennis experienced a massive stroke soon after the hotel was completed about seven years ago, and died before they could get him to an emergency room from the hotel's relatively remote location. Carly had run the successful business on her own ever since. This year, however, COVID had put a damper on the business. Despite being in peak season, the hotel was operating at only a quarter of its capacity due to the pandemic.

Ross and Lilith were escorted to their table by a young man with the name "Mark" written on his nametag. It wasn't long until Carly came by the table, wearing a white mask with the state flag of Texas embroidered over the mouth.

"Good morning and howdy y'all," Carly said with an exaggerated southern accent. "I hope you don't mind the Texas accent. It helps with business down here in the south. Now get out of those seats and let me give the two of you more hugs this morning!" As she gave Lilith a hug, she said, "Lilith, when you arrived last night, in the dark, I didn't fully appreciate the extent of your tattoos." She continued to hold Lilith's upper arms as she examined her from head to toe in disbelief. "I can't believe it's you. Back from the dead. It's just so unbelievable. And you have all of your memories from before your death?"

"So far as we can tell, Carly, yes," Lilith said.

"Do you eat normal food? Do you have a heartbeat? Do you poop?"

"Yes, yes, and we all know girls don't poop," Lilith said.

"That's right," Ross agreed with a wink.

"Alright, so I had a husband years ago," Carly started her pop quiz. "What was his name?"

"You mean Dennis?" replied Lilith.

"Do you feel pain?" Carly asked.

"Yes, but I seem to recover from injuries really fast," Lilith said.

Carly continued, "It's going to take me some time to get used to having you back in the family. It wasn't very long ago that I attended your funeral, and as if being dead wasn't enough, they cremated you. It's pretty hard to understand how anyone could come back from that! Don't get me wrong, praise the Lord, I'm really glad you're back from the dead, but it will take me a minute or two to stop doing a double take when you walk in the room."

"It's good to be back with my family, Carly," Lilith said, "and I find it all very hard to believe myself, every day.

Carly gave Ross a hug and said, "You can stay here for as long as you need to, baby brother. Fair warning, though, I don't think you and the family have ever visited us here in August. Texas is a different animal come August."

"Now you know how desperate we are," Ross said with a grin. "Better to be safe and sweatin' our tails off than out on the road. I just hope we won't put you out too much over the next few months. Oh, and we are *all* willing and able to work and help you out. Well, except for me. I'm more the supervisor type."

"Supervisor huh, well, I may take you up on that last offer," Carly said. "Could use a few extra hands around here. But I'm serious, stay as long as you want – you're all family, including Rabbi Rosenburg, who, by the way, is staying out in one of the honeymoon cottages, and as far as I'm concerned, is now officially a member of the family, too. And speak of the devil, or speak of the angel, here he comes now."

Carly put her hand next to her mouth and whispered, "Is Rabbi Rosenburg single? He's sort of cute, aside from the big bandage on the side of his head. What happened there?"

Ross also cupped his mouth and whispered back, "Careful with the man who brought my wife back to life, Sis. But to answer your questions – yes, he is single, and could probably act in an official capacity to marry people here at your wedding destination. As for your second question, a mercenary ripped his ear off with his bare hand, but they managed to sew it back on."

"So, a handsome miracle worker with a rough streak," Carly whispered. "What's not to like?"

Wendell was being led into the breakfast area by the young host. He saw them at a distance and waved, smiling.

"Please join us, Wendell," Lilith said. "And congratulations are in order! Carly has just made you an official member of the family. Carly, have you had breakfast yet?"

"As a matter of fact, no, I have not. Give me a second to let Mark know that I'll be taking a break, and help yourselves to coffee and the buffet."

"Wow, thank you, my adoptive family," Wendell said. "I feel like a New-man."

"Hey, he's even got the dad jokes!" Ross said with a smile.

"I must say," Wendell continued, "that I can't fully express the gratitude that I feel for how you have all welcomed me into your homes and your lives. You have truly made me feel like a part of your family."

After they all had visited the buffet, and more importantly, grabbed cups of steaming java, they all sat down around a table next to a large window with a view of old oak trees lining the driveway for about a half mile out to the country road providing access to the hotel. The stables could be seen off in the distance with horses in the pasture grazing near a grassy creek that flowed through the property. Beyond the distant fence line rolled gentle hills covered in live oak, mesquite, acacia and hackberry, with patches of yellow and pink wildflowers sprinkled across the land.

"This is such a beautiful location that you have here, Carly," Rabbi said Rosenburg. "What an incredible view! It just takes your breath away."

"Thank you, Rabbi Rosenburg," Carly said. "It is beautiful, but it's a lot of work. Don't get me wrong, I love it here, and I love the steady income it provides – present pandemic being the exception – but I go to bed every night with the kind of tired that guarantees a good night's sleep."

"Please, call me Wendell," the rabbi said. Wendell took a polite moment to observe Carly: about five foot five, with long, straight, nearly black hair, a year-round tan, and a lean, muscular frame—125 pounds, he guessed—reflecting the hard work required to manage the hotel and ranch. To Wendell, she was one of the most beautiful women he had ever seen.

"Thank you, Wendell," Carly said, holding up a mug of coffee. "Here's to the man who brought Lilith back from the dead – a true miracle worker. God bless you, Wendell." The four friends clinked their mugs together and dug into the delicious breakfast buffet.

It was about this time that Brian and Emily were led into the dining room by Mark, who pointed out the four who were already engaged with conversation and breakfast. As they approached, Carly got up and said, "Well, if it isn't my favorite nephew and niece in the whole wide world!"

Brian replied, "But we are your *only* nephew and niece in the whole wide world..."

"Still counts!" Carly said, as she hugged Emily and then Brian. "Why don't you kiddos help yourself to the buffet."

"Thank you!" Emily said enthusiastically, as she headed toward the food.

"Thank you for letting us stay with you, Aunt Carly," Brian said as he gave her another hug.

"El gusto is mio, sobrino," Carly said.

"Uh, right back at ya," Brian replied with a chuckle.

Ross swallowed the last of his sausage link and gravy.

"Carly, Wendell had a very interesting idea on the drive down from the 'cold, dark, expensive north,' as you refer to it," Ross said. "Wendell, since it's Carly's ranch, we'd need to get her approval for your idea. Would you like to share it with her?"

Wendell began to describe what he had in mind, "Well, you've heard about how Lilith was recreated – how it required a lot of special, hard-to-get 'ingredients.' The Sefer Yetzirah Scroll. An elaborate ritual. And –"

"Brian's blood, a dead man's rib, Lilith's ashes, clay, and water under a full moon, yes," Carly whispered, cutting him off. "I don't care if you had a back-to-life cookbook in front of you, I still think that what you did was a miracle."

"Thank you, but I was merely an instrument of the Almighty—and I happen to be able to read Hebrew," Wendell said. "Honestly, I think that what you have done in the creation and running of this ranch must have been more difficult than what I did."

"Thank you," Carly said, blushing like a teenage girl. "That's a very generous compliment."

"I think that you said earlier 'El gusto es mio?'" Wendell said. "Anyway, all of those ingredients are not needed to create a very simple golem – essentially a robot soldier whose job it is to protect, but who also follows simple commands. All that is needed for that sort of golem is clay, water, and the Scroll."

"What are you proposing, Wendell?" Carly asked.

"Before I tell you, let me remind you – as Ross has already done – that you, your family here, and your property are all at risk of being attacked by soldiers from an Israeli weapons company who want to capture the Scroll and Lilith and take them both to unknown locations to make super soldiers to fight Israeli wars. So, my *first* question before we proceed is to ask again – are you sure us staying here with you here at your place of business and livelihood is a good idea?"

"Y'all are *my* family on *my* ranch at *my* invitation," Carly said, both hands firmly planted on the table. "If they come to *my* ranch and *my* land with malice in mind, then they'd better be prepared for armed resistance, because I've got an armory in this hotel that puts the National Guard's armory in Fredericksburg to shame. But to answer your question, you're *all* welcome to stay here for as long as you'd like."

Wendell noted that Carly's eyes met his for longer than anyone else's as she scanned those around the table.

"And all of that will definitely be helpful if they show up, though they have the backing of a company that is worth billions of dollars, and they are very determined," Wendell said. "I have a suggestion that might help us even the odds, but it will require preparation."

Over the next 15 minutes, Wendell shared his detailed plan.

When he finished, Carly put her hand on his back.

"Sounds like fun," Carly said. "When do we start?"

41

A WALK IN THE HILL COUNTRY

7:31 AM
AUGUST 3, 2020
WHITE DRESS RANCH, GREYHILL, TEXAS

Lilith, Emily, Carly, and Wendell walked in pairs of two down the horse-riding trail that had been crudely carved into the hard dry earth and rock of the ranch property. The path had recently been "mowed" by Ross and Brian, using a pair of gas-powered walk-behind devices that had the appearance of a giant weed eater on wheels. It was a dirty job, with vegetation and bits of rock and sand flying everywhere all at once at crazy velocities, causing both Ross and Brian to wear safety glasses, leather gloves, a surgical mask for the dust, long sleeves and long pants during the process in the hot Texas summer sun. They both had also purchased cowboy boots to protect against the aggressive and venomous rattlesnakes that seemed to have infested the arid landscape.

Since they were in Texas, Carly insisted they carry Sig Sauer P365s loaded with CCI shotshells—9 mm rounds that fire shot like a shotgun. Each shell was tipped with a transparent blue plastic dome that showed the tiny pellets inside the aluminum cartridge, and if you shook them, they audibly rattled. The ranch had eight of these guns, which could be rented by wedding parties for use on the trails.

Carly made Ross and Brian practice with the guns on her make-shift gun range until they both felt comfortable enough to quickly draw the weapon from a holster and pull the trigger to be able to hit a steel "rattling varmint" target. Carly never walked around the property without one holstered at her side.

They talked as they walked down the horse-trail, sometimes between boulders, sometimes up steep inclines to the tops of low-lying hills where they would stop and view the arid vistas. Frequently the discussion gravitated to the Scroll, to Lilith, and to the nature of the Scroll. Today was no different from others, except that Lilith and Emily had joined them on their hike.

"Wendell, how do you think the Scroll creates living things from something as simple as clay?" Carly asked.

Wendell had acquired a bear-head walking cane, left behind by one of Carly's customers who never returned for it. He didn't need it, but preferred having something other than a gun in case of a snake.

During their hikes together, Carly referred to Wendell as "My wandering Jew," and Wendell embraced this term of endearment. Wendell had also adopted cowboy boots as a manner of protection from the "rattling varmints."

"So, your question is sort of like asking how the Almighty created Adam," Wendell replied. "I think that the Scroll perhaps somehow taps into the creation power of the Almighty, Himself, to create life. I don't know exactly how, but I do believe that He is far beyond our ability to understand. If you think about the chemical composition of clay or mud from a river, the list probably includes things like water, silica, alumina, with some minor traces of organic materials, along with trace elements like iron, magnesium, and such. If you compare that ingredients list to what a person is made of – mostly water followed by carbon, oxygen, and nitrogen along with a few trace elements like iron and magnesium, this means that the act of creation involve transmuting the very elements of clay into those that we need for life, much less the very formation of every microcellular structure in that body from something having absolutely no cellular structure whatsoever, much less all of the blood vessels, nerves, bones and organs in that body."

Wendell continued, "Now as for a simple golem, one made from clay and having the appearance and perhaps the composition of clay after it has been created, it is almost as though the Scroll enables that sort of 'being' to be connected to the power of HaShem, or the Almighty. Even scientists are saying that everything in the universe is connected through quantum effects that they don't completely understand. Perhaps the Scroll allows for the golem to draw the power of life through that connectivity from the universe surrounding it."

"So, basically, you're saying that the Force in Star Wars actually exists? In the words of the late great Obi-Wan Kenobi – it's 'an energy field created by all living things. It surrounds us and penetrates us. It binds the galaxy together?'" Carly said, doing her best British-accent impression of Alec Guinness.

"I don't think that Obi-Wan, or perhaps more accurately, George Lucas, was too terribly far from the truth with that description," Wendell said, "with the exception that the 'Force' we are talking about is the Almighty. I'm also a bit skeptical about people moving boulders with their minds or shooting lightning out of their fingertips, just to be clear."

"But I do find it interesting that there are so many references to animals or golems being created from clay," Wendell said. "Lilith, I must admit that I've been researching golems ever since – well – you."

Wendell held up his index finger and began to count on his fingers, one by one.

"Starting with God creating Adam and Eve in the Torah. Next Abraham is reputed to have created a calf in order to feed three angels announcing his wife, Sarah's pregnancy. There is also the account that Jesus created a bird from clay and then breathed life into it as a child according to the Quran.[1] Fast forward and you have Rav Hanina and

1. According to the Quran, Jesus (referred to as "Isa" in the Quran) is described as

Rav Hoshaiah creating a calf to eat *while studying the Sefer Yetzirah*[2], emphasizing the connection to the Scroll and its contents. In the 11th century, there's Solomon ibn Gabirol, creating a female golem for household chores[3], then Rabbi Eliyahu of Chelm created a golem in the 1500s that grew out of control until he destroyed it[4], and finally, Rabbi Loew in the 1600s in Prague created a golem out of clay from the banks of the Vltava River to defend the Prague ghettos from anti-semitic attacks[5]. There are a few others that I can't remember off the top of my head, but if these seven events alone are true, then historically, the creation of life by righteous men seems almost commonplace. I must admit that I am humbled that HaShem was able to use me, a thief who stole money from his own congregation, as an instrument to bring Lilith back to life."

"God is all about second chances, Wendell," Carly said. "Goodness knows you felt horribly remorseful about what you did."

"I just know that I do not consider myself in any way equal to the righteous men that I just mentioned," the rabbi said.

"And that statement is the true nature of repentance," Lilith said. "I'm just grateful for the second chance that you have given me."

"So am I," Emily said.

"Me too," Carly said, reaching out to squeeze Wendell's hand.

The foursome continued hiking in silence through the mesquite trees, boulders, and arid landscape for quite some time, until a high-pitched rattling erupted nearby.

"No one move!" Carly said in a loud whisper, whipping her Sig Sauer from its holster in the blink of an eye.

A large, thick rattlesnake was coiled next to Emily under a bush, his rattlers at attention and vibrating, his head cocked over a spring-loaded muscular neck. Emily was the last hold-out in the family against wearing cowboy boots on the ranch. She said they made her

---

creating a bird from clay and then breathing life into it as a child, demonstrating his divine power; this story can be found in Surah Al-Ma'idah, verse 110.

2. Sanhedrin 65b and Sanhedrin 67b.
3. https://wjudaism.library.utoronto.ca/index.php/wjudaism/article/view/34940
4. https://mishpacha.com/the-original-golem/
5. https://www.jpost.com/jerusalem-report/a-golem-into-gold

feel too hot. Her tanned calves were exposed to the rattler, and well within striking range. Lilith stood on the opposite side of Emily, away from the snake. Suddenly time slowed for Lilith. She grabbed Emily with her right arm and twisted her away from the snake. The snake unleashed the lightning-fast muscles of its strike, fangs bared. As it flew towards where Emily's calf used to be, an explosion of mycelium shot out from Lilith's left palm towards the snake, blocking its strike. As Emily was thrown away from the snake to the other side of the path, Lilith grabbed the snake's neck just behind the head with her right hand, which had made a complete orbit during Lilith's fraction of a second pirouette. Coming a little late to the action, a shot rang out from Carly's gun and a 4-inch spread of pellets blasted through the snake as well as through Lilith's arm. A crunching sound issued from the neck of the snake as it desperately wrapped its pellet-filled body around Lilith's arm.

"Oh God! Lilith! Are you alright?" Carly exclaimed as she realized what had happened.

The snake went limp around Lilith's arm, and she allowed it to drop to the ground. Wendell stepped towards Lilith and reached out to examine her arm.

Lilith warned him away, "Stand back, Wendell. Just give me a moment."

As the three watched, Lilith's body extruded the pellets back out of the holes from which they had entered, with tiny white fibrils wrapped around the 0.9 mm pellets. A dozen fibril-wrapped pellets fell to the ground from her forearm. The holes then closed themselves with skin and soon no trace remained of the wounds that were there.

"Sorry, Wendell, I'm still unsure whether the fibrils that heal me are toxic to others or not. To be safe, we probably shouldn't touch them," Lilith said.

"Lilith, your abilities seem to have been activated by you alone this time, and not by the Scroll," Wendell said.

Lilith paused thoughtfully, then replied, "You're right. This was in response to protecting Emily rather than the Jews or perhaps even you, Wendell."

Emily asked, "Is it ok to hug you now, Mom?"

Lilith brushed her right arm with her left hand and then brushed her hands together thoroughly, then said, "I think so, honey."

Emily embraced her mother and said, "Thanks for saving me."

Carly added, "Sorry for shooting you, Lilith."

"Well, it didn't hurt as badly as a point-blank round from an assault rifle. For what it's worth – if I hadn't gotten in the way, you would have probably blown its head clean off," Lilith said.

"If you hadn't done what you did, we'd be rushing Emily to the ER right now – and that rattling varmint was a big one, too!"

"I guess this means that I'll be getting a pair of cowboy boots when we get back?" Emily conceded.

"Yes, you will, young lady," Lilith said.

"Welcome to Texas, sweetheart," Carly said.

Lilith and Carly were amused at how hypervigilant Wendell and Emily were on the walk back to the ranch. Carly made rattling noises between her teeth, causing both of them to jump the first time she did it, resulting in the pair nearly jumping out of their skins and gales of laughter to the point of tears from Lilith. Wendell playfully punched Carly on the arm every time she did this during the rest of the hike.

Once after being punched by Wendell, Carly said seductively, "Careful, I bite, too," causing Wendell to blush bright red.

42

COPY

4:45 PM
August 18, 2020
IDS Research Facility, Tel Aviv, Israel

Rabbi Hazan examined the copy of the Scroll very carefully using a lighted magnifying glass. Prior to the Scroll being "re-acquired" by the Newman family, it had been subjected to a series of measurements, and spectroscopic analyses – 3D scanning via laser imaging, FTIR spectroscopy, UV-visible spectroscopy, mass spectroscopy, NMR spectroscopy, atomic absorption, and gas chromatography/mass spectroscopy designed to allow Israeli Defense Systems to be able to reproduce the Scroll. The idea was that these careful measurements and analyses could act as a back-up plan in the event that the Scroll was damaged or destroyed during the creation of further golems. The copies might also be used to create a super soldier factory in Israel. The copy that Rabbi Hazan was examining represented their first attempt to reproduce the original Sefer Yetzirah scroll.

A great deal of effort had been invested in reproducing the Scroll.

The parchment had been prepared from sheepskin according to recorded historical documents from the 22nd century, B.C., when Abraham was believed to have written the Scroll. In this process, freshly acquired lambskins from flawless lambs were soaked in water for a day to remove blood and other contaminants in preparation for a dehairing liquor. The initial dehairing liquor consisted of fermented vegetable matter, similar to beer, supplemented with lime to make the liquid alkaline in nature. The liquor bath was contained by a wooden vat and the hides stirred with a long wooden pole just as people would have done during Abraham's era so as to avoid contact with the caustic solution. The liquor was kept at a temperature thought to occur during an average summer in the 22nd century B.C. Middle East – 29 degrees Centigrade. The skins were kept in the dehairing bath for eight days and stirred three times a day to ensure the solution's deep and uniform penetration. The alkaline liquor was replaced once at the mid-point of the process.

After soaking in water, the skins were mounted on stretching frames so as to expose both sides of the hides for scraping with a sharp, moon-shaped knife to remove the last of the hair and adjust the skins to the correct thickness. To make the parchment smooth and white, thin pastes of milk, lime, flour, and egg whites were rubbed into the skins, as was a known practice of the time and validated by spectroscopy.

After allowing the skins to dry thoroughly, the parchment was cut to exactly the same shapes as the pieces sewn together in the original Sefer Yetzirah scroll and the pieces sewn together using sinews from the muscles of a calf's leg. Hebrew calligraphy specialists were then employed to duplicate both Abraham's writing style in the main text, and Rabbi Loew's writing style in the marginalia. Even the compositions of the two types of ink used were recreated as closely as possible using results from the spectroscopic analyses combined with ancient records of ink compositions. Skilled craftsmen were engaged to duplicate the Scroll's roller, including the coatings used to provide the glossy finish found on that of the original roller.

Finally, the most educated and talented Kabbalah rabbi in Israel – Rabbi Volozhin – was enlisted to conduct the most important step of the process – the enchantment of the copy of the Scroll in the fashion estimated to have been used by Judah Loew ben Bezalel, the Maharal of Prague. This latter step contained the biggest unknowns, since the only documents in existence that related to this process were only tangential in nature, and not directly related to how such a scroll might become supernaturally empowered. The scroll was scheduled for the creation of a simple golem on September 1st, when a full moon would occur.

43

WHERE THERE'S SMOKE

10:33 PM
August 19, 2020
Ulaam Synagogue, Tel Aviv, Israel

Ivan Sokov stood on the women's balcony of the synagogue, watching as Rabbi Volozhin began the empowerment ritual. The copy of the Scroll lay fully unrolled on the bimah, the special table where the Torah is traditionally read to the congregation. To Ivan's right sat Rabbi Hazan, and to his left, Eva Fischer. All three wore surgical masks, partly due to the recent airline travel of both Eva and Ivan. An empty seat separated each of them, though not enough to meet the six-foot requirement of CDC guidelines. They were close enough to speak quietly to one another during the ritual.

A cantor was quietly singing praises to the Almighty in Hebrew while two other rabbis quietly prayed in unison, rocking their upper bodies in a gentle bow on either side of Rabbi Volozhin, while he read the marginalia of the copy of the Scroll.

"I continue to be concerned about the intentions for conducting this ritual, Mr. Sokov," Rabbi Hazan whispered. "To put it politely, you have been rather vague about what, exactly, you intend to use the Scroll for once it has been empowered."

"What difference do my intentions make to you, Rabbi?" Ivan whispered, his tone sharp. "I'm donating a significant amount of money for a holy ceremony in this sacred place of worship, in the middle of the week when your congregation isn't even here."

"Your intentions for the Scroll could adversely affect the outcome of the empowerment ritual, and they must be completely righteous," the rabbi said. "For example, if your intentions are to protect our sacred land of Israel from invasion, then this is a noble and righteous intent, and this would align with the will of the Almighty. However, if you have other intentions beyond this, say, for example, to sell golems created by the Scroll for a profit to other nations, then this would not be aligned with HaShem's will, and the results of the empowerment ritual might fail, or even worse, yield an unholy abomination."

Ivan straightened his shirt forcefully. It was apparent that the rabbi had struck a nerve with him as he crossed his arms and faced him.

"My company, Israeli Defense Systems, has supplied the Israeli military with the equipment that it has needed to defend our nation for decades," Ivan replied, his tone becoming more stern and hardly a whisper anymore. "Further, IDS has donated tens of millions of dollars to synagogues and Jewish causes for decades. There is no company that has done more for the defense of our nation than IDS. Its intentions are righteous and beyond reproach."

"Please don't take offense, Mr. Sokov, but intent is quite critical to the overall outcome of the ritual. Your contributions to our country's defense are well known and unquestioned."

"And you weren't quite as vocal about my intent until after you had cashed my check to your synagogue," Ivan said, a little too loudly.

"It's not like that at all, Mr. Sokov," the rabbi whispered.

"Perhaps we should focus our attention upon the ritual," Eva whispered. "No one can question Mr. Sokov's intentions after he lost his wife in pursuit of defending his country."

As they watched the ritual unfold, the ten-foot replica of the scroll began to smolder and smoke, causing Rabbi Volozhin to cough during his recitations of the marginalia. The smoke became dark and thick. This was followed by coughing from the two rabbis on either side of him, and eventually the cantor. Despite the coughing, they continued to vocalize their support for the ritual. Soon after the smoke began, it stopped, and with it, Rabbi Volozhin, the prayers, and the singing came to an abrupt halt. Everyone on the platform continued to cough, but the ritual was complete. The smoke, smelling of acrid sulfur, rose up above the platform, forming what initially looked like medium grey dough – opaque and yet dimly lit from within. The grey cloud slowly took on the form of a face , but instead of eyes, a nose, or a mouth, there were only gaping black holes. From deep within the smoke, tiny purple spots of light sparkled in the places where those features should have been. The hollow eye sockets glowered at Ivan for several seconds and then a hungry maw formed below the nose, complete with needle-sharp black teeth and a thick, forked tongue. The ghoulish apparition slowly dispersed, and the resulting smoke made its way up into the women's balcony.

The trio also began to cough, and their eyes began to water and burn. A smoke alarm began to squeal loudly as the three rose and made their way down the steps of the balcony and towards the stairs leading to the foyer. As Ivan looked down upon the product of their efforts to empower the copy of the Scroll, he saw that the parchment had changed from off-white with black lettering to medium grey with blood red lettering. He also saw that the marginalia were sparkling in purple.

44

FORMATION

10:33 AM
August 20, 2020
White Dress Ranch, Greyhill, Texas

The flatbed truck kicked up a trail of beige dust as it bounced down the road that led to the main building of the White Dress Ranch wedding venue. The truck rolled to a stop in front of the main entrance, and the African American driver popped open the door and deftly slid off the driver's seat onto the step of the truck and then down onto the dirt and gravel driveway, raising a small cloud of dust. He adjusted his face mask – colored in yellow and black with the words Norton Antivirus printed in bold letters – up over his nose as Rabbi Rosenburg and Carly came down the steps leading to the front door. Rabbi Rosenburg wore a simple blue surgical mask, while Carly's featured the Texas state flag with the words "DON'T MESS WITH TEXAS" stamped across the middle, like a brand on a steer.

Although his mouth wasn't visible, it was plain from his eyes that the delivery driver was smiling. "Howdy y'all! I got a delivery of beige clay for Ms. Carly Smythe today. Where would you like me to put it?" The driver handed Carly a clipboard describing the bulk shipment as being two tons of beige modeling clay from Amarillo Art Supply at a cost of $0.25/lb for a grand total of $735.63, including shipping.

"Look okay to you, Wendell?" Carly asked.

"I think that this should do nicely," Wendell said.

Carly signed the invoice on the clipboard and the driver tore off the top page, handing it to Carly. "Point me to its final destination and I'll take it off the truck for you," the driver said.

Wendell walked down a hard dirt path leading behind the chapel with the driver and he asked him to put the pallets of clay on the ground back there.

"I think I'll be able to make it down that path, but if not, can I put them in front of the chapel?" the elderly driver asked.

"I don't think Carly has any weddings scheduled for the next few weeks, so that should work out okay as a backup plan," Wendell said.

The driver walked quickly to the rear of his truck, where a forklift was mounted. He climbed up into the lift and lowered the forklift to the ground and drove it around to the side, scooping up the first pallet of clay. He drove to the path and easily traversed the hard path with the three wheeled lift carrying the first ton of clay, deftly dropping it behind the chapel exactly where Wendell had indicated. He repeated this process for the second pallet, reloaded the lift onto the back of the truck and headed back down the dusty driveway, beeping his big truck horn twice to say thanks for the business.

* * *

The next day, a big blue Amazon van pulled up to the front door of the hotel and the driver hustled up the steps carrying a package, again addressed to Carly, thereby keeping the Newmans and Rabbi Rosenburg completely off the grid. The host accepted the package and set it on a table in the front lobby.

Carly later opened the package and exclaimed, "What the heck is this?" and then, "Of course. Wendell! I think this is for you."

Wendell came running down the stairs, looked at the contents, and with a grin, said, "Shhhh! That's for my plan, but I'm saving this as a surprise, so don't tell the others."

"My lips are sealed," Carly said.

"Say, since you already know this part of the surprise, do you think you might be available to help me with the first ritual this evening?" Wendell asked.

"Like I said when I heard your plan the first time – sounds like fun – sure!"

"Do you have a commercial blender?"

"Yes, but what could you possibly want with a commercial blender?"

"I'll show you tonight, but don't bring anyone else. Like I said – I want this part to be a surprise for the others. I'll meet you in the chapel after dinner.

"It's a date!" Carly said. "Oops, I mean, I'll see you then."

"If I can borrow a bottle of your favorite wine from the storeroom, then–"

"Part of the ritual too?" Carly interrupted, with a flirtatious grin.

"Well, perhaps after our work this evening is finished, we could take the opportunity to get to know each other a little better," Wendell said. "And if it's okay with you, we could call it a first date. How does you and me sitting in the starlight with a glass of wine sound?"

"I would like that," Carly said.

"Then it's definitely a date," Wendell said.

* * *

After dinner, when Wendell arrived at the chapel, Carly was there with a commercial kitchen blender. Wendell set two bottles of wine and two wine glasses off to the side along with some wildflowers in a glass vase.

"Why Wendell, are those flowers for me?" Carly asked.

"Oh, sorry, no. There is a point in the ritual that requires the sprinkling of chicken blood onto the forming golem using local wildflowers."

Carly looked disappointed for a moment but recovered quickly.

"Of course these are for you, you big goof," Wendell said, laughing. "Though the flower choices were a bit sparse."

Carly smiled, stepped over and hugged Wendell warmly, and said, "Thank you. Yeah, springtime is the best time for wildflowers here in Texas, but I like what you were able to find."

"You're welcome. So, would you like to make a golem?"

"I think so. . . What can I do to help?" Carly asked.

"Take these six cans. Drain them and then puree the contents.

"Seriously? Puree them?"

"Seriously. I hope you're not squeamish."

"Nope, not in the least. Consider it done."

"After I get dressed, I'll begin work on sculpting the clay outside. I'd like you to remain completely quiet during the ritual, but I'll need you to assist in unfurling the Scroll as I read."

Wendell unzipped a small airplane roller bag, pulled out a pair of nitrile gloves, put them on and then removed the Scroll, laying it out on the altar of the chapel, unfurling it as he read a few words in Hebrew and then stopped.

"Now I will not be giving you verbal directions during the ritual because I need to focus all of my spoken words on the ritual without interruption, and so I will give you hand signals, instead. So, when I make this circular hand motion," Wendell rotated his Torah pointer in a counterclockwise circle, "it means to unfurl the Scroll to the left and roll it up a bit the right side – right meaning from my perspective. Hebrew, unlike English, is written from right to left. If I need you to get the puree, I will point to you and give you a motion like this." He put out his hand, index finger up and curled it towards him. "Also, since Texas is hot, even at night, I may ask for you to towel off my forehead occasionally, so I don't accidentally drip onto the formation ingredients."

"Sort of like a nurse helping out a surgeon, then?" Carly asked with a smile.

"That's an interesting way to think about it," Wendell said. "I don't know how long it will take – maybe a few hours? – but once we start, we have to press forward until we are done, or it won't work.

Unfortunately, because of the size of this golem, we don't have enough space to do this in the chapel. If it starts to rain, all of our work will come to an end, and we will have to scrap the materials. The most important thing of all is for us to protect the Scroll from the elements, from damage, and from becoming soiled. It is a holy artifact, and we have to treat it that way. So, when you handle the Scroll, please wear these nitrile gloves."

"Rain?" Carly asked as if she'd never heard the word before. "In August? Here in Texas Hill Country? That'd be a miracle of a different sort! I can pretty much guarantee that won't be an issue tonight."

"Good. Well, let me put on my 'scrubs' and we can finish setting up outside."

Just as he did for Lilith, Wendell placed his white silk yarmulke rimmed with gold embroidery upon his head, wrapped his white shawl around his shoulders and then set his two tefillins containing hand-written texts from the Torah on the altar and recited a blessing in Hebrew. He strapped the arm tefillin around the bicep of his left arm and hand and recited another blessing in Hebrew as he placed the head tefillin on his head around the yarmulke with the fabric box positioned on his forehead. Carly watched all of this in silence and with great fascination.

The two of them moved the altar from the chapel out of a side door and to the rear of the chapel, where they placed it on level ground near the blue tarp holding the clay. Unlike Lilith's formation ritual, the moon above was barely a sliver of a crescent, as Wendell believed that a full moon was unnecessary for the formation of a "simple" golem like the one they were about to attempt. Instead, a pair of flood lights had been turned on to illuminate the ritual area.

Rabbi Rosenburg repeated most of the readings and prayers that he had performed for Lilith's ceremony, but this time, no rib was used, no blood from Brian was used as the ink for tattoos, no soil was used, and no cremation ashes were used. Near the beginning of the ritual, Wendell requested that Carly bring him the puree, which he mixed thoroughly into the clay until it was as homogeneously blended as he could practically achieve. His hands ached at the end of this step, and his head required toweling by Carly several times due to the heat the exertion of this process. The rabbi again produced a set of sculpting tools and used these to produce details that his hands and fingers alone were simply incapable of achieving. After several hours, the clay sculpture was complete.

Carly was fascinated by the entire process, and once the sculpture lay finished upon the tarp, she was stunned both by Wendell's imagination and his artistic abilities.

Wendell held up the annotated Sefer Yetzirah and began reading in Hebrew, walking around the prone clay figure, gently bowing as he spoke. The annotations around the margins of the pages glowed red, visible even under the illumination of the floodlights.

Wendell removed his nitrile gloves, tossed them away from the tarp onto the ground and washed his hands in a blue and white bowl of water resting on the altar, and dried them with a ceremonial white towel. He reached into his pocket and pulled out a necklace identical to the one worn by Lilith, forged from silver with the Hebrew letters:

אמת.

Which translates to "emmet," meaning "truth." Wendell gently fitted the necklace under the back of the golem's neck in a tunnel between the neck and the tarp. He fastened the clasp, centered it upon the creature's chest, and breathed the Hebrew word onto the effigy's face. He then took a small paint brush and carefully painted the letters of the Hebrew alphabet using a Kosher ink containing water, oak gall nut, gum Arabic, soot, logwood, and iron sulfate that he had previously prepared for the ceremony. Finally, in English, and under the creature's right arm, Wendell painted the name "OctaJoe."

Upon completing this task, he motioned to Carly for another pair of nitrile gloves, which he donned. He picked up the Scroll and read the glowing red marginalia in Hebrew again, walking around in a circle around the clay sculpture lying before them both, chanting and repeatedly bowing as he walked. Then he knelt and read from the Scroll for the last time, ending with "Amen." He then rolled up the Scroll and placed it in a white plastic bag on the altar, believing that the Scroll needed to be close to the golem during its formation. He tied the bag shut and weighed it down by placing a lump of clay on each side of the plastic bag to protect it from possible wind and rain during the night.

Wendell and Carly slipped back into the chapel where Wendell removed his ceremonial garments and placed them back into the airline roller bag.

"I'm not sure how long the formation event takes, but with Lilith we were so exhausted that we got some sleep while the formation was occurring. It's late, so I would completely understand if you'd like to reschedule our first date."

"You can't get off that easily, Rabbi Rosenburg. I'm holding you to your original invitation – a glass of wine while watching the stars and getting to know each other better."

"That still sounds very nice to me, and I'm happy to keep my promise, even though I'm dead tired. Just don't expect me to have the rapid-fire wit of Robin Williams or the romantic charm of George Clooney tonight."

"I'm tired, too, so 'a loaf of bread, a jug of wine and thou' sort of sums up my expectations for the rest of the evening."

The two then gathered up the wildflowers and the two bottles of wine and walked over to one of the honeymoon cottages furthest from the hotel, sitting side-by-side in the two Adirondack chairs on the front porch. The light from surrounding cities was nearly non-existent, making the Milky Way visible across the night sky. Every now and then a shooting star would flash across the darkness of the night sky. The wine and an unexpected loaf of bread with cheese courtesy of Carly were delicious, and the conversation felt like two friends catching up after a lifetime of being apart.

"Don't take this the wrong way, Carly, but I'm about to fall asleep sitting here. I think we should call it a day."

Carly reached into the reusable grocery bag and pulled out a key attached to a large red plastic heart. "I don't want to seem too forward or anything, but there's a room with freshly changed sheets, two robes, fresh soap and toothbrushes right through the teal door behind us," Carly said.

"That sounds very, very nice, on two conditions," Wendell said.

"What's that?" Carly asked.

"That our second date is me bringing you breakfast from your buffet, which will definitely include coffee."

"Coffee? Of course! If you didn't drink coffee, then I'm afraid that would be a deal breaker, sir, and we might as well call this whole thing off right now. But that being said, I'm listening . . ." Carly said.

"And then, our third date – well, you know what happens after third dates, right?" Wendell asked.

"We check to see if you've made a golem?" Carly asked, with a smile on her face.

"I can do that on the way to pick up breakfast and report back with how things went," Wendell said.

"Like heck you will! I want to see it too! How about – I go *with* you to pick up breakfast, and then we *both* check in on the golem? You can even make *that* our third date if you want to, that way we don't have to wait for breakfast for the fun part," Carly said.

"All this talk about what happens after a third date is starting to make me hungry, but not for food. What would you say to moving up the part that usually happens after the third date to after the first date? We can worry about the golem, and breakfast, tomorrow morning."

"I say – here's the key to what happens after the first date," Carly said, handing Wendell the key to the honeymoon cottage. Then she reached up and pulled Wendell's face to hers, kissing him long and slow.

45

OCTAJOE

8:14 AM
AUGUST 21, 2020
WHITE DRESS RANCH, GREYHILL, TEXAS

"Wow," Wendell said as he looked at Carly lying next to him under the white sheets, smiling back at him as a beam of sunlight gently illuminated her face.

"Wow right back at you," Carly said.

"You are amazing. I feel as though I've been given a gift of the most precious kind, or that a curse has been broken and I've been brought back to life," Wendell whispered.

"And you feel like the missing piece that I've ached for all of my life. I feel like a teenager again."

"What date number are we on now?" Wendell asked.

"I don't know about you, but I stopped being able to count after about date number five," Carly replied

"Me too. Would you like to go check on OctaJoe, and get some breakfast?" Wendell asked, pulling on his pants.

"Oh, so you named him, did you? You're pretty confident in your abilities, Rabbi Rosenburg," replied Carly, closing the front clasp of her bra as her legs dangled off the side of the tall bed.

"I tattooed his name under his right arm. And as for my overconfidence, I'm simply an optimist. I happen to be on an incredible streak of great luck at the moment," Wendell said with a grin.

The two finished getting dressed, and Wendell made coffee in the room while Carly brushed her hair.

Cradling their cups of pecan roast coffee, Wendell opened the front door of the cottage, and the two of them walked to the rear of the chapel eager to see if their efforts from the previous night had been successful. The blue tarp was empty, save for a golem-shaped clean space surrounded by a thin layer of clay. The Scroll remained on the altar in the plastic bag weighed down by the two clay bricks.

"Well, that's interesting . . . Where on earth would a 500 pound golem go?" the rabbi asked.

"Where is it?" Carly asked.

"I'm not sure. Say, Carly, was that dead oak tree there last night?" Wendell asked, pointing to the tree trunk.

"I'm pretty sure that the only trees around the chapel are those that I intentionally planted. I would have cut down any dead ones because photos are constantly being taken both inside and all around outside of the chapel. A dead oak tree would simply be bad for business."

"Then let's try something – OctaJoe, show yourself!" Wendell said loudly as they both watched the dead oak tree carefully.

The dead tree, with folded, greyish-brown bark, hollowed branch ends, and roots that extended into the ground, changed rapidly before their eyes. The dead color of the tree changed from greyish brown to beige. At the same time, the folded bark texture changed to a featureless smooth surface. Two large branches that forked from the upper portion of the trunk converted into large arms with fingers. The apparently fused lower portion of the trunk with roots extending into the soil converted into two large legs with over-simplified feet as they pulled themselves out of the soil. Four tentacles, complete with suckers, loosened themselves from the trunk and extended, wavering from the central abdomen of the golem. A lump extended itself upwards out of the top of the abdomen, revealing two oval eye sockets and a nose socket. A curved black beak surrounded by a short, protruding pipe of flesh extended about five inches outward from where a mouth would exist on a man.

"So *that's* why you needed the pureed canned octopus," Carly said.

"Yes, but I wasn't expecting *this* kind of result!" Wendell exclaimed. "He's better than I could have imagined."

The sound of distant laughter and conversation came from around the corner.

"OctaJoe! Quickly, hide yourself near those rocks," Wendell whispered to the golem.

OctaJoe leaped over near the pile of boulders and *became* one of the boulders. Wendell and Carly both looked at each other with raised eyebrows, then Carly started giggling uncontrollably. Wendell soon joined her, and the two of them were laughing as Ross and Brian, then Lilith and Emily rounded the back corner of the chapel.

"Well, here you are!" Ross cheerfully greeted them. "We missed you at breakfast. Where have you two been hiding?"

Spurred on by the word "hiding," the conspirators looked at each other and spilled coffee from their cups as they laughed even harder.

Everyone smiled at the laughter until Brian finally chimed in, "Wendell, did you make a golem last night?" pointing to the empty outline on the blue tarp.

"Oh, we made a golem," Carly said, smirking.

"Guilty as charged, Brian," Wendell responded. The Newman family immediately became very interested.

"Wow, based on the silhouette on the tarp, he must be a big one!" Brian said. "What on *earth* are those tentacle-looking things extending from his chest area?"

"You nailed it on the first guess – they're tentacles," the rabbi said.

"Where is he?" Lilith asked.

"At the moment, he's playing hide and seek. See if you can find him," the rabbi said.

"The roof?" Ross asked, backing away from the chapel to get a better view.

"He's part octopus or squid, isn't he?" Lilith said.

"Very good, Lilith. He's part octopus," Wendell said.

"Where did you find an octopus in Texas?" Emily asked.

"Amazon, of course," Carly said. "You can get anything on Amazon."

"You ordered a live octopus from Amazon?" Lilith said.

"Nope. He ordered *canned or bottled* octopus from Amazon," Ross said. "I don't think that the animal needs to be alive for the formation ritual to work."

"Well done! You've solved part of the puzzle, but now can you find him?" Wendell asked.

The Newmans looked around, walked around, and even felt the trees, mounds of earth, the wall of the chapel, and even the boulders where the golem was located.

"Come on, guys," Wendell said, part encouraging, part teasing, "he's 500 pounds. How hard can this be?"

Eventually, Ross said, "We give up," and raised his palms and shrugged his shoulders.

"Everyone, watch that boulder over there," Wendell said pointing to the hiding golem. "OctaJoe! Show yourself!"

Instantly, the golem stood up from his hiding place as a boulder, changing his color from a mottled granite appearance to a smooth beige color, revealing his appendages and appearance to the Newmans for the first time.

Everyone, including Wendell, exclaimed "Whoa," at nearly the same time, as though they'd just witnessed the grand finale of the New York City fireworks exploding in the sky on the 4th of July.

"So, OctaJoe has taken on some of the capabilities of an octopus during his formation?" Ross asked.

"Exactly," Wendell replied, "but not just any octopus – octopus vulgaris – one of the best camouflage artists of the animal kingdom. This species is capable of duplicating the coloration, texture, and shape of objects they are near, in less than a second. I must admit I was concerned about the octopus's need for water, but so far, OctaJoe doesn't seem to have such a need."

"In the Texas heat?" Carly said. "I'll go grab the poor guy a glass of ice water. Or start the world's biggest bubble bath."

After the family, which now included Wendell, stopped laughing, they all stood together admiring the wonders of what could only be called the children of the Scroll.

46

TESTING, 1, 2, 3

9:46 PM
SEPTEMBER 1, 2020
ULAAM SYNAGOGUE, TEL AVIV, ISRAEL

Rabbi Hazan held the copy of the Scroll, reading the sparkling purple marginalia in Hebrew as he walked around the clay sculpture lying on the black plastic tarp. Chanting softly, he bowed repeatedly with each step. The copy of the Scroll had slowly generated a faint acrid smoke during the entire ritual, causing those present in the synagogue to cough occasionally. Then Rabbi Hazan knelt and read from the copy of the Scroll for the last time, ending with an Amen. He rolled up the copy of the Scroll and placed it on the bimah, which was near the clay sculpture, thereby ending the ritual.

Ivan Sokov, Rabbi Volozhin, and Eva Fischer sat in the women's balcony of the synagogue, watching the formation ritual quietly. Several video cameras were recording from the balcony, and one was recording from the platform. The fire alarm system had been disabled to prevent it from automatically calling the local fire department during the ceremony as it had at the end of the last ritual. Instead, the doors and numerous windows were opened by assistants the moment it became clear that smoke was being generated. Below, a clay effigy had been sculpted by Rabbi Hazan. It was a relatively simple golem – taller than an average man, made from dark gray clay, with eye and nose sockets and a simple slit for a mouth.

Eva whispered, "Is the silver amulet the shem for the golem?"

Forged in silver, lying upon the chest of the golem was an amulet consisting of the Hebrew letters:

אמת.

Ivan replied quietly, "You are correct, Eva. However, this shem is high-tech. It is an Israeli Defense Systems custom design, specifically for this project. The amulet contains a micro-explosive charge positioned between the first letter, aleph, and the second letter, mem. A phone application installed on my phone allows me to, in the event of an emergency, detonate the micro-explosive charge, thereby separating the aleph from the mem, and changing the word hanging from the golem's neck from 'truth' to 'death,' thereby killing the golem. At least that's according to Rabbi Hazam and Rabbi Volozhin."

"Yes, according to both legend and written accounts, the separation of these two letters in the shem causes the golem to simply crumble into pieces," Rabbi Volozhin confirmed.

Two armed guards with Uzi submachine guns stood at either side of the golem off of the platform. Rabbi Hazan looked up into the women's balcony of the synagogue at Ivan and nodded his head as he exited the platform.

"What do you think?" Eva whispered. "Will it work?"

"I think we have done everything humanly and spiritually possible to reproduce the Scroll and to empower it," Rabbi Volozhin said.

"At this point, nothing else can be done," Ivan said. "Now we wait."

"Will the guards be staying for the night?" Eva asked.

"The guards will be quietly changed out at 4 AM, and the cameras will be running all night, as well, in case something unexpected or interesting happens," Ivan said. "After we leave, the doors to the synagogue will be locked until the guards are changed at 4 AM, and then unlocked again when we reconvene tomorrow morning at 7:30."

"Hypothetically, if the golem comes to life during the night, he will remain near the copy of the Scroll and wait for the owner of the copy of the Scroll to come and give him orders," Rabbi Volozhin said.

"Who's the owner of the copy of the Scroll – Ivan?" Eva asked.

"That's correct," Rabbi Volozhin said. "The soldiers have been given strict orders to simply stay out of the golem's way and to not speak to it if he awakens."

"Well, friends, I don't know about the two of you," Ivan said, "but I'm gonna get some sleep. I'll meet you two and Rabbi Hazan here tomorrow morning. Good night, sleep tight."

47

THE CONSEQUENCES OF INTENT

7:30 AM
September 2, 2020
Ulaam Synagogue, Tel Aviv, Israel

Rabbi Hazan stepped quickly from his car in the parking lot to Ivan, Eva, and Rabbi Volozhin, who were waiting for him at the entrance of the Ulaam Synagogue.

"I've always said that the definition of 'on time' is five minutes early, and that 'on time' is actually late. I believe that you are now officially late, Rabbi Hazan," Ivan Sokov said as the rabbi approached.

"Apologies, Mr. Sokov. I will keep your valuable lesson on punctuality forever in my future practices," Rabbi Hazan said.

Ivan held a walkie-talkie to the side of his face and pressed the talk button. "Benjamin, we are waiting outside the front door. Please report your status."

A deep voice sounding as though it were a chorus of voices rather than one voice replied, "I've been waiting since 3:56 AM. I thought your definition of 'on time' was five minutes early? Your 4 AM relief team was 'on time,' for example. They arrived five minutes early."

"Benjamin, please report your status immediately," Ivan said, annoyed with the voice that he didn't recognize.

"Benjamin, shall we say, left the synagogue earlier this morning," the voices calmly replied.

"Then who is this?" Ivan asked, becoming more impatient.

"My name is Legion, for I am many," the voice said.

Rabbi Hazan said, "You're speaking to the golem that resulted from our work last night. You should use your phone app to destroy."

"Before I destroy a potentially valuable IDS resource, I'd like to at least meet it first," Ivan said. "But perhaps we should keep the phone app front and center and active on my phone."

Rabbi Volozhin said, "Give the golem a simple command. Let's see who's in charge of this 'Legion'"

"Very reasonable," Ivan said, as he clicked the talk button on the walkie-talkie. "As the owner of the Scroll, I command you to come to the front door, so that I can see you."

The golem strolled into the foyer and up to the glass door of the synagogue, posing an imperious figure. The golem's face no longer had the appearance of a slit for a mouth and simple holes for eyes and nose as it had been sculpted. It had a quite handsome face complete with eyebrows, a Roman nose, full lips, high cheekbones, and a slightly cleft chin. The face was looking at them with mild amusement. The face wasn't the only thing that contained additional detail – there were now fingernails, muscles, nipples, no belly button, a completely bald and shiny head, and a generous penis and scrotum – all colored in dark grey. Legion was smiling through the glass at them with arms crossed and pearly white teeth. The walkie-talkie resided in the creature's left hand. The small silver shem swung from his neck on his chest.

Rabbi Volozhin turned his back on Legion and faced Ivan so the creature could not read his lips and said, "Give him another command, perhaps even a ridiculous one."

Ivan was now holding his cell phone in his left hand with the app for remotely exploding the shem open. A red flashing button lit up the screen. Ivan clicked the walkie-talkie with his right hand again and spoke, "I command you to bend over and touch your toes, and then stand on one leg until I tell you to stop."

Legion clicked his talk button and said, "As you wish, though this is becoming tiresome. Please come inside so that we can discuss our very profitable future together."

The golem bent over and touched his toes, then stood on one leg in such a way that his right foot pressed against his left thigh. He held both palms and fingers flat against each other above his head in what is known in yoga as the asymmetrical tree pose, almost as a means of showing off.

"Rabbi Hazan, please unlock the door," Ivan said.

"You realize that your guards are likely dead inside, don't you?" Rabbi asked Hazan.

Ivan nodded his head to the rabbi, then gestured to the door.

The rabbi reached under his robe into his pants pocket and produced a set of keys. Peeling off a shiny brass key imprinted with the star of David, he walked to the glass door alongside the others, shakily inserted the key, opening the main door to the synagogue. The golem remained in his yoga pose as the four entered the synagogue.

"At last - companionship worthy of my intellect," the golem slowly said. "Please accompany me to the bedsheets of my birthplace, so to speak. I understand that you require proof of value for your military products. Allow me to show you a sample of my value."

"But I have not released you from standing upon one foot yet."

"Is it normal for you to have talk business with your future valuable and knowledgeable business partner while he is standing naked on one foot?" Legion asked.

"Fine. You may walk on two feet again," Ivan said.

"Thank you. Oh, I don't suppose anyone brought a spare set of clothing with them?" Legion said, over his shoulder.

"I'm afraid not. We were expecting you to be rather simple, both in intellect and appearance," Rabbi Hazan said.

"Yes, I watched the video of the ritual," Legion said. "Honestly, a 7-year-old could have sculpted better than that, Rabbi Hazan! Gumbies everywhere are rolling over in their toy boxes. I must be quite a surprise to you all. In order to speed up your military evaluation process, I used the synagogue as my testing ground and during the shift change, I used your four highly trained military operatives as my challenge opponents. Unfortunately, the synagogue did not fare so well. I was working for speed, not the avoidance of collateral damage. Honestly, the vast majority of the damage was done by your soldiers and their Uzis. You should send their families the bill for the repairs."

Eva, Ivan, and the two rabbis stared in disbelief at the formerly beautiful synagogue. Every single stained-glass window had been pierced with bullet holes. The interior walls were pock-marked with bullet holes. The speaking podium had been used as a club and lay in splinters. Many of the pews had bullet holes in them. But the piece de resistance lay piled in the center of the platform – four dead IDS operatives – and lying upon this pile of death, their four Uzis had been carefully bent and twisted together to form a Star of David.

As the four gazed incredulously at the interior of the synagogue, Legion stepped up to the four dead soldiers, selected the tallest, and began to remove his clothing, dressing himself as he did so.

"Final score: Legion – 4, IDS operatives – 0," Legion intoned. "Most importantly, I seem to have the ability to rapidly heal, so your newest military asset is completely undamaged, even though they managed to hit me with 6 of their shots – pathetic for four Uzis in the hands of trained soldiers, I might add."

Legion finished tying the dead soldier's left boot onto his own foot and continued, "Now that I'm properly dressed, I have a proposal for our strategy moving forward, assuming there are no objections from the owner of the copy of the Scroll?"

Ivan continued to hold his phone with his thumb over the red button which would disconnect the golem's shem and said, "Legion, why did you refer to yourself as being 'many'? And why have you chosen the same name that was used by the demons that were exorcised by Jesus from the possessed man?"

"I refer to myself as being many because I *am* many. I have chosen the name Legion, because it is an accurate description of both my abilities and the source of my life force. We *were* the demons that possessed the man described in the Christian Bible," Legion said in his deep choral voice.

"But that man was insane. Why is it that now, instead of insane, you are coherent? One would even describe you as intelligent and well-spoken," Ivan said.

"Rabbi Hazan can answer that question, can't you, rabbi?" Legion said.

"Well, I suppose I can hazard an educated guess, Ivan. I believe I mentioned to you that your intent was very important to the final result of the formation ritual. Hence, if your intent is righteous, then the golem's life force will be from a righteous source. However, if your intent is not righteous, or perhaps motivated by revenge or a lust for power or greed, then the source of the golem's life force will be from an unrighteous source, perhaps even an evil source. As for why the man possessed by Legion as described in the Christian books of Mark, Luke, and John was insane – I would venture to say that it was because Legion was present in his body *against his will* creating insufferable mental conflict. In this case, the only presence in this body is Legion, so there is no mental conflict in this vessel."

"Well done, rabbi! Correct on all accounts. The word 'vessel' is very appropriate for this situation. I must admit that I do like this 'vessel' very much," Legion said.

Ivan replied, "Thank you, Rabbi Hazan. This is very helpful in our understanding of the copy of the Scroll. IDS will begin restoration – with improvements – of Ulaam Synagogue as soon as possible. Legion, could you please enlighten us with your business proposition for moving forward? I'm interested in what you have to say."

"I thought you might be, Mr. Sokov," Legion said. "But would you mind taking your thumb away from that 'kill' button? I don't want an unintentional sneeze to end the very short life of my 'vessel'."

"Of course, Legion. I wouldn't want that to happen either."

"I suppose you'd like me to go and find a closet to stand in until you need my services further," Legion said, with sarcasm.

"Legion, you have instantly become a very valuable member of my team. How, exactly, would you like for me to make your life better?" Ivan asked.

"So thoughtful of you to ask! Oh, just a few minor requests – nothing too outrageous. Let's see, I'd like my own apartment downtown with private access to the beach, a nice car similar to the Porsche that you have in the parking lot, except perhaps in blood red, an identity, and a paycheck to spend," Legion replied.

"That's a rather lengthy and expensive list. Just a question or two - how will you explain your grey skin to the rest of the world?"

"Let's just say that I will be a nocturnal creature. I will dress to cover my skin and face and stay mostly at my place during the day, unless I'm needed here, of course," Legion said.

"Will every super soldier that we produce at our new 'super soldier factory' have similar requests? If so, then I'm not sure that we can afford you and all of the new soldiers that we intend to produce. Obviously, we *need* the soldiers to be subservient and obedient, with minimal upkeep, and minimal expense. I'm slightly tempted to press this button if all of you will have these kind of expenses involved. Can you guarantee that future soldiers will meet my cost and subservience requirements?" Ivan asked.

"I'm planning for us *both* to be very profitable, and for that to happen, we will *both* need for the super soldiers to be subservient, obedient and low cost. Here's what I'm thinking . . ." Legion said in his multi-tonal voice.

48

HOSTAGES

8:05 AM
September 5, 2020
Greyhill, Texas

Ahmed Bukhari finished loading his sixth AK-47 assault rifle magazine for the morning, carefully lining it up in his backpack with the other magazines and two grenades. He then jammed a seventh magazine into the rifle in preparation for the morning's task – elimination of the Jews from the Beth Israel Synagogue. He looked around his one-bedroom apartment in disgust. While he rotted in this 650 square foot shit hole, the Jews and Christians of this town lived in ranch homes and on actual ranches. Even his job downtown washing dishes at the Rusty Bucket Grill was an insult to his abilities, his intelligence and his Islamic faith, especially the dishes contaminated with the meat of pigs.

He had come to the United States with the dream of a university education in international studies at the University of Texas, but ironically, he soon flunked out with a marginal ability to speak or read the cursed English language. His student visa had expired and now he was simply trying to fly under the radar to avoid being deported. Back home in Pakistan, he was a member of the Muslim Rajput caste, giving him few prospects for advancement in society there. Lack of hope wherever he had turned had ignited his hatred of the Jews. He was ready to give his life for Allah to create a last meaningful memorial from his miserable life. Ahmed went down on his knees, faced Mecca and prayed what he believed would be his last prayers to Allah.

Ahmed rose from his prayers, put on an unseasonably long jacket that nearly reached the floor and slid his AK-47 into a special slot that held it hidden under the jacket. Pulling the backpack on over the jacket, he stepped out of his apartment, walked down the dark, squeaky interior stairs to the dirt-floor courtyard of his apartment complex, and began his walk to what he believed would be his last stand – The Beth Israel Synagogue of Greyhill, Texas.

* * *

9:12 AM | SEPTEMBER 5, 2020 | BETH ISRAEL SYNAGOGUE, GREYHILL, TEXAS

Ahmed Bukhari parked his car along the street about a block away from the Beth Israel Synagogue in Greyhill, Texas and looked up at the small white wooden building. At first glance, the building gave the appearance of a small Baptist country church, save for the absence of a cross at the peak of the roof. A small simple sign on the front lawn read: BETH ISRAEL SYNAGOGUE.

Ahmed opened the door to his car, swung his legs onto the asphalt, and walked along the sidewalk to the front door. There he slipped through the door, slid quietly into one of the seats at the back in the synagogue and listened to the cantor finish a song in Hebrew.

There were about 30 people in the small synagogue. There weren't nearly as many synagogues in Texas as there were in Illinois, nor were the congregations very large in Texas, which rested firmly in the middle of the Bible belt of the country. In Ahmed's mind, however, Jews were Jews, and many more Jews than this would make it difficult to accomplish his mission.

As the cantor ended his song, Ahmed stood up, pointed his assault rifle at the ceiling, and fired eight rounds in succession. A small stream of concrete and glass rained down around him.

People began to scream and yell, and he yelled loudly with a thick Pakistani accent, “Everyone! Walk up onto the podium, sit down, and keep quiet, and no one gets hurt! Put your phones and guns on the floor at the front of the synagogue, where I can see them!”

He pointed to the cantor with his rifle and said, “You! Go to the entrance and lock the main doors! Now! If you aren’t back in one minute, someone will die!” The cantor went running, head bowed, to the front door to obey the command.

He pointed the rifle at Rabbi Mastowitz and said, “You! Pick up one of these phones, dial 911 and tell them what is happening here. Count the number of Jews that I have taken hostage to share.”

Within 10 minutes, the synagogue had attracted the attention of every police car on duty in the city bringing the grand total to two, emergency lights flashing brilliantly.

* * *

9:33 AM | September 5, 2020 | White Dress Ranch, Greyhill, Texas

Wendell stood next to Carly, OctaJoe, and Lilith in the hotel’s common area, watching the live news feed of the synagogue hostage situation as it unfolded.

As soon as he heard the Rabbi’s name, he looked at Lilith and said, “Lilith, as the owner of the Scroll, I command you to remain on the White Dress Ranch property. I know Rabbi Matsowitz from rabbinical seminary. We’re going to send OctaJoe on this mission, and we are going to try to keep this under the radar, if at all possible. We don’t need your face on TV.”

She became silent and nodded to Wendell.

“Carly, can I borrow your truck?” Wendell asked.

Carly replied, "You're not going to like what I'm going to tell you, but we don't have time to argue. You can borrow the truck, but I'm driving. I know exactly where that synagogue is, and we're only about five miles away."

"Fine. Let's get a bale of hay and OctaJoe," Wendell said, reluctantly.

Ross rushed outside to the truck. Nearby was a covered pile of hay. He uncovered one of the bales, grabbed it and tossed it up into the bed of the F150 Texas Edition pickup truck.

"OctaJoe, show yourself!" yelled the rabbi.

The golem had flattened himself against the sand, pebbles, and dried grass and created the appropriate texture and colors needed to render himself nearly invisible against the ground features. On command, his skin immediately changed to a beige-mottled surface, and he rose from the ground and reformed into a very large clay figure with four tentacles, two arms, and two legs.

"OctaJoe, get in the back of the pickup and hide yourself there," Wendell said.

OctaJoe leaped up into the back of the pickup and camouflaged himself to have the appearance of another three bales of hay next to the one that Ross had thrown aboard.

Wendell jumped into the passenger seat and put on a cowboy hat and sunglasses. Carly started the engine, spinning the wheels on the gravelly surface. Ten minutes later, they arrived near the rear of the synagogue, but due to the police presence, they were forced to remain about a quarter of a mile away.

Wendell jumped out of the pickup and spoke to the bales of hay, "OctaJoe, as the owner of the Scroll, I command you to do your best to remain concealed as you free the hostages in the synagogue. Don't allow anyone to get hurt or killed with the exception of the gunman."

The bales of hay became taller, and his eyes protruded upward from his Gumbie-like face as OctaJoe looked around to ensure that he was out of sight from anyone save for Wendell and Carly. Wendell opened the rear tailgate and OctaJoe poured himself out of the truck, flowing under the truck and moving swiftly low across the ground, camouflaging himself as he moved, first across the side of a brick house, then over a green, grassy yard, then along a wooden privacy fence. His colors and texture changed to match the background almost perfectly as he went.

Wendell and Carly lost sight of the golem as he moved quickly through a field of dry grass but picked up blurry movements as he entered the rear parking lot, where police were actively staged behind their vehicles with weapons drawn and pointed towards the synagogue. Slowly but steadily, he inched his way towards and then up the synagogue wall, eventually flowing onto the roof of the building.

He pressed his ear against the roof and made out the voice of the Pakistani antisemite. Continuing to use his camouflage as part of the roof, he flowed to the point where the sound of the voice was loudest. He estimated correctly that it would be difficult to break through the roof without loss of hostage lives. Maintaining his cover, he made his way to the edge of the roof, his suckers silently giving him stability on the sloping surface. An open window awaited him below, and he slowly flowed his way down the wall, through the window, matching his coloration and texture to the interior wall of the synagogue.

Wendell, meanwhile, had taken a seat back inside the truck, leaned his seat back and was watching everything progress through OctaJoe's eyes, courtesy of his connection to the Scroll.

Soundlessly, OctaJoe made his way to the floor, then across the carpet under the pews, and finally to just behind the Pakistani. OctaJoe rose slowly to his full height behind the kidnapper, continuing his efforts to confuse the hostages via camouflage as he arose. Soon, however, the puzzled looks on the faces of the hostages caused the Pakistani to turn around, also presenting a puzzled look.

For Ahmed, however, it was too late. As he struggled to understand what he was seeing, OctaJoe snatched the AK-47 from the hands of Ahmed, and bent it in half, tossing it to the side. The golem then grabbed Ahmed using his tentacles and tossed him across the room, breaking his neck against the brick wall. OctaJoe dropped back onto the carpet and quickly retraced his path back out of the open window. Retracing his path back to the truck, he flowed back into the bed of the truck and resumed his camouflage as four bales of hay.

Carly drove the speed limit back to the ranch.

* * *

10:40 AM | September 5, 2020 | White Dress Ranch, Greyhill, Texas

Wendell and Carly watched the live interviews of several of the congregation. An attractive brunette described the rescue as being a miracle from God, and that the rescuer was a very tall figure who wore some sort of super camouflaging suit, making him very difficult to see at any point in time. An elderly gentleman with glasses and a goatee suggested that the rescuer had surprised the hostage-taker – and in fact surprised everyone – so much that he wasn't even able to shoot his weapon before the rescuer had bent the gun barrel. This feat alone seemed to indicate that the rescuer had superhuman powers.

Finally, Rabbi Mastowitz weighed in by saying that whoever the unknown and incredible rescuer was, 32 people owed him their lives that day, because that man had the "hatred of a demon in his eyes and was only moments from shooting them all." The hostage taker was not being swayed by the efforts of the rabbi to make the congregation look like helpless people worthy of his compassion, as he was taught to do in a recent training course that he had taken, and in fact, the gunman was only becoming angrier and more aroused as they attempted to mollify him.

As the interviews concluded, Ross said, "Not that we would have done anything different, but I think that our cover was just blown wide open."

"I think that you are correct, Ross, though you've got to admit that in spite of that, OctaJoe probably couldn't have done any better staying out of the limelight," he said with obvious pride. "Do you think that they'll leave us alone?"

"Not a chance," Lilith said.

"By the way, please accept my apologies for ordering you around, Lilith. OctaJoe's expendable and you're not," Wendell said.

"I'm quite happy to stand back and cheer OctaJoe on from the sidelines. I'm glad that the Scroll is putting decisions like that into your hands lately. Do we need to go on the run again?" Lilith asked.

"Not as long as we've got Wendell making super golems for us," Carly said.

"We shouldn't underestimate these guys," Ross said. "They've got deep pockets, mercenaries, and military grade technology."

"That's not what worries me..." Wendell said.

49

WOLF IN SHEEP'S CLOTHING

4:05 PM
September 7, 2020
White Dress Ranch, Greyhill, Texas

Anatoly Dezhnyov drove his rental car up the driveway of the White Dress Ranch with his new bride, Katarina Dezhnyov, or at least that's what they planned on saying. The couple got out of their Kia Telluride, put on surgical masks, and strolled into the main lobby. Anatoly was middle-aged, pudgy, short, and balding with brown hair and brown eyes and an air of abundant calmness. He wore a dark blue Cuban shirt with two large beige vertical stripes – one on each side of the shirt – khaki pants, sunglasses, and a straw fedora hat with a narrow rim, and narrow blue band.

These were all tools that Anatoly used to compensate for his disfigured face, which was a completely different story. Horrible burn scars projected from underneath his surgical mask, across his eyes, over his forehead and about halfway up across his skull. His left ear was completely missing, replaced by mottled scarring. The flames had effectively removed all of the hair in the scarred areas, including both of his eyebrows, and about four inches into his hairline, beginning from over his right eye to behind his left ear. Anatoly's left eye was now made of glass, the color matching his right eye, but never blinking. Underneath the surgical mask, about 1/3 of his nose was completely missing, and his lips were severely deformed.

In complete contrast, Katarina was a young, attractive brunette with blue eyes, wearing short khaki shorts with a cuff, dark brown sandals and a red low-cut shirt tied in the middle to reveal both a generous cleavage and a slim midriff. Katarina also wore a pair of dark, oversized sunglasses, occasionally peeking over the rim as though to ensure that she was being properly appreciated by all who might be within eyeshot.

Mark, the host, saw the couple approaching the glass entry doors. This provided him with the opportunity to react with an uncomfortable, involuntary grimace before they saw him. He recovered quickly as he greeted the couple warmly at the desk, "Welcome to the White Dress Ranch, y'all. This is our hotel lobby. Would you care to check in for the evening?"

"Da, I mean, yes, we would like check in," Anatoly said.

"If you could provide me with your driver's license and a valid credit card, that'll get us started, sir. Would you prefer a honeymoon cottage, a regular room or a honeymoon suite?" Mark asked. "Ah, thank you . . . Mr. Dezhnyov. Am I saying that correctly?"

"Let me see, what is colorful saying here in the USA? Close enough for hand grenades and horseshoes? Where do most guests staying during pandemic?" Anatoly asked.

"Well, thanks to the pandemic, and our off-the-beaten-trail location, we only have a few rooms booked at the moment, so the hotel is pretty much yours for the taking," Mark said.

"Then nothing too good for beautiful new wife – Katarina!" exclaimed Anatoly with a flourish in her direction. "We become married two days ago, in Austin, Texas, at Maria's Ridge. We read it won beauty award online."

"Perhaps room away from other guests? Honeymoon can be loud, if know what I mean?" Anatoly said with a wink.

"Well, congratulations to you both," Mark said, wincing internally at the mental image. "How many nights will you be staying?"

"One night, then off to next location," Anatoly said. "By the way, please excuse Katarina's silence, she still learns English."

"Here are your keys. You are both now booked in the VIP Honeymoon Suite. Check out time tomorrow is 11 AM. The restaurant has a delicious dinner menu and a hearty breakfast buffet, and it's located just down the hallway to your right." Mark said.

The couple walked back to their car and picked up a few roller bags. Katarina opened hers in the trunk and pulled out a Nikon digital single lens reflex camera and took pictures of the front of the hotel, the stables, the chapel and the honeymoon cottages. She then slung the camera over her shoulder and she and Anatoly made their way back into the hotel and up to their room.

Once they were in the room with the door locked, Anatoly and Katarina began to speak in Russian.

"I can't believe that I missed the fact that the husband had a sister here in Texas! I feel like I'm beginning to lose my investigative edge, Katarina. Not to worry, they basically broadcasted where their golem was described by witnesses on national TV from the Jewish hostage rescue," Anatoly said.

"Don't be so hard on yourself. It only took three months for you to find them. The sister has insulated them from detection until now by keeping them off the grid," Katarina said.

"I suppose. We have a busy evening ahead. We will go down to the restaurant at about 5:30 and then settle in for a few hours. If they are staying here with his sister, then that is when we are most likely to see them. If you do see them, be sure to discreetly take photos of them, perhaps using the guise of us wanting a picture of each other while having them clearly in the background," Anatoly said.

"Of course. Whatever you want, my 'handsome husband,'" Katarina continued sarcastically in Russian.

"Very funny. I don't pay you for your sense of humor, but I do intend to make some noises later this evening. Hopefully, we might even disturb the other guests," Anatoly said.

"If you pay me just a little extra, I'll make *sure* that we disturb the other guests," Katarina said seductively.

"Hasn't your Papochka fattened your bank account enough to get whatever he needs from you?" Anatoly asked.

"Yes, Papochka, but your little Devochka loves money."

"Fine. Let's get to work. Take some pics of anything that might be of use from these windows. They should provide a reasonable vantage point. Launch a drone out of the window, as well, and make sure that you get photos of the inside of each room where the curtains are open. I want to find that Scroll. These folks should have no objections to a drone from a couple of honeymooners, though hovering at the windows might seem a bit creepy. Oh well, what is the American saying? 'You have to break a few eggs to make an omelet.'"

Continuing in Russian, Anatoly said, "After you finish with those items, let's go for a walk to see what or who we find wandering around or working on the property, but we have to be done with our walk by about 5:15 PM, so you'll need to hustle with the window shots and the drone photos."

The sound of a shutter clicking came from behind Anatoly, and then a window opened. Anatoly turned to see a drone rising from the floor and then buzzing quietly out of the window over the property. After 10 minutes of drone activity, the drone returned through the window and landed on the floor.

The two "honeymooners" took the elevator down the 4 floors to the lobby and walked casually outside towards the chapel. Nothing seemed too unimportant for them to photograph – the chapel, the horse stables, the number of horses in the corral, the inside of the chapel, the honeymoon cottages, and the rear of the chapel, where they found a blue tarp held down by a rock. Unfurling the tarp, they photographed the interesting and somewhat worse-for-wear clay silhouette, though still clear enough to allow them to make out the size and shape of the figure that had been sculpted. After taking these photos, they folded the tarp and replaced it under its rock.

A few minutes later, the couple had drinks and dined by a set of windows with an excellent view of the hills. Around 6:30 PM, the Newmans, Rabbi Rosenburg and Carly met for dinner at their usual spot, where three tables had been pushed together to allow them to eat together if they wished. The Russian couple took individual photos of each other with the group clearly visible in the background of each photo. Then Anatoly put his arm around Katarina and walked by the family's table saying something to her quietly in Russian.

The couple stopped on the opposite side of the group at the table and again, each took a photograph of the other, trying to get all of the faces captured at the table.

Politely, Brian stood up and said, "Would you like for me to take a photo of the two of you together?"

Anatoly replied, "That very nice of you. Da, please. Thank you."

Back in the room, Anatoly pulled Brian's fingerprints from the camera to provide forensic evidence in the event that it might be needed. The next morning, Anatoly sent photos of the ranch, the Newman family at dinner, Brian's fingerprints, the address of the White Dress Ranch and a clipping from the local newspaper with the story of the rescue of the Jewish hostages in the synagogue to Eva Fischer via email. What he neglected to send was the photo of the inside of Rabbi Rosenburg's third floor room from outside his window, complete with a view of the Scroll laying on his nightstand.

"Katarina, go down and make sure that the rabbi is still engaged with dinner and then come back. We have a Scroll to steal," Anatoly said. "We may have to leave our things here to make a hasty exit."

A few minutes later, Katarina returned to their fourth-floor room. In Russian, she said, "The rabbi, his girlfriend and the Newmans are just beginning dessert. We have about 15 minutes."

"Let's assume seven minutes, just to be safe. Here is your crowbar and lockpicking kit. Let's get down there, quickly!" Anatoly replied in Russian.

Exiting the elevator on the third floor and based upon the location of the drone when the photo of the room was taken, the two followed the sign to room 308. Katarina unzipped her lockpicking kit as they approached the door, and wasted no time, kneeling in front of the door handle and inserting a pair of picks into the lock. In under a minute, the door opened, and the two entered the room.

Anatoly walked quickly to the nightstand and grabbed the Scroll.

In Russian, he said, "Shit! This thing is scalding!"

As he dropped the Scroll on the bed the bedspread began to smolder where the Scroll was touching the fabric, releasing thin trails of gray smoke.

Carly entered the room and said, "What the hell are ya'll doing in Wendell's room? You two Russian scumbags need to get the hell out of my hotel and off my property, now, before I call the police!"

As Carly said the word "police", Katarina lifted a small handgun and pointed it at Carly's head. She walked quickly across the room to Carly as she raised her hands and removed the handgun from her shoulder holster, tossing it in a corner of the room.

In Russian, she said, "Get that Scroll in a pillowcase and let's get the hell out of here!"

Katarina then grabbed Carly's wrist and twisted it hard behind her back with her left hand while pressing the gun to her ear.

At that moment, Wendell stepped into the frame of the door.

Anatoly looked into Wendell's eyes with his last functioning eye and quietly said, "Step out of room. Now. Quietly. Don't want gun going off into pretty girl's head, correct?"

Wendell saw the gun pressed against Carly's head and nodded, backing out of the room as Anatoly wrapped a towel around his hands, grabbed the Scroll and shoved it unceremoniously into a pair of pillowcases, which began to release a thin stream of smoke.

"Don't follow us," Anatoly said to Wendell.

Katarina led Carly, with her left arm painfully twisted behind her back, down the fire escape stairs with Anatoly behind her streaming a thin stream of gray smoke from the white pillowcase. The pillowcase was beginning to brown near the bottom.

Finally, they reached the bottom of the stairs on the ground floor and Katarina roughly pushed Carly against the crossbar of the exit door, then through the door next to the main entrance to the hotel. The threesome walked quickly onto the asphalt of the circular driveway in front of the hotel and made their way towards the parking lot. A shot rang out from the direction of the hotel and Katarina's forehead exploded right next to Carly's cheek. Katarina slumped down onto the asphalt, dropping the pistol. Carly screamed loudly and ran away from the dead Russian.

Ross was perched in the third-floor window over the hotel entrance with his 30-ought-6 rifle. Lilith leapt from the hotel window down to the asphalt and bounded towards Anatoly, then stopped just as she reached him, concerned about damaging the Scroll. She raised her hand to shoot Anatoly with poisonous fibrils, but her hand froze in mid-air, fibrils dropping to the ground from her hand in front of her.

"No!" Lilith yelled and then composed herself with some difficulty.

"Today is not your day to die, Anatoly," Lilith said, spitting the name of the man from her lips with contempt.

"Give me the Scroll or . . . I beat you to within an inch of your life, and then I *take* the Scroll from your nearly lifeless fingers," Lilith said.

"How I know you won't kill me when you get Scroll, golem girl?" Anatoly asked.

"For some reason, the Scroll won't *let* me kill you, though I'm not sure why. But it's not discouraging me from *hurting* you, assuming you take this limited time offer to give me the Scroll, take your dead 'fiance', get in your car and never let me see your face again," Lilith said. "If you do these things, quickly, I will let you go unharmed. Five. . . Four. . . Three. . . Two. . ."

"OK! You have deal! Here is Scroll!" exclaimed Anatoly.

The Russian handed the Scroll to Lilith, then dragged Katarina's body to his rental car and placed her in the trunk, leaving a trail of blood on the asphalt. Then he got in the car and drove away.

Later, Ross Lilith asked, "Why do you think that the Scroll wouldn't let you kill him?"

Her reply, "I don't know, Ross, but the Scroll was very clear about its desire to let him live."

* * *

10:28 AM | SEPTEMBER 8, 2020 | WHITE DRESS RANCH, GREYHILL, TEXAS

Ross was angered and disturbed by the email sent through the hotel WiFi to Eva Fischer from Anatoly Dezhnyov. Unknown to his sister, Carly, he had set up software to copy, but not interrupt, incoming and outgoing emails from guests, believing that the day would come when someone would come looking for them. That day had arrived, nearly costing Carly her life, and it raised the urgency of their preparations to a new level.

He sent a group text message to his family, Carly and Wendell that read, *Family meeting at noon in the small conference room. Bring your lunch with you. I have important news.*

Ross was sitting in a chair near the front of the conference room eating a turkey sandwich with his laptop open as everyone arrived.

"Thank you all for interrupting your day to join me at this meeting. I have a confession and some bad news," Ross began.

"Carly, first the confession. Soon after we got here, I began looking at guest emails going out of the hotel, to make sure that we weren't being spied upon or compromised," Ross said.

"Ross Newman! What the hell were you thinking? I could be shut down if someone discovers that and reports it to the authorities. I could lose my business and my reputation!" exclaimed Carly.

"I realize that, and I have been very careful to avoid detection, and I permanently delete everything after I review it. Also, I sincerely apologize to you Sis for doing this behind your back. By doing so, I was giving you plausible deniability if I was caught. Unfortunately, yesterday, my subterfuge provided us with some very bad news. Yesterday, the Russian 'honeymooners' that stayed here reported our location to Eva Fischer," Ross said.

"Oh, dear God, no," Lilith whispered.

"They sent pictures of OctaJoe's tarp, our family around the table at dinner, Brian's fingerprints from when he used their camera, drone photos of the ranch layout, photos of the various buildings on the property, your vehicles, the horses, the layout of the interior of the hotel, and a clipping from the local newspaper with the story of the rescue of the Jewish hostages in the synagogue," Ross said. "I'm guessing the newspaper clipping and the national news reporting of the camouflage-suit-wearing, super strong man that killed the gunman holding hostages in a synagogue probably prompted them to fly down here and begin snooping around."

Wendell said, "We're going to have to move faster with our plan."

"Much faster," Ross said.

50

GRENADE ENGINEERS

9:37 AM
September 9, 2020
White Dress Ranch, Greyhill, Texas

Ross, Brian, and Wendell inspected the prototype for their "sticky grenade." It was a 17 oz transparent plastic flask – relatively flat and narrow and similar to those used to hide whiskey in one's clothing – filled with black gunpowder. A hole was drilled through the top of the lid, and through this hole a small spark generator had been inserted. The spark generator was connected to the leads from a burner cell phone's vibrator, which was activated by calling the unique number of the cell phone. The entire apparatus was wrapped with plastic wrap and inserted into an extra-long athletic sock.

A handle was fashioned at the end opposite the toe of the sock by wrapping that end with colored masking tape, making the entire sticky bomb about two feet long, while the bomb itself was only about 6 inches long. The color of the masking tape indicated the phone number to be called to activate the sticky bomb, which was entered into each of the three grenadier's cell phones under "Color-blue" or "Color-green", etc. A simple search for the term "color" in the phone would find them all, ready for a push of the call button to activate.

Finally, a very tacky industrial adhesive had been applied to the exterior of the sock. A YouTube video showed a worker applying the adhesive to a large brick followed immediately by pushing the brick against a wall. The 20 lb brick instantly stuck to the wall and did not budge after the worker released it. However, in order to prevent the adhesive from drying out or curing prior to the need to stick it to an enemy, the three amateurs placed the sticky grenade inside a plastic bag, pushing all of the air out and sealing it with a small metal tie. To use the device, the user grabbed the handle, removed the tie, pealed the grenade out of the bag by the handle and threw the sticky grenade where they needed destruction to occur. The bomb adhered to the surface was then detonated by a cell phone taped to either Lilith's forearm or from the phone of Ross, Wendell or Brian. To protect against accidental scam calls or misdials while in storage, the shade-tree explosives engineers were storing each grenade in a Faraday bag - $13.95 each from Amazon.

"Well, what do you think? Is it going to work?" Wendell asked.

"It's a little clunky to use and there is some delay pealing the grenade out of the bag," Brian said.

"I think you're probably right, but we don't have access to real grenades. I'm also concerned that the adhesive will cure while it's wrapped in the plastic," Wendell said. "Let's store one of them and test it in a week or so just to be sure."

"I want to test the adhesive with a rock in the sock, first, so we don't mess it up on the first throw," Ross said.

"Sounds like a nice first step before we ruin a burner phone and a grenade," Wendell said.

Ross slipped a flat rock into one of the extra-long athletic socks, taped off the top of the sock with generous length of green tape, and slathered adhesive out of the Constructo Super Tack Adhesive bucket using an old paint brush onto both sides of the sock. "Sticky grenade prototype X1. Brian, you're up," Ross said.

The shade tree grenade engineers had assembled several blast test dummies using chicken wire and hay stuffing with an exterior layer of clay. The dummies were shaped like simple chest-sized cylinders mounted on poles to speed up the testing process. Brian grabbed the purple tape handle of the X1 prototype and began swinging it around his head in a circle, running towards one of the stuffed clay dummies. As he ran past, he let the sticky grenade wrap itself around the dummy and kept running. It wrapped around the blast test dummy and remained stuck, with very little movement.

"Woo hoo! One blast test dummy down!" Brian exclaimed.

"Yeah, but how hard is it to remove?" Ross said, as he slipped his hands into a pair of nitrile gloves.

He grabbed the masking tape handle and pulled. It was possible, but the adhesive resisted removal from the dummy leaving long strings of rubbery polymer as it pulled away, delaying the ability of the subject to avoid damage from the grenade. It was very close to what they were hoping for.

"Now it's time to test the Sticky Grenade prototype X2 and blow one of these blast test dummies up!" Ross said with a grin on his face.

Ross put his Bluetooth earpiece in his ear and dialed Brian's phone number.

Brian slid his finger across the screen. "We're connected, Dad."

"Yes, I can hear you fine on my end. Can you hear me, ok?"

"You're good to go," Brian said.

"Gentlemen, don your face shields and take cover." Ross proclaimed in his best NASCAR announcer voice, as he pulled on his plastic, protective face shield. Wendell and Brian followed suit and stepped around the corner of one of the honeymoon suites for cover. "I'll be using Green for this test!" Ross said.

Ross grabbed the green masking tape handle of the sticky grenade wrapped in a plastic bag. He untwisted the small metal tie and pulled the sock out of the bag, holding onto the bomb portion at the bottom of the bag until the sock stretched out to its full length. Casting the plastic aside, Ross began swinging the grenade and ran towards the same test dummy Brian had used earlier, slapping the sock around the cylindrical dummy as he continued to run by, shouting, "Green is a Go!"

Brian's phone was on speaker, and once Wendell heard Ross' signal, he pressed the call button on his phone for the Color Green. Wendell and Brian watched the phone's screen as it dialed, and then they heard a loud BOOM, followed by the sound of pieces of chicken wire mixed with clay falling through a cloud of disintegrated hay.

"Woo hoo!" Brian yelled, giving Wendell a high five.

"Dad, are you ok?" Brian spoke into his phone. "Dad?"

Wendell and Brian looked at each other with alarm and ran around the corner of the honeymoon cottage, noting that one of the windows had been broken by the blast. Ross lay still on the ground, face down about 25 feet from the blasted dummy, of which little remained. Smoke was clearing from the area as the two ran to his side. Blood was dripping from the back of his shoulder and a variety of red spots dotted the back of his shirt. His Bluetooth earpiece lay on the ground about 10 feet away.

"Dad! Dad! Are you OK?" exclaimed Brian.

Wendell felt for a pulse in Ross' neck and held his hand in front of his mouth and nose to check for breathing.

"He's alive and breathing," Wendell said.

He then examined the largest wound on his back. A small wad of chicken wire was stuck under the skin.

"Ungh," moaned Ross.

"Dad?" Brian asked.

Ross lifted his head, then slowly rolled himself over with a little help from Wendell.

He removed his face shield, coughed and wheezed and said, "Slipped on some loose gravel. Blast hit me from behind as I got back up to run away. Knocked the wind out of me."

Thankfully, after a few minutes, Ross was nearly back to normal save for some ringing in his ears and a headache.

"Brian, would you please escort your dad back to the hotel and see if you can get your mom to clean him up and pull out all those slivers of chicken wire?" Wendell said.

"Absolutely. Take it slow, Dad," Brian said, as they walked back to the hotel.

After they left, Wendell examined the blast test dummy. Chicken wire, lumps of clay and small pieces of hay, sock, cell phone and plastic flask were strewn in a circle around the pole to which the blast test dummy was originally strapped with nylon zip ties.

"What were we thinking? We should have waited for Ross to take cover prior to calling the grenade. I could have killed him," Wendell whispered under his breath.

51

ORINA

8:20 PM
October 16, 2020
IDS Synagogue, Outside of Tel Aviv, Israel

The first IDS synagogue was still radiating heat from the day into the night air as the all-but-invisible new moon floated silently in the dark sky. The synagogue structure was erected at record speed using wood and a simple concrete foundation with no built-in utilities. In spite of its simplicity, the architecture was well-suited for the purpose – a square building with a three-dimensional star of David filling most of the roof of the two-story structure.

Printed vinyl windows substituted for stained glass windows on the walls and over most of the six-sided star. The interior temperature was controlled by mobile air conditioning units. Power was supplied by mobile generators. Water was supplied by a large truck outside and port-a-potties sufficed for bathrooms.

Legion and Ivan watched from a small viewing area as two men wearing odor masks fitted with an activated carbon cartridge on one side brought in a gurney containing a beige body bag. They carefully lifted the body bag onto a table covered with a shiny golden-metallized table covering. Six more of these covered tables glinted under the hastily installed overhead lights on the periphery of the circular platform below the giant star of David above them. A circular table in the center of the platform was also covered with the golden metallized film. Upon the circular table lay the partially unrolled copy of the Scroll with grey parchment, red letters and sparkling purple marginalia. Ivan closed his eyes and massaged his temples with his fingers as the men unzipped the body bag.

"Tell me when they are done placing Orina's body onto the table. I can't watch this," Ivan said.

"Of course, Ivan. They are being respectful and gentle," Legion said with his strange, multi-tonal voice. "They are done."

Ivan opened his eyes and looked down onto his dead wife's body in the early stages of decomposition lying on the table. "Dear God! Are you sure that this will work for Orina? She will be like she was before?" Ivan asked.

"Don't forget, it worked very well for Lilith Newman. I don't need to remind you that Ross Newman was so enamored with his reanimated Lilith that he ended up killing Orina to rescue her," Legion said.

"Don't even mention that bastard Newman's name in connection with my wife! I want that man's head on a platter to give to my precious Orina as a gift when she is back in my arms again," Ivan said.

"Dare I say that Orina might enjoy helping you fulfill that wish?" Legion replied.

"She would indeed," Ivan said.

Legion continued, "And don't forget that *they* didn't even have her actual body! They used the ashes remaining from her cremation! And not to toot my own horn, but your copy of the Scroll worked quite well for *me*. In fact, I ended up being *far* more capable and intelligent than the Gumbie animatron that I was intended to be. I have every confidence that this will work for your Orina," Legion said.

Rabbi Volozhin, also wearing a rubber odor mask, entered the IDS synagogue and walked to Orina's table, giving instructions to the two men who had brought her in and offering them a large pair of scissors, a bucket of water and several towels. They looked at each other, then looked up and Ivan.

"What's going on?" Ivan asked.

"The rabbi has asked them to cut her clothing away from her body so that the items don't contaminate the formation process. She also needs to be washed," replied Legion. Ivan thought that Legion almost had an eager, hungry look on his face, like a man watching the beginning of a strip club dance.

Ivan was disgusted by his dangerous ally and struggled not to react in anger. He often wondered where this collaboration with Legion would ultimately take him, and at what price.

Ivan spoke loudly to the men below, who looked doubtful, "Please proceed with the rabbi's instructions. This is necessary for the ritual."

As the men turned to the task of cutting away Orina's rotting clothing, the rabbi climbed the stairs to where Ivan and Legion were sitting, pulling his odor mask off as he came near.

"How can we help you, Rabbi Volozhin?" Ivan asked.

"I'm need you to leave the property for the night, Mr. Sokov," the rabbi said.

Ivan's face flushed red as he stood up, poked his index finger into Rabbi Volozhin's chest and said, "I will sit right here and watch every moment as you bring my wife back to life!"

"Then I cannot conduct the ritual," Rabbi Volozhin said. "There are things that we need to do tonight to Orina's body that you will find difficult to watch. If I have a synagogue with you as a distraction, I could make mistakes. If I make mistakes, you will not be happy with either me or the end result. You of all people, should know that we are all trying our absolute best to bring her back to you. Your presence is intimidating to both your team below and to me. You have done everything you could do to help us – you've provided a pint of your own blood, Legion has somehow acquired a man's rib by means I do not wish to know, and you've exhumed Orina's body. There is nothing more that you can do for Orina tonight, with the exception of going home. The Almighty willing, she will be here for you tomorrow morning."

As Ivan listened, his demeanor softened. He thought for a moment and then said, "Orina is in your hands, Rabbi Volozhin. Take good care of her. I'll be back at 7:30 tomorrow morning." Then he walked down the stairs, got into his car and drove off into the night.

* * *

7:23 AM | October 17, 2020 | IDS Synagogue, Outside of Tel Aviv, Israel

Ivan's Black Porsche 911 GT3 growled onto the gravel parking lot of the IDS synagogue and parked near the entrance, leaving a cloud of dust dissipating in the warm gentle morning breeze. Ivan nervously stepped out of the vehicle and walked into the synagogue. Rabbi Volozhin was waiting for Ivan just inside the door.

"Was the ritual successful?" Ivan asked.

"Yes, yes it was! She is still foggy, mentally, but Legion has been very helpful in helping her recover. I should also prepare you for her appearance," the rabbi said.

Ivan impatiently stepped past the rabbi towards where Legion was seated, his back turned towards him. As he approached, he saw Orina sitting naked across from Legion, her eyes looking blankly at the floor.

"Orina?" Ivan said. "Orina, are you alright?"

Orina raised her head and met Ivan's gaze. Her hazel eyes were no longer hazel, but grayish green. Her skin was no longer tanned, but gray, and similar in color and shade to Legion's. Blood red Hebrew letter tattoos covered her body. She did not respond to Ivan's question but seemed drugged and disoriented, her eyes glazed.

Legion responded gently with his crowd of voices, "Ivan, you may need to be patient with her awakening. Thanks to Rabbi Volozhin, the ritual was conducted perfectly in every respect. Recall that we talked about how the use of her entire dead body would undoubtedly yield an excellent reproduction of Orina, including her memories. But you must also remember that this approach might cause a lengthening of the time during which the new body is healing and knitting together. I'm certain that this is what is happening to her now. Let's see if she will eat or drink something, then put her to bed to rest and recover for a day or two?"

"Rabbi, get me the overnight bag that I brought for her yesterday. Legion, please get her something to eat and drink next door at the cafeteria while I get her dressed," Ivan said.

Legion gave Ivan a dark look at being asked to fetch something but rose from his seat and walked towards the cafeteria.

Ivan helped to get Orina dressed in some simple, but comfortable pajamas that she liked. As he was buttoning the last few buttons of her shirt, Legion entered with a breakfast tray from the cafeteria. There was fruit, cottage cheese, scrambled eggs and toast, along with orange juice and an espresso.

"Thank you, Legion. Soon, we will begin making soldiers," Ivan said.

"I have an operation tonight, but I trust that the rabbi will conduct himself well without the need for an observer. Won't you, Rabbi Volozhin?" Legion said.

"Of course, Legion. As always, I will do my best for both of you," the rabbi said.

"Who is the target for our new Dark Operations Division tonight?" Ivan asked.

"An Iranian spy in Tel Aviv – Ibrahim Nazim."

"Interesting. Isn't this the third one this month?" Ivan asked.

"Yes, but the other two were Hamas and Hezbollah operatives. This should be a relatively easy five hundred thousand shekels, or about $160,000 US dollars – and right down the street, so to speak," Legion said.

"You definitely have a mind for this business, Legion. I had completely ignored the services sector of the global military market," Ivan said.

"Well, first, you didn't have me to provide those services, and second, I have a relative who has been working in this area for a very long time," replied Legion.

* * *

1:23 AM | October 18, 2020 | Residence in Tel Aviv, Israel

The black Israeli Blitz electric motorcycle whined quietly up the deserted street traversing up a hill in the dimly lit neighborhood. The five-story apartment building had been constructed on the side of a stony hill, and Mr. Nazim's apartment on the 5th floor provided a beautiful view of the skyline of downtown Tel Aviv with the Mediterranean Sea as a backdrop. Legion wore a deep hooded jacket the same color as his skin to reduce the likelihood of having his face photographed by a security camera and thin leather gloves to avoid leaving fingerprints. He parked the bike in an alley next to a dumpster and began climbing up the side of the building, one terrace at a time. The apartments attached to the 1st and 2nd floor terraces were dark, with residents sleeping at this hour of the morning.

Light from the 3rd floor apartment, however, streamed outward and into the night from all of the windows. Legion lifted himself up and peeked through the patio door from just over the handrail. A young naked couple was making love on the couch, facing away from the patio. He watched for a moment with interest, then shimmied around the patio near the wall, where he was only visible from the lighted, vacant bedroom window, and continued his climb upwards. The 4th floor apartment was also dark.

Slipping over the railing of the 5th floor terrace, he peeked into the darkened apartment's living room through the floor-to-ceiling sturdy patio door. The living room contained two leather sofas and an easy chair, all with a view of the 60-inch flatscreen TV LED. Seeing no movement in the home and no security bar in use, he tried to slide the door open, but it was locked.

He pulled a sturdy flathead screwdriver from a pocket in his jacket and inserted the blade of the screwdriver under the sliding glass door at the bottom of the door under the metal frame and below the door handle. Using his right hand, he then levered the door upwards about half an inch with the screwdriver, raising the hook of the latch up and over the catch while he pulled the door open with his left hand. The door opened with an audible, but unavoidable, clunk. As quietly as he was able, he slid the door open and stepped into the apartment, leaving the screwdriver on the patio floor.

"Hello?" came a voice from an adjacent room. "Is someone there?"

Legion walked to the room from which the voice came. The door was cracked open slightly. He pushed the door inward and stepped into the small bedroom.

Bullets and flame erupted from a handgun held by a man sitting on the edge of the bed in the dark, hitting Legion squarely in the chest three times and briefly lighting up the dark room with each shot. Legion pounced on the man as he fired a fourth round, grabbing the gun and twisting until a satisfying crunch emitted from his wrist as the man yelled in pain. A woman next to the man began screaming, pulling the sheets up over her breasts. Legion pulled the gun from the man's hand, causing more screaming, and shot the woman in her left eye, causing her head to snap back against a bloodied bed board and pillow.

"I've made reservations for you at a table in Hell tonight, Ibrahim," Legion said, pulling the trigger one more time for a shot to his forehead.

Legion threw the gun on the bed and turned on the bedroom lights. Gray matter, blood and bits of skull and hair spattered the backboard. He looked at the gore with interest, reached out, pinched a piece of Ibrahim's brain between his thumb and fore finger and popped it into his mouth, chewing it and swirling it about with his tongue like a bit of foie gras at an expensive French restaurant.

"Surprisingly buttery and creamy, with a few strands, probably nerves. Interesting," he said.

After swallowing the piece of brain, he unzipped his black hoodie and looked inside at his chest in the mirror. One of the bullets had grazed his shem, leaving a nick in the silvery pendant. The bullet hole was nearly healed.

"Well, that was a little too close for comfort," he said to himself. "We really should do this whole shem thing a little differently."

He pulled out his phone and took a photo of the faces of both Ibrahim and the girl. A laptop rested on the nightstand next to where Ibrahim had been sleeping. Legion took the laptop, walked back onto the patio and looked at the night-time skyline of Tel Aviv, taking a deep relaxing breath of the fresh night air. He picked up the screw-driver and threw it about a 100 yards away from the building onto a deserted street. Cradling the laptop to his chest with his left hand, he leapt over the edge of the railing to the sidewalk, five-stories below. Police sirens wailed in the distance as Legion mounted his electric motorcycle and rode off into the night.

52

AN UNWELCOME VISITOR, SOLDIERS, AND A DRUG DEALER

9:15 AM
October 18, 2020
White Dress Ranch, Greyhill, Texas

Sergeant Glen Mitchell of the Gillespie County Sheriff's Department parked his police truck in front of the main entrance of the White Dress Hotel. He reread the file describing the murder of Ahmed Bukhari, a Pakistani immigrant, and former resident of Greyhill, Texas. He thought that this was perhaps the strangest case he had ever investigated, straight out of the X-files or Twilight Zone – an anti-semitic Pakistani immigrant brings an AK-47 into a synagogue, takes 32 Jewish congregation members hostage, and before the police can even begin their response, some extremely well-camouflaged "thing" flows into the synagogue through the window, kills the gunman and then flows back out of the window. The witnesses said that the "thing" was so good at camouflaging itself, that they couldn't tell exactly what shape it was, though it apparently had tentacles.

The only other clue they had about the "thing" was that an elderly woman waiting for her dog to poo saw some "thing" "flow" into the bed of a white Ford F150 at which point the hay bales in the truck became visibly "larger". The driver of the truck, a white male, closed the tailgate and drove calmly away with a woman in the passenger's seat. The vanity license plate, according to the dog walker, appeared to spell something like "WH DRESS1". None of the details about the "thing" had been released to the press, but in Sergeant Mitchell's professional opinion, if you multiply the wagging tongues of 32 frightened hostages by about a thousand, that would approximate the number of folks who had heard about the "thing" at this point.

Sergeant Mitchell stepped out of his truck with a notepad clipped onto the surface of a Plexiglass board and walked over to the stables where a white Ford F150 truck was parked. There, on the rear license plate was printed "WH DRESS1". In the back of the truck was a single bale of hay. He stepped closer to the truck and examined the bed a little closer from the side of the truck.

"Howdy, Officer, how can I help you today?" Carly said.

The officer turned slowly to see an attractive, petite brunette dressed in white boots, jeans and a red checkered button up shirt. Her hair was pulled back in a ponytail.

"Good morning, Ma'am. I'm Sergeant Mitchell with the Sheriff's Department," he said.

"Nice to meet you, Sergeant Mitchell, I'm Carly Smythe. I own this ranch."

"Ms. Smythe, I'm hoping you might have time for a few questions this morning?" the officer said.

"Sure thing, Officer," Carly said.

The officer pulled his pen from his shirt pocket and held the clipboard firmly in his left hand. He looked at her through his mirrored sunglasses. "By any chance, were you in Greyhill on September 5th when that hostage situation at the synagogue occurred?"

"Let me think about that for a second," Carly said. "Hmmm, you know, I think we went downtown to pick up a few groceries that day."

"We? So, you were with someone else that day?" the officer asked.

"Yep. We had a down-on-his-luck drifter who stayed with us a few weeks. I paid him to do some maintenance work and let him eat in the restaurant while he was here. He was pretty handy with a shovel in those stables, I'll tell you that for sure," Carly replied. "He drove me into town that day and helped me carry the groceries."

"What was this gentleman's name, ma'am?" The sergeant asked.

"Hank Fokker. That man was one of the hardest working helpers I've ever had. I was real sorry to see him leave," Carly responded.

"I don't suppose you might have a photo of Hank or a copy of his ID, would you?" Mitchell asked.

"No sir, I don't usually take photos or require ID from the help," replied Carly.

Mitchell asked, "Do you recall stopping by the side of County Rd. 544 near the intersection of Sand Lake Road, with Henry that day?"

"As a matter of fact, we did stop there. He told me he was feeling sick to his stomach, and he pulled over, thinking he might puke. He didn't want to mess up the inside of my truck," she replied.

"Any reason he might have opened the tailgate during that time?" Mitchell asked.

"Yes sir, he wanted a place to sit while his stomach calmed down enough for him to drive again, so he sat on the back of the tailgate. That was the only problem that I did have with Hank – he hit my wine cellar pretty hard, if you know what I mean. Had a hangover or a stomach issue about half the time," replied Carly.

"So, you didn't see anything unusual climbing onto the bed of your truck?" The officer asked.

"No sir, what kind of unusual thing did you have in mind?" Carly replied.

The officer pulled off his reflective sunglasses, folded them and put them in his pocket. He locked his steely blue eyes with Carly's brown eyes. "The kind of unusual thing that might leave sucker marks on the floor of your truck bed. About the same size as the circular tracks we found near where your truck was parked," responded Sergeant Mitchell.

Carly could feel the man's gaze slicing through her deception.

Sergeant Mitchell waited, watching and listening for what sort of bullshit Carly would feed him next.

She regained her composure, turned and looked into the bed of the pick-up and said, "Well, I'll be! I wonder where those came from. Maybe someone's kids got in there playing with suction cup arrows or something?"

Sergeant Mitchell pulled out his phone and snapped a few photos of the circular marks in the bed of the pickup, and said, "Could be, I suppose. But if you know anything about a 'thing' that may have saved 32 hostages at the Greyhill synagogue on that day, I sure would like to thank them in person, because that 'thing', if it exists, is a genuine hero, as far as I'm concerned."

"Here's my card, Ms. Smythe. If you decide that you want to remember the events of that day a little differently, please give me a call," the sergeant said.

"I will, Officer. I surely will," Carly said.

* * *

4:23 PM | October 18, 2020 | White Dress Ranch, Greyhill, Texas

Ross hammered the last nail into the makeshift ladder leading to the bell tower of the chapel. The bells were relatively heavy, but OctaJoe made short order of carrying them down the ladder and storing them in a loft in the barn next to the stables. Ross had just completed the conversion of the bell tower into a sniper's nest.

The bell tower was about 4 stories tall – not the tallest structure on the ranch, but it commanded a view of nearly every part of the ranch with the exception of a blind spot on the opposite side of the hotel. Ross had secured rifle rests on each of the four sides of the tower. A trap door opened up into the bell tower and had been modified to bolt closed from inside the sniper's nest. Stained glass windows had been replaced by heavy steel bars bolted into the window frame to provide some semblance of protection to the sniper from the golems that they were expecting to defend against.

"Are you nearly done?" Wendell asked.

"I just finished the access ladder. The 30-ought-6 is up here in a waterproof case along with about 50 rounds," Ross replied.

"You really think that we're going to need 50 rounds to defend ourselves?" Wendell responded.

"I don't think that ammo will be the limiting factor. I'm worried that we're simply going to be overwhelmed by larger numbers and better equipped forces, some of which don't really care about bullets at all," Ross said.

"Then you should come take a peek at what I've been doing while you've been playing Bob Vila on *This Old Chapel*. I've been creating the White Ranch Army," Wendell said with a grin. "Come on, let me introduce you to our new friends from the golem factory."

The two men walked towards the barn. Along the way, Carly joined them, grabbing Wendell's hand as they walked. Ross gazed at the two of them as they walked and smiled, enjoying their contagious happiness at being a couple.

Wendell opened the barn door to find Lilith already inside.

"Hi, guys! I thought I'd swing by to take a look at my 'brothers.'"

"Interesting choice of words, honey," Ross said.

"Well, they are *sort of* my brothers," replied Lilith.

"Perhaps you should consider them distant relatives," Carly said.

"I see that you've made another OctaJoe," Ross said.

"His name is CamoRon. Get it?" Wendell said.

"Aarrrggghh," groaned Ross. "That is absolutely terrible!"

"Hey, it's a lot better than 'Squidward,'" Wendell said. "Brian simply refused to allow me to name him that."

"And does the giant feathered hawk actually fly?" Ross asked.

"Absolutely! And it is a beautiful thing to see," Lilith said.

"I'm going to regret asking, but what is *his* name?" Ross asked.

"MoeHawk," Wendell said.

"Aarrrggghh," groaned Ross again. "Does he have a friend named LarryByrd, or CurlyBird?"

"Ha! See! It's sort of fun, right?" Wendell replied.

"Holy crap!" Emily said, joining the review of the troops as she stared at the golem that looked horrifyingly like a giant wasp. "Does this one's stinger really work?" pointing to the next golem over.

"Language, young lady," Lilith said.

"Oops, sorry, Mom," Emily said.

"Yes, I got him to sting a javelina yesterday. Dead as a door nail in about 10 seconds," Wendell said.

"Serves those destructive bastards right – rooting up my potato plants and carrots last week," Carly said.

"Language, Sis," Ross said, wagging his finger at her with a smile.

"I suppose you're going to call this one 'Sting'?" Lilith asked.

"Exactamundo, dear Lilith!" the rabbi exclaimed, laughing.

"So, what I want to know is who's under the blanket over in the corner," Brian said, joining the inspection of the troops.

"Hi Brian, you are a little late to the party, but you've seen all but this one, anyway," the rabbi said. Wendell walked over to the corner and with a "Voila!" he theatrically whipped the sheet from over the golem.

"Whoa! He's scary." Brian said.

Ross pointed at the belly and chest of the golem. "Is that what I think it is?" he asked.

"When in Texas, do as the Texans," Wendell replied. "Yes, it is an armadillo crossed with a grizzly bear."

"Where on earth did you get a grizzly bear?" Lilith asked.

"One of Carly's nearby ranch neighbors is a hunter, and he had several stuffed grizzlies from an Alaska hunting expedition and some 6-year-old frozen grizzly meat in his freezer. The hunter passed away a few years ago and the wife is trying to pare the taxidermy collection down. We got the bear and the meat for $200. The armadillo – well, I'm not proud to say that he was taken from roadkill."

"That is the most Frankenstein-looking aggregation of animal parts I've ever seen," Ross said. "God help me for asking, but what's *his* name?"

"Bearmadillo," Wendell said.

"Wow. That one is terrible! What about Armagrizzly? Grizzadillo? I see what you mean, Bearmadillo is probably your best bet," Ross said. "Aside from the name, he looks really formidable."

"I hope so. Ok, the show's over for the moment. I need to talk privately to Lilith and Ross, so could the rest of you kindly give us the room?" Wendell asked.

Carly gave Wendell a puzzled look, but he shooed her out of the room with the rest of the family.

"What's the big secret, Rabbi?" Ross asked.

"So, we all remember when Eva and her IDS goons used tranquilizer darts to put us under. The interesting part is they were able to put *Lilith* down with those tranquilizer darts."

"You have a very good point, Wendell. Though I don't want to test it, I bet I could walk through the crossfire of a dozen commandos and, though it would hurt like hell, I would probably recover fairly quickly. On the other hand, the four tranquilizer darts that they used knocked me out for several hours," Lilith said.

"And this may be the edge we are looking for in any battle against a team of golems. That being said, we don't have access to the tranquilizer formulation that was in those darts. Nor do we have access to carfentanyl, which is also used as an elephant tranquilizer. What we *might* have access to is fentanyl, which is now commonly sold by drug dealers on the street, frequently blended with heroin, and 100 times more deadly than heroin," Wendell said.

"So, you'd like Lilith to buy some fentanyl from a drug dealer?" Ross asked.

"I suppose that is what I'm asking, Ross. I completely understand if you think that it's too dangerous for her. I'd use OctaJoe, but I think that the mission requires more mental firepower than he is carrying," Wendell said.

"Sounds fun!" Lilith said.

"Lilith, come on. I don't want you to risk being hurt by dangerous men," Ross said.

"Sweetheart, by now you know that a drug dealer armed with an AK-47 doesn't really represent a threat to me, right?" Lilith said.

"Well, when you say it that way, I'm not sure whether I should feel inadequate or turned on," Ross said.

"There is no reason whatsoever why I can't easily handle a drug dealer or two by myself, and this could give us a huge leg-up on any golems that IDS might throw at us. Any advantage we can acquire over a military hardware company might save the lives of our family," Lilith said.

"I can't argue with you on that. I suppose this also means that Carly will need to go shopping for tranquilizer guns," Ross said.

* * *

10:22 PM | OCTOBER 18, 2020 | GREYHILL, TEXAS

Lilith rode slowly down Mason Avenue in the White Dress Ranch Ford F150 pickup truck, which was, of course, white. The downtown portion of Mason Avenue was lined with stone and pole buildings with 'old west' styled facades. Signs for antiques, art, barbeque, saloons, and live music littered the well-lit tourist trap downtown area, with people strolling along the wooden sidewalks holding margaritas and beer in plastic cups. As she drove away from the downtown area, the avenue devolved away from carefully maintained and well-lit to dark, run down and littered.

She passed a small gas station containing a store where signs on the small building advertised lottery tickets and cigarettes and the price of gas was $2.27 per gallon. A man with torn, dirty jeans wearing an old AC/DC t-shirt slept propped up against the side of the building with a plastic bottle of whiskey.

She was looking for a drug dealer – one who preferably sold fentanyl, as pure as she could get, and as much as she could get. A little further, she passed the "Greyhill City Limit" sign, and then spotted a Hispanic man in an abandoned parking lot making an exchange with a black man dressed in a black hoodie. The overhead streetlights had long ago been shot out, rendering the parking lot quite dark. She parked the truck on the street nearby and waited until the client had exited the lot before she got out of her truck.

Also wearing a black hoodie with the hood over her head, Lilith walked confidently towards the man leaning against the gray lamppost and said, "First of all, are you a police officer?"

"Oye, coño blanca, you got some cojones walking onto my parking lot asking me a question like that. Who the fuck do you think you are?" The man replied, pulling a snub nose, 0.38 caliber revolver from the front of his pants and pointing it at Lilith.

"Don't you know it's bad for business to pull a gun on your customers?" Lilith asked as she snatched the man's wrist and pointed the gun away from her. The man pulled the trigger twice, raising a cloud of gravel and bits of asphalt, prompting Lilith to crush his wrist bone and pull the gun out of his hand. She opened the cylinder and dumped the remaining three 0.38 caliber bullets onto the parking lot, then threw the revolver across the lot into an alley.

"Ahhhhh! ¿Qué quieres, tu perra loca?!" the man yelled.

"Quiero que me digas si eres policía. ¿Comprende, amigo?" Lilith said.

"¡No! ¡No soy un maldito cop!" the drug dealer exclaimed.

"There. Now that I know that you are not a police officer, we can do some business," Lilith said. "Next time, just answer the simple question so you can avoid getting beat up by the next 'white cunt' that walks onto your parking lot."

"How much fentanyl can you get for me tonight?" Lilith asked.

The man was cradling his right wrist gingerly and moaning, but sensing a deal in the making, he said, "I can get you 250 birria pills later tonight."

"No. I'm not interested in fentanyl mixed with heroin. I want *pure* fentanyl in either pill or powder form, and I want 10 grams of the stuff," she replied.

"Are *you* a cop?" the dealer asked, angrily spitting out the word.

"No. I'm just a girl who will end you if you try to screw me over. I personally think that drug dealers are the scum of the earth, but tonight, it just so happens that I need one. Can you get me what I need, or should I look for another dealer on the other side of town?"

"I can get you that, gringa, but it will have to happen the night after tomorrow night. I don't keep that much on me."

"How much will it cost?"

"Twelve hundred dollars. Shit, bitch, why did you have to break my wrist?"

"Fine. I'll meet you here the night after tomorrow at 10:30 pm with the money. Be sure you bring me the 10 grams of fentanyl. Now, would you like a ride to the emergency room?"

53

ASTRAL PROJECTION TO TEL AVIV

1:05 AM / 9:05 AM
October 19, 2020
White Dress Ranch / IDS Tel Aviv Facility

Wendell woke with an involuntary jerk and turned his head to see if he had awakened Carly. She lay on her side, her head nearly covered by the light bedspread, snoring ever so lightly. He smiled at this and looked up into the moving blades of the ceiling fan. As he was closing his eyes to go back to sleep, his sight glazed over, and he briefly wondered if he was having a stroke, but as his vision refocused, he found himself floating near the ceiling in the corner of a conference room watching a scene play out beneath him. Eva Fischer was about to read a section of a newspaper article to four other people who sat in conference room chairs around a long table built for about 12 people.

The four other people were Eva, a man who the Scroll recognized as Ivan, and two golems, similar to Lilith, not Gumbies, but exquisitely formed golems, both grey in color with blood red tattoos. The final attendee was a rabbi – the name Rabbi Volozhin came to him.

On the table lay an open file containing photos, and a copy of their Sefer Yetzirah, their Scroll! The copy of the Scroll was unfurled slightly providing a view of a medium gray parchment with blood red lettering. He also saw that the marginalia were not sparkling, but a dull purple.

Eva Fischer began to read from the news clipping, "Rabbi Mastowitz said that the rescuer was essentially invisible due to some sort of camouflage technology that almost perfectly mimicked the background behind him. He was incredibly quiet and the only thing that alerted the hostage-taker to his presence was the puzzled looks on the faces of the congregation trying to figure out what or who was standing behind him. He turned around, and the still-camouflaged 'thing' snatched the assault weapon from his grasp and bent it in half. Then a tentacle came out of nowhere and threw the terrorist against a brick wall, instantly breaking his neck. The 'thing' then flowed out of the window almost perfectly camouflaged and out of sight," Eva said, as she stopped reading the article. "And this all happened in Greyhill, Texas, USA."

"So, they have a golem based on an octopus?" Orina asked.

Wendell hadn't recognized the gray colored, tattooed woman from his position in the corner, other than to note that she was a golem. The Scroll gave him the name of this woman.

"Orina!" Wendell tried to say, but then he realized that he was simply an observer from afar, and that the best description of his state at the moment was an astral projection. He knew he was somewhere near Tel Aviv in Israel, and that he was in an Israeli Defense Systems conference room. The fact that there was not one but two golems sitting around a conference room table could only mean that they now also have a formation Scroll, a fully functioning copy of the original!

"My private detective, Anatoly Dezhnyov, and his assistant tracked down Ross Newman's sister, Carly Smythe, and found that she owns a wedding destination ranch and hotel in Greyhill, Texas, in the heart of the Texas hill country," Eva said.

"Then Orina will soon have the opportunity to kill Ross Newman, preferably slowly," Ivan said.

"Yes, sir," Eva said.

Eva pressed a button on her laptop and the front screen lit up, showing a series of pictures taken by the private investigator.

When the photo of the tarp came up, Orina said, "Wait! Let me look at that one more carefully. See the clay residue shaped like tentacles and suckers coming from his sides?"

"But where the hell did that damned rabbi get a live octopus in Texas?" Ivan asked.

"It doesn't *have* to be alive. People *eat* dead octopus all the time," Legion casually replied in his usual multi-tonal voice.

Orina paused, thinking, then slowly said, "Well said, Legion, they must have used bottled octopus chunks."

* * *

1:20 AM | October 19, 2020 | White Dress Ranch, Greyhill, Texas

"Ross! Lilith! I can't wake Wendell. Please come quickly!" Carly said, as she pounded on Ross and Lilith's bedroom door.

"Copy that!" Ross yelled as he slid into his plaid pajama bottoms, and a short sleeve light blue T-shirt. Lilith responded in kind, but Ross beat her to the bedroom door.

"It's like he's had a stroke or something! He's breathing, his eyes are open, but he won't respond when I shake him," exclaimed Carly.

"Let's go," Ross said, walking quickly down the hall.

Upon entering the bedroom, Ross, Lilith and Carly looked at Wendell, who's eyes were open and moving around, but no other part of him was moving.

"Wendell? Wendell?" Ross said loudly, shaking him, but without response.

He reached down and pinched the rabbi in the upper arm, hard. Still no response from Wendell.

"How long has he been this way?" Ross asked.

"I'm not sure, I know that I slept through some of it. He woke me when he said something, and when I rolled over to check on him, he was like this."

"What did he say?" Lilith asked.

"Something like 'Orina,'" Carly replied.

"He's having a vision," Lilith said. "He's OK, but the Scroll may be showing him something."

"Where is the Scroll?" Ross asked.

"It's now in my gun safe in the closet," replied Carly. "Why do you need it?"

"If the marginalia are glowing red, then the Scroll has projected his consciousness somewhere else," Ross said. "If that's happening, he should be OK when the Scroll shows him what it wants him to see."

"Open the safe and let's take a look," Ross said.

Carly opened the drawer to her nightstand and pulled out a flesh-toned vibrator. "Well, that's not what I was looking for, damn it." It took every fiber of his being for Ross not to laugh, instead he channeled the laugh into a disguised cough. Even Lilith was looking at the ceiling with her hand over her mouth.

She put the vibrator back and turned on the lamp on the nightstand. This time she found what she was looking for – a 9-inch black Maglite flashlight. She clicked it on and walked quickly into the bedroom closet, where the gun safe was bolted to the wall from the inside of the safe. She punched in four numbers and turned the handle. The safe was about 6'x 3'x 3' and the open metal door revealed a large collection of guns and ammo. But in addition to all of this, the Scroll lay rolled up on a shelf near the top, and from between the gaps in the rolled parchment, a gentle red light shone.

Just to be sure, Ross carried the warm-to-the-touch Scroll back into the bedroom and unfurled it carefully on the floor. The marginalia clearly glowed red. Wendell continued to look out into the distance while moving his unfocused eyes.

Within a few minutes, Wendell's astral projection returned to his body and his vision returned to normal. He blinked several times and looked up to find Ross, Carly, Lilith and Brian bent over him with concerned looks on their faces.

"Welcome back," Ross said.

Carly bent down and kissed him on the lips and hugged him.

"Carly, please stop. Orina has been reformed! The IDS must have made a copy of the Scroll. She seemed sentient and 'normal' in her behavior, but, Ross, they want to come here and kill you slowly! There is another golem, also intelligent. His name is Legion, like the Legion mentioned in the Christian New Testament," Wendell said.

"Slow down. Slow down," Ross said. "Orina is alive?"

"Yes, but she is gray with blood red Hebrew letters, so she was definitely created by a formation ritual," Wendell said.

"And Legion, from the Bible?" Ross asked.

"Yes, Legion is the name of the multitude of demons that Jesus cast out of the possessed man, sending them to live in a herd of pigs," Wendell replied. "The Scroll gave me his name during my astral projection."

"So, you are talking about *the* literal Legion, the group of demons that Jesus cast out of the possessed man 2000 years ago, and sent into a herd of pigs," Ross asked again, holding his hand against the side of his head.

"Yes, it's hard to fathom – or, is it?" Wendell thoughtfully said.

"What do you mean?" Carly asked.

"Just think about it for a moment. Our Scroll is empowered by the spiritual forces that were part of the individual who empowered the Scroll to begin with. Our Scroll was created by Abraham himself and further empowered by the marginalia of Rabbi Judah Loew ben Bezalel, the Maharal of Prague with the intent of creating a Scroll for the good and protection of the people of Israel, the Jews. Both of these men lived, breathed, walked and sacrificed themselves for the Almighty.

Abraham, of course, was even asked by the Almighty to give his first-born son as a sacrifice to the Almighty, in order to test the *intentions* of his heart. Thankfully, an angel stopped Abraham just as he was about to slay his son Isaac and replaced Isaac with a ram. His intentions were therefore found to be pure in the eyes of the Almighty," Wendell said.

"So, by implication, you're saying that since the intentions of the CEO of Israeli Defense Systems were *impure* and perhaps even evil, then the copy of the Scroll is empowered by evil spiritual forces driven by those same impure intentions?" Ross asked.

"Those intentions allowed a legion of demons to give themselves a living body through the IDS scroll and, yes, also to give power to their scroll. What worries me is what *other* abominations it might create," replied Wendell.

54

ABOMINATIONS

3:35 AM
October 20, 2020
IDS Synagogue, Tel Aviv, Israel

Orina watched as one of her two sculpted creations began to smoke and reform itself from the molding and sculpting of her hands into life. She lay on her side next to her creation, watching the dark energy pulsing through the clay as it formed arteries and veins, individual hairs and follicles. She held a lighted magnifying glass near the hand to watch keratin forming on each fingertip, first making a fingernail, then growing further to form razor-sharp, black claws. She watched as the lips of the creature parted to reveal black, shark-like, serrated teeth. With each passing moment, the smoke grew thicker as it emanated from the forming entity. She stood and turned on a set of recently installed overhead ventilation hoods to suction the smoke out of the building and vent it over the roof so that she could see better, also allowing her video cameras a clear view for their recordings.

The copy of the Scroll lay open on the bimah in the center of the

IDS synagogue. It also emitted a dark gray smoke as the marginalia twinkled in purple. Rabbi Kohn had departed from the ritual hours ago, allowing Orina to complete the final steps of the process herself.

She lay back down on her side and watched the formation of the right ear of the creature. Not knowing herself how the ear would ultimately present itself, she had fashioned an ear similar to that of a human or an ape, but the being coming to life before her had other intentions. The ear grew outward and upwards towards the top of the creature's head, finally coming to a point, with vascular structures similar to what one might find on a gargoyle or a bat. In fact, the nose of the creature had formed at the same time as the ear, resulting in exactly what one might find on a bat – comprising four cavernous openings roughly shaped as irregular semicircles in a flattened, upwardly pointed cup.

To her great delight, the creature inhaled its first breath suddenly. This breath was followed by more sporadic inhalations and then coughing, resulting in a spray of dark gray phlegm. The creature's eyes remained closed, but the breathing continued. Orina reached out and stroked the fur forming on the golem.

"There you are, Jack. Come to me, my little ripper," Orina whispered as the creature slowly began to stir.

She crawled on the floor near to the other on-going formation. It was similar in structure, giving the overall impression of a gargoyle, with a short, dark spike projecting from each knee, at each elbow and from each heel. Each finger and toe of the creature was tipped with a black claw. Dozens of serrated black canines filled the gaping maw of the gargoyle as it smoldered and smoked its way to life. She stroked the fur of this creature, as well.

"Arise Mr. Gacy, and bring us your special talent for killing," she whispered, as the creature opened its eyes and writhed, rising up to a squatting position. Roughly the size and shape of an average man, the creature sat on its butt with its hands flat on the ground and its clawed feet and legs stretched out, steam and smoke still wafting from its body. It bent forward and vomited up a small puddle of grey ooze and then coughed hoarsely several times. Still waking, it panted and looked threateningly at Orina.

Ivan sat in the observation section above the platform and watched Orina's unusual attentions to the new soldiers, thinking to himself that these two looked more like gargoyles than soldiers, and that Orina had not been quite herself since being reformed.

"Orina, why have you chosen the names of two serial killers for the new golems?" Ivan asked.

"I didn't choose them, darling. They were chosen by the copy of the Scroll. These are the souls that were sent to inhabit these two golems – Jack the Ripper – now 'Jack', and John Wayne Gacy – now 'Mr. Gacy'. I was informed of their names in a vision, and I have tattooed those names on the inside of their thighs. You wanted ruthless super soldiers equipped for killing? You will have difficulty finding more ruthless killers than these," she replied. "Powerful, effective killing machines, built to deliver death and destruction at the command of their owner, my love."

"You're telling me that these two gargoyle-golem monstrosities are inhabited by the souls of serial killers?!" exclaimed Ivan.

"Yes, darling. They are perfect soldiers – as you can imagine, they derive great pleasure from killing, and because of that, they are also *enthusiastic* soldiers. Just as they were in real life, they might be a little *too* obsessed with killing. So, we shouldn't let them get bored. The world is *filled* with people who deserve to be killed, so that kind of boredom shouldn't be too much of a problem," Orina replied.

Legion stepped out of the shadows just underneath where Ivan was sitting on the elevated platform and waved to Ivan, silently.

"Hello, Legion. I was not aware that you were here tonight. I thought you were on another contract mission," Ivan said.

"You should know that I wouldn't miss the formation of our first two super soldiers. Now why would you call them monstrosities? Aren't they simply perfect?" Legion asked.

"I don't approve of using the souls of serial killers to inhabit the bodies of our super soldiers. This will render them uncontrollable in a military action. And no, they're not perfect. They're hideous!" Ivan exclaimed.

"That brings us to a small matter that we need to discuss," Legion said. He walked over to Orina, put his arms around her and kissed her passionately. The two gargoyles stood up and began to watch them kissing, sniffing the air around Orina and Legion, and then looking back up to Ivan, expectantly.

"Get your hands off my wife!" Ivan shouted as he reached into his jacket pocket for his phone and its special kill switch app.

Legion stopped kissing Orina, reached into his pants pocket and pulled out a military grade cell phone. He lifted it into the air and asked, "Are you looking for this?"

Ivan looked at the phone in Legion's hand and the color drained from his face as he began to realize the price that he was about to pay for the copy of the Scroll.

"Orina lifted it from your jacket as she was kissing you just prior to the formation ritual. You were so distracted by where her hand was while she had her tongue down your throat, you didn't even notice what her other hand was doing," Legion said.

"We have decided that an organizational change is needed. Due to your untimely demise during a training exercise with two of your new super soldiers, the board will be appointing me as the new CEO," Legion said. "Mr. Gacy, Jack, you must be starving after your formation. Please enjoy Mr. Sokov as your first meal." He then crushed the cell phone with his right hand.

The two gargoyle-golems leapt up the stairs towards Ivan, snarling and snapping at each other, racing towards their meal. Ivan pulled his beloved 45 caliber Jericho 941 given to him by Yitzhak Rabin from its holster under his left arm and began firing at the two creatures as they peaked the stairway leading up to the viewing area. In spite of his excellent marksmanship landing numerous hits to both head and chest of each creature, Mr. Gacy tore Ivan's throat open, while Jack grabbed Ivan by the thigh with his serrated black teeth and disemboweled him with his clawed left hand.

After watching the gory spectacle with interest, Legion said to Orina, "Let's talk about removing this annoying explosive charge from my shem, now, shall we?"

55

DRUG DEALERS, DARTS, CAMERAS

10:20 PM
October 20, 2020
Greyhill, Texas

Lilith again rode slowly down Mason Avenue in the White Dress Ranch Ford F150 to the edge of the parking lot that she had frequented a few nights before. Parked on the lot was a black Chrysler 300 with deeply tinted windows. The drug dealer from the night before was now wearing a dark gray cast, leaning against the same broken streetlamp as the night before. She parked the truck in the same spot that she had the previous night, stepped out of the vehicle, and walked towards the pusher. The two front doors of the Chrysler 300 opened, and a Latino man stepped out of each side – a man with a goatee and a black tracksuit and a tall muscular man with a bald head wearing a short sleeve t-shirt. The man with the t-shirt had an intricate sleeve of tattoos on each arm. Each man brandished a handgun.

"Hola, amigos. I am just an unarmed little girl. I'm not looking for trouble or a fight. I just want to do a little business and then we both go on our ways," Lilith said.

"Do you have the money, gringa?" the drug dealer asked.

"Yes. Do you have the product?" Lilith asked.

The man with a goatee said, "Yes, but the price went up since yesterday. It is now $2,000 for the 10 grams of product."

"That's too bad. I made a deal with your representative, here. Now if you'd like to tarnish your company's reputation by breaking that agreement, that's your business, I suppose, but since we made a deal for $1200 for the 10 grams of product, as a loyal customer since yesterday, I'd really appreciate it if you would honor that agreement," Lilith said.

"And if we don't want to honor that agreement, little Chica with no gun, what'll you do about it?" the bald muscular tattooed man asked.

Lilith licked her lips suggestively, put her hand on her hip, and then said, "Perhaps I can make up for the difference in some other way, boys?"

The two men from the Chrysler 300 looked at each other and smiled. The bald man holstered his gun and both men walked closer to Lilith, who raised her right hand and shot fibrils into the face of the man with the goatee and the gun. He managed to fire two shots into Lilith's chest before he succumbed to the Death Cap poison and dropped forward on his face. The bald tattooed man reached for his gun, but Lilith shot fibrils into his face, blinding him. She stepped out of the way as he began to fire at where she last stood, then he, also, fell to the ground on his face.

Lilith looked at the last man standing, the drug dealer with the cast. He stood by the lamppost, holding the same revolver from last night in his left hand. Lilith wagged her finger at him, and he dropped the gun.

"Now, where is the fentanyl?" she said.

"It's in the car. There's a hidden compartment under the console," the dealer said.

"Open it up. Get the fentanyl out and show it to me," Lilith told the man.

He sat in the driver's seat, reached under the middle console and lifted it upwards and to the back of the car. There under the console, were bags and bags of pills and powders. He picked up a bag that looked like it was about 10 grams of powder and held it out to Lilith.

"Give me a second," Lilith said, pulling a pair of nitrile gloves out of her pocket and slipping them on. "You can't be too careful, these days. Ok, hand it over."

With his left hand, he complied, and she took the bag with a gloved hand. "Is this fentanyl pure?" Lilith asked.

"Yes, about 90 percent or so," the dealer said.

"Is it laced with Xylazine?" Lilith asked.

"Si, señora," the dealer said.

"Well, that shouldn't make much difference for our purposes."

"What are you going to use it for?" the dealer asked.

"I need to kill some wild elephants," Lilith said.

"You have enough to kill a herd of elephants there."

"Perfect. Here's the money that we agreed to. A little life coach suggestion for you – stop dealing drugs and find a new profession before you end up like your bosses, here," Lilith said as she handed him the $1,200 in a white envelope.

She took three steps towards her vehicle and then turned back. "By the way, what is the name of the man that your two former bosses here get their drugs from and where is he located? You are safe from your bosses now. They can't harm you anymore."

"The name of the distributor for most of our drugs is a man named Anatoly. He is located somewhere in Chicago," the dealer said.

"Anatoly? As in Anatoly Dezhnyov?" Lilith asked.

"Si, señora, I think that's right," the dealer said.

* * *

8:37 AM | October 21, 2020 | White Dress Ranch, Greyhill, Texas

Lilith handed Wendell the fentanyl bag from her night's adventure. Both of them wore gloves and surgical masks to avoid the possibility of exposure to the deadly effective sedative. Wendel weighed the fentanyl into a small beaker.

"Eleven and a half grams! Was the drug dealer having a Tuesday night special? The guy gave you extra fentanyl for your $1,200 of hard-earned cash!" Wendell said.

"By the time I collected the product, the dealer was pretty shaken up and ready to get me out of his life. His drug lord friends tried to charge me extra. Let's just say I made them an offer they couldn't refuse."

"Ever considered becoming a drug lord? With your abilities, I think you could do quite well for yourself," Wendell said with a wink.

"No thanks, I'll stick to accounting, if we can ever settle down to a normal life again. Spreadsheets don't try to kill you," she replied.

Wendel placed a small Teflon-coated, magnetic stir bar into the beaker with the fentanyl, and then carefully poured paint thinner grade methanol from an Ace Hardware can into a graduated cylinder until the meniscus matched the 45-milliliter mark. He then poured the methanol into the beaker and turned the white knob on the front of the magnetic stir plate. The white magnetic bar began turning rapidly in the small beaker, creating a liquid vortex, and the fentanyl dissolved quickly to form a solution.

"I had no idea that you had chemistry skills," Lilith said.

"I'm not sure that you can call Googling 'what is fentanyl soluble in' combined with my freshman Chemistry 101 lab where I learned how to use a graduated cylinder and a magnetic stirrer 'chemistry skills' exactly, but I'll take the compliment, thank you," Wendell replied.

"Isn't methanol poisonous?" Lilith asked.

"Yes, as a matter of fact, it is. It can cause blindness and death. But it is also one of the best solvents for fentanyl. Since we aren't exactly concerned about the health of the IDS golems, methanol poisoning might actually be a good thing," replied Wendell.

"Good point," replied Lilith.

Brian stepped into the cottage where the two were making their batch of golem tranquilizer gun cocktail.

"Hey guys, do you need any help?" Brian asked.

"We are just coming to the point where we load the darts. I'm guessing that neither your mom nor dad would appreciate you handling fentanyl. It is quite deadly in very small quantities. You can watch if your mom is ok with that," Wendell said.

"Probably best if we all put on face shields, but after that, you can watch from a distance," replied Lilith.

"This is where we all should put on face shields. I have to work with pressurized syringes, and if some squirts out, enough could get in your eyes, mouth or nose to potentially be fatal," Wendell said.

The three all put on face shields and Wendell got to work. He took a hypodermic syringe and filled it to the 2-milliliter mark with methanol solution. He then inserted this syringe through the tip of the dart, injecting the contents into the dart, capping each short injection needle with a tiny plastic tip. When fired into an animal, the force of the dart hitting the animal activated a firing mechanism that shoved a plunger forward, delivering the contents into the animal. Wendell loaded two of the darts and placed them all tip side up in a special box specially designed to safely hold them.

"Ross can test one of them on a javelina or deer later this evening. We want to make sure that the methanol doesn't gum up the plunger mechanism. It's a pretty strong solvent, and not normally used in these types of darts," Wendell said.

* * *

8:27 PM | October 21, 2020 | White Dress Ranch, Greyhill, Texas

Ross loaded the Air-Dart long-range tranquilizer rifle with one of the darts that Wendell had loaded. He wore the blue nitrile gloves that he had been provided with a warning from Wendell – that he most certainly did not want to expose himself to the contents of these darts at the possible risk of his life. As an added measure of safety, Ross put on a pair of gun range safety glasses. This was about the time of year when javelina preferred to feed at night, when the temperature began to cool from the 90s and 100s down into the 80s.

The sun had set in the west about 15 minutes ago, but the clouds remained lit by the pale pink light of the sun below the horizon. Ross slowly inhaled the night air through his nostrils and smelled the smoke from the never-ceasing California wildfires. It was those wildfires that had produced the spectacular sunsets during the time that they had lived there with his sister.

A snorting noise from below interrupted his reverie. He looked down to see a pair of javelinas sniffing and moving their way towards Carly's vegetable garden. The pair was soon followed by a group of five more, taking their time as the first pair pulled up the netting and rutted their way into the garden. Ross rested the rifle on the rifle pad and took aim through the scope on one of the larger peccaries in the group of 5 bringing up the rear. He slowly breathed in until his lungs were about half full, then stopped, holding his breath while he initiated the trigger pull at a slow steady rate.

The rifle kicked into his shoulder as a charge of carbon dioxide was released into the barrel behind the dart. The red fletching of the dart briefly became visible as it traversed the distance from the end of the rifle to the javelina's hind quarters, lodging firmly in the muscle due to the barbed delivery needle.

The javelinas surrounding the target were startled by the brief squeal of their sibling, jumping away a short distance while looking towards their brother. The brother, now clearly tagged by the red fletching of the dart began walking in circles while limping. The limping became more pronounced, and the animal fell over onto the hip carrying the dart – twitching, but unconscious. All total, the 70-pound creature required about 6 seconds to go down. After a few more seconds, even the twitching stopped.

* * *

9:38 AM | OCTOBER 22, 2020 | WHITE DRESS RANCH, GREYHILL, TEXAS

Brian mounted the final security camera on a fence post near the north extremity of the property using a rechargeable screwdriver and a pair of deck screws. He then painted the assembly with a light coat of adhesive, taking care not to coat the lens, and gently applied some of the nearby topsoil and dried grass to camouflage the camera.

"Dad? Does this unit look good to you?" Brian said into the walkie-talkie. "Are you receiving a picture?"

"Not too bad, but it looks like there is a piece of grass over part of the lens," Ross said.

"Sorry about that. It shifted in the wind before the adhesive locked it in place. Brian pulled the offending piece of grass away from the lens and sprayed insecticide all around where the camera was mounted to help repel insects and reduce the number of false alarms.

"Yep. That took care of the problem," Ross responded. "Looks like we have the entire perimeter covered."

"Great! I'm headed back on the ATV," Brian said.

"Hey, on your way back, could you please swing by and check camera N5 to the west of you? It keeps alerting me that something is there, and I can't tell what it is. It looks like the lens might be covered with something," Ross said.

"Sure thing, Dad. On my way."

Brian straddled the ATV, turned the key to start the engine and twisted the handle, spinning the rear wheels as he steered the vehicle back onto the path and away from the property line. A rare cloud cover had cooled the day to below 80, and there was a faint mist dampening the normally arid region. A rainbow stretched from horizon to horizon in the distance, presenting a stunning spectacle. He stopped the ATV and turned off the engine, sitting there for a few moments to simply watch it in silence, arched against a backdrop of grey clouds. He had never seen a full rainbow before, only the partial rainbows that appeared near cities, where buildings and rooftops competed with rainbows for space against the hidden horizon.

As the rainbow filled him with wonder, he wondered when his family would ever be able to stop hiding, to stop being afraid of evil people who wanted to harm them. He wondered if perhaps next year he could begin attending high school again and make a few friends, maybe even a girlfriend.

He pushed these thoughts aside, turned the key and continued his ride to the misbehaving perimeter camera. Upon arriving, he discovered that a nest of fire ants had built a mound from the bottom of the fencepost, up and over the security camera, completely blocking the lens. He took a photo of the mound and the fencepost and sent it to his dad with the caption *N5 has fallen to the enemy*.

Brian found a dead branch of a mesquite tree nearby and used it to level the mound, causing an incredible outflow of the tiny red ants from deep within the earth. It became difficult to reach the mound after about a minute of leveling, as the ants were rabidly seeking the source of the desecration of their city. Two of the tiny red devils found Brian's boot and crawled up and over the boot, eventually reaching his bare shin underneath. The two soldiers clamped their mandibles into his skin and injected a toxic mixture of alkaloids and proteins, causing Brian to stomp his boots free of ants and to reach into his boots to find the source of the pain.

After searching for further ants on his clothing and a lot of scratching at the two bites, Brian reached into the plastic box strapped onto the rack at the back of the ATV and found a plastic bottle of Endem Fire Ant Mound Blaster. He twisted the plastic lid and sprinkled a generous portion of the granules all around and atop the mound. Finally, he pulled a long thin leafy branch from a Mesquite tree and brushed the dirt away from the lens of the N5 security camera.

"I was wounded in the battle, but the mound has been cleared. Is the security camera back online?"

"Back in business, son. Nice work. Are you OK?"

"A couple of the little devils bit me on the shin, but they won't be biting anyone else in a day or two," Brian replied. "On my way back."

56

ARRIVAL

10:20 PM
October 22, 2020
Greyhill, Texas

Ross wrapped himself in his sleeping bag in the bell tower and began to settle down for a night's sleep. His laptop rested open on a shelf plugged into a multi-strip, its screen displaying a grid of views from the cameras and motion detectors positioned around the ranch perimeter. Next to the laptop sat a walkie talkie nestled in its recharge station, listening for communications from his team. His 30-ought-6 rifle was loaded and wrapped in plastic against the elements. His Air Dart long range tranquilizer rifle stood next to it, also loaded with a single dart and wrapped in plastic.

Lilith looked over at where Emily was sleeping in the bed in Cottage 4 and picked up a walkie talkie. She pressed the talk button and said, "Hey handsome, are you asleep yet?"

Ross replied, "Just getting settled into my sleeping bag. I wish you were here to warm me up."

"Me too. Thank you for being so vigilant in the sniper's nest, darling," Lilith said.

"Well, since Wendell said that they want to kill me *slowly*, I'm sort of motivated," Ross said.

"I keep hoping that they will simply give up on the thought of revenge or destroying our Scroll, or both, and set about the business of making billions of dollars creating super soldiers," replied Lilith.

"I can't believe that Orina would hold a grudge for so long. I mean, all I did was blow her brains out in her military testing center conference room. Some people just don't know how to forgive and forget or live and let live. After all, to err is human, to forgive is divine," Ross said.

"Sarcasm and humor noted, darling, but I'm really worried about all of us," Lilith said.

"We *should* be worried. With demons, golems, billions of dollars and mercenaries at their disposal – we *should* be worried. That being said, we are about as prepared as we can be with the resources that we have available to us," Ross said.

"Do you want me to bring you a snack or something to drink before you go to sleep? Maybe a little snuggle?" Lilith offered.

"No but thank you, darling. It has been a long day, and I'd like to get a little shut eye," replied Ross.

Wendell and Carly looked at each other on their inflatable air mattress in the barn and smiled. Wendell pressed the talk button. "You both realize that these are community walkie-talkies, right?"

"Oops, yes, sorry. Bri-Bear are you alright in Cottage 3?"

"Doing great, Mom. Good night," Brian said.

"Over and out, and goodnight, Lilith, Wendell, Carly, Brian, Emily, OctaJoe, Sting, MoHawk, Bearmadillo, and CamoRon," Ross said.

A series of goodnights came from everyone save for the golems in the barn with Brian.

* * *

12:05 AM | October 23, 2020 | Mesa Vista Regional Airport, Austin, Texas

The black Israeli Defense Systems Airbus 320 touched down at the Mesa Vista private airport southwest of Austin, Texas, visible in the darkness only from its navigation lights. Orina awoke as the wheels squeaked against the asphalt tarmac and the thrust reversers roared. She opened her window shade and looked out into the blackness. In the distance, the city lights of the Austin skyline were visible as the plane rolled down the runway. She raised her seat and looked across the aisle, where Legion sat looking at her.

"Good morning, darling. Welcome to Austin, Texas, home of Willie Nelson and Matthew McConaughey, where never is heard a discouraging word and the skies are not cloudy all day," Legion said in his eerie, multi-tonal voice.

"Good morning to you, as well. Did our three pets give us any problems during the flight?" Orina asked.

"None whatsoever. The titanium cages held up nicely. As for our corporate operatives, they all survived as well." Legion turned and looked behind him to see an unusual sight - 12 corporate operatives, suited up with body armor, helmets, and black uniforms, all buckled in their seats.

The plane came to a stop next to a hangar containing an MH-6 Little Bird helicopter, which resembled a black egg with windows equipped with a helicopter rotor and a tail. Mounted to the side opening of the Little Bird was a "plank" – a sideboard where one to two soldiers could sit – and to this plank was mounted a 7.62 mm machine gun.

"Roll the golems out of the cargo hold," Legion said to several of the operatives.

"Right away, sir," one of the soldiers said.

The soldiers opened the cargo bay of the plane and rolled a conveyor ramp up into the opening. Two of the men crawled up into the hold of the plane. Soon, a single, large cage with thick bars rolled onto the conveyor and made its way down to the bottom of the ramp. Snarling, the gargoyle golem within tried to bend the bars open, but they were too thick and strong. The golem stuck his clawed hand out between the bars. One of the soldiers at the bottom of the ramp used an electric cattle prod to shock the creature as his cage was near the bottom. The creature screamed and pulled his clawed hand back into the cage.

"Be careful with Mr. Gacy!" yelled Orina to the soldier.

"Yes, ma'am," the soldier dubiously said.

Legion walked over to Mr. Gacy's cage and spoke to him through the bars of the cage, "I'm going to have this soldier open the door to your cage. I want you to leave our soldiers alone. Leave the workers at the airport alone. Do not harm them in any way. Leave your cage and go find a deer, cow or a horse to eat. Once you have had your fill, return to me." The gargoyle golem became excited and began to pant quickly, drooling onto the cage and the tarmac.

Legion walked to the soldier with the cattle prod and said, "Open Mr. Gacy's cage and let him go eat dinner."

"But sir, that thing will tear me apart," replied the soldier incredulously.

"Do it!" replied Legion, his voice sounding like an angry lynch mob.

"Yes sir," the soldier said.

The soldier walked closer to the cage, holding the crackling, sparkling cattle prod in front of him, then pulled a key from his pocket, reached over, and unlocked the cage, allowing the door of the cage to fall open. Mr. Gacy leapt out of the cage, looked at Legion and then turned to the soldier with the cattle prod, who was still holding it in front of him. He then raced away into the darkness to find dinner.

The soldier looked at Legion and said, "I think that was the most terrifying thing that I have ever done in my life."

"I'm sorry, was your name Benson?" Legion said.

"Yes, sir," the soldier said.

"Goodbye, Benson," Legion said. At that moment, Mr. Gacy rushed from the darkness and grabbed Benson by the throat with his teeth, nearly decapitating him. He fed hungrily on the soldier, leaving a small pile of guts and bone next to the conveyor.

"Legion, can we really afford to waste operatives that way?" Orina asked.

"After Benson, there, we now have one to spare," Legion said casually. "They need to learn not to aggravate the premium assets of the mission, especially you and me. Now, do we have any volunteers to take Benson's place?"

By that time, the rest of the operatives had quietly melted into the darkness.

57

THE INEVITABLE

6:20 AM
October 23, 2020
Greyhill, Texas

The Scroll woke Wendell from his slumber and astrally projected him into a small helicopter. He saw a soldier straddling some sort of "plank" on each side of the helicopter, one manning a mounted machine gun, another manning an assault rifle, while a third flew the helicopter.

"They're here!" he tried to speak while floating in the chopper.

After this revelation, as though a switch were flipped, he now found himself floating above two military Humvees containing soldiers. Legion and Orina stood next to three large gray metal cages, which contained creatures straight out of a nightmare – monsters resembling bats, or perhaps demons, or gargoyles. They snarled loudly as he passed over them, all of them looking directly at him. Legion looked up, as well, and made eye contact.

"Hello, Rabbi Rosenburg. We thought we'd stop by for a friendly visit. Perhaps you'd like to conduct a wedding ceremony for Orina and me in your chapel before I let Mr. Gacy, Jack and Mr. Bundy disembowel you and your little girlfriend?" Legion intoned with many voices. He then raised his radio to his mouth and said, "They know that we're here. Commence the air attack now! Humvees roll!"

At that moment, Ross was alerted on his laptop that the perimeter to the property had been breached. He watched as two Humvees entered the White Dress Ranch property. "Humvees?! What the hell?!" he said.

The Scroll brought Wendell back into his body with a disorienting lurch. Wendell grabbed his walkie talkie, pressed talk and shouted "Wake up! Wake up! They're here!" Adrenaline surged into everyone, and wakefulness was instantaneous.

Wendell raced to the barn door, opened it with a great pulling effort and shouted, "All my golems! If you encounter an enemy golem, try to break their shem! MoHawk! Find and destroy the helicopter, now!"

The enormous red-tail hawk golem, with a combination of hopping and running on its taloned feet, exited the barn door, flapped its wings hard and took to the air. The whirring of helicopter blades soon followed, but the hawk had disappeared into the dark pre-dawn sky. The Little Bird chopper came in low, and the machine gun opened up, spraying the second floor of the hotel with 7.62 mm bullets, blasting out windows and shredding the walls. The second gunner aimed higher, at the third floor, leaving a layer of bullet holes in the walls and broken windows on this floor, as well.

As this was happening, Wendell shouted, "Sting and Bearmadillo, leave the helicopter alone. Find and kill enemy golems."

The golem derived from a large nest of yellow jackets began to vibrate and hum, and its wings lifted it into the air as it whizzed through the opening in the barn door. Its black wings blurred as its yellow body flew out into the darkness. The giant Bearmadillo followed Sting closely, loping quickly on all fours, plates of armor covering its back and belly.

As the helicopter gunship released bullets into the hotel, Wendell yelled into the walkie-talkie, "Ross, no time to explain. Mercenaries will be next. Be ready with your 30-ought-6. Be informed – the mercenaries have body armor."

"Copy that, Wendell. Thanks. I just saw two Humvees crossing into the ranch across the northeast perimeter." Ross said. He followed this up quietly to himself with, "Damn it! I guess that body armor limits me to face shots."

Wendell shouted, "OctaJoe, protect Cottage 3! CamoRon, protect Cottage 4!" The two oversized octopus-derived golems camouflaged themselves and flowed out of the door into the darkness, one going one way and one going another, each vanishing in the darkness.

Wendell pressed the talk button and yelled, "Lilith, this would be a good time to see if what you've been practicing works."

Lilith put on her earpiece and replied, "Copy that, Rabbi." She turned to Emily and said, "No matter what happens, lock the door after me and do not unlock the door. Close the curtains and hide under the bed, sweetie. I love you."

Emily replied, "OK, Mom. I love you too. Be careful."

Lilith shut the door behind her and heard the deadbolt click into place. She then looked towards the hotel, still under siege by the gunship, lifted her head and arms and closed her eyes as though she were trying to summon something. Almost ten seconds passed with her in this position, and the skin of her arms began to deform and move, as though something buried and crawling under her skin was trying to get out. The head of an insect poked its way out of her skin, and then another. Out from each opening in her skin came a small wasp, pure white in color. Several spread their wings and began flying angrily around her. Soon the air around Lilith was abuzz with a cloud of buzzing white wasps. Lilith opened her eyes with burning anger and said, "Go, find, and kill our enemies." The flying white wasps flew off, twisting like a whirling dervish mid-air, then fanning into the night towards the northeast.

Lilith knelt on the ground for a moment, as the formation process had taxed her. The ruptures in her skin quickly began to heal as she knelt on the ground gently panting.

As the machine gunner targeted the front of the chapel, a dark form swept in from the night and long sharp talons penetrated his right arm and his abdomen, then dropped below the whirling blades of the chopper as the soldier screamed, falling to the ground from about 4 stories up. A cloud of brown feathers swirled in the air – many of them sliced into pieces – as MoHawk flew away from the helicopter.

"What the hell was that?!" called out the pilot over the helicopter communications to the soldier.

"It looked like a giant hawk. I think we should get the hell out of here," replied the soldier. As the pilot considered his proposal, MoHawk swooped up to the cockpit, grabbed the left skid with his talons and bit his left arm off mid-bicep. Blood sprayed out of an artery and dispersed into a pink mist as the wind from the propeller blades whipped the pumping red stream. The hawk-golem held onto the skid as the gunner fired his assault rifle into the creature. Another bite from the hooked beak of the hawk-golem landed on the pilot's neck, ending his life, and sending the chopper into a spin. The chopper hit the ground hard and broken blades whistled through the night as the aircraft caught fire, lighting up the area in front of the chapel. The remaining gunner was crushed as the chopper took the hard landing on its side. The gunner, his left leg nearly amputated by the very plank that was his seat of destruction earlier, began to moan and cry for help. MoHawk, severely injured, crawled away from the burning chopper, calling out with screeches and squeals in pain.

As soon as MoHawk had crawled free of the wreckage, Ross sent a tranquilizer dart into his back, either killing him or putting him to sleep – Ross wasn't sure which. Considering that the moaning soldier was attacking his family, he thought about letting him suffer, but then realized that he could use the moaning soldier as a test for his shells versus their body armor. Ross switched back to his 30-ought-6, took careful aim at the back plate on the soldier and fired. The soldier was immediately silenced.

"Thank you, God in Heaven, for giving me the means to protect my family from these evil men," Ross quietly prayed.

* * *

To the northeast of Ross, the swarm of white wasps came upon a Humvee, rolling quickly across the dead grass and rocky terrain of the ranch property towards the hotel. A gunner rode atop the Humvee, manning the machine gun. The cloud of white wasps swirled around the vehicle once, then dove towards the gunner and down into the cabin of the Humvee. They landed on the bare skin of their faces and hands, when possible, but also on their black uniforms. They buried their stingers into the men, injecting Lilith's death cap venom, killing them quickly. The Humvee, lacking a living driver, plowed into a large boulder, crumpling the front end of the vehicle, releasing steam from under the hood. The gunner was thrown away from the vehicle upon impacting the boulder and lay prone over the front of the Humvee hood. As steam rose from the vehicle, the white wasps also rose, and dissipated like snowy ash, floating gently downwind.

58

WAR IS HELL

6:40 AM
October 23, 2020
Greyhill, Texas

Wendell again felt himself slip out of his body to another location. He floated inside the cargo hold of a jet plane, which the Scroll informed him was an Airbus 320 at the Mesa Vista Regional Airport southwest of Austin, Texas. He looked at all of the cargo within the hold of the plane and saw black plastic gun cases shaped like assault rifles, metal ammunition boxes, luggage, webbed yellow strapping hanging from the walls to which some of the boxes were secured, and one large red metal box.

This box was definitely different from everything else, because it was emitting a dark gray smoke and purple light from the edges and corners. He turned and saw that the cargo hold door was open and an industrial fan had been placed in the doorway, to clear the smoke from the hold. He knew that this box contained the copy of the Scroll. His Scroll made it clear that he needed to destroy it.

Instantly, he returned to his body, which now lay akimbo on a pile of hay. Carly had her fingers on his neck, checking his pulse. Wendell refocused his eyes on hers.

"Thank God! I was worried about you. You almost hit your head when you passed out," Carly said.

"I'm OK. The Scroll projected me again. I saw their copy of the Scroll and it's at the Mesa Vista Regional Airport southwest of Austin. Our Scroll wants me to destroy it." Wendell said.

"Sounds like a plan to me! Let's roll!" she exclaimed.

"No. I'm not sure why, but this is something that the Scroll wants me to do alone, and now!" Wendell said. He got to his feet, ran to a worktable, picked up a plastic 5-gallon container of gasoline, a blue grenade, and checked to make sure that he had his cell phone. He cracked the barn door open just enough to slip through, kissed Carly through the opening and said, "Hide the Scroll and guard it! Close the door and bolt it, quickly!" Then he ran to the truck next to the barn, got in and spun the tires as he drove away.

Carly swung the bolts closed to lock the door and immediately heard a harsh sniffing noise near the bottom of the door, followed by an inhuman growl. She ran to each of the doors to make sure that they were closed and locked, then saw the hayloft door up high, cracked open on the side of the barn opposite to where the golem was snuffing. She heard scratching and clawing on the walls of the barn as the golem began to climb to the roof. Running now, she raced to the wooden stairs leading to the hayloft. As she ran, she pulled the tranquilizer gun from her shoulder holster.

A scrabbling sound on the roof began, and it was apparent that the creature was now making quick progress across the roof to the back of the barn. Near the top of the stairs, a nail used to hang cord stood out from the left side of the handrails. Carly caught her jean blouse on the nail, and it scraped across her ribs as she staggered backwards on the stairs. She grabbed the handrail, frantically ripped her blouse off, leaving it firmly entangled on the nail and streaked across the hay-strewn floor of the loft in her red bra.

Dark black claws jammed themselves through the wood under the hay beam. Carly dropped the tranquilizer gun, steadied herself against the door that was properly bolted and gingerly reached out for the other door. A claw swept across her bare forearm, drawing blood as she pulled the door. Frantic scratching noises on the outside of the door continued as she bolted the door shut. Then she heard the creature scream. The scream was a scream not of frustration, but of pain.

Outside on the hay beam, the gargoyle golem gripped the beam with the claws of its feet and fought desperately to pull Sting off of his back, who had implanted his stinger into Mr. Bundy's lower back. His stinger was pulsing downwards as he injected the abomination with massive quantities of toxic venom. Mr. Bundy continued to growl and scream as Sting held firmly to him with his six legs, all equipped with small claws of their own. Then Mr. Bundy reached backwards with both of his claw-filled hands, groping for purchase on his enemy. He was rewarded as his claws gained hold of the wasp-golem's head. Straining, the gargoyle-golem pulled and twisted as the wasp-golem bit at his hands in an effort to free himself, but Sting's head detached from his body, and Mr. Bundy angrily crushed the head and cast it aside.

The toxins were beginning to take effect, however, and the gargoyle fell three stories to the ground, parting himself from the wasp's stinger mid-air. He rose and tried to walk and immediately met the fury of Bearmadillo, who buried his teeth in the neck of the gargoyle and pulled out a great chunk, shaking his head and flinging the meat aside. Mr. Bundy was still now, as Bearmadillo roared in victory. He looked around for other golems, then remembered the words of his master – "break their shem!" There on the chest of Mr. Bundy, lay the silver shem. He sniffed it, used a claw to pull it between his teeth and bit the shem in two. Mr. Bundy crumbled into small black chunks of smoldering clay. An image of Ted Bundy's face formed in the rising smoke – a handsome, smiling face, which looked at Bearmadillo and then formed into a rotting, angry skull, reaching for him with bony fingers. The pungent smoke dissipated in the gentle morning breeze.

The Scroll then spoke to Bearmadillo, and he lay down, face up on the hard scrabble ground. He felt himself changing.

* * *

Ross held the 30-ought-6 pointed at the ceiling and ready to move wherever he needed it, depending upon the direction of the threat. He heard the growling before he saw the creature. Coal black skin with claws, teeth, and muscle, the creature came at a trot from the parking lot in front of the now demolished hotel. Keeping his eyes on the enemy golem, Ross carefully and quietly leaned the 30-ought-6 in a corner and gently pulled up the long-range tranquilizer dart gun containing a fresh dart filled with fentanyl and methanol solution. As the butt of the dart rifle came round into position, it bumped into the 30-ought-6, sending it clattering noisily sideways.

Jack's large ears turned, as though on ball pivots, towards the sound, and the eyes of the creature followed, spotting Ross in the sniper nest. The bat-faced gargoyle-golem lifted its head and roared a hideous, rasping, gurgling roar, as though it were warning or calling its comrades. As the gargoyle roared, Ross took aim through the tranquilizer rifle scope and fired the dart, hitting the beast in the left shoulder. The roar turned into a scream, which almost sounded human. The creature grasped the dart with its right "hand" and pulled it out, tossing it aside. Then it cast its eyes on Ross again and began racing towards the chapel.

Jack clawed his way up onto the roof of the church and rushed the bell-tower-turned-sniper's-nest, as Ross frantically reloaded the rifle. As he grasped for another dart in the morning darkness, his finger was pricked by one of the other needles in the box. The dart tip was wet.

"Damn it!" Ross said, as he pushed the syringe dart into the gun and closed the stock and barrel together.

Jack slammed against the exterior bars of the makeshift sniper's nest and shoved a black clawed hand in to disembowel Ross, but Ross slammed the butt of the dart gun down on the wrist of the creature, forcing it down at a ninety-degree angle. The creature pulled its hand back out of the bell tower and screamed in pain. It looked at its wrist and then back at Ross in rage into the barrel of the tranquilizer rifle. Ross pulled the trigger and fired the dart point blank into the eye of the creature, who again screamed and rolled off the roof of the church, clawing at its eye to pull the dart out.

Ross could only hear Jack the gargoyle-golem below; his view blocked by the roof of the church. The creature continued to whimper and pant, and then grew silent as the two elephant-herd-sized doses of fentanyl finally took effect.

A gentle wave of relaxation washed over Ross, and his senses numbed. He touched his earpiece and said "This is Daddy-Bear to Emmy-Bear. Are you OK? Over."

"I'm OK, Dad," Emily said.

"Hey, sweetie, where did your mom end up stashing you?" Ross asked.

"I'm in Cottage number 4. Are you OK?" Emily asked.

"Yeah, you know, getting a little tired, but aside from that, doing OK," Ross replied.

A Humvee pulled rolled noisily between the corral and an outcropping of rocks.

"Bye Emmy-Bear, gotta go, lub you," Ross said.

"Be careful, Dad. Love you, too," Emily said.

Ross pulled the tranquilizer dart rifle back into the sniper's nest and exchanged it for the 30-ought-6. The feeling of relaxation that he had, began to give way to drowsiness. His ability to aim the rifle was becoming impaired. He knew that he *must not* go to sleep, his family was depending upon him to protect them, and he carefully targeted the soldier manning the machine gun atop the Humvee and pulled the trigger. Fire instantaneously lit up the bell tower as the bullet exited the barrel. Ross watched as the soldier slumped onto his side.

"Got the basdard!" he slurred to himself. He had the passing thought that he was very high as he re-aimed the semi-automatic 30-ought-6, waiting for one of the occupants of the vehicle to get out.

Instead, someone inside the Humvee pushed the dead mercenary out of his perch and off of the roof. The black-uniformed soldier fell unceremoniously to the ground, landing on his helmet. The turret then adjusted itself so that the shield was facing him, and another soldier crawled up and took his place.

Ross shook his head trying to clear the cobwebs and said with a voice that sounded like Scooby Doo, "Ruh roh, rooks rike I gotta shoot him in the face." Then he imitated the laughter of the Three Stooges "Nyuck, Nyuck, Nyuck."

The machine gun opened fire on the sniper's nest as Ross calmly took aim and fired, hitting the soldier in the left cheek and blowing a pink spray out from under the back of his helmet.

Ross sang the words, "Another one bites the dust, na na nah na na. Owww! I think he got me." He put his rifle down and saw blood pouring from a hole in his thigh.

"Let's see, now, what would Bear Grylls do? Ooo – that's what we coulda called Bearmadillo – Bear Grylls. Hah! Focus, Ross, Focus! Uhhhhhhh, what's that thing called? Seems like it was some sort of Fench word - a tourniquet. Thaaaat's what Bear would do, yeppur," Ross said. Fumbling with the fastener, he pulled his belt out from his pants loops, wrapped the belt around his thigh, struggled to reinsert the end back into the fastener, then fumbled to tie a knot to hold the belt tightly in place.

The machine gun fire from the Humvee resumed, tearing into the roof of the church. Ross's gun rests exploded, showering sand all around him. One of the bullets penetrated Ross's left bicep, causing Ross to say, "Looks like I'm losing this one. Ima sleep now."

Lilith jumped on top of the Humvee and grabbed the soldier's helmet with both hands, twisting hard and snapping the man's neck. She then leapt to the driver's side door and pulled it off of its hinges, throwing it like a frisbee across the corral. Flashes of fire came from inside the cabin as the driver pumped round after round into Lilith's chest from his Glock. She grabbed the man's gun and twisted hard, causing him to release the weapon, which she cast aside. Lilith grabbed his lapel, picked him up and slammed him down onto a corral fence post, partially impaling him.

He gurgled blood from his mouth as he died, and Lilith briefly watched to ensure that he was no longer a threat. Seeing that there was no one else inside the Humvee, she walked weakly to the chapel, still recovering from the bullet wounds she had taken.

She leaned against the chapel and called up to Ross.

"Ross! Are you OK? Ross?" but received no answer. She felt the hot slugs pushing outward courtesy of the mycelium fibers that she had been given by the Scroll, thinking to herself "These certainly do come in handy." She untucked her blouse so that the hot slugs could fall to the ground as she healed.

59

LOSS

7:07 AM
October 23, 2020
Greyhill, Texas

A loud voice came to Lilith from the direction of the White Ranch Hotel. "Your husband looks like he's in really bad shape, honey. I think he's bleeding out as you sit there and recover. But that's OK. You can know that he will die while I keep you busy with some major payback," Orina said loudly.

Lilith stepped away from the chapel wall and looked in the direction of the voice. There in a decimated fourth floor room, where part of the wall had collapsed, including one of the windows, stood Legion and Orina. Lilith opened the storage shed next to the chapel and grabbed one of the sticky grenades hanging in the shed. She then touched her earpiece and said, "Brian, be ready with red. Leaving the channel open after you reply. Respond."

Brian replied, "Copy that." Lilith pushed another button on her earpiece that left the channel open.

When Lilith looked back at the window, Orina had jumped to the ground and was walking in her direction, casually, as though she had all of the time in the world. Legion now sat in the opening, smiling and swinging his feet gently as he watched Lilith. As she walked towards Lilith, she swayed her hips suggestively and dragged a sword through the dry sandy soil, eliciting a ringing sound. The sword was about three feet long and reminded Lilith of a weapon that a Roman soldier might carry.

"Like my new toy?" Orina asked.

"A sword? What's so special about a sword?" replied Lilith.

"It's for cleaving shems," Orina said, as she took the pommel in both hands and swung it towards Lilith's head.

Lilith ducked and dove out of the way and shot fibrils from her fingers, hitting Orina in the neck. She smiled and brushed them off.

"You know, as a nerd scientist, I made sure to test a concentrated extract of the Death Cap mushroom on Mr. Gacy, one of our golem pets. It had no effect, meaning your pathetic fibrils have no effect on me," Orina said.

Orina again walked towards Lilith, swinging the sword around the pommel with one hand like a cheerleader with a baton. Lilith circled and began to swing the sticky grenade with practiced purpose.

"What's special about your toy?" Orina asked.

"It's sort of like yours – it sticks things, too," Lilith said, and she swung the improvised explosive device onto the belly of Orina's black uniform, releasing the sticky red handle to allow it to wrap around her.

"Now, Brian, call red!" exclaimed Lilith as she jumped away from the device, while Orina struggled to unstick herself from it.

"Hey, your belly is ringing. I think you should take that," Lilith said. The grenade exploded, leaving a bloody hole in Orina's abdomen and throwing her 6 feet onto her back.

"Leave it to a nerd scientist to bring a knife to a grenade fight," Lilith said, pulling a tranquilizer dart pistol from a holster in the back of her pants and shooting Orina in what remained of her chest with a fentanyl dart.

Orina's mouth gaped open in surprise and then closed along with her eyes as the fentanyl took effect. Lilith ripped open what remained of Orina's body armor and positioned her silver shem flat onto her chest. She then picked up Orina's sword, took the pommel in both hands and slammed the tip of the sword through the shem, through her chest and deep into the ground. She watched as cracks formed in Orina's face and hands, crumbling into small pieces of black clay that smoldered with an offensive smelling black smoke. Lilith looked back up at the fourth floor opening in the wall of the hotel. Legion was gone.

"Orina's dead," Lilith said. "Thank you, Bri-Bear."

"You're welcome, Mom. What about Legion?" Brian asked.

"I'm not sure where he went, but I'll find him," Lilith said.

* * *

Mr. Gacy heard voices coming from the cottage and sniffed loudly at the base of the front door of Cottage 3. Brian heard the sniffing and moved to ensure that the windows were locked. Brian parted the curtains to check the lock but was greeted instead by a horrific bat-faced gargoyle-golem staring back at him. He gasped and backed quickly away from the windows, which promptly shattered into the room. The gargoyle-golem roared in rage as his claws became entangled in the curtains and as his shoulders wouldn't quite fit between the sliding aluminum frames. Suddenly the creature disappeared from the window and squealed like a pig as OctaJoe grabbed him by the rear legs and began beating him against the wall of the cottage, and then against the ground as though he were a rug that needed cleaning.

Brian opened the curtains and looked outside while this was happening. "Yeah! Beat the crap out of him, OctaJoe!" he yelled.

Mr. Gacy's rear legs slipped from OctaJoe's tentacles during his struggles, however, and he clamped his jaws on the octopus-golem's abdomen and tentacle, shaking OctaJoe like a wolf attacking a moose. OctaJoe released a high-pitched screaming noise as the gargoyle-golem ripped away one of his tentacles with his teeth. Brian looked frantically around the room and found his tranquilizer pistol. Unlocking the front door, he rushed outside to find Mr. Gacy attempting to disembowel OctaJoe with his razor-sharp talons. He quickly aimed and fired the fentanyl dart, hitting Mr. Gacy in the rump. The resulting roar was enough to cause Brian to run back into the room, locking the door behind him.

After chasing Brian to the front door and losing that race, he reached back and pulled the dart from his hip with his clawed hand and ran back to the window that he had begun to traverse the first time. OctaJoe was no longer in sight as he rounded the corner and attempted to jump through the smashed window of the cottage. OctaJoe stood up quickly from his camouflaged position flattened on the ground and pulled the beast away from the window again by his legs. Brian parted the curtains and yelled, "Hold him still for a second!"

OctaJoe complied, and in spite of the blood draining from his dismembered tentacle, he managed to hold Mr. Gacy up by the feet, clawing the air to allow Brian to take a second shot at the beast, which he did with great anger. Mr. Gacy, already showing signs of slowing his frenetic bestial pace, soon went to sleep.

* * *

As Orina began her quest for revenge with Lilith, Legion jumped to the ground and made his way in the shadows of the hotel towards the west, then north, towards a row of three honeymoon cottages each nestled near a streamlined with trees, each one painted white with teal painted doors. Based upon the careless walkie talkie chatter that he had overheard on his own earpiece, he was on a quest for cottage number 4.

"Well, isn't this romantic. Let's see, now – 6, 5, and here it is – 4," Legion whispered with his many voices.

The dead oak tree in front of the cottage suddenly reached out with two tentacles and grabbed Legion, pulling him towards the waiting arms of a now very visible and very large, CamoRon, who grabbed Legion around the throat with his oversized hands and began to squeeze. Legion gasped, then slowly pulled his arms free of the tentacles and grabbed the two massive wrists of CamoRon. He pulled the hands away from his neck and broke both of his arms. CamoRon yelped in pain and released Legion, trying to flow away from him, but Legion leaped onto him and grabbed his shem snapping it in two as CamoRon struggled beneath him.

"No fuss, just - dust to dust," echoed Legion's voices, as CamoRon whimpered lightly and crumbled into small beige clods of dried clay.

"Time to meet sweet, defenseless little Emily," Legion said.

Legion kicked the door to the cottage in and entered. He looked around the room and called out melodically as a choir might sing, "Emily? Where are you hiding?" then lifted the bed over onto its side to find her sprawled on the floor.

He put his finger to his mouth and said "Shhhh. I'll take this, thank you very much," as he removed her earpiece and crushed it in his hand.

He pointed to his own ear and said, "See, I've already got one, and it will be more than enough for both of us."

Eva Fischer stepped through the open door of the cottage. "I hope that I'm not late to the party, Boss," she said.

"Not at all! You've arrived just in time, Eva! Put your gun to this little one's head, bring her outside in front of the cottage and stand behind her. We are expecting a guest soon. If Lilith makes a move towards you or the girl, put a bullet through her brain. I'll be right back," Legion said and he stepped quickly out of the room.

* * *

Lilith kicked the door to the chapel open and rushed in, racing to the back of the building where the door to the bell tower was. The door was locked, so she kicked this door in, also. She reached for the ladder and pulled her hand away. Her hand was covered in blood, and there was a pool of blood at the bottom of the ladder. She climbed the ladder frantically to find Ross at the top, leaning back in his make-shift chair. He was barely breathing; he was pale, and his heart rate was barely detectable. She touched her earpiece and said, "Brian, call 911 and get an ambulance to the chapel, your dad needs help right away.

He's been shot in the thigh and the arm, and he's lost a lot of blood. I'm counting on you, Bri-Bear. I've got to go check on Emily now."

In a quavering voice, Brian replied, "Copy that, Mom," then, "God please don't let him die."

Carly's voice came on next, "Lilith, I'm on my way to the bell tower."

Lilith replied, "Thank you, Carly."

Lilith examined the tourniquet around his leg and cinched it a little tighter. His arm wasn't bleeding much, so she left that for the ambulance crew. She had to get to Emily before Legion did.

She raced out of the back door of the chapel, and as she ran towards the cottage, she saw Emily with Eva holding a gun to her head. Her heart dropped in her chest, and she slowed to a walk as she approached the two.

"That's far enough, Lilith," Eva said.

And from behind her Legion said, "Yes, that *is* far enough, Lilith."

Legion was holding a yellow handled sticky grenade, swinging it like Lilith had done earlier with Orina. He said, "Throw me your earpiece."

Lilith reluctantly reached up and pulled off her earpiece and threw it to Legion, who caught it with his left hand and crushed it.

"If you want sweet little Emily here to live, you need to tell me where the Scroll is, right now," Legion said.

"How do I know you won't simply kill Emily once I tell you?" Lilith said.

"Just like every movie that has ever asked that question, the answer is that you don't, but what kind of monster do you think I am? The only reason your little girl has a gun to her head is because I need you to answer a simple question," replied Legion.

"It's in the barn," Lilith said.

"Since I don't have all day, exactly *where* is it in the barn?" Legion asked.

"I don't *know* where. Wendell and Carly have probably hidden it, though there aren't too many places to hide a glowing scroll in a barn, so it shouldn't be too hard to find," Lilith said.

"Fair enough," Legion said, as he released the swinging yellow sticky bomb, hitting Lilith squarely in the chest, wrapping the long sticky handle around her left arm.

Emily yelled "Mom!" and tried to run to her, but Eva held her by the arm firmly.

Lilith began to struggle, but Legion said "No, no, no . . . Don't move a muscle or we will paint the honeymoon cottage with Emily's brains. Now, neither of you say a *single word* while I enjoy myself, just a little." Legion's voices took on the sound of talons raking against a chalkboard when he said *single word*.

Legion reached up to his own earpiece and pressed a button, then with perfect mimicry of Lilith's voice said, "Brian, call yellow, now!"

Brian's voice came back into Legion's earpiece, "Copy that."

Legion looked into Lilith's eyes and said, "This time, just stay dead, bitch."

The sticky grenade exploded against Lilith's chest, leaving a gaping bloody hole. Lilith was thrown onto her back, staring lifelessly up at the sky.

Emily began screaming and crying "No! No! Mom! No! Let me go!" and at that moment, Eva saw an enormous brown furry "thing" rounding the corner of the chapel, thundering towards Legion.

Eva yelled "Behind you, Legion!" but her words were largely drowned out by Emily's screaming.

Legion turned and found himself being thrown into the air by giant claws. He landed at least a hundred feet away from where he was. Eva began running, but Bearmadillo had grown to gigantic proportions, and he swatted her aside, slamming her into the cottage. Legion managed to get back on his feet and was running away from the massive, armored creature into the desert. As Emily knelt by her mother and cried, Eva limped away, north through the rocky terrain, and towards escape.

60

TRUTH, AND BURNING THE DARK BRIDGE

7:57 AM
October 23, 2020
Mesa Vista Regional Airport
Southwest of Austin, Texas

Wendell arrived at the airport worrying that he would not be able to secure access to the Israeli Defense Systems Airbus 320 private jet, but his concerns were mostly unfounded. He simply drove through the gate of the small airport, and slowly down a row of corrugated sheet metal hangars, finally arriving at the airplane he was searching for, where a single, black-uniformed mercenary was smoking a cigarette, assault rifle strapped over his shoulder.

He said to himself, "Just like the days before 9/11, no driver's license needed, smoking in the airport, and I didn't have to take off my shoes or walk through a metal detector. The only difference is that I have an armed mercenary to deal with."

The plane's luggage compartment door was still open with an industrial fan blowing inside in an attempt to mitigate some of the smoke being generated by the copy of the Scroll in the red box, just as he had seen during his astral projection.

Wendell flopped the passenger seat forward and reached behind the seat, finding his prayer shawl and yarmulke. He put these on, stepped out of the Ford F150 pickup truck and walked over to the soldier.

"Shalom aleichem," Rabbi Rosenburg said using his best Hebrew.

"Aleichem shalom," replied the soldier, and then continued in English. "This area is restricted. I'm going to need you to get back into your truck and leave the area immediately," pulling his assault rifle off of his shoulder.

"I am Rabbi Appelbaum. One of our golems was severely injured during the mission and I'm here to reform him using the copy of the Scroll. Where is it?" Wendell asked.

"No one has informed me of any of this, rabbi. Stay where you are and I'll radio my chief to confirm," the soldier said leaning his rifle against the ramp and unclipping his radio from his belt. The soldier's rifle started sliding to the ground causing him to turn to catch it. Wendell pulled his tranquilizer gun from his shoulder holster, stepped forward and shot the man point blank in the neck. The soldier reached up towards the pain, dropping his radio, and then slid to the ground unconscious, and soon to be dead.

Wendell walked back to the bed of his truck and grabbed the 5-gallons of gasoline and the blue sticky grenade and walked up the luggage compartment ramp. As he passed the industrial fan, he unplugged it from its power source with a quick tug on the cord. He continued into the compartment, opened the red metal box and poured the 5-gallon container of gasoline over the copy of the Scroll and into the compartment of the airplane. He then placed the sticky grenade on top of the copy of the Scroll and exited the compartment.

He drove out of the airport, parked his truck where he could have a view of the fireworks and gave the color blue a call, just to say hello. The plane released an initial orange fireball from the luggage compartment and began to burn. In about 30 seconds, a much larger fireball issued from the plane with a satisfying boom as the fuel tanks erupted and began to burn.

When he heard sirens in the distance, he drove the speed limit back to the White Dress Ranch, where the property was lit up with the red and blue flashing lights of an ambulance. He sped the truck up as he entered the driveway and skidded to a stop near the front of the ravaged hotel. Jumping out of the truck, he spotted Carly near the chapel and ran to her. She immediately hugged him with tears streaming down her face.

"What happened?! Who's hurt?" Wendell asked.

"Ross has lost a great deal of blood and may have been exposed to fentanyl. They have given him Narcan and a unit of blood, but they need to take him to the hospital to do surgery. He was hit in both his thigh and his arm by a machine gun," replied Carly.

"Will he be OK?" Wendell asked.

"They're not sure, he lost a great deal of blood. They say he's gone into hypovolemic shock, whatever that is," replied Carly. "Ross is not the only one hurt. Lilith took a direct hit from one of our own grenades – Legion found one and somehow imitated Lilith's voice to get Brian to detonate it. Wendell, Lilith's dead! She's dead! That bastard Legion *killed* her!" Carly sobbed angrily as she spoke.

As they passed the Chapel on their way to Lilith, Ross was being loaded into the ambulance. He was unconscious, taking both oxygen and blood intravenously and his face was as pale as bleached bones.

"Where is Lilith?" the rabbi asked.

"I got OctaJoe to move her into Cottage #6. She's there on the bed with the curtains closed," Carly said. "OctaJoe lost a tentacle to one of the gargoyles."

"Where is the Scroll?" Wendell asked.

"It's hidden in the barn," replied Carly.

"I need to get two pair of pliers from the barn. Make sure that Emily and Brian are in Lilith's cottage when I get there." Wendell said.

"You got it. But why the pliers?" Carly asked as she started to head for the barn.

"Although the gargoyle golems should be dust after I burned the copy of the Scroll, I'm guessing that there are a few of our golems who haven't had their shems broken," Wendell said.

"You would be guessing right. Oh, and the police are on the way." Carly said.

"What about Legion and Orina?" Wendell asked.

"The best I can tell, Orina is a pile of crumbled clay with a sword stuck into the middle of it, thanks to Lilith. The last that I saw of Legion was him being chased down by a 30-foot tall Bearmadillo," Carly said.

"What?" Wendell asked.

"Seems like the Scroll felt like we needed a little extra help, and so it grew him to Ice Age-sized Bearmadillo," Carly said.

"Thanks to the Almighty. I've got to get those pliers now, or the internet will be buzzing with photos of our golems. That sort of publicity might not be good for the honeymoon business," Wendell said, breaking into a run towards the barn with Carly.

Minutes later, Wendell had made good use of the pliers, permanently turning MoHawk, Sting and CamoRon back into the earth from which they came by breaking their shems and preventing the soon-to-arrive police from seeing the golems. He wondered where Bearmadillo ended up, hoping that he didn't return as a 30-foot monster during the interviews to come.

He then hurried to Cottage 6, where Brian, Emily and Carly awaited.

Wendell entered the cottage and walked over to the bed, leaning over Lilith to carefully examine the large hole in her chest.

"Look very closely at the area where she was wounded," Wendell said.

Everyone looked at the gaping hole in Lilith's chest. It was barely visible, but tissue was beginning to reform. Minute traces of new lung tissue, heart tissue, nerves, veins, and tiny white fibrils were everywhere they looked.

"Will she come back to life after I killed her?" Brian asked, his voice trembling.

"First of all, you were tricked by demons. Not just one demon, but an entire *legion* of demons. *You* didn't kill her. Second, yes, she will heal, but it will take time," replied Wendell. "Look at her shem.

Only the Almighty knows how, but her shem was only bent ever so slightly, and it wasn't broken during the explosion."

Emily rushed to give the rabbi a hug, quickly followed by Brian and then, of course, Carly.

"Wendell, I see red and blue flashing lights again," Carly said, looking out of the window.

"Then we should go talk to the police and the other ambulance drivers, by the look of it," Wendell said. "I suppose the extra ambulances are here for all of the dead mercenaries." He looked through the window a moment longer. "Did you invite the government guys in the black SUVs?", Wendell asked.

"No, I most certainly did not," replied Carly. "What are we going to tell them?" she asked.

"Unfortunately, this time, we're going to have to tell them the truth," Wendell replied.

EPILOGUE

Months Later
Greyhill, Texas

Ross and Lilith survived. It took several weeks for the two of them to heal and return to normal health, though Ross continues to walk with a limp. They decided that, in spite of the summer heat, they liked the seclusion that the Texas hill country offered. Ross has put their home in Skokie on the market and the two of them are looking for a property somewhere near the ranch, where they plan to build a home.

OctaJoe regrew his tentacle. Bearmadillo came back about a week after Legion and escaped. By that time, he had shrunk back to his usual large size again. Being unable to talk, he wasn't able to provide an update on the status of the two fugitives. Wendell ordered him to pose absolutely still in plain sight in the lobby of the hotel as an entertaining example of fantasy Texas wildlife. After all, if Wyoming can have the jack-o-lope, then it only seemed fair that Texas could have a Bearmadillo. Besides, he was great for business.

The pandemic continues to ravage the world, but a new vaccine is now available, and the people who remember how polio, smallpox, measles and a variety of other diseases were prevented and very nearly eliminated are receiving the vaccines. Other folks who don't are taking their chances.

Questions from the police were quickly shut down by the FBI, the CIA and representatives from the United States military. Sergeant Glen Mitchell of the Gillespie County Sheriff's Department was about to question Carly about what had happened there at the ranch but was asked to leave immediately by several men with the letters FBI on the back of their jackets. He just nodded, took off his white straw cowboy hat with a badge on the front and wiped the sweat off his forehead. He then looked at Carly, winked, and sauntered off towards his police truck, shaking his head at what appeared to be the result of a major military battle.

Wendell and Carly told the feds *almost* all of the truth. One of the mistruths that was necessary was that the Scroll had been taken by Legion during his escape. If Wendell had handed over the Scroll, it might become damaged, which could cost Lilith her life. The truth was that it was still hidden in the barn under one of the bells from the church tower. A few weeks after all of the excitement subsided, Wendell rented a safety deposit box at the Greyhill First Bank and Trust and placed the Scroll there for safe keeping.

The other mistruth that was necessary concerned Lilith. The truth was that as Wendell was leaving the cabin to meet the authorities, he instructed OctaJoe to take Lilith to the nearest outcropping of rocks, make her comfortable, cover her with his body and camouflage himself. If he hadn't done that, the feds would have confiscated Lilith's body-under-reconstruction as a national security concern and then dissected her. The mistruth that Wendell told was that Lilith's shem had been broken by Legion during the battle and her crumbled remains were scattered across the battlefield. The plan was to give her a new identity once she had healed.

The United States government held numerous high-level conversations with the government of Israel about how an Israeli weapons company was able to launch what essentially amounted to an invasion of a ranch on sovereign U.S. soil. The damage to the White Dress

Ranch was a bit hard to hide, and the papers picked up a story about the weapons company attack, but the story soon grew cold as those concerned, especially the U.S. government, Israeli Defense Systems and those living at the White Dress Ranch refused to fuel the fire with answers to questions.

Wendell and Carly are engaged to be married in June, after the reconstruction of the damaged chapel and the hotel is completed. Brian and Emily, like many children in the rural areas of Texas, are being home-schooled by Lilith and Ross. Brian now has a girlfriend.

Lilith eventually concluded, perhaps with the Scroll's help, that without Anatoly being alive to supply this region of Texas along with a variety of other areas of the United States with fentanyl and heroin, they might never have succeeded in defending themselves from the abominations that were thrown at them by Israeli Defense Systems. For this reason, she understood why the Scroll had prevented her from killing Anatoly when she had the chance.

Knowing that people were dying every day from fentanyl poisoning, Lilith decided that it was time for Anatoly to stop distributing these drugs. Ross conducted his own private investigator work and eventually found evidence of Anatoly and his whereabouts, and Lilith and he drove back to the Chicago area to do their small part to shut down the national flow of fentanyl. This time, the Scroll didn't seem to mind at all.

Wendell is *almost* certain that Legion crumbled into dust when the copy of the Scroll was destroyed, and every so often, Wendell wonders what happened to Eva.

ACKNOWLEDGMENTS

Thanks to my smart, beautiful wife for encouraging me to retire so that I could have the time to write this book and find something new and fun to pursue in addition to polymer science consulting. Thanks also to her for her patience with my unending fountain of creativity, some of it filtered, much of it not.

Thanks to my father-in-law, Barie Fritz, for reading several drafts of this book, providing me with tons of encouragement, information about the comings and goings of a funeral director during the Covid-19 pandemic, finding typos and making a variety of recommendations that panned out very nicely.

Thanks to my daughter, Samantha, who helped inspire this novel, and still likes the original title - The Mud Woman - best, because I tried to give her a scare at dusk one day when we saw a dark silhouette of an old woman hunting for something in a ditch. I told her that it was the Mud Woman, searching for children to absorb, after it becomes dark.

Thanks to Chris O'Brien and Professor Seth Strickland of Carnegie Mellon University for reviewing and editing the novel and providing feedback on pacing, writing style and expansion of certain segments.

Thanks to Long Overdue Publishing for believing in me as an author.

Thanks to my son, Glen Tabor, for validating a variety of facts on guns and grenades, and for providing information on standard police procedures.

Thanks to Darren Pryke for answering questions related to IT issues in the novel.

Thanks to my friends and family, Angela Tabor, Darren and Colleen Pryke, Bill Reid, Jodi Reid, Jonathan Zarych, Barie Fritz, my daughter Karen Sepolio, Chaz Sabon and Logan Tomaszewski for reading this novel and providing encouragement and suggestions for improvement. Thanks, Logan, for "gua gua" and getting me to fix the "As you know, Bob," issue. Thanks Bill and Jodi for suggesting the final title.

Thanks to Pengxu Qi, for information about Chinese medicines and for sharing his knowledge of the area around Wuhan, China.

Thanks to Matthew, Samantha and Charlotte, for being patient as I spent many days and nights writing this novel.

ABOUT THE AUTHOR

Rick Tabor is a semi-retired polymer scientist who has co-written and co-invented 85 patents, 22 scientific articles, two scientific book chapters, and commercial products that have generated more than $100MM in revenue for the companies he has worked for.

Rick lives in the northwest suburbs of Chicago with his lovely and smart wife, Angela, and their three children – Matthew, Samantha, and Charlotte.

This is Rick's first novel.